The Persian Jesuit

A Romance of India in the Age of Akbar

by

Ray Thomas Smith

Note for Librarians: A cataloguing record for this book is available from Library and Archives Canada at www.collectionscanada.ca/amicus/index-e.html

Printed in Victoria, BC, Canada.

ISBN: 978-1-4251-4523-1 (sc)
ISBN: 978-1-4251-4525-5 (e-book)
ISBN: 978-1-4269-2368-5 (dj)

We at Trafford believe that it is the responsibility of us all, as both individuals and corporations, to make choices that are environmentally and socially sound. You, in turn, are supporting this responsible conduct each time you purchase a Trafford book, or make use of our publishing services. To find out how you are helping, please visit www.trafford.com/responsiblepublishing.html

Our mission is to efficiently provide the world's finest, most comprehensive book publishing service, enabling every author to experience success. To find out how to publish your book, your way, and have it available worldwide, visit us online at www.trafford.com

Trafford rev. 3/8/2010

www.trafford.com

North America & international
toll-free: 1 888 232 4444 (USA & Canada)
phone: 250 383 6864 • fax: 812 355 4082

Table of Contents

ACKNOWLEDGMENTS: RAY SMITH

I wish to dedicate the novel to the memory of Gordon C. Roadarmel, able translator of the Hindi novel Godaan, who at his death was instructing at the University of California, Berkeley; Dr. P. C. Gupta, Vice-Chancellor of Jadavpur University, Bengal, whom I first met when he was Visiting Professor of History at Berkeley; and Professor Prabhakar S. Aiyar, an outstanding member of the Department of Politics, Bombay University, Mumbai. The three had a deep love for India and shared it in all their work and friendships.

Special thanks are also due to a longtime colleague and friend Dr. Issa Khalil, Professor of Religious Studies at San Diego State University, for his particular advice on technical matters. His knowledge of the Arabic language and of comparative aspects of Christianity and Islam were exceptionally helpful, especially his well informed approach to Arabic vocabulary and calendrical matters.

For the novel's cover I owe much appreciation to graphic artist Helen Sonneborn of Springfield, Ohio, for her skillfully evocative line-drawings of my Muslim protagonists Aziz Ahmad Khan of Bijapur and his beloved Mira Bartolomeo of Christian Goa.

I am especially grateful to writer Nancy Kress for the encouragement of her outstanding columns in Writer's Digest. She has been for me, unknown to her, a great help in every structural and stylistic aspect of writing, including practice at adapting one's style to varied genres.

I wish to thank Elizabeth Bennett of Trafford Publishing, Victoria, British Columbia, for advice on several chapters of The Persian Jesuit. Since the recent transfer of Trafford from Canada to Bloomington, Indiana, and resulting delays in publication, I appreciate Matt Hunckler and his Design Team for their devotion to final production of the novel. My thanks go also to Ashley DeVol of Author Solutions, Bloomington, and Mrs. Geneva Quinn of Author Solutions, Indianapolis, for their help and encouragement.

Last, I owe great gratitude to my wife Joan Smith for her very professional support of my writing efforts, especially for backing my experiments with poetry, plays, and short stories over the years, and for her expert help in "vetting" the current novel. Every writer would be fortunate to have such effective "in-house" editing and advice.

Chapter 1

Seventy Years: A Memoir

In the Name of Allah

the Beneficent, the Merciful,

here begins the life story

of Aziz Ahmad Khan.

Thanks to the Creator and Judge of all men, Who has allowed me long life, I stand now at the opening of my seventieth year. Blessed with good health, and with eyesight and power of memory still undimmed, I look back in awe at the times through which I have passed. Especially am I blessed to have at my side a daughter who remains with me to guide my hand and restore my concentration when they falter. I therefore dip my pen in the inkwell of resolution and begin this remembrance of a Muslim life.

I was born in the Hijra year 968 in Bijapur, capital of one of the five most important Muslim states in the Deccan plateau of central India. My father, a general in the service of the Sultan of Bijapur, was a Turk of the Sunni tradition of Islam, and I was therefore raised in that religious tradition. My mother, on the contrary, was of a distinguished Persian, Shi'a family that had migrated to India's Deccan, like so many Persians, insearch of better fortunes. My mother cooperated in my being raised a Sunni and, thanks to my father's tolerance and generosity, was never forced to abandon her Shi'a beliefs and practices. It was also due to my father's tolerant attitude-- for, as he said, "Are we not all Muslims united in praise of Allah and in gratitude to the Prophet?"-- that her widowed sister, "Aunt Bibiji," was also allowed to live with us and retain her Shi'a identity.

As a result of all this was that as a child I never conceived a dislike of Shi'as, and this carried into adulthood. In fact, my Aunt Bibiji was an example of the educated Muslim woman who read both Persian and

Arabic, and she often regaled me with tales of Persia's great poets Hafiz, Sa'adi, and Rumi! I never thought of her as anything but the wise and devout Muslim she was.

As with many another Muslim boy of good family, I was set at the age of five to study Arabic, the language of the Qur'an, and to recite long passages from memory-- as well as learning the custom of Shahada, which was to hail Allah, especially at each of the five customary times of prayer, and "bear witness" that he is the One and Only God and that Muhammad is His rightful Prophet or "messenger." Thus the Shahada and the Five Prayers became a part of the daily fabric of my life.

My father, though a lifelong soldier, was also strict in his observances of Islam. Especially he wished me to become fluent in both Arabic and Persian, and he made me certain that I was weekly instructed in both languages by qualified teachers. Arabic, of course, was the key to the Qur'an, but Persian had become the language of cultivated men in all Muslim courts and governments, and he wished me also to be able to serve at the court of the Ali'd sultans of Bijapur. By the age of ten, indeed, I had shown such talent for languages that I was regarded by my father, like my teachers of Arabic and Persian, with much praise. It appeared that upon this path I would guarantee for myself a place among the most distinguished men of Bijapur and the Deccan.

To the age of ten, therefore, the course of my life had run smoothly. In my education it only appeared that I needed training in the arts of horsemanship, archery, and the uses of the sword to become a man of military promise. I was gradually attaining all the fondest hopes of my father and family.

It is from that perspective that I continue with the story of my life, just as changes were about to occur that would complicate my future and turn it in directions for which I was untested and unprepared. I loved and respected my mother. I regarded my Aunt Bibiji with something like holy awe. But it was father who most had given direction to my thoughts and ambitions. I looked upon him as if he were equally emperor, sultan, and the sun of my existence. One learns only as an adult, perhaps, that life is always pregnant with events unexpected.

And even as a boy I knew that only God--only Allah in His Wisdom--could know what any man's future might be.

As I continue my account of my youth and early experiences, it may be asked how a Muslim of the Deccan might become known as "The Persian Jesuit!" The matter can be discussed in detail at a later time, but I may briefly explain it here.

In the Christian year 1510, almost half a century before my birth, the Portuguese had established a stronghold at Goa, formerly called Govepuri, a port on the Sea of Arabia that had belonged to Bijapur. Christian missionary orders rushed to take up residence there, among which was the Society of Jesus, better known as the "Jesuits," wearing their customary black capes and wide-brimmed black hats. In the Christian year 1575, when I was seventeen, I was exploring the Deccan on horseback to the south of Bijpur when I met a travelling Jesuit priest, Brother Antonio Monserrate, who was returning to Goa from a mission to towns that bordered the Bay of Bengal!

The Jesuit and I talked at length as we rode west toward the hills of the Western Ghats, and I found him to be a surprisingly decent and knowledgeable man. In an adventurous mood I finally allowed myself to be persuaded to descend the Ghats with him and proceed to Goa, where I might spend something between one and three years studying Christianity-- and Latin, language of the Christian scriptures-- under Monserrate's auspices! Even before accepting his offer of protection in that Christian outpost, I realized that he would attempt to convert me to his Faith. But I planned, while studying Christianity, to follow the dictates of my conscience and remain Muslim!

Monserrate and I gradually reached an understanding, and by the Christian year 1578 we had developed a warm and long-lasting relationship-- even though I never did become a Christian! He and his monastic order the Society of Jesus, did gain however from my growing command of Latin and Portuguese, together with my fluency in Persian! When a Jesuit mission set out in November of the Christian year 1579 for the "Mughal" realm of North India, in the hope of making a convert of its great Muslim emperor of the day, Jalal-ud-din Muhammed Akbar, I went as Monserrate's personal secretary!

Here I may as well explain, in brief, how I acquired the unlikely name "The Persian Jesuit." Not I, but a proper member of the Jesuit mission of 1579-1782, Brother Francis Henriques, who was Persian in origin, was supposed to be the group's translator. Yet, facing hostile insults from Muslims at the Mughal court, and feeling that the great Akbar was simply toying with us, he soon went back disgusted to Goa. I then found myself acting as accidental translator of the mission! Being Muslim, however, with a command of both Persian and Arabic, I could deal better with criticism and invective. Soon I was translating from Persian to Latin, Arabic to Latin, and the reverse.

It was now that I began hearing hostile Muslims calling me "The Persian Jesuit." Yet I was clearly Muslim-- and from Bijapur in the Deccan-- and was not a Jesuit at all! In simple fact, many of my Muslim countrymen at court, angry at being criticized by the mission's zealous Italian leader, Brother Claudio Acquaviva, were not using the words "Persian Jesuit" in a friendly way. But when the emperor Akbar humorously adopted the phrase, and even Monserrate chuckled over it, the name stuck.

What more can one say about the strangeness of fortune, fate, or destiny?

I return now to the first great change that came to me as if by fate or the Will of God. I would later understand that it may have been the most decisive event of all. It occurred when I was ten years old.

In recounting this event and others over the course of my life, I continue to place my hope in the eternal kindness and compassion of God, that I may fullfill my purpose, the vow I made these many years ago.

By the Mercy of Allah,

And in the name of the Prophet,

On whom be Peace.

Chapter 2

A Father's Blessing

The last time I saw my father was the day he stood next to me, his strong archer's hand on my shoulder. He was talking of honor. The subject was not strange to me, since he had always made much of our family's name and reputation. His voice this day, though, held a depth of tension that I had never heard before.

I was a ten year old boy, more concerned with my studies of Persian and Arabic than the thought of reputation. Here I was, seated sleepily before the page of my tutor's last assignment, and my father had come to the entrance of my room, pushed the curtain aside, and gazed at me a long time.

Hearing him come and expecting his voice, I looked up. He was gazing at me as if committing my face to memory. By habit I rose and stood with my head turned slightly to the left.

The leftward turn was my instinct when anyone looked at me, because I could slightly hide the scars left when a cauldron of hot oil in the bazaar had tipped and splashed on my five-year-old's body where I stood watching sweets being made. People thought it a miracle that I had survived. Truly I had been lucky not to lose my left eye. But the oil had permanently marked me. A cicatrix of red welts ran from the left edge of my jaw up past the corner of my eye, across the stump of the ear, and down to my left shoulder.

I knew that my father hated to see those scars, but there was nothing to be done now, and he had learned like most other adults not to stare or comment. The worst of it was from children of the street who stared, made faces at me, and called me names. But even those I had learned to ignore or tolerate, and if the jibes went on too long I would thrust my face close to theirs and dare them to stare at me until they backed away and left me alone.

I tried not to think how the oil had burned me, tried not to look at myself in any mirror. I hated it when I saw myself reflected anywhere, including the faces of people who had never seen me before, the gazes of strangers, the sympathetic eyes of friends. I kept trying to train myself not to turn my head, not to look away and pretend there were no scars. To bridge the gap between reality and denial I would put on a turban when going into public places. The turban covered my ruined ear and the corner of my forehead. Often I wore a shirt with a high collar.

But this was my father at the door. For him I could only stand, my head uncovered, and wear a smile of gratitude. He was my father whom I loved and worshipped. He stood now dressed formally in full armor--the double cloak of chain-mail, the shining steel helmet, the greaves on arms and legs, the curved scimitar girded at his waist. I basked in the glow that seemed to surround him.

And now, truly, his gaze did not waver or rest on my scars. He looked deep into my eyes, as if he wanted to lay open the pages of my heart.

What could I say but "Yes, father?"

"It is…nothing," he stammered. He attempted a smile. "You are studying your Persian today?"

"No," I answered honestly. "My lesson in Arabic. It is more difficult than Persian. I like Persian better."

His smile broadened at my child's logic. "You will be a scholar, my dear Aziz, before you are a soldier!"

Coming from a man who had been a soldier his whole life, it might have been an unpleasant thing to say. But I knew him better. He had always respected scholars, and had been the first to insist that I study both Persian and Arabic.

How many languages can you speak now," he asked boldly; "at least a few phrases?"

For the first time I could relax. Even at the age of ten I took pride in the discovery that learning any one language made the others easier.

I proceeded to count on my fingers, looking up each time for his approval.

"Turki," I began, "which we speak often at home." Half Turk and half Persian that he was, I knew my father would approve this beginning! With the blessing of his smile, I sped onward. "Deccani, which I hear in the streets. Phrases of Tamil and Konkani spoken by merchants.

Barely stopping for breath, I plunged onward. "And of course," I said, drawing on my reserves of dignity, "I study Persian, which you have told me will do well for a position in government. And Arabic, so that I can read the Qur'an and converse with holy men."

"Excellent," he said, clapping his hands. But he sobered again. "It is well to know the classic writing of our Muslim people-- and the poetry of great men."

"Yes," I admitted, "it is well." Somehow his last statement seemed stiff, as if he were lecturing some third person. The duty of a son, however, was to agree.

Slowly my father's expression turned to sorrow. It was then that he laid a hand on my shoulder. He was silent awhile. I exulted in the warmth of the hand.

His voice was suddenly gruff, the words awkward. "I may not see you again, boy."

I looked up startled.

He was staring over my head. His thoughts seemed to reach me from a distance. "Bad things happen in this world. Often one is not prepared." The grip on my shoulder hardened. "You must always remember to study and advance your mind, son Aziz." His gaze returned to mine and held it captive. "Do not let anyone persuade you that becoming a soldier and achieving victories will end in success. Do not believe the lie that taking a position with much promise of wealth and respect must end happily. The world is cruel even to those who are brave, who act well, who have done nothing shameful."

I heard the words. I could remember them-- and still can. But I comprehended nothing.

He gave my shoulder a rough squeeze. "Now-- back to your studies."

Quickly he walked back to the doorway, pulled the curtain aside, and disappeared. I watched in silence. My last impression was of his strong-muscled legs and broad, squared shoulders. I stood there a long time, torn between admiration and strange uneasiness.

The next morning he rose early. Still half asleep, I heard my mother in quiet, anxious talk with him. I heard words about the Shah's "darbar." There, as I knew, honors were heaped on the fortunate, positions of command assigned, punishments decided, and matters of great policy announced. I had often heard of such royal convocations. More than once my father had been granted honors or given new posts! I wanted to creep close where I could hear better, but this time I could not make myself get up. A fear seized me. I lay straining my ears. The conversation ended.

My mother was too nervous to have breakfast, but on me she forced the usual things. When I asked about the words she had exchanged with my father, she stiffened and left the room. Sometimes our servant Riaz Bahadur would share the adults' talk with me, but this time he only shook his head at my questions.

I could not bring myself to finish my bread and fruit. My Arabic lesson with the tutor went badly. So did the rest of the morning, then the afternoon. It was early evening, just before sunset, when a messenger arrived. My mother rushed to the gate. I tried to follow. Riaz Bahadur, more a friend to me than a servant, gently took my arm and pulled me back.

My mother was crying when she returned to the house. I did not have the heart to speak to her. She sat alone all evening, pretending to sew.

My father never returned.

A ten-year-old is not supposed to be told dreadful things. Yet he, too, worries and listens. Later I heard, not from my mother but from boys on the street, that my father was a criminal, a traitor, and had been executed. Since he had no male, adult relatives at hand, his body had been turned over to slaves who had the duty of burying Muslim criminals.

Only one man, a soldier of advancing years, dared to ask for my father's belongings at the execution. That man had saved my father's rings, a bracelet or two, a chain from his neck, the oval earrings of gold that he liked to wear, an ornament from his turban, a beautifully scabbarded small knife that had never been used in war.

My father's clothing was not returned. Riaz Bahadur told me later that after my father was condemned he was whipped. His tunic and undershirt had been thrown up over his head while he was lashed until the blood drenched his clothing. The executioner's sword-blade had then left his beheaded body gushing the rest of his life's blood. He was buried unwashed, in a common grave of common criminals, with no effort to have his feet facing the direction of Mecca.

When I heard more facts it was from boys, the eldest of whom was only too glad to tell all the details. I was so angry that I shouted, cried, and wanted to fight. The eldest evaded me. All of them quickly walked away. I heard no laughter or calling of names. Nothing had been said about my scars, my disfigurement. I was alone with my anger and tears.

The humiliation went on for days, for almost a month. I saw my mother sink under her burden of grief. I tried holding her, clinging to her. I spent hours standing and kneeling and prostrating myself in prayer to Allah.

When the old soldier came with my father's few belongings, my mother would not let me see them at first. She cried and prayed by turns. It was left to the old soldier to take me aside and let me know the truth. My father, he said, had been accused of consorting with the enemy, of exchanging information with agents of the Shah of Ahmadnagar. Of course he had denied it. The soldier, who had long known and admired him, denied it also. But, he added, my father was an orthodox Sunni who had Shi'a enemies at court. The Shah favored the Shi'as. He may have had other, more private reasons for condemning my father, who always spoke his mind in conference, even when it meant criticism of the Shah's policies, especially in things military.

So my father stood no chance when his enemies, armed with "secret" correspondence, brought charges against him. "Treason," said the older soldier—himself a Shi'a, but a man with clear and honest eyes—was just a convenient label for difference of opinion! He warned me to be quiet, to aid and support my mother, to bear with her in her unjust suffering and humiliation.

I begged the soldier to do what he could to restore some part of my father's honor and reputation. Tears came to his eyes. He had done what he could during these weeks—without effect. When he saw opportunities, he would do more. Not once did he look at my scars.

He took a deep breath. "Think of your father's last words to you," he said, "the ones you told me of. Remember them! Hold them tight against your heart! Someday you will restore your father's honor. Your own honor will be his best epitaph." He placed his right hand on my shoulder as my father had done that last day. "Grow to be a tribute to him. Never forget!"

For weeks I treasured the soldier's words. I committed every one of them to memory.

I drew myself up to my full ten-year-old's height and vowed to do as the soldier had said. In my honor would be my father's honor.

Seven days I vowed it—five times each day at the hours prescribed for prayer.

Chapter 3

Aunt Bibiji Presides

Now, even at the age of ten, I began to look with new eyes at the city of my birth. My father had often told me stories of Biapur's greatness. This Muslim city and state had long been a power on the plateau of the Deccan. Men like my father—Persian, Turk, Arab, Ethiopian, and many another—had flocked to Bijapur's service. The state had expanded its borders west to the Sea of Arabia, with valuable seaports at Goa and other places, and Goa—originally known as Govepura—had for a time been the capital. Slowly the state's Muslim sultans had enhanced Bijapur's wealth, served by able men.

In recent years one of those men had been my father, recognized for his military skills and record of victorious actions. He had gained fame especially in the war that destroyed the powerful Hindu state of Vijayanagar, which had threatened our borders on the south. That war had enriched Bijapur beyond our dreams. But now? The whole story dimmed and seemed a lie.

The death of my father brought my whole family the bitter taste of dishonour. Those who once had sought happiness in the reputation of being our friends became silent, fearful, and distant. Others, more bold, became carping tongues that dared now to defame us. Poverty we could accept, but the loss of honor, marked by whispers and excuses, lay heavily on my mother and weighed me down as well. Our tears dried, but downcast looks and long silences became our commonplace.

My beautiful mother began to wilt like a rose bereft of the life-giving water that had been my father's love and protection. Of course I know that most mothers are beautiful in the eyes of their small sons. My mother however was beautiful by any measure, her Persian birth a natural dowry of large eyes, intensely black but fine-textured hair, skin pale and perfect, slender limbs, and refined fingers upon which any gem gained more value. Now she seemed only frail and vulnerable. I did what a ten-year-old boy could do to comfort her. I held her hands, sat as close to her as I could, and gazed desperately into her eyes.

Yet my efforts only made her more sad. For when I was five years of age I had suffered an injury which seemed to damage my life's chances forever. I was playing in the bazaar at my favourite sweet shop when the owner's halfwit son clumsily allowed a kettle of hot oil to slop it contents over the side of the charcoal-fed oven. Screaming, I was terribly burned on the left side of my face, neck, and shoulders. The shop's owner leaped to save me, but by the time the oil could be wiped away I was hideously scarred. Even a month's treatment with unguents and poultices could not undo the harm.

My own face, divided since then into its unharmed and damaged sides, became a kind of reproach. My mother especially felt guilt that she could not have rescued me. Strangers, upon seeing the unharmed and damaged areas like bright and dark regions of the moon, would often turn away in disgust. And now my mother, gazing at the unhurt side with its Turkish contours like my father's, would always see his visage there and give way to tears.

She began to pray much. She asked for a mullah to come and recite the most comforting passages of the Qur'an. I would stand nearby and try to remember the most glowing lines. It was now that my slow and unwilling studies of Arabic gained determination and depth. Words and phrases lodged in my brain, and I never forgot them. My tutor in Arabic applauded my recitations.

Then my Aunt Bibiji Maham, my mother's elder sister, came to me one morning with tear-filled eyes Even before she spoke I knew that my mother had died. It shocked me to see the body of my mother, so shrunken and fragile when the mullah came to wash and enshroud her. Even as they bore her away I stood sorrowing and recited soundlessly a verse of the Qur'an promising Heaven to the virtuous, loyal, and pure servant of Allah. It did not matter to me that most readers of the Holy Book might be thinking only of brave and virtuous <u>men</u>. In my mother, beautiful to me again in my memory of former days, I saw the perfected being worthy of God's recognition and reward.

Aunt Bibiji, my mother's elder sister, became my guardian, there being no male in the family but myself. My aunt had always been a kind of puzzle to me. The only member of our family to have come with my mother from Persia, Aunt Bibiji had always had a stiff, undying sense of honor and would insist on it in all circumstances. Like my mother she was of the Shi'a sect of Islam and kept all the holy observances, including the Fast of Ramadan observed also by Sunnis. Aunt Bibiji's character was so strong-- and normally silent-- that she came near to suppressing any raillery or fun in life.

It was only my father, the soldier, who could make an occasional joke about holy things. I followed in his footsteps as far as I dared.

My Aunt Bibiji, however, immediately began to have a powerful impact upon me. She came from a Persian, Shi'a family of high intellectual achievements. Her brother my maternal uncle, who lived in Belgaon to the southwest of Bijapur, had become a Sufi of the Chisthiyya order, and resided at the subordinate Khanaqah of that order situated in the trading town of Belgaon.

My aunt would not leave my fate to accident. She decided that I must be well educated, a man of ideas and command of languages, a diplomatist in speech and ambition. Besides, I should be a fighter and have the skills to defend myself. I must create, when I needed it, a distance that other men feared to narrow too much. I was to gain a respect for my abilities that would overcome my scars and was to acquire not only reputation but office and wealth!

It may have seemed a mad scheme, but my aunt set out to do all this with rare determination and zeal. Thanks to her confidence and her energetic ways I soon realized that I did not have to fail because of an injured face. At her insistence I began to see success as my natural future.

Nor did my Aunt Bibiji limit herself to big talk and happy dreams. She was a woman who loved details. She was quite clear about what I was to study, what skills I would learn, and how I was to advance step by step.

She seized first on my evident skill in acquiring languages. I would have to perfect my Persian for the access it would give to service in government-- any service, any government! I would raise my command of Arabic to a level that I might not be ashamed to express myself to men of religion, be they simple mullahs or sophisticated ulama, and to debate on equal terms! I would of course keep my command of my father's Turki speech as well as my opportunity in Bijapur and the wider region of my birth. I would study the Qur'an-- and the poetry of great men like Hafiz and Sa'adi. It would not be enough to speak well. I must read in all my languages. Especially Persian I must read and write elegantly.

Realizing that I would sometime falter or resist, Aunt Bibiji made a lecture of her plans for me. "You have mourned long and well for your father, nephew. To continue this mourning will not suit the rest of life. You must honor your father by what you achieve! It was his wish. It is your duty. Do not make excuses or expect the slightest sympathy from the world. Discipline yourself. Take up your energies and shape them."

For a start, I was to cease hanging about in the streets. I was to ignore the insults of the street urchins that I had been accustomed to roam with. I would concentrate on the lessons given by the teachers she would hire for me.

The very next morning a new teacher arrived-- an ustaad whose expertise was music-- and the three-stringed dilruba. I had not sent for him, had never imagined this kind of skill. By the end of an hour, however-- with my aunt watching, I knew, from the curtained entrance to the room-- my fingers were hurting from the tension even of one string of the dilruba's three, my legs from strict positions that I was to learn, seated like this with bent knees as if in yoga. I had been given already the intervals of a "raga"-- the strict tonalities of its basic octave, the scale and mode chosen by the teacher. The next day's lesson was set.

And my aunt had other surprises in store. Scholar and musician I was to be, but not without the skills of marksman and soldier. She announced that I would learn all the ways of weapons and war. The Portuguese had brought new weapons, especially the musket, to our coasts. I was to combine our traditional command of Turko-Mongol archery with the handling of firearms.

There again Aunt Bibiji would not leave things to chance. She would hire for me a famed Turko-Mongol teacher of riding and shooting. It began with horsemanship. I would learn to rely not on common horses bred in the Deccan but to ride the best of Arabian coursers, their endurance and smooth gait the marvel of east and west. I must shoot from the saddle with either bow or musket as well as from a kneeling or standing position on the ground. My swordsmanship, in and out of the saddle, must begin with our Muslim scimitar, its one-edged, slashing blade curved and deadly from much 'working' by the swordsmith.

My aunt had always seemed so tranquil and without violence in speech or action! Her interest in military skills continued to astonish me. "Ah, if I by Allah's mercy had been a man...," she sometimes said with obvious envy. But if it were not her destiny, then she would make of me, her nephew, one of the best horsemen and musket-men in the Deccan!

The teacher that Aunt Bibji hired was an old Turko-Mongol who had been a companion of my father's in earlier years. Even before the man arrived at the gate of our house, my aunt brought me a bow of my father's, an old one that was not too stiff. And as I fumbled with it I realized what she wanted of me. I was going to learn how to string and draw that bow and to release its arrows with true aim. With the full strength of a man's bow I was later to hit a mark at a hundred paces, even while riding at a gallop, and from a kneeling position I might succeed at two hundred as the Mongols had been known to do! And yes, I would be able to bring down a hawk, an antelope, or-- a man on horseback. The last image bothered me. I was still too young to contemplate the real facts of death.

I turned my mind to thinking of the Portuguese muskets that were becoming common in the Deccan. Shooting with a long-barreled musket, this latest of weapons-- that would be a challenge! Already I had heard that the so-called "matchlock" musket, in spite of its slow wick and problems of priming and firing in wet weather, was to be preferred in the hunt of large prey like the tiger, the lion. I could hardly wait to get that musket in my hands. How easily a child shifts from one ambition to another, as if in a game, and does not think of the consequences!

I asked about my father's matchlock, trying to make it seem just a casual idea. It made me wish my father were there. My aunt thought a moment. She smiled. "The musket will come in its place, when you are ready."

I hesitated to ask her more questions. I only knew that she was planning to enjoy this whole business of "educating" me. Silently, as I sat at my next Arabic lesson, I thanked her for including a man's business of war and the hunt.

Yet I genuinely intended to be both an Arabic and Persian speaking man of learning, fit to join the foremost ranks of the scholars of religion and literature that had always been much respected among Muslims-- not to omit being a poet, perhaps a musician. All this my father, though a man of war, had wanted for me. Aunt Bibiji desired the same. Unusual for most Muslim women, Sunni or Shi'a, she was both literate and scholarly. Many were the nights I glimpsed her in her room reading by candlelight from some tome, often a book of Persian poetry by the famed Sa'adi or Hafiz. Poetic phrases and lines were often on her lips.

To ride well, shoot well, speak well. Heady ambitions for a boy so young! But they were the ambitions of my father, as of my aunt. And therefore they were mine.

Chapter 4

A New "Brother"

By the time of my twelfth birthday I had settled into a routine of language study-- still both Persian and Arabic-- and had begun to think of myself only as a scholar, perhaps on my way to becoming a mullah. Yet things changed quickly the morning when Aunt Bibiji called me to her sitting-room. She never did this unless she had some important message to convey.

Normally if I had a few minutes, I would drop from the low terrace outside my room, aim some pebbles at crows or mynahs perched on our rooftop, and sit awhile in the shade of a favorite pear tree.

This time I bounded off the terrace and went directly to my aunt where she was sitting propped at ease against a single large cushion. I bowed low to touch her bare feet with a respectful hand and took a seat on the rug in front of her.

She arranged herself more comfortably in the summer day's mid-morning heat and, languorously waving a hand-fan of figured silk from Persia, looked me over. Even today, in her fifties, Aunt Bibiji wore a delicate cotton kamiz and wide Muslim pantaloons in the best of taste.

"I hate to interrupt your studies, Aziz Ahmad, but I have had an idea. I have begun to worry about your lack of a companion your age. My inquiries among friends have found a boy about your age who might do well. Though two years older than you are, Nephew, he seems of suitable intelligence and good manners. Tomorrow the young man will come at my request."

She looked to see if I were alarmed or showed interest. To tell the truth I was in a state of shock.

Aunt Bibiji smiled ingratiatingly. "He is of a princely family, I am assured. Rama Raya is his name. He calls himself 'Raya.' I have personally spoken with him, and was impressed with his dignified bearing and honorable mode of address."

A Hindu name! This news alarmed me. I must have paled.

"He has had some unfortunate experiences," my aunt said, "having been captured in the war with Vijayanagar two years ago. At present he is living as a servant in the home of a Muslim family of good character, but they no longer need his services. Rather than turn him out on the street or try to apprentice him to a trade, they have agreed to transfer him to my care and employment." She paused. I was silent-- even deeper in shock.

"Like you, Aziz Ahmad, he is unfortunately an orphan," she continued, "and when captured after the fall of Vijayanagar was he made a slave. After several attempts at escape he convinced his owner-- a man of importance at the Sultan's court-- that he should be sold, on condition that if he gave offence to his new owner he would be submitted to the Sultan's justice!"

After such remarks my aunt seemed rather out of breath. But, to forestall any outburst from me, she went on.

"I made further enquiries about the boy and talked with him in his honorable owner's presence. I concluded that he was of good character but had experienced mistreatment. At last, impressed with his gentility, I concluded that, if he would agree to behave himself, commit no outrages, and live peaceably in my household, I would purchase him and-- upon a year's evidence of his good qualities-- give him his freedom and consider his adoption."

I sat in stark silence. This Hindu-- a prisoner and slave? Now to be my "companion!" And, after a year, to be freed and-- become my cousin? Or worse, be regarded as my brother!?

But my aunt ignored my coolness. "I know this may seem to you a hasty decision. But I believe it is for the best. The boy is clearly intelligent. He has agreed to a course of studies and improvement similar to your own. And he understands my terms! He must show that he has the qualities I expect and does what I ask of him. If I am right, he will earn your trust as well-- and become a friend, as would befit any son of mine. To be freed is a very desirable goal, and he admits it. To be adopted, he knows, would be even more honorable."

It was a speech that stunned me. I had been prepared to hate this Hindu prince-turned-slave-turned...what? My companion? Now I realized that aunt Bibiji Maham would not allow me the freedom to show enmity or make any trouble over this business.

My aunt was looking at me expectantly.

"Well...what can I say?" I grumbled. "I will do my best." But I had a few conditions of my own to demand. "Only please, allow me to dislike him if he makes too much of his claims to be a 'prince' -- and do not keep him on if he sneers at Muslims!"

Aunt Bibiji was startled, but then laughed. "Very well, Nephew. I accept those conditions. Merely give him a fair chance to prove that he has the good qualities I expect of him."

The next day the Hindu 'prince' arrived. There he stood in my aunt's sitting-room, a little distance from her, yet close enough to show her approval. I was surprised how short he was. Yet he had a proud manner that made him seem taller than I was! And in spite of my wishing to think him ugly, he was handsome-- better looking than I in many ways, even were it not for my scars. I was inclined to stare at the curly darkness of his hair and the deep brown of his skin. His dark eyes seemed to combine uncertainty with a challenge.

We were staring at each other like young lions considering the chances of attack. His stare included my scars. Yet we both quickly averted our eyes and looked toward my Aunt Bibiji. My aunt, I could see, had counselled him as she had counselled me. Young lions or not, we were expected to be at peace. I was just thankful that we were not true brothers!

When my aunt introduced us, it was quickly and with a slight gesture. She said only "Rama Raya" and "Aziz Ahmad." His eyes probed mine. "I prefer 'Raya,'" he said, forcing a smile.

My returning smile came no more easily. "I am 'Aziz.'" I noticed that his Dakkhini speech was impeccable.

He gazed at me further. "I am Hindu," he said.

I felt no inclination to be more informative. "I am Muslim."

I could see Aunt Bibiji becoming uneasy. She leapt into the breach. "There is no reason why you cannot cooperate-- even be friends!"

"Yes," said Raya after a moment, his brow furrowing. His gaze at me hardened. "But Aziz Ahmad must never mention that I have been a slave."

I lurched into my own kind of honesty. "And you must never sneer at my scars! And never say that I enslaved your people-- or say that all Muslims are bigots." I raised my chin.

Raya snapped back. "Very well. But you must forgive me if I still hate Muslim for ravaging my country!"

Aunt Bibiji spoke up sharply. "I do not like the path the two of you are taking. Treat each other with more civility, or I will teach you some sharp lessons of my own!"

She glared at us in silence awhile. "And I have a new rule for you. From this moment I expect you in fact to treat each other as brothers. Within this family I will tolerate no trading of insults. Do you both understand that?"

Raya and I both drew a long breath. Neither of us, clearly, wished to yield much ground in the name of a relationship we did not feel-- brothers!

Aunt Bibiji, too, could see that this whole fabric of pretence could easily collapse. "I am not asking either of you give up all your hostility right away, but I do expect you to keep it under control and not keep speaking ill of each other-- or speaking ill of each other's religions."

And she made a decisive move. "Salute each other now-- each in the custom of your religion!"

Slowly my brother-in-making placed his palms together at eye level, as Hindus did, and allowed himself a direct, serious gaze at me. I raised my right hand to my forehead, palm upward in the Muslim salute, and bowed over the hand.

Another surprise came from my aunt. "Now-- embrace each other as brothers would! I want no more displays of hostility!"

Raya and I stiffened. In both of us a tremor seemed to find its way from head to foot. But we were dealing with this lady of unyielding will. We embraced quickly and stepped back.

The shock came of hearing my aunt's voice one more time. "Now promise to treat each other in every way as brothers. Let me hear it!"

For a long moment Raya and I gazed at each other, trying to read our futures. A destiny was being thrust upon us. Our two religions, our two societies, could not be reconciled. In many ways we were fated to be rivals, even enemies. But we were going to have to get on together. We would have to find a way.

"We will treat each other as brothers," my companion said. "We will treat each other as brothers," I echoed. And then, silently, I led in exchanging salutes again, and Raya followed--the Muslim and the Hindu.

And now that Aunt Bibiji had been bold enough to force Raya and me to treat each other as brothers-- as competitors, yes, but also brothers-- she would need a plan to succeed. Fortunately she did have that plan!

She made us sit down, only a little space apart, and hear her out. It was at times like this, under my aunt's forthright gaze, that I had learned to respect the lady.

We were to be given the same education-- the classic Persian education of language and culture in which she was already training me. She admitted that Raya might not see its usefulness at this point, but my aunt knew better. We were to remain neither unbending Turk nor Hindu, but be trained up as gentlemen capable of any post or career in a government. We would learn from both Muslim and Hindu traditions. We would scorn no kind of learning.

In her words, "Neither of you is to be a barbarian nor trust only to your strength, wile, or wit. You will earn respect. You will be men of culture not merely soldiers or adventurers. I am not saying you will be only men of classical learning. You will at the same time be masters of practical affairs, equally comfortable on horseback and in a library, masters of men as well as masters of thought. I would have you be also students of the natural world, its animals and plants, as ready to speak of birds and flowers as you are of battlefields, and to write the poetry of love as well as you report a triumph of war or diplomacy! You will scorn no man-- and no woman-- who knows something you do not, or who has a skill that you lack. You will never be satisfied with yourselves when you are ignorant."

She paused for breath, but also waited for us to respond. "Do you understand, young men?" We stared at her, and I sensed that we were both awed and a little terrified. Raya had started listening with a little smirk of self-assurance. Now even he looked sober.

"Do - you - understand - me, - the - two - of - you?" my aunt intoned. Raya was first to summon up a "Yes." I, being two years younger, but also better acquainted with my aunt, echoed him firmly. "Good," said Aunt Bibiji in triumph. "We begin tomorrow."

And when the next day dawned, we found ourselves each with a two fierce new tutors in Persian-- a father and son. Even more awesome, we were confronted by Qarah Khan, an ancient Turko-Mongol from Badakshan who was to train us in riding and shooting. We also found that neither the two Persians nor the hard-handed old Turk would permit any laziness, smart rudeness, or inattention-- and that Aunt Bibiji would not tolerate any complaints.

When not occupied with our lessons under our teachers of Persian or our new mentor Qarah Khan, Raya and I often quarrelled. At first I let him dominate and provoke me, but I soon began to fight back-- in words if not physically. It was when he began to make fun of my five-times-a-day Muslim prayers that our relations almost came to blows.

Still proud of his Hindu heritage and resentful of my aunt's often bold attempts to "introduce" him to Islam, Raya began to watch me with amusement when I prayed in his presence-- and then to chant his favorite Hindu prayers aloud while I attempted to concentrate on my words. At last it was too much for me. One day I paused awhile, then resumed praying and carried through to the end of my prostrations and risings again. Then I stopped and asked my tormentor if his "gods" required him to be obnoxious to other people's beliefs.

This new "brother" of mine announced that if I prayed silently it would be just as pleasing to any "god" I claimed to worship-- and it was frankly he who had a right to be annoyed, and not me!

I promptly told him that surely his "useless" number of deities did not require him to shout me down while I was sincerely worshipping in my own fashion. Or did he just want to make fun of Islam? He started to say something else cynical, but I cut him off. "Well then," said I, "I will interrupt and mock your prayers and your religion!"

"Try it," he shot back. "Just try it. I am not afraid of you or this 'Allah' of yours!" I was astonished he really wanted to fight me.

"So," I said, "you must want to go back to your miserable life as a slave or somebody's servant-- the miserable life you've told me about so often. Frankly I'm sick of your lack of gratitude to my aunt, not to say more about your insults to me and to Islam."

Having seized the initiative, I pressed on. "Would you like to repeat these things to Aunt Bibiji Maham? Or would you prefer to have me do it? And then you can stop living in our house and eating at our table!" I waited a moment "What are you waiting for?" I challenged him. "Why don't you just pack up and go?"

He had fallen silent. I could see that he was in turmoil inside-- and did not want to say anything that would lead to a challenge to my aunt. She would be a bigger, less easy target!

His silence continued. Now he was thinking. "All right," he said at last. "Keep to your prayers. I will keep to mine. Just do not expect me to become a Muslim!"

Now I realized how deep his resentment at my aunt's efforts to soften him up for a conversion to Islam! But I was too angry to relent. "You expect me or Aunt Bibiji to ask you to convert? Just keep to your faith and stop making fun of mine."

Raya stood awhile in silence, frowning. "All right," he growled again. "I apologize." But he looked unrepentant.

I could see that he really meant no apology. He simply did not want to antagonize my aunt! Still, I waited to see if he had more to say. Nothing. He turned to his Persian lesson-- which, I knew, had too many Muslim elements to appeal to him.

So he did not intend to become a Muslim? Fine! Let him continue his prayers to this and that god. The test would come when I returned to my open, verbal prayers. I waited a day, and unfolded my prayer mat again. I could see Raya getting restless as the Arabic phrases went on. I persisted. Raya kept silent.

When I finished I stood rolling up my prayer mat. "Your turn," I said casually. "Thank-you so much," he announced-- and went into his room. In a few moments I could smell the incense burning in front of the altar where the images stood. I felt an air of finality. We had arrived at a truce.

Once we stopped trying to be critical of each other's religion, things began to settle down. Thanks to my Aunt Bibiji's wisdom in keeping us busy at one lesson or another, we slowly began to accept each other. And she stopped openly trying to nudge Raya to convert.

Raya and I went ahead and found ways to cooperate, especially in horsemanship, weaponry, and other skills suited to soldiers rather than men of religion. We no longer engaged in a war of ideas.

We were doomed as Muslim and Hindu, I knew, to have a sense of conflict over our beliefs. Slowly, however, we did begin to think-- and feel-- as if somehow we were brothers. We just never talked about some things.

I thought it all over. This was life. To live in anything other than a state of war we all needed a certain amount of tolerance. The truth was that simple. No two of us, even if we tried, could live without differences. And in this case? It was not just Raya's doing. We would accept each other because we both had to accept Aunt Bibiji!

Chapter 5

Ready For Adventure?

Four years passed. Raya and I lived at close quarters. We studied together, played together, competed together. Aunt Bibiji would tolerate no fighting between us-- when she knew of it. But some fighting and arguing did occur, and out of my aunt's sight and hearing we were normal boys.

These were the years when Raya and I studied the Persian language every week under our two appointed tutors. Both of us being competent readers, writers, and speakers, although I kept a slight edge from having started earlier. Raya, proud of his reasoning abilities, would often discuss the writings of Sufi masters like Hafiz and Rumi, and it sharpened both our habits of thinking. But we avoided any major conflict of ideas about the Qur'an, Mohammed's prophecies or the religious pronouncements of the Sunna and Hadith, because even Raya knew that he could not make headway there with our tutors-- or with Aunt Bibiji!

It was fortunate that Aunt Bibiji had stopped trying to use Raya's Persian studies as one of the several tools, some subtle and some more obvious, to convert him to Islam! He remained determined to be Hindu. He would observe the Muslim fast-times, especially the month of Muharram, so as not to offend my aunt, and would normally wear Muslim clothing, but he also kept to his Hindu gods and celebrated quietly his Hindu feast days-- which, also to avoid conflict with my aunt, he treated as fast-days!

When I summoned the courage one day to ask why he was so steadfast a Hindu, he took the occasion to inform me bluntly that his patron god was Lord Rama, just as his proper name remained "Rama-Raya." I could hardly argue about that, since so many Muslims were named "Muhammad" out of respect for the Prophet! Again I decided to tolerate what I considered his wrong-headed beliefs.

Raya still would twit me sometimes about my five daily prayer-times and their elaborate rituals-- but I would remind him that if I must sometimes refer to Allah, the One God, by one of his ninety-nine Holy Names, or Divine Qualities, Raya seemed to see nothing odd in there being ninety-nine Deities (or ninety-nine thousand!), some of which were male, some female, and others a little of both! We would then argue, but briefly, until we exhausted ourselves or had to go back to our studies. If we continued to disagree, we also learned that our religions were both beset by complexities which the average person could neither explain nor resolve.

Fortunately we did make progress in another area of our lives. That was our training, under the discipline of Qarah Khan, in the many skills of parts of our daily and weekly training that Aunt Bibiji insisted upon. The physical and mental demands that Qarah Khan made part of our lives were easier to face than the intellectual demands of a language or a religion, and often we were simply too tired to argue!

The old Turk was tough and expected us to follow his instructions exactly. Sometimes he humiliated us-- calling us "girls" and worse when we made mistakes or thought too highly of our accomplishments with the Mongol bow or our riding lessons. But step by step we became adept as archers and riders. To show us that he could learn things that were new to him also, Qarah Khan took up one of the matchlock muskets which Aunt Bibiji insisted become part of our training. He quickly made himself as expert a marksman as these cumbersome weapons would allow-- while he remained unconvinced that the musket was really a better weapon that the light, quick-firing compound bow of which he was a master.

The Khan was so expert an archer that he would have left musketry alone, though he did practice himself until he had mastered the Portguese matchlock musket for our benefit. Once I realized how much a change of habit and thinking that required I respected him more and more. However, he never accepted the musket as equal or superior to the bow and arrow. He disliked the inaccuracy of the smoothbore, its lighted wick that could cause too early a discharge and the priming powder that could easily become damp and useless.

He capped his argument by saying, "I can put three arrows in your heart at fifty paces with my Mongol bow while you are still priming, loading, blowing on your match and sighting your weapon. At a hundred paces at least one of my three arrows will find you! Be sure that you, too, are adept with a bow." And that was his justification for hundreds of hours of archery as well as the matchlock-- hours more and more of which were spent shooting from horseback!

Whenever our spirits sank, which they did about once a month, old Qarah Khan would cheer us on with stories of his youth on the plains of Badakshan. It was a faraway world, in distance as in time, north of the Hindu Kush mountains, adjoining the high plateau of the Amu Darya and Syr Darya rivers. I thought of the Deccan, the southern plateau mixing broad agricultural lands with rough and rocky, hilly and dry country. Did this old man ever wish he were again in Badakshan? His stories were rich with hard and daring men, fast riding, sudden fighting, and then again silence and the wind and emptiness.

It was not long before my fingers and hands became sun-browned and calloused-- especially my right thumb with its archer's ring! But Raya and I could both see how our shoulders and arms developed the muscles of the professional archer, and we became as able as Qarah Khan to heft, load and fire the Portuguese muskets that my aunt managed to acquire for us!

By the time Raya was eighteen and I was sixteen, we had grown up together both as scholars and speakers of Persian and as students of riding, weapons, and the skills of war and the hunt. Our Turkish boots and spurs were as familiar to us as the rumpled pages of our textbooks. We were ready, we felt, to go out into the world and make a name for ourselves.

Thus it was that one day, after many efforts to persuade my aunt to let us ride forth on some kind of adventure, Raya came bounding across the garden to our rooms. "We can go!" he shouted happily. "Aunt Bibiji has given the word!" We spent the rest of the day imagining the glory of it all.

The truth was that Aunt Bibiji had decided to let us ride to the town of

Belgaon to visit her brother the Sufi philosopher! It was not quite the "adventure" we had expected. Raya had made clear that he wished us to be able to ride rather far to the south-- to the remains of the great capital city of Vijayanagar-- and to indulge in leisurely hunting along the way. Instead we were to ride directly to Belgaon-- and, after a short "family" visit, return straight to Bijapur!

Aunt Bibiji had in fact promised that when Raya reached eighteen and I was sixteen she would allow us our first big trip on horseback. But a three day ride southwest to the town of Belgaon where her brother, my uncle, lived in a Sufi khanaqah? That was not quite the "adventure" we had in mind, which would have been to go hunting in the hills or else-- Raya's preference-- visit the ruined city of Vijayanagar where his father the 'prince' had served as a high-ranking officer. But my aunt as usual was firm about her decisions, and Belgaon it would be!

"Besides," said Aunt Bibiji, "I will be better able to know your location and activities, and my brother will acquaint you with something you, as yet, know little about-- the life of a devout group of Muslims whose spiritual lives bring honor to our Religion." What sixteen or eighteen year old boy-- or recently fledged "man"-- could argue with that wisdom?

Raya and I departed at last, before the rains of summer and fall could begin in the Deccan. We knew now that our Mongol bows and quivers of arrows were likely to be our best defense on the journey by road-- a "road" so rough that it was hardly more than a half-overgrown cart track. At least we could do some hunting, we told each other.

The muskets slung across our saddles did contribute a lot to our confidence-- "in case," the Khan told us, "you meet with bandits." Having absorbed that information, we were less likely to complain about our heavy coats-of-mail and the steel helmets and round Turkish shields with which my aunt had burdened us.

We were almost sorry when no bands of brigands appeared.

Aunt Bibiji's letter six months earlier to my uncle in Belgaon had received a welcoming reply just before we departed Bijapur. We could stay several days in the Khanaqah where my uncle resided with a community of Sufis! I did know something of what a "Sufi" was. Now, maybe, I would find out why my uncle had taken up residence in a small town like this.

In just over three days, without incident, Raya and I reached Belgaon. We soon found our way to my uncle's khanaqah. The place turned out to be constructed of two stories built around a central courtyard, as almost any building in the Deccan would be, whether public or private.

Approching from the street, which had widened into a square, what impressed me was not the khanaqah but a whitewashed tomb within a wall with an imposing gate. The tomb was probably that of the Sufi who had founded this Chisthiyya khanaqah so far from the master's seat at Ajmer. It would be the shrine from which the spiritual power of the founder would continue to radiate after his death. That much I remembered from seeing a similar tomb in Bijapur. Now I realized this must be a place of pilgrimage for devout Muslims. The tomb would attract donations from the faithful and might be a source of considerable wealth for the khanaqah. I also noted that grouped behind the khanaqah stood perhaps half a dozen smaller buildings, including rooms for guests, a row of storage places, and a stable for horses. Hence the khanaqah was a place of security and accumulation of wealth.

Raya and I rode to the stables to dismount and find someone to take charge of our horses. A young syce appeared and made the stabling arrangements. He then led us to a large rear door of the khanaqah where heavy gates stood open on rusty hinges. An elderly gentleman appeared there and escorted us to one of the rooms for guests. He suggested that we wash away some of the grime of travel and then go with him to meet my uncle.

Feeling refreshed but a little nervous, we emerged and found the gentleman still awaiting us. We followed him into the inner courtyard of the khanaqah. This surprisingly wide area we found shaded by big old orange trees.

Here was the customary Muslim charbagh or "fourfold garden" plan similar to my aunt's in Bijapur but much larger. At the garden's center a large stone fountain splashed and sent water into little stone channels that fed the orange trees. In the corner of the charbagh a stone well with rope and buckets made clear that the khanaqah was nicely supplied with water.

Passing into an arched corridor at the opposite side if the charbagh, we found ourselves walking on large flagstones that glowed with the high polish given by many feet. At the center of the corridor, awaiting us with folded hands, stood the man who must be my uncle. Offering my salaam, I tried to intone correctly the Arabic phrases of the Shahada. My uncle also formally welcomed us and introduced himself.

Raya had learned to sound as proper as I, and my uncle's smile of welcome broadened. He ushered us into a large, heavily carpeted, but otherwise very simply appointed room. Soon all three of us were seated on the carpeted floor. Sherbet was served in simple bowls, and I found myself slipping into a tired but happy frame of mind.

After customary questions and answers about Aunt Bibiji's health, our ride from Bijapur, and our impression of the khanaqah, I suddenly felt a kind of expectant silence. Sufism seemed to surround and command us, awaiting some inevitable response. What had we to say in reply? We sat in the silence of our ignorance.

My uncle surveyed the two of us. "I see in your armor and weaponry that you have not come here to study Sufi beliefs," he said quietly. "You are more soldiers in search of excitement and the rewards of life than seekers of ideas and the contemplative life. Is it not so?"

I felt like a statue of myself, unable to speak. I had really come here with no definite thought-- except to meet this middle-aged man and convey to him my aunt's message! And already I knew that I would not find my father's spirit here. For he most surely was a soldier, and I could remember him in no other way. My uncle had found a new path here, a new way of perceiving the world and understanding his Muslim faith. And I had not come ready to learn from him, whether of Sufism or anything else. Was I "seeking" anything at all?

Strangely, in the silence that I could not pierce, it was Raya who found his tongue. And what he said astonished me!

"We would be soldiers, honorable Shaikh," said my companion, "but we are not without a care for ideas. Would you not be willing to explain something of your discipline and faith to us?"

I had become Raya and he had become me-- or what each of us was supposed to be! And I felt, miserably, that he was the one with a mind that could learn, while I sat alone in isolation and blankness-- no, not in blankness but in the past. I could think only of my father now, how he was gone and I was bereft of the warmth of his love, even the warmth of his hand.

In the fresh silence where Raya's questions echoed, waiting, I could only listen. I had nothing to say. And whatever my uncle in his wisdom might say, I felt I had no part in it.

My uncle looked Raya over carefully. He must have noted the unusually dark skin and curly hair that gave Raya's Muslim clothing an exotic flair. Did he realize that he might be speaking to a Hindu who had converted to Islam? He cleared his throat and adjusted his tunic.

"It will be some years, I think, before you young gentlemen are seriously ready to consider joining our brotherhood. The beliefs and practices of our men of the patched woolen robe are not for everyone." He raised a hand in caution. "Do not misunderstand me. I do not count your lack of interest as a failing on your part, because the world is full of attachments and temptations, and even men of great piety and zeal are often content to follow the main path laid out by the Qur'an and by Sunni or Shi'a custom. But if you begin to see the ordinary ways of the world-- or indeed the ordinary beliefs of Islam-- as an unsatisfying way to seek and know God-- then you may be ready to take up the Sufi way."

He paused, obviously intending to give us a way out of further questions. Here I sat, letting Raya seize the initiative, I who had framed all sorts of questions that I wanted to ask-- questions about my uncle's past, about my father! Now I was jealous of this companion of mine.

Raya broke the silence again. “Then you have no members who are young?”

My uncle smiled. “The youngest in our khanaqah is just over thirty years of age-- which at age fifty-six I do admit that I find ‘young.’ Most of us, indeed, are of forty years or older and have seen a great deal of the world. Some have been soldiers, others scholars and students of the Qur’an, and still others men of ordinary employments. We do not discriminate among the backgrounds of those who come to us. Ours is an association by free choice, and we may come and go or become lifelong wanderers if we wish. While we stay, however, we are bound by the rules of this our particular Order and khanaqah.”

“But, Shaikh-ji,” said Raya, looking for argument, “would you not be glad to have younger men, as they might bring fresh ideas?”

My uncle stiffened. “It depends, my young friend, on what kind of ‘fresh ideas’ you have in mind. Sufism welcomes questions, and new questions do arise. But ours is a path of worship and devotion, not a way of debate. We wish to praise God using all the Ninety-Nine Names-- and other names and attributes that the Sunna offers us.”

He quickly went on. “I do ask your pardon if I seem too dependent upon tradition, but Sufism is a path dating some eight or ten centuries past, and many very wise and scholarly men-- including philosophic poets and God-inspired rulers-- have contributed to its ideas. We enjoy looking to the sayings of saintly men in our tradition and finding ways to apply those sayings to the world as it is today!”

I knew Raya too well, however, to expect that he would let this conservative viewpoint reign without a challenge.

“I have no argument against wise words from the past, and I do beg your pardon, Shaikh-ji. I would only wish to feel, if I joined your Order, that the ideas of apprentices, even if young, would not be rejected out of hand.”

My uncle chuckled at this effrontery. “Perhaps you would forgive me if I corrected any reference to me as “Shaikh,” for that is the little that I and my Sufi comrades reserve for the very wise man who directs our rituals and worship. I myself am only an apprentice who, like the other members of the khanaqah and of whatever age, regards the Shaikh as my spiritual master and guide. For example, in our sessions of dhikr, he leads us in remembering the beauty and power of the Divine attributes."

"I see," said Raya, not to be put down. "And the Shaikh gives shape to everyone's ideas?"

My uncle picked up the challenge again.

"I would prefer to say that he helps us think more clearly about the beauties and powers of God-- or, if you will, of Allah, May His Name Be Praised. Even though we repeat one of the Ninety-Nine Names ten times, or a hundred, we do not simply think alike. Each of us has his moments of Divine inspiration and discovers-- and repeats-- new ways of expressing our love for our Creator."

This silenced Raya for the moment. To express any other challenges, whether of Sufi ideas or practices, would be rude. And I knew that Raya, typically of him, had only been curious-- and bold and blunt-- but not trying to antagonize this man who was so sincere and so much his elder!

It was my time to speak, if ever.

"Uncle," I said, "your way of describing Sufism makes me realize that you and your comrades are no ordinary Muslims-- and certainly not ordinary men! Let me say I have grown up an "ordinary" Muslim of the Sunni faith, and I have tried to follow the way of the Shahada and the most basic teachings of the Qur'an for our daily lives, yet I see that many a Muslim-- how like myself!-- do these things only by habit and without reflection. Clearly you and your Sufi brothers are much more serious than that. Your daily devotions impress me. I am ashamed of myself for my lack of faith."

My uncle had shifted his gaze to me, perhaps trying to understand why I had-- yes-- interrupted. Was it merely to pacify him and find a way of apologizing for Raya's manner?

"You are revealing," said my uncle, "that you are both young men of thought and presence of mind. Someday, I believe, you will find more of value in our Sufi path. You will want to see our Faith, the way of Islam, fulfilled more devoutly. I truly believe that one or both of you will join our fold as wearers of the woolen robe. You will understand that men's behaviour in the world, even when they are sincere Muslims, is often lacking in true gratitude and love of God, and that they are often drawn into paths that ignore or defy God."

He seemed to be tiring of his responsibility to lecture us, but he pushed on. "You will not expect perfection, of course, either of yourselves or of others, even of Sufis. But you will want to be surrounded by men of faith truly seeking Divine inspiration and attempting to express in every way their love of the One God who, in His love, created them and sustains them in every breath every day."

What had started as an explanation, or perhaps a reassurance, had indeed become a sermon! Yet I-- and even Raya, I could see-- was affected by it. Raya had asked the first question, which was a request to know something about Sufism. My uncle, even though pressed for patience, had let us know some of the most essential features. And I realized, too, that he had spared us from a description of every small thing, yet had imparted the essence of his philosophy.

The mood had changed. From thinking that I had no part or advantage in anything my uncle might say, I had found a way to appreciate it.

Still, I was not ready to become a Sufi. It was a path of much tradition and ritual. It meant giving up much that made life interesting. It meant retiring from the world and living in a much more narrow one, where every other thought and action-- indeed, all thoughts and actions!-- were to focus on the worship of God. Would I ever reach the point of worshipping God the Sufi way?? Just now I could not say.

"Very well," said my uncle. "You are both tired after your journey, and I have pressed things upon you that probably should have been saved for another occasion. Please retire awhile and rest. Then, if you wish, join in one of our short sessions of worship where you will learn more about our ideas and practices."

During the two days following it became clear that Raya, for all his first show of interest in these Sufi matters, was at this point even less prepared that I to join a Sufi order!

For yes, we wished to be soldiers-- soldiers of fortune. Our quivers held many an unspent arrow. Our muskets had yet to bring down a foe-- or even an antelope.

I could tell that my uncle was glad to see us depart the next day from his orderly way of life. If he were right, and religion held the best answers, we would have to discover that for ourselves-- later.

Raya and I knew that we craved adventure. As we rode back to Bijapur, we set our imaginations free to speculate on our future. Most important was this new sense of opportunities. We were developing a mental map of our surroundings in the Deccan. We now knew more about my family, and Belgaon and its Sufis would remain on our map of awareness.

Next year, at seventeen and nineteen, we would ride forth again. As my aunt had finally agreed, we would ride south to explore the city of Raya's ancestors-- the ruined city of Vijayanagar.

Chapter 6

Qarah Khan's Death

I would remember the year of our journey to Belgaon for another reason. It was the time when a prolonged southwest Monsoon brought more than the usual rain to the Deccan during the summer and fall months. That was the year when our demanding old teacher of the arts of horsemanship, archery, and the musket fell sick.

I look back now with the eyes of an adult, and I am shocked to realize that a man like Qarah Khan might live in shoddy conditions far beneath families like my own that could claim wealth and status. In this respect old Qarah Khan was merely a servant and, for all I knew, lived like other servants in run-down, "kaccha" houses or even in tent-like structures leaning against the back walls of houses. How could I, living in the better part of the city of Bijapur, appreciate how the old Turk might live-- what lodging he would return to after a day of riding and shooting with me and Raya? I should have been ashamed-- as I am now-- to have given no thought to the old man's poverty. Thanks to my aunt's wealth Raya and I lived healthy, protected lives and paid no attention to the kind of life lived by Qarah Khan-- or gave any thought even to our better-paid language teachers.

One day when the "Rains," as we called the Monsoon, kept on fitfully throughout the day, I noticed Qarah Khan was coughing and sometimes had to clear his throat and, as politely as he could, expel the phlegm. Once when he spat on the ground, I noticed that the color was not white but a yellow-grey. Even then I refused to let my mind accept the fact that he was ill.

It was when he did not appear of a morning a week later that some idea of his illness came to me. Aunt Bibiji sent me to check on the reason for his absence. For me it meant riding halfway across the city and entering a district of shabby buildings and muddy dirt streets wholly unlike my own neighborhood. And when I located the Khan I was all the more surprised because he lived in a hut built against the wall of a house whose owners deigned to "rent" the space to him rather than leave the street clear.

I remembered how Raya once grumbled about house or shop owners who rack-rented even parts of the common street to someone. It shocked me, too, that the Khan kept his horse tied in a small enclosure covered by hides that withstood water only a little better-- for he did love that horse as a brother or friend-- than the boards serving as a roof over his own flimsy shack.

He had himself stitched the hides carefully together, but his own roof consisted of boards that had been chinked with leaking straw and plaster. His one piece of furniture was a cot of interwoven rope.

When I arrived this rainy day to inquire about his health, the Khan was lying down on a thin mattress that lay, with a blanket or two, across his cot. He coughed, cleared his throat, and sat up on his mattress. I could see that he was embarrassed, because there was no place for me to sit except the bed, which was not inviting.

Later I would realise that everyone of his class had only such "beds" as this. He was fortunate to have even the mattress and blankets that some others lacked.

The Turk, coughing again, would have tried to stand up to welcome me, but I quickly motioned him to keep seated. My polite salaam was returned with embarrassment, for he was hardly in a position to regard himself as a householder like my aunt. But by now I was determined not to treat him as an inferior.

He motioned to a boy who was crouched in a corner of the hutch where I had hardly noticed him. The boy, he said, would go and bring fruit or a melon from the bazaar. It would have been rude for Qarah Khan not to offer me some kind of refreshment, and equally rude for me to excuse myself of consuming some portion. Shortly the boy returned with two small melons. The Khan gestured for me to join him in sitting on his cot. As a guest I would not really be justified in refusing. We sat while a knife was produced and cleansed by pouring water over it from a large clay jar. The same supply of water was used to wash our hands. The melons were somewhat out of season and slightly bitter. I nevertheless praised them and thanked the Khan for his welcome.

Then at last I could ask about the old man's health and make small talk about the prolonged season of the Rains. Every time the Khan coughed I felt more regret for disturbing him and requiring the purchase of the melons. I felt as if Allah were judging us both and finding me the worse. Qarah Khan assured me that he would return to my aunt's the next day, and said we were not to worry ourselves about his cough. He would be better, he added, when sunny weather arrived. That was all I could get from him.

As I excused myself and rode away I was feeling miserable-- and not because of the rain. I hated myself, and all the circumstances that separated me from the Khan. When I reported to Aunt Bibiji, she had little to say besides thanking me. It was as if the Turk had only a small, passing illness and would be quite all right within the week.

That night I slept badly. Hearing what I thought was a cough, I sat suddenly upright in my warm bed with its thick mattress. It took me awhile to realise that I was quite alone. The rest of the night an old man's cough kept waking me.

The next morning I told Raya about my visit to the Turk. Raya listened politely but showed no sympathy. Finally I asked why he, who like myself owed so much skill at horsemanship and weaponry to Qarah Khan, seemed to care so little about the old man's health. I can still remember the casual cruelty in Raya's response.

"Why should I feel anything about him, or any sympathy for the embarrassment you seem to have felt, when he has been riding me about every fault he can think of for the past month?"

For a long moment I sat astonished. "But," I said, "he is supposed to teach and train us, Raya, and everything he does is dictated by Aunt Bibiji-- or supported afterward if we complain. And he has been sick. Isn't it just that he is easily worn out recently by any exertion, and his patience is thin?"

Raya looked me over. "All the same, he has no excuse for insulting us when we make a mistake. The fact is, we are doing everything we can to please him. And he rides us hard, both of us, and will not let up! If he has a cough, let him go to a hakim for a remedy and not come infecting us with his breath every day."

After that little speech I had nothing more to say. When the Khan returned I concentrated only on doing better at any task he gave us. If he criticized us-- and he did!-- I bent myself to working harder. Raya, if I allowed him to catch my eye, clearly thought me to be an amusing slave to this wizened old man. But afterwards I only worried. And when Qarah Khan had gone to his hovel again, I found myself praying for him. Five times that day, and every day after, I prayed to Allah for this old man. "Let him not sicken more," I begged. And I knew what lay at the doorstep of my mind. Let him not die!

But the Khan did sicken more, coughing frequently now and hardly trying to keep his old body under control. I tried to let him see that I was concerned, if only by the expression of my gaze, and yet I also felt that he did not want my sympathy, any more than he wanted Raya's.

Fortunately the clouds overhead cleared, and sunny days began drying the air and the ground around us. The Khan had survived another Monsoon-- even, I realized, when the next might be his last! And I began to think that this plateau of the Deccan, however healthy it might usually be, must never have become a real home for him. How sadly he must miss the cool, dry air of the grasslands of Badakshan from which he came so many years ago!

I consoled myself with the thought that, now more than ever, he needed this employment to regain his health, and that my aunt although lacking in visible sympathy was not like Raya, who simply wished to be rid of him. She in fact still had need of the Khan, I concluded, as long as Raya and I talked of riding south to the ruins of Vijayanagar the next year. She could be persuaded that keeping the old Turk at work for her was good for him-- and even better for us fledgling birds who hopped around thinking we were ready to abandon this nest!

I found myself laughing cynically at my own thought. Oh yes, here we were, Raya and I, two strutting crows-- or more likely two chattering mynahs-- aching to spread our wings on the winds of adventure and independence. Well, good for us! Qarah Khan, that brutal taskmaster, would soon be gone-- and there would be no one to enchain us and make us labor for them. Free, free! And I repeated the mockery.

But a day came when, even as the air and the land dried, the Khan was ill again with his mysterious cough, and his breath grew shorter. He had less strength now. He grew leaner and seemed to shrink within his leathern old skin. His step, like his archery, was losing its quickness. His eyes were losing their light. And now I prayed for him again and begged for Allah's mercy. But deep inside I knew that Qarah Khan could not last.

Finally one day the old man sent us a message by the boy who tended him. Would I come to see him? The message was only clear in that. I went.

The Khan lay on his back even when I arrived. I had heard him cough before I entered, but now he seemed deeply composed. With a crooked finger he signalled to me to sit next to him. His mouth barely moved under his beard.

"I had this dream," he said. "It kept returning. That was why I called you." He started to cough now, but stopped it with what seemed a pure act of will.

"A young boy stood beside a man," he said. "The man turned and walked away. The boy ran after him, stayed near him again. The man walked away a second time. And a third. I saw that the boy was you, Aziz Khan. You wished always to be beside that man, Maybe...it was many men. You needed someone to stand beside, learning from him, having him instruct you. But always someday he would leave you. And you would turn everywhere, looking."

The Turk had barely controlled his cough again during the last two or three sentences. Now he yielded to the cough once more-- but clenched his fist. Again he won the contest. "What do you think of all this?" he asked, tensing his fist.

I knew the answer. Perhaps the one true answer-- or many of them.

The dying man was right. It was I he spoke of. I would always seek my father, or someone like him. I would always want to have him near, teaching and encouraging. This old Turk, Qarah Khan-- he was such a man. He had come and stayed awhile, and I had taken strength from him. Now he, too, was going away-- where I could not cling to him.

I took the weakening hand nearest mine. Somehow, without quite knowing why, I held it while we gazed at each other.

"I have heard," I said, "that dreams sometimes prove true. If it is so, I will have much to remember of you." I drew a long breath that came hard for me. "For yes," I went on, "you have become a father to me, and I am sad-- almost angry-- to be losing you. You are the father I keep seeking."

Slowly I laid his hand back to rest beside him. Qarah Khan lay still. He had closed his eyes, his breathing quiet. I thought I could detect a tiny smile.

I returned to my aunt's embracing walls and strolled in her garden awhile. I was remembering Qarah Khan in he days of his vigor, when he enjoyed pushing me and Raya to the edge of exhaustion and sometimes farther. In our exercise with the Turko-Mongol bow, both while running and shooting or riding at a gallop, he would sometimes let us rest. He would then tell us a tale of Turkish stamina and bravery in the heat of the battle, most often battle on horseback.

As the details heaped up, he would see us growing impatient, and he would tell us to renew our exercises. After those and displays of marksmanship with bow and musket he would again relate some story. He told us about the rough games among Turkish young men and how they often charged and wheeled and circled in mock combat-- or just raced their ponies for the fun of it.

Now as he lay dying, I wondered if the Khan were having a vision of himself as a boy, riding and shooting with the others his age, filling his lungs with the fresh air of the northern plains. Ah, if he could just breathe that clean air again! And I remembered his telling us that the women of his tribe had learned to ride as well as the men, though keeping to their own circle. Yet sometimes one of the younger women would ride close to the men and let her eyes give the message that she wished to race him. And this would be how, often but not always, there was a pairing and later a marriage.

The old man had told many such stories. He had also told us about one girl who caught his eye-- that "special one," he would say-- who rode better and faster than could most boys and men. Yet with those words he had always stopped and changed the subject.

In my mind I could see the young Qarah Khan galloping to be near that girl. Lying now in his narrow cot-- did he still remember showing off for the girls? I wondered if he ever fell into place again with that "special" one and could see the flash of her eyes, the laughter on her lips, her long hair streaming in the wind.

Chapter 7

"City Of Victory"

It was winter, with the days short but warm, well after the monsoon rains had ceased. The rivers and streams that gushed among the rocky beds of the Deccan were again subsiding. At long last Raya and I were about to fulfill our plan of riding south to see the ruins of Vijayanagar, the Hindu "City of Victory."

Raya had the habit, whenever he thought of Vijayanagar, of lapsing into a moody silence. By his account he belonged to a branch of the ruling Vijayanagar clan. His father had been recognized as a prince, he said, whenever any grand royal event brought together the leaders of royal lineages. Orphaned when Vijayanagar fell to an alliance of Muslim states, including Bijapur, Raya had a deep resentment of Muslims. He could barely tolerate the fact that he was living now with me and my Aunt Bibiji-- a Muslim family. A sadness haunted him. But now, after hearing so much from Raya about Vijayanagar, I was ready to join him in seeing the "City of Victory" myself.

The journey had been long, through barren and insecure country, and my Aunt Bibiji had told us she would approve the adventure when we were experienced enough with horses and weapons. At the ages of nineteen and seventeen, Raya and I were sure that we were now quite mature and able to take care of ourselves. My aunt, I knew, was sceptical about this confidence, but she had honored her word and sent us on our way.

She had only one little speech. "Just remember, you are brothers now, bound to each other's care. Never forget that, even when you disagree or go far apart."

Riding our Arabian horses and leading shorter-legged, stocky Deccani geldings laden with packs, Raya and I were trying to reach Vijayanagar by midday. Rising to the crest of a low hill just north of the river

Tungabhadra, we stared across the valley beyond. For a moment we did not recognize the ruined capital!

We could easily see the sprawling river Tungabhadra, with the many channels of its rock-strewn bed. Across the river, near its south bank, we also saw the high-gated gopuram of a large, antiquated Hindu temple we had been told to expect. On the peak of the temple hung a yellow banner that told us it was a place still housing Brahman priests and drawing active worshippers.

But beyond the temple, on the southern side at the foot of a large hill, cloaked in he faint haze of noonday, we saw only granite rocks piled here and there. Some of the stones were huge, standing alone. Others, almost as large, seemed to have been propped upon each other, as if the gods of the region had been playing some obscure game. The scene did not look to us like a desolated city. Whatever was there spoke of chaos.

We looked closer. What seemed a desolate wilderness consisting of piled and scattered granite boulders slowly resolved itself into structures-- or the ruins of structures. I murmured in astonishment. Raya's face wore a kind of rigid disappointment.

The remains of unidentifiable structures along the south bank of the meandering riverbed must once have teemed with merchants, craft workers, soldiers, religious pilgrims, Hindu mendicants, and priests in the service of temples large and small. The one still active temple within its rectangle of walls presided hugely over the scene.

I could not speak of Raya's feelings just then, but the wasteland of destruction and transience sent me into a deepening mood of sadness. I could imagine grandeur and prosperity, but only in small pieces, like the fragments of some magnificent sculpture-- and now the masterpiece was gone. The scene shocked me, too, because I knew it had been "my" people, the Muslims of Bijapur, Ahmadnagar, Bidar, and Golconda who had found this place thriving-- this huge city and its suburbs-- and had reduced it to ruin and desolation.

It took us almost an hour to cross the Tungabhadra. There were some small boats made of hides sealed with pitch, but they would not carry our horses and packs as well as ourselves. The river was flowing fast in several places where the channels were wide and deep. We saw the remnants of a bridge, but the stone pilings were all of the structure that remained. At last we found a place not too deep to ford-- if we were able to coax our horses into the water. We rode the horses across half swimming, half clambering over submerged rocks, to the river's southern side. We and our mounts were exhausted, the horses snorting and heaving.

Ahead of us loomed the rocky flanks of two large hills. Both the hills were strewn with ruins of temples and watchtowers. Raya observed the ruins with a frown.

He turned to me in his saddle. "This," he said with a cynical sweep of his arm, "Must be what we came to see."

Not wanting to aggravate him further, I gazed left and right. "Shall we ride along the river first?" I asked.

He said nothing, so I reined up my horse and started downriver with my pack-horse. At almost every step of my Arabian the path was obstructed by large rocks or stone fragments.

Raya stared after me gloomily and did not budge. "Well," I thought, "if he wants to be alone it is his privilege."

At a distance downstream the ruins of a fine cluster of granite-hewn buildings came into view. I seemed to see the remains of a half-shattered temple and other structures within the walls around it. I looked back and found Raya following slowly at a distance. I resolved to ride on to the enclosure with its broken walls and explore what remained. If Raya wished to join me, that was his choice.

Soon I observed that almost half of several buildings remained. I rode in among them and dismounted. Although overgrown with rank bushes and grass, while the roots or trunk of a sapling issuing here and there from a crevice or a broken area of pavement, the design and execution of the buildings revealed an astonishing elegance.

I felt dwarfed by the heights of stone platforms, pillars, and the remains of wide-roofed buildings set in expansively paved courtyards. A large stone chariot, its wheels head high, stood near the entry-way of a long, columned walk. At the end of that passage a crumbling shrine survived, rousing me to an imagine of some royal procession that accompanied a gorgeously clothed, solid-gold image carried forth from the chariot.

Among other structures that had survived stood pavilions with almost complete rooftops that rested on thin columns of stone, the columns giving an effect of airy lightness. Again my imagination supplied the actors of some ritual event. In these shaded, cool pavilions a royal party might sit enthroned, with space enough for guards to stand, priests to attend, musicians to play, and servants to come and go. I stood awhile basking in the sound of imagined music and voices, half expecting to hear the jingle of bells on the ankles of arriving dancers.

Just then Raya appeared instead. He dismounted and looked around him as I had done. "So," he said, pretending cheerfulness, "how do you like it?"

I smiled indolently. "You interrupted my dream of musicians and dancers!"

He snorted. "And visions of dead rulers?"

"And of course dead rulers," I said, "if it makes you happier!"

"I see these palaces and shrines as shells only," retorted Raya. "Empty shells left to flaunt our humiliation and defeat."

"Well, then," I came back, "enjoy your outrage." I started pacing. "Do you think I hate Hindus? Was I the killer of your father or mother? Did I despoil these places!? You are an idiot. What did I do to earn this attitude of yours? No, I do not hate Hindus, my dear Raya. And I know too little of their religion to hate that either!"

With that I mounted and turned my horses. Raya aimed a last look of annoyance at me. "Enjoy your adventure," he said.

I looked up at the nearest of the two large hills that defined the shape of the devastated city. I vowed to ride up that hill, cross it, and go down the other side.

Raya caught up before I could ride far among the shattered rocks. "Enough!" he said. "I am behaving badly." He rode close and touched my arm. "Please know, Aziz Khan, that I do not blame you for what your rulers did-- they and their armies I am only sad for my people, humiliated for them, angry for them. I think you will understand that."

I relented, feeling his grief. "I should apologize also. I misjudged how all this would affect you."

We rode on toward the nearer hill. The sun baked down upon the stones scattered and heaped around us. Threading our way up the hill, we found more ruins at the top but only looked-- did not speak-- and went down the other side. We were facing a vast array of broken structures spread across the wide valley ahead.

We kept coming upon the chipped or chiseled walls and floor of what must have been noble pavilions. Along the lower walls of one or two shrines that had partly survived were sculpted panels that contained scenes of processions, including dancers, foot-soldiers, and riders on horseback. Even then the lower panels were almost hidden by piles of rubble. The scorn and hatred of Muslim victors was like a welling up of dust around us.

Suddenly my companion drew up his horse and shouted. "No more of this, brother! I cannot bear seeing it!" He threw me a look distorted almost to tears. He jerked his bridle reins and turned his horse my way, almost shoving my animal back on its haunches. "Do you understand, Aziz Ahmad? I am leaving this place. Now!"

This time his reaction, even to me, seemed right.

I, too, the Muslim, the offspring of victors and despoilers, wanted to leave. Our eyes and minds could not restore a view of the city's royal greatness. For Raya, and for me also, there was too much pain.

We started riding away as fast as the terrain would admit. Raya kept his pack-horse close roped behind him. I had to do the same. We proceeded over the nearest shoulder of the smaller of the two hills that stood between us and the river Tungabhadra. I could see that Raya was set on returning to the place where we had forded the river. We would go the way we had come.

Our path led between some huge boulders that narrowed the way, threatening to close off the path altogether. Raya was still leading. Abruptly he came to a halt, his horse half rearing before some obstruction. A curse floated back to me.

Then a statement. "Holy Man, you are blocking our way. Please give us space to pass"

In a moment I had come to a stop behind Raya's two horses. I dismounted and squeezed my way forward between horses and rocks. In the middle of a very narrow space squatted an old man-- almost naked, one of those holy men called by Hindus "saddhu"-- who had been worshipping at a circle of small stones surrounding the crudely carved stone image of a god. As I arrived the saddhu was stolidly finishing a prayer. The man evidently had not bothered to look up at my demanding companion.

I quickly took in the rest of the scene. The saddhu had made some kind of residence for himself in the nearby cleft between two giant rocks. A staff bearing a trident stood thrust into the hard ground next to the cleft. I had as yet no great knowledge of Hindu sects or practices, but I guessed that the saddhu might be a worshipper of the god Shiva. In any case it was clear that Raya and I would either wait for the man to complete his prayers, or we would back ourselves out of the narrow space where he squatted and find another way to the river.

In fact I found the confrontation almost amusing, as Raya was after all a Hindu and should be preparing to give alms to the man rather than railing at him like some misbegotten Muslim.

Something in me decided to teach my friend a small lesson-- which was that Muslims, like good Hindus, were much accustomed to the giving of alms, it being one of the main points of our Muslim religion.

Raya had not dismounted but was trying to control his conflict of annoyance and respect. I slipped past him on foot and took up a kneeling position near the saddhu, whose advanced age was betrayed by long grey hair drawn up roughly in a bun, his leathery skin and deep facial crevices, and his rheumy old eyes. The old man uttered some last phrases of prayer and sat on his heels with eyes closed for a time. I said nothing.

The saddhu opened his eyes and peered at me. There was annoyance in his gaze but also a hint of amusement.

"You wished something?" he asked in a cracked voice with strong Dakkhini accents. The voice could have cut through impertinence like a knife.

"No, old father," I said, "we were only passing though and did not realize that we would disturb you."

Yellow teeth regarded me with a grin. He looked up, giving Raya the benefit of the same grin. "I am no one's father," said the cracked voice, "and you are at leave to pass as soon as I have collected the things with which I worship. Only give me yet some time and a little politeness, and you may go your way."

Abruptly he reached out and took my right hand in a strong grip. He turned the palm up and studied it, followed by fingers and thumb. My hand looked pale and weak in his leathery, imperious grasp. The saddhu was silent awhile. He merely studied the signs that might disclose my character-- and future.

At last the voice rasped again. "You will travel far, young man, and pursue high ambition. You are not greedy but of great curiosity. Your intellect will commend you to a great man, whom you will serve and follow for many years. I see much of war and danger in your future, but you will become respected by many who at first do not know your value."

He looked up at my face and scars. "The wounds you bear will keep you from your highest goals, for those wounds will often be misunderstood for a sign of weakness. But you have hidden strength and will receive many a confidence from those who see beyond appearances."

He stared at my hand again, especially the thumb. "You have a good heart and will find true love. You will be rewarded with long life, though you suffer many disappointments. Also you will receive much friendship and survive the traps set by enemies. Trust your fortune and do not be afraid."

He released my hand and sat back on his haunches. At first his gaze had unnerved me, but now there was a kind of benevolence in it. I must reward him! But with what? A handful of Bijapuri coins would not do.

I had almost forgotten that Raya was still in the saddle. Glancing his way, I realized that he had watched the whole episode with a look of forced patience. Slowly I rose and returned to my horse. I decided that I had only one thing that the holy man might value. It was a cloak of fine Persian wool that my Aunt Bibiji had given me when Raya and I departed for Vijayanagar. I pulled the cloak from the rolled-up blanket in which I had been carrying it.

I returned with the cloak to the old man, who remained as immovable as the stones around him. I turned back some folds of the cloak for him. "Sometimes the nights are cold," I said. "Please take this as my gift."

The old fellow took the cloak and looked at it carefully, fingering the fabric and its finely stitched sedge. After a long silence he smiled. "Not one night, but many, are cold among these stones. Your gift is good. It comes from a man of honor."

And with that he rose, a movement more flexible and strong than I had expected, and disappeared into the cleft between the stones that he had made his residence.

Trying not to look smug, I threw Raya a glance. He smiled, half by indulgence-- and shrugged, half by dismissal.

The old saddhu returned. He was carrying a small, silken pouch, the silk old and faded. He took my nearest hand, placed the pouch in it, and closed the fingers under his own. "It is something of little value to me," he said, "distant as I am from the world you are destined to have within your grasp." He gave me a look of surprising warmth. "Take it. Do not refuse it."

His eye caught Raya's before returning to me. "But do not open the pouch now, young rider. Wait for a time when you can reflect upon it. If it suits your need at some unexpected time, Lord Shiva will be satisfied."

Without another word the old man took up the small bundle of items with which he had been doing his prayers of puja. He turned and disappeared again into the cleft between the rocks. The wind seemed to acknowledge his finality with a little swirl of dust.

Raya eyed the pouch in my hand. I could see that curiosity had seized on him and made him its prisoner. I carefully put the pouch away in an inner pocket and, without a word, returned to my horse and remounted.

Having descended the hill, we found that fording the river Tungabhadra was still no simple matter.

We crossed, struggling again to keep ourselves and the horses upright among the boulders in the water's rush. This time, tired as we were, the crossing was even more difficult. Raya's mood, though, was like a force of nature. We succeeded without losing ourselves or our animals.

There was the a village close by, north of the river. I would have stopped there to rest. Raya ignored the village and kept riding. At a crossroad he turned west. I fell in behind him, not caring to attempt conversation. He had withdrawn into himself.

By nightfall we had reached another village, a larger one. There, in a grove of banyan trees, Raya had us stop. We were both happy to be well north of the great river and its ruins.

The grey light before the dawn found Raya up and ready, re-saddling the horses and loading them again while I was still half awake. I lay listening to the sound of mynahs croaking and calling among the branches of a banyan tree. I did not want to waken. Sitting up at last, I observed how the long air-roots of the banyan had created a large, shady grove around us.

"Up!" said Raya, not unpleasantly, when he saw me gazing at the banyan.

I moaned, rolled over, and got to my feet. There was a well nearby. Probably it was a caste well for Hindus that I, a Muslim, would foul by using.

I turned to Raya. "Would it, my dear Hindu friend, be beyond your mercy to procure from yonder well some water for my Muslim ablutions, in order to avoid a riot or some such event?"

"I suggest this water-bag of ours," said Raya, tossing its considerable weight in my direction. "It will lose us no friends among my fellow Hindus!"

I knew I could have used sand or dust as ritual cleanser if we lacked water, but I washed my face, hands, and forearms gratefully. In a few moments, having done my prayers in the direction of distant Mecca, I felt ready to go.

"What do you think?" I inquired. "Would you have us return through the wilds to our north, or continue on this road-- for such the rutted path we came by appears to be? In a day, perhaps two, we should be able to reach Dharwara, where we can turn north to Bijapur."

Raya shook his head in mock sadness. "I take it, my Muslim friend, that you prefer the ease of the road. You have no stomach for more rocks and hills?" But I could see that he was happy to go in any direction other than the road to Vijayanagar.

We stayed on the road west. Raya, for a change, was willing to banter about anything that avoided too much seriousness. "You could open that pouch the holy man gave you, friend Aziz," he said after awhile. "Surely our benefactor the saddhu did not mean to keep it an eternal secret."

I was curious myself, frankly. But I suggested that we wait for a place to rest the horses. Raya could hardly argue with that, but I could see he was still impatient. Let him suffer, I thought! It was almost the noonday when we halted in shade of a convenient tree.

I retrieved the pouch and proceeded to open it. Through the silk I had already guessed that a stone lay inside. I emptied the content into my palm. It was a ruby of amazing size, brilliant with what seemed a liquid inner fire!

Raya and I both stared, speechless at first. I hefted the stone. "Dare I ask," I said to him, "if it appears genuine to your practiced eye?"

"It could only have been a king's possession," he murmured, "or it could have been extracted from the space between the eyes of some divine image sculpted of stone or fine metal."

"I suppose you are right," I sighed. I turned the ruby over in my fingers. It was faceted to make a play of light-- and could hardly have been pried from anything less than a masterpiece of sculpture.

"Surely," I said, "it is not meant to be sold." I hefted it again. "I will just have to keep it, I suppose." Raya looked at me strangely. This was no longer curiosity. It was envy. But he restrained himself and was silent.

"Here," I offered, "you certainly should touch it-- before I put it away." Slowly Raya took the ruby. He kept turning it over in his hand, as I had. At last, sadly, he handed it back.

"It is worth a fortune. Keep it safe," he said. I could see that he hated to return the stone, be it to a thieving saddhu or to a Muslim whose people had despoiled his country.

Carefully I returned the ruby to its frayed silken pouch, tied the drawstrings, and tucked it into a secret place within the seam of my jacket. As we rode on, Raya was silent. It was another hour before he could be his normal self. We did not speak of the stone again.

I was remembering the saddhu and his prophesies-- and basking in the day's warmth and the thought of the long, adventurous life I had been promised.

Chapter 8

Two Jesuit Travelers

We continued westward for about an hour when I realized that it was past time for my midday prayers. I glanced at Raya, whose look of gloom suggested caution. I decided that I would do well to say my prayers from horseback this time-- especially as I had seen no nearby tree that would provide my companion with at least some shade. So I muttered the Shahada and proceeded without the standings,kneelings, and prostrations.

Suddenly my companion, who was riding ahead, turned in his saddle and gave me a sour look. "Oh, for God's sake, stop mumbling! I will gladly stop when we can find a tree, any tree, and let you spread your rug in the shade!"

I tried a grin. "I thought you were in no mood for it!"

He laughed. "Forget my mood! It is likely to last awhile. And besides, this is your midday prayer, the most important one you have told me over and over."

I sighed. "All I really need is to say the prayer with sincerity. That I can do in silence. I forgot I was mumbling!"

Raya shook his head. "So why all this about the prayer rug and facing Mecca? Would not silence and sincerity just be enough?"

"Well," I said, "I think I told you more than once, it's not absolutely required by Allah, it's the...."

"I know, I know," he cut me off. "It's the custom!

"But when traveling, or at war, or in the face of obstacles, we may sometimes compromise."

We rode silently awhile. "All right, he said. "I accept the compromise. Go ahead and mutter!"

And that was how we finally settled the question of the Muslim five daily prayers-- whenever the two of us were riding together-- except that, by agreement, I would not 'mutter' but ride a little apart and speak in a low, clear voice that did fundamental justice to the Shahada and the rest of my Muslim prayers. In that and other ways Raya and I kept learning how to avoid conflict by the small compromises that made living and traveling together just a bit easier.

As the afternoon wore on under a hot, clear sky we were scanning some hills ahead. Suddenly our attention was caught by a low cloud of dust rising over the road.

"Horsemen!" said Raya, squinting. "Maybe a dozen, maybe twice that!" It became clear that we, who were riding faster, would soon overtake them.

"Can we ride slower and not approach them?" I asked. "They may be traders with with a train of pack animals. Or they could be soldiers-- or bandits!"

"A little cautious of you, dear Aziz," scoffed Raya. "Our quivers are thick with arrows and this morning our muskets were reloaded and primed. Our horses are more or less fresh. What is to be feared?"

It was a challenge I could not let pass me. I gave my Arabian a light spur and increased our pace. If the dust-making column were peaceful, we could easily pass them and ride on. If they seemed hostile, we could fall back or take another way.

As we closed on the riders, Raya counted twenty-four in the main column, with an equal number of pack horses following in train. More than half the riders held lances at the vertical, but Raya noted that the whole cavalcade rode without much order.

"Not much leadership going on there," said my companion. "I suggest we just pass them as if they hardly existed. By the time their leaders decide what to do we will be gone!"

But soon, as we looked toward the head of the column, we saw two figures strangely dressed-- in long black cloaks and black, wide-brimmed hats. We stared.

"You know," I said, "those could be Europeans. Traders or missionaries. And maybe-- to judge by what little I have heard about their way of dressing, Jesuit missionaries."

Raya snorted. "Good! We can be past them and gone before they bother to notice us either."

"That may be," I said, "but it could also be interesting to learn their destination, which I suppose is Goa, and why they are crossing these barren parts of the Deccan."

Raya threw me a look. "I see where your thoughts are going, dear Aziz Khan. You would like to ride with them, I take it."

I grinned. "Thank-you for the idea, my dear Raya! In fact, now that my curiosity is aroused, I would like very much like to have their company awhile. It would make this trek a lot less dull!"

Raya shook his head but grinned. "Since we are dressed as armed Muslims, they may not be too happy with our company, Aziz Ahmad. Let's make their acquaintance short!"

I shrugged. But I had won the contest of wills. We would fall in with the two Jesuits if we were able.

As we moved ahead, Raya busied himself counting the exact number of riders. "Twenty-four," he said presently, "counting the two Jesuits. I am not impressed by the discipline of the other twenty-two. They could be soldiers of fortune-- not much above bandits. I wonder why the Jesuits would trust them."

I was looking mainly at the pair of Jesuits with their black cloaks and broad-brimmed but low-peaked hats of strange design, also black. The two were chatting easily and seemed to be without weapons. Such, I thought, was their trust in divine protection!

My gaze shifted to the rough-looking commander of the riders who rode before and after the Jesuits. The other riders, like their commander, wore mismatched pieces of armor. Only the commander and two companions riding directly behind him carried muskets of the Portuguese type. Most carried no weapons other than swords and lances. A few carried quivers and bows. Some wore helmets, others only turbans. I had to agree with Raya that I would not have committed two holy men, let alone ourselves, to the protection of such a gathering.

We came up behind the cavalcade but kept a careful distance. Eventually someone noticed us and spread the word. We faced some very hostile stares. The two Jesuits turned in their saddles and regarded us. They slowed to a stop.

Our own two muskets, loaded and primed, lay across our saddles where a free hand held them balanced. Raya murmured angrily that we would expose ourselves to twenty or so men by simply riding up to them.

We halted. One of the Jesuits turned his mount and rode back to us. I gave Raya a terse look. "Just keep your eyes open if you don't mind," I told him. "Let me do the talking."

The Jesuit, who seemed to be the older of the two, looked us over carefully and seemed to judge that we were inoffensive Muslim travelers, not hardened adventurers.

"I am brother Monserrate of the Society of Jesus," he said in good Persian, "and my companion is Brother Castro, also of the Society."

"We regret if we have startled you," I said in my own best Persian-- and repeated it in Dakkhini. "I am Aziz Ahmad Khan of Bijapur, and with me is Rama-Raya of the recent Vijayanagar kingdom."

Interest flickered into view in the Jesuit's eyes. "May I assume you recently would have been enemies, but are now friends?"

I was uncertain how this conversation would progress, and answered only "That is so." My glance beyond the Jesuit told me that everyone else, including Raya, would like to see an end of this talk and be on their separate ways.

"We are returning to Goa from Saint Thomas Mount on your country's eastern coast," said the Jesuit Monserrate. "You may ride with us awhile if it is your pleasure," he added.

I explained with similar diplomacy that Raya and I were returning to Bijapur by way of Dharwara, and that we could accompany the two Jesuits to the parting of roads at Dharwara.

Surprising me, Monserrate offered me his hand and a smile. "Brother Castro and I would be glad to have you ride with us," he said. I could almost fee Raya stir unhappily in his saddle as I took the Jesuit's hand. Monserrate's hand was strong, and the pressure of his fingers promised good fellowship and natural friendliness. My only doubt was about Castro, whose eyes held no such welcome. Monserrate must have seen the same stiffness in Raya. But, like myself, the Jesuit was prepared to ignore it.

The thought passed through my mind, too, that Monserrate was no more sure of his accompanying riders' intentions than Raya had been. At any rate, my seizing a chance to talk with the Jesuit had come about as Raya predicted.

We started west again, with Raya and I arrayed beside the two Jesuits. The twenty-two other horsemen fell in behind us in ragged order, headed by the truculent commander and his two lieutenants.

It soon became clear that I would have Monserrate to myself. The two of us were soon deep in conversation. It almost amused me that Raya and Castro kept to the silence of hostile listeners.

I stole a look at Monserrate's face. His eyes were rather small but spaced well, and a look of intelligent concentration enlivened them. His mouth, though small like his eyes, turned up slightly at the corners as if he were always ready to smile, and the small teeth were even and white. I had known no Europeans with such agreeable features, not handsome perhaps, but of an alert mind and friendly disposition.

The Jesuit quickly set me at ease by asking about my town of origin and the places my trip had taken me. When I named Bijapur he recognized it as the Muslim capital that had previously ruled Goa after taking it from Vijayanagar. I noticed Raya's mouth tighten, but he remained silent. Monserrate then asked further about Vijayanagar and the impression I had of it. Feeling myself under Raya's scrutiny, I kept to a few bland remarks about the ruins. I could see my Hindu companion poised on the brink of some hard words about Portuguese interference in our country.

To avoid an outburst from Raya, I hurried to ask Monserrate about the origins of the Society of Jesus, how its members worked, what its goals were. The Jesuit's face brightened. I quickly saw that he could not resist this chance to woo a Muslim to the Christian faith. I not ready for such a choice, yet my curiosity was aroused. If Raya would hold his tongue I might learn something.

Monserrate spoke glowingly about Ignatius Loyola, founder of the Society, who had been a soldier and courtier but had turned to a more peaceful kind of career, a monastic one. The Jesuit told eloquently how Loyola had recruited his followers among men who were students and intellectuals, many of them clergy-- how he preached a revived and more potent Church-- the Roman or Catholic "church universal"-- in a time of increasing challenge from certain churchmen who were coming forth as "Protestants." And what were Protestants? Men who protested against weaknesses and defects in the Church and started calling for a "Reformation." And if they could not reform the Church from within, they would split away to form churches of their own. But fortunately Ignatius found allies, too, and in the end he created an order of monks and won the support not only of a Pope of the Church but also the kings of several countries.

Ignatius, said Monserrate, flung himself into opposing any Reformation which abandoned and opposed the true Church. His creed called for strengthening the Church from the ground up, with the Society of Jesus in the lead. All of Europe-- and now parts of the "New World" found by Columbus the mariner, and parts also of Africa and Asia opened up by Portuguese and Spanish captains-- became areas into which members of the Society of Jesus poured their energies and lives in order to win people everywhere to the Church and the Christian faith.

To achieve his goals, added Monserrate proudly, Ignatius especially worked to bring men of intellect and energy into his Society, men willing to go anywhere, regardless of the part of Europe from which they came, regardless of the language they spoke. Like members of many another Order-- Augustinian, Dominican, and Franciscan, to name only the most prominent-- the men of the society were to use Latin, the Church's Latin, in communicating with each other, both for its efficiency and because it was the language of the Holy Bible and of the version approved by the Church. The Jesuits, he said, were dedicated to exceed all other monastic brotherhoods in spreading the Word of God through education and to do so widely among the peoples of the world.

Monserrate's enthusiasm was so lively that I became more and more impressed, not merely with his Society but with the man himself. I wondered how it would be to ride to Goa, to see the Society at work and to make him my guide and teacher. It was not, I told myself, that I was ready to "convert." But could this man, whose intellect and sense of mission I was finding more and more admirable, help me understand Christianity rather than simply oppose it? At least, if I remained a Muslim, I could develop what I now lacked-- a reasoned and knowledgeable view of either Christianity or my own faith.

I began to have a strange sense of elation. Fate had brought me into a whole new realm of thought and choices-- here on this road-- inspired by this man's vision and devotion to his cause. I needed something like this, this life that now might have a shape and a cause, rather than wandering vaguely in search of military exploits or some post in government!

What did it matter, I asked myself, if this man Monserrate were a Christian? No doubt if I went to Goa under his guidance he would hope for my conversion. Yes, he could educate me in his faith and try to convert me to it, but it did not mean that I must abandon mine and take up his. It was the chance to see Portuguese rule up close in Goa, to explore new ideas, and to make my own decisions about them. All this had suddenly taken hold of my imagination.

The Jesuit was silent a few moments as we jogged ahead. He was studying me, I knew. He sensed my excitement.

"You are a young man of intelligence, I believe," he said. "You are also disciplined and, it seems, on the way to becoming a soldier." He paused. "I was a soldier once-- as was our 'General,' Ignatius. But we both saw, after awhile, that the best battles are of the mind, the best discipline that of the heart, the best cause that of Christian faith and God's cause! We had studied how to fight men and kill them. Now we studied a new discipline-- how to win men's souls and commit them not to the destruction of other men but to their Salvation!"

Monserrate waited awhile, silent again.

"Forgive me if I am too forward," he went on. "But I feel, Aziz Khan, that you may understand what I have said. You will of course follow your own path, which may be to remain a Muslim and a soldier. But if what I say interests and compels you, I would be most ready to have you accompany me to Goa, reside there under my protection, and provide yourself with whatever knowledge you wish. Then, if you find Conversion the right step for you, I will do whatever I can to assist you in making that step.

"If you find that, even when you are in some measure satisfied with what you have learned, you nevertheless feel that our Christian way is not acceptable to you, I will see that you safely return to Bijapur. Whatever your decision, I believe you will have become even more a man of knowledge and discipline. As long as you remain a man of honor and principle, I will remain your friend."

I rode awhile silently, stunned by the Jesuit's offer-- and his honorable attitude toward me as a Muslim. Could it all be true? Was I really at the point of the choice he offered me? Did I have the courage to do this-- and take the risks? What must Raya be thinking? Even more, what would my Aunt Bibiji make of such a daring venture with all the risks attached? Was I being ungrateful to her, a self-deluded fool even to consider going to Goa-- with or without Raya?

I hardly stumbled through these thoughts when I found Raya's horses moving very close to mine. Raya leaned and whispered in my ear. "This group of men is riding too slow, and night is coming. I would not like to be caught among these travelers at night." He straightened and gave me a look with some message in it. It was not about religion or the Society of Jesus, I decided.

I turned to Monserrate. "My friend Raya believes the two of us should ride ahead and see what would be a good place to spend the night. There is supposed to be a village not far away. He wishes us to ride faster and have a look at it."

It was a lie, but a convenient one. Monserrate considered a moment, and then agreed. "I did not mean to say so much about our Society, but as you can see, it means much to me. Please ride ahead and see what you can find for yourselves."

He hesitated and gave me a pleased look. "I believe, Aziz Ahmad Khan, that you will find success in any venture you choose."

Again a hesitation on his part. "If we meet again, I will be most happy to repeat my welcome to our society in Goa."

Monserrate did not expect us to meet again! That much I could see.

I gave my farewell with a salaam-- and returned his gaze a moment. His eyes were serious, yet somehow still held out to me the hope he had expressed. I turned reluctantly and spurred my Arabian.

"What," I asked Raya as we separated ourselves from the group, "is this all about?"

Raya could have smiled at the triumph of tearing me away from Monserrate. I saw no smile. "I know some pieces of the Tamil language, and I heard something pass between the commander and his two friends-- who, incidentally, were behind our backs and could have killed us at any moment."

Now I was not smiling either. "You are always suspicious, Raya!"

"They are planning something," said Raya emphatically. "Or they have already planned it. They will attack those two Jesuits in the dark of night. And can you guess? The two of us, who are armed, and are seen as sympathetic to these Jesuits, would be the first to fall."

I had a vision of myself pitching forward with a bullet in my back. I picked up my pace. Then I thought-- "but this is a coward's way." We could really be killed, if what Raya heard was true. Was the logic of it therefore to abandon the Jesuits to their deaths?? It made me angry, and I told Raya so.

Raya took a long breath. "You would rather stay behind and have the miscreants kill us all?"

"We might have warned the Jesuits," I burst out, "and attacked the treacherous dogs behind us when <u>we</u> were ready!"

Raya smiled as if dealing with an idiot. "When we were only two, and they have three muskets between them? I don't think so."

"So tell me what you <u>do</u> propose!"

"We need to stay within hearing distance, and maybe achieve surprise-- also in the dark of night. It would then be we two who had the advantage. And we have not only two muskets but quivers full of very accurate arrows! In the dark the bandits would not know where they were being attacked. Our advantage again."

I turned the idea over as we rode. Bold, but it might work. I sighed.

"You know, Raya, sometimes I have to bow to you. I know. Laugh! But it's true. I only worry about our staying close enough to be ready in time-- and able to get around by foot on unfamiliar ground."

Raya did laugh. "I appreciate your gratitude." He paused. "But they will have to stop sometime soon-- before sunset if they are smart. We can set up a sort of camp near them, and attack by road if we have to!"

I meditated on that. "All right, wise one. Your great logic again stuns me. You lead, I follow."

We kept riding ahead. Not too far ahead, using the rolling slopes of a few almost barren hills to hide our presence. Finally, as darkness descended, we had to find a place to camp. We tried the crest of a hill. We could not see the cavalcade down the road, but we reasoned that neither they nor we could afford to ride much farther. We stopped and listened hard. There might be distant voices, or.... Nothing definite.

There were rocks exposed on the barren ground around us. So, apart from any defensive value they might have, our best thing was to clear the ground of any snakes, scorpions, or centipedes. We did our best--and laid out our blankets.

"I don't like this," I said. "We need a campfire."

Raya agreed. "You build the fire. I will watch it."

I said my evening prayer to Allah. Raya and I would need His help. I lay fully dressed while Raya sat poking at the fire.

The only sounds other than the low, crackling fire were a few crickets and the distant yips and yowls of a pack of Deccani jackals. Declining westward, barely visible, was the thin crescent of a new moon.

Chapter 9

Defending The Jesuits

The stars of midnight were approaching the zenith when I suddenly awoke. A scorpion scrambling nearby? A pair of foraging jackals? I listened. Faint sounds. Distant faint sounds coming in ragged bunches. The report of a musket? I listened harder. Yes, I was certain. A second shot. The neighing of a horse. Men's voice shouting. I tried to judge the direction. From the east, carried on the faint night breeze! I scrambled to my feet and stared eastward, into the darkness.

Raya was sitting up now, though I had heard him curse me. But he was listening, too. "At least one gunshot. Maybe two. And shouts. Men shouting."

"We need to get back to the road, head toward that hamlet we passed!" said I. I was almost shaking in the night air.

Raya was not so enthusiastic-- or close to panic. "The country is full of bandits," he said; "what did you expect?"

I could barely make out his profile in the dark, but my sight was improving thanks to the brilliance of starlight spread across the sky. "And there are two Jesuits," I said firmly, "with twenty horsemen whom I would not trust to defend anyone! I beg of you, Raya. We have to go. With our muskets and bows and arrows. Go with me, please. Otherwise I will have to go alone!"

My little speech annoyed Raya, but he agreed to join me. We saddled our Arabians to cover as much distance as possible on horseback, but we knew it could be foolish to make a charge, especially at night. Our tactic, if we found the Jesuit party under attack, would have to be to dismount and make our last approach on foot. Though only two, we might have the advantage of surprise. We could spread slightly apart. Ten, twenty paces. We agreed that would mask our numbers. Our ridiculous numbers!

Arming quickly, we led our horses to the road, mounted, and set out at a canter. The cart-path of a road had a high crown between the wheel ruts, and we could keep to the center of the road with fair confidence. Naturally I led, but a few words settled the question of how we would approach the fight. We could now hear it clearly in the distance, though now we heard only shouts, no more

Whoever had the guns, and why there were only two shots, mystified us. The shouting wavered and died. Whatever had happened… had already ended.

As we came within a gunshot's distance of the sound, a pall of silence seemed to have settled. The darkness was still almost total around us, but our gazes pried it open.

We were young and, if foolish, would have been impetuous enough to close the distance on our horses, but we quickly reined in, dismounted, and advanced at a fast walk. Soon we heard voices. Men's voices in a Dakkhini dialect. The sounds were not promising. Our horses were well trained for hunting, and we hobbled them loosely.

The scene we came was surprisingly bright. A fire within a circle of stones still burned. Men stood in two or three clusters. Others lay scattered on the ground, their shapes twisted. The two Jesuits sat with their hands freshly tied behind them. From the position where Raya and I lay crouched in some dry grass it was evident that attackers had taken over the encampment of the Jesuit priests and their escort. Their escort? Or was it… an attack <u>by</u> the escort? Only one thing pleased us. The attackers had made no attempt to set out pickets.

We already had a plan, Raya and I, agreeing to use a good many of our arrows first, gaining from the relative silence of our own attack to create more the surprise. Our muskets, reloaded and primed again, could give us only two shots for sure-- and would betray our positions-- and limited numbers!-- with their muzzle flashes. If we were careful, the whirr and impact of our arrows might be enough to panic the attackers and drive them running into the dark.

Now we would see whether old Qarah Khan's training and our constant practice would guide our shafts to their targets.

Raya remembered another thing about the old Turk's advice. "Count their guns first," he said.

Two men who stood forward, facing the Jesuits, were holding muskets. We could make out the shapes of no other weapons but swords and lances.

Now it was clear that the men before us, living and dead, were all members of the horse-guards that the Jesuits had trusted to defend them. And now we recognized the body of a man lying face down between the fire and the two Jesuits. He had been the horsemen's leader. Someone had killed him first. We were staring at a mutiny.

Standing with his feet apart, the most prominent man with his musket was surveying the two seated and bound. Monserrate was looking up and talking. I could hardly hear his words, but he was speaking in broken Dakkhini, in which he was asking for God's mercy. The leader of the attackers told him, in pungent Dakkhani dialect, to shut his mouth. "They may have money-- or jewels," said the leader. "Strip them." He jerked his chin toward two horsemen standing nearby. The two men came forward. Raya and I exchanged glances.

"Time to move apart," I muttered. "Make it twenty paces-- ten apiece." Raya touched my arm and pointed. "What about the two in the saddle there are the rear, the ones with the rest of the horses hobbled behind them in the middle of the road behind them? They could rally a defense."

I followed his pointed finger. So," I agreed, "we take down the leaders, then the two men on horseback-- if they're not too far away." Raya smiled in the shadows. "Have we recently missed a hawk at that distance!?" We separated, moving slowly, ten paces each. My first arrow would be the signal.

The bandit captain moved to stand over the Jesuits while stripped-off cloaks and undergarments were flung to the ground.

Monserrate was not asking for mercy now, but praying. "Dear Savior, forgive us our sins. We beg your mercy on all your children, be they Christian or gentile. Thy Will be done." At this moment, I had no such thoughts of compassion. I was about to kill half a dozen men. But then, without our arrows, the two Jesuits would be among the dead.

Unfortunately my first arrow only lodged into the leader's shoulder. He turned my direction, staring, though he could not see his assailant. My second shaft struck his chest but seemed to have lodged in a rib. With a curse I aimed more carefully. The third arrow went deep above his heart. He pitched forward-- just as he fired into the dark and I heard the ball whip past my head.

Raya did better, bringing down the second of the leaders with one well-placed arrow-- taking him below his breastbone as he, too, turned our way staring. Men were moving now at the center of the circle, looking this way and that. Raya's second arrow felled a third man who seemed to be giving orders. I aimed now at the one of the commanding horsemen in the road behind the scene. Without waiting to see the hit I sent another arrow after the first. It was a wise move, because the first arrow chipped a collarbone and flew wide, but the second found his chest, leaving him teetering in the saddle a moment before he careened to the ground. I did not see Raya's arrow until the second mounted man stood in his stirrups and began tugging at the shaft in his chest.

Bereft of their leaders, the miscreants ran back and forth shouting and trying to peer into the night. One man snatched up a fallen musket, fired wildly, and tried to reload. An arrow from Raya brought him to his knees. A second one from my bow, already in flight, finished him.

Like my friend I kept looking for men who seemed too alert or reasonable to panic. Suddenly I heard a weird sound from Raya, like an animal keening in the hunt. The sound chilled me. I added cries of my own. The tactic worked. Men started running away into the darkness.

Raya and I had our muskets, but with only two loads between us we instinctively kept to our bows. Soon the whole crowd of the surviving attackers were making for their horses, unsure whether our force on the hill were few or many. Only when the disorderly survivors mounted and started riding away in crazed terror did Raya and I, as if by a joint decision there in the dark, take up our muskets and fire, felling one slacker and wounding another. The sound of firing we had guessed-- even with only two muskets-- would be enough to keep the survivors riding quite a while.

And all through this the Jesuits, stripped naked and crouching low near the fire, could do nothing but look, listen, and keep their heads down.

Slowly, moving crouched over, Raya and I approached the fire that had almost burned away to coals. I was first to reach the missionaries. The two men were still almost naked, clutching their clothes to their chests, trying for privacy. It amused me how white, both in skin tone and in the color of his face, Castro looked. He was thoroughly alarmed and must have thought me a demon from hell, whether Hindu or Muslim it made no difference! Monserrate almost immediately recognized me. He was on his knees now, searching for the belongings that lay heaped around him.

Monserrate slowly straightened. "Why did I think of you suddenly?" he said to me in Persian-- "just before you appeared like this? It must be God's work!" I smiled. "Everything is in God's sight," I said, using the word Allah; "but are you all right, Father?"

He put a hand on my arm. "Brother Castro is hurt," is said, "but thanks be to God I am well." I turned to see Raya, as we had agreed, keeping a close watch on the prostrate forms around us and glancing apprehensively into the night. "They could be back!" said Raya-- "Hurry."

I was going to help the two men get dressed. Castro pushed me away. His expression said to me, "You rescued us, but you are still a Muslim dog. I want nothing more to do with you."

I turned to Monserrate. As I helped him dress he thanked me. "God knew our desperation. Through you He came to our aid." I needed no gratitude but that.

There were horses wandering about. I found two that were still hobbled, with light Deccan saddles, and brought them as mounts for the Fathers. Helping get Castro horsed was not easy, but I managed-- while he looked glum. Monserrate gazed around, his face full of anxiety. "What can we do for these fallen men around us?" he asked. I caught a glimpse of Raya's stern face, and I knew what the verdict had to be. We were in the open, exposed to a group of armed horsemen who might rally and return at any moment.

I looked at the Jesuit priest squarely. "We can do nothing for those dead or dying, Father. We must leave this place as soon as possible!" Then I thought about the Christian principles that ennobled this man Monserrate. "But of course you may pray for their souls." Monserrate's eyes moistened but he kept his peace. As the four of us rode away, toward the next town and toward Goa, he prayed for the dead and those who still lingered dying.

We led the Jesuits' horses, including their pack-horses, back to where ours were hobbled. Raya suggested we return to the hill where the two of us camped, where the barren ground gave us a defensive view. As an afterthought I had picked up the two muskets left by the attack. I would clean and reload these weapons, making us stronger.

Raya led our little group of horsemen to that hill we now claimed. I followed, keeping watch at the rear. The sliver of new moon had long ago sunk below the horizon. The stars overhead were like beacons to us, though. How many events like this had they lighted in the history of men?

One other truth-- no, several truths-- came to me as we bedded down again for the night.

The elation of attack and victory had drained away. I felt puzzled about that. I could reflect that Raya and I had proved ourselves this night, but at a price. In half an hour we had become men. Dealers of death could no longer have the luxury of being boys.

Chapter 10

Dividing At Dharwara

The rest of the ride west to Dharwara, the major town above the Western Ghats, did not suffer from another attack. I knew that Raya would have preferred striking north toward Belgaon and then on to Bijapur, and he realized that I aimed at riding on to Goa with the Jesuits. As a result we said little to each other, and I made more conversation with Monserrate.

I told the Jesuit of my decision-- that I would depend upon his view of it. It was not that I had made up my mind to become a Christian, I told him. But I wanted to study his Faith under auspices, or at least with the permission, of his Jesuit fellows. Could it be done? It meant really, I supposed, that he would become my guide and mentor of a sort, and I was prepared to make myself responsible to him.

He quickly assured me that I would be most welcome in his own view, though he could not vouch for "Brother" Castro. But he would be happy to present my proposal to to the Jesuit's Order's "Provincial" in Goa, Brother Alexander Valignano, who would probably be well disposed, and that he would also undertake to have the approval of the Bishop of Goa. I was impressed with the discipline, almost military, to which the Society of Jesus was accustomed-- reaching up to the "General" of the Order in Rome-- so that things were done in a systematic, orderly way. I also began to realize that Monserrate was a highly influential member of the Order in "India," as the Jesuits and other monastic orders were calling my country, and that if he approved a proposal it stood a good chance of being instituted.

It disturbed me that I was asking not for a small boon but for a very large one-- but if Monserrate would commend it.... My spirits rose. My father, who had been a soldier, had always valued discipline. Well, so would I. Monserrate therefore stood even higher in my estimation-- and my gratitude.

I also saw that I would have to dedicate myself to a course of study that would be Jesuit in discipline, and that I would do well to have Monserrate as not only my advocate but my guide and friendly advisor. And in the manner of families and communities in "India," this Spanish Jesuit would also in some sense be my patron and "master," equivalent to a "guru" among Hindus and a "shaikh" among Muslims. These were heavy thoughts, full of implications, and Monserrate was also both "Brother" to his colleagues and "Father" insofar as he was a member of the Clergy.

It was with thoughts like these that I occupied myself during this day's ride to Dharwara, and while I was resolving any lingering doubts about my decision to accompany Monserrate to Goa, Raya and I logically had little to say to each other. To him, as a few remarks of his assured me, I was placing at hazard all my childhood and adult 'Faith' as a Muslim. And truly, I was beginning to enjoy the thought, as Monserrate expressed it, that I would be welcomed to the College of Saint Paul as a lay, daytime student and could reside in their hostel and take meals in their refectory. And, as Monserrate said, I could later decide whether I wished to undergo Conversion and apply for the status of a Jesuit Novice.

I thought of the approximately one hundred Jesuits that Monserrate had earlier told me were associated with the College of Saint Paul at this time-- and the several hundred lay, "day" students at the College. Side by side with these students, many of whom were already Converts, I would be studying Latin and the Christian Gospels, would study the "Roman" Church's Catechism and would therefore be quite busy, if I chose, for three years or more unless I withdrew! I told Monserrate that I could not yet commit myself to the entire program but that I would be happy to enroll, submit to whatever discipline it involved, and give my best effort.

With this I became, in my mind, attached to Monserrate as my patron, mentor, and teacher-- and yes, in his role as both advisor and priest, the nearest person to a father that I could have had in… very well, in Goa and in "India."

At the moment, of course, there was a practical problem of a much different nature. How were we to deal with "Brother" Castro's wound-- the iron arrow-point still imbedded in his right knee? The wound would lead to permanent damage to the leg -- or worse, loss of a gangrenous leg and possibly his life-- if the point were not removed soon.

Monserrate cleaned the wound as best he could with hot water and applied a wet poultice which had been made up 'dry' several months earlier in Goa for such an eventuality. I bent over the wound in what I thought was the helpful role of an apprentice in this medical treatment. Castro, however, spoke abruptly to Monserrate in Spanish. Monserrate looked at me apologetically. "If further treatment is to be done by a Muslim doctor," said he in carefully chosen Dakkhini phrases, "I am to tell you that Brother Castro will wait for a Christian doctor in Goa."

Monserrate and I both knew that Castro's knee, even with changes of poultice, was likely to fester before reaching Goa and could cause permanent damage to the Jesuit's leg. Monserrate conveyed the message. Castro angrily rejected the notion. He would die before he submitted to some "Moor" for treatment! I announced in good Dakkhini that after all it was his "Christian leg" that was at stake. Monserrate fell silent and made no more conversation on the subject.

The wound did fester, and by the time we reached Dharwara the stubborn Castro was feverish. "We will at least have to lance the wound," I observed. Monserrate considered awhile, looked at me cautiously, and offered that he had seen gunshot wounds lanced in Spain and would take care of the matter for his Jesuit partner until we reached Goa. But he thanked me for my offer. I must have raised an eyebrow, because he then apologized for Castro's behaviour.

He smiled and spoke again in Dakkhini. "You will not find all of us so difficult a patient." The smile faded. "And I apologize for my Brother's use of the term 'Moor.' He seems to have forgotten that this is not Spain. Can you forgive us?"

"Yes," I said, and I thanked him for his more liberal and correct understanding that I and my countrymen were Muslims, not "Moors."

The conversation gave me one more reason for respecting, indeed admiring, Monserrate. I could trust him, I felt. The incident made me surprisingly more confident of riding on to Goa.

Raya, of course, had heard the whole exchange. I cast a smile his way. He did not return it. Our silence continued almost the entire way to Dharwara.

Finally, when we had paused to rest our horses and the two of us were sitting a little to ourselves, I asked him what might be wrong.

He grunted sourly. "I am beginning to see what you are aiming at, friend Aziz. You really want to keep riding west in the company of these two Christians, especially this Monserrate whom you have begun to worship. You discount the hostility of his comrade 'Brother' Castro, who hates us 'Moors' and Hindus. You imagine that by following Monserrate to Goa he will protect you, and you can drink at the well of his wisdom every day. And maybe someday you can wear the black cloak of the Jesuit!"

The rancor in his voice startled me.

I sighed. "I suppose I have not heard the last of your lectures, Raya. But I ask myself, what had brought us so far from Bijapur? Are we only to turn and ride quickly home again? Or is it something braver? Isn't there a curiosity to see more of the world and find places for ourselves?" He started to interrupt, but I would not let him. "What, I ask myself, is the value of returning to Bijapur? Except for the safety of my Aunt Bibiji's walled house and gardens, it is a place of rejection and closed doors as far as I am concerned. My father's miserable, unjust death has raised a wall against my hopes of employment at the court of Bijapur. Many men who betrayed him are prominent, rich, and in possession of high posts. To them I am only a rival, and they will block me at every turn! And I have more positive reasons for continuing with these Jesuits to Goa. It is almost the only way that I will ever have an opportunity to see that Portuguese port and learn under Jesuit protection the strengths of the foreigners."

Raya had listened to my speech with varied expressions of doubt, annoyance, and amusement. "It is good to know what high principles you have, dear Aziz, and why you burn to leave Bijapur behind you. Even better is it to learn in what great regard you hold your Aunt Bibiji's kindness, her wisdom, and my worthless companionship! If you feel as you say, then of course you must go and seek your fortunes elsewhere. And I, for one, will be better to be rid of your unhappy company!"

"Look," I said, almost shouting, "I know that my aunt may be puzzled at first, and angered that I seem to have abandoned her. But it was she, after all, who urged me to go out and "'see, listen, and learn!'" These Jesuits-- Monserrate at any rate-- are, as I said, my best opportunity to do what my aunt urges! If you wish to be angry and hold me in contempt, so be it my friend. But which of us is being more practical? I who will take my chances by riding on to Goa, or you who can only think of falling back on the security offered my aunt? And if I would rather follow these Jesuits to Goa and try my fortunes there-- to fight, even, and maybe to die if I must-- I would prefer that to sitting frustrated in Bijapur!"

"I can see," said Raya, "that you are not about to accept any voice of reason-- or warning-- other than your own, Aziz Khan. You think it a safe challenge to ride to Goa with these men, in the hope that one of them will protect you and be your mentor. Well, have it your way! We have reached a split in the road. But I must still remind you that you are being unfair to your aunt-- and leaving me to explain this bold course of yours. How long do you expect to be under this man Monserrate's safe umbrella? How will you communicate with your aunt-- assuming that you do care?" He took a deep breath. "I could go on and on, but do you care?"

I was silent awhile, thinking of the last challenge. "I will will find ways to keep in touch with Aunt Bibiji," I said. "And will even find ways to stay in touch with you-- if you care. But I see my main chance here, and I will take it!"

We stared at each other, truculence ruling us. Now I realized that Raya had expected me to value his companionship more-- to need it. And yes, we had proven that we were good at any joint effort and could expect many an adventure together. Yet we saw our prospects differently. Perhaps we had never thought of it before, because we had been thrown together by my aunt in constant cooperation and alliance. Until now we had not seriously thought of going different ways. But the moment of truth was upon us. The juncture of two roads at Dharwara, one leading on westward to Goa, the other leading north to Belgaon and Bijapur, would make us decide.

"You may not accept this," I said to Raya, "but perhaps it would be best, now, if each of us went his way. At the least we would find other causes to fight for, other pathways to hew out of our lives, without making each other the target of each disappointment, failure, or mistake." I tried to use a tone that would help us relax. "We aren't quite twins, after all and never had been-- despite my aunt's best efforts to make us inseparable. And now, being seventeen and nineteen, almost eighteen and twenty, we really can take different paths. Isn't that true?"

Raya fell into a strange, quiet rage. "And I had put myself to the task of being your daily companion and friend-- for this! I sacrificed my independence, my Hindu identity and the things I desired, for this. And now you, playing the fool, are going to tell me what to do. Well, be a fool! I do not need to have such a friend!"

He was gazing hard at me, his face contorted with anger… and… grief?

Suddenly I had to relent. I seemed to be savaging my best friend. My only friend, to say the truth. And maybe I was a fool to go chasing after this man Monserrate-- the feringhi Spaniard, Christian, and Jesuit.

"Stop!" I said. "we have to stop this!" I was feeling a kind of pain, a grief, myself. "I am sorry, Raya, I have wronged you-- wronged my friend. Please!"

And we stopped. We stopped letting anger fountain and grow. Each of us were silent awhile. I was ashamed.

Raya did not apologize for his part-- not in so many words. He seldom, by habit, apologized for anything, but I knew him well. He would find a way to patch up the torn fabric.

When we returned to our horses we rode without speaking. We looked anywhere but at each other. We had been raised thinking that a man did not expose a weakness, or an innermost feeling.

At last he did speak.

"I will go back to Bijapur and explain to your Aunt Bibiji-- our Aunt Bibiji-- what you have chosen. As well as I can. As for what I will do with my own life I cannot say yet. I may be much changed, friend Aziz, when next you see me. And you will see me, because I cannot just forget the things we have done together. I know that I will care what happens to you-- for good or ill."

He paused and could not seem to go on into this territory of affection.

I picked up the thread. "I, too, don't know what will happen to me, or how I may change. What I have chosen may be all wrong. But I will ride to Goa. With these Jesuits, with Monserrate-- with luck and the mercy of God-- I will find a path of honor. And someday, when we meet again, I will tell you everything I have learned, or suffered, and hear your own story with a good heart."

We did not talk again of these differences until we parted at Dharwara, I to the west and he to the north. But I did have a message for my aunt.

"You will please give Aunt Bibiji my best wishes-- and not turn her too much against my choice?"

Raya shrugged. "I will give her your best wishes-- and tell her you are a great fool!"

I jerked in the saddle, my heart rising. He laughed.

But he had a second, more serious thought. "I almost forgot. You will sit down somewhere-- now!-- and write Aunt Bibiji a note explaining this crazed decision of yours! Tell her at least that you found one of the two Jesuits a man of intelligence, and that he persuaded you to go with him. Tell her you probably are a great fool-- and that you will find ways to get other letters to her-- and that she should be proud of you for taking so much to heart her advice that you "see widely, listen well, and learn much!"

He dismounted smugly and went and sat in the shadow of a scraggly tree. "I perceive, dear Aziz, a fairly flat, big stone over there. You always bring paper for your 'travel notes,' I have observed. This is an excellent place to use it!" And he would not budge until I had written the note in ragged Arabic strokes-- and signed and dated it.

My companion then tucked the illiterate looking letter into his waistband. "Thank-you," he said, remounting. I hated the little smile he gave me.

"Actually," he said, "I almost feel sorry for you, brother Aziz. You had better stick close to that friend Monserrate of yours. Otherwise, those Portuguese crocodiles will make a quick meal of you. Do let us hear from you again some way or other!"

He rode off.

Sitting listlessly in my saddle, I considered "those Portuguese crocodiles" with a discomfiting thought that Raya was right. There was a very possible finality of this parting.

But I took a deep breath and turned my Arabian to rejoin the two Jesuits. We were to start tomorrow for Goa, descending the Western Ghats. I had to get into a ready state of mind again.

I turned once to see if Raya was still in sight. The road to Bijapur had risen to a low hill. I watched as Raya reached the top. He, too, turned in his saddle to see if I were visible. We both gazed awhile. He waved. I waved. He rode out of sight.

For a moment I wished I could think of an appropriate Persian verse about parting or loneliness or something. The only words I could think of were less poetic.

"Damn him! He didn't have to leave like that!"

Chapter 11

From The Ghats To Goa

Dharwara lay still some distance from the western Ghats, those hills and ravines that separated the Konkan plain from the Deccan plateau. The Jesuits therefore rode to a village just near the Ghats from which we could start to descend.

Unsure what our experience of the Ghats was likely to be, I had found a caravan-master who had just come up from Goa and claimed to have made the trip many times. Seeing that I was a novice, he enjoyed spending the better part of an hour telling me stories calculated to make my hair stand on end and my heart beat faster. He told of a leopard encountered in the twilight between sunset and night, and recounted other men's stories of having to keep a tiger away from their horses and camels. He told what he claimed were his own experiences of bands of long-armed langur monkeys that would swing with loud crashes among the branches on a steep slope, then leave behind a silence that was almost as disturbing as their passage. By the time he was finished with me I was prepared for the worst to happen, especially since my Jesuit comrades seemed to be innocent of any untoward happenings when they, several months before, had come up from Goa, and we would be a small group-- only five or six persons, including the attendants employed to manage the Jesuits' pack-horses.

In consideration of all this I decided to make myself the possessor not only of my own matchlock but the two weapons I had acquired two nights earlier. I would feel much more secure having three matchlocks loaded and ready-- for what I could not quite know, but I would have them! And of course I would have my bow and arrows. Aside from that I was mainly concerned with keeping a close watch and tight rein on my two horses-- my Arabian, that was well disciplined in the hunt on the plains but lacked experience in negotiating mountain trails or jungle, and my pack-horse which I usually could control but was inclined to balk or shy away from almost anything unusual. Just thinking of it all, I did not sleep well the night before our descent of the Ghats!

At the earliest light before daybreak the two Jesuits and I set forth. The "road" we would take was hardly more than a trail where two men might ride abreast. My Arabian and two sturdy geldings carried the three of us, and I would lead my own pack-horse. A syce I had hired cared for the Jesuits' three pack-horses. We did not reach the main descent of the ghats until mid-morning. I let Monserrate and Castro go ahead, making what conversation they cared to. Their energy seemed to grow with each turn and twist of our path. I tried to keep alert for any strange sounds, and make sure that my two horses would not stumble or fall. We did move fairly fast, given the Jesuits' eagerness to get through the Ghats before nightfall.

At first there were trees with light branches that admitted flickering rays of the sun. Then we entered glades of tall trunks and thick branches where only the occasional patch of sunlight pierced the canopies overhead. Unsettling thoughts insinuated themselves into the shadows around us. I had to admit that the caravan-master had done well his frightening of me the unseasoned traveler. But I concentrated on the downward pitch of the road with its unexpected angles, which at the speed of the Jesuit descent was really quite enough to concern me.

Soon I turned my thoughts to how I would deal with the risks of being a Muslim in a Christian city. I was glad to have Monserrate as my sponsor. I had in effect become his student, and it was from him that I hoped to learn more about his Faith, about the Christian missions in Goa, and how the Jesuits lived and pursued their calling. I was getting prepared, I realized, to give Christianity the compliment of hard study, not to exclude learning the Latin that Christian scripture required. But also, after a little thought, I vowed to learn enough of the Portuguese tongue to make my way among the streets, shops, and varied buildings of this port and capital.

My thoughts shifted to the Hindus and Muslims who had lived among the coconut groves of the Konkan. Many of them, I guessed, and been forced to make their peace with their Portuguese conquerors. A great many must have converted to Christianity in order to save their lives and properties! And those who were sincere in taking up this foreign religion? Thinking of Raya, I wondered how former Hindus had bridged the gaps in belief and custom that were so wide. I ended by lecturing myself on keeping quiet about these matters and learning by observation, not by challenging my Jesuit patrons. I would see if I could get to know any Hindu or Muslim converts at first hand!

My first glimpse of Goa was from a stony ledge about halfway down the Ghats. My Jesuit companions stood awhile in joy, pointing out this part of the scene and that. If it had not been for the Portuguese ships at the docks on the Mandovi River I would have had trouble making out anything but white church spires and the red-tiled roofs of a few large buildings.

Most of all I was intrigued by the bellying sails of a ship in mid-river. But dominating the scene was the Sea of Arabia stretching blue and calm to the immense horizon. I could see the tiny shapes and two caravels faraway on the blue expanse. Painted ships on a painted sea, I found myself thinking.

Monserrate turned to me in his saddle. “I will tell you much about our Jesuit mission, Aziz Ahmad, when we arrive in Goa,” he said proudly. “We still have several hours’ travel to reach our College and Residence, and it will probably be after dark when we arrive.” I decided to concentrate again on the trail, not count the hours. So far, at any rate, we had come upon no leopards, no tigers, and no noisy langur monkeys! I was almost disappointed.

It was just after sunset when we emerged from the Ghats. A Portuguese guard post loomed before us. I counted a troop of about twenty men under arms, but except for their bored, bearded captain they appeared to be a lackluster band of half-breeds. In any case my Jesuit companions moved ahead with hardly a word, and while I received some stares, no one challenged Monserrate’s assertion that I was a new Convert!

With the Ghats behind and the lush plain of the Konkan before us, I turned to the emerging scene of tree-shaded streets, houses and churches built of the local stone, walls heavily whitewashed, and red-tiled roofs. Coming closer to the center of the city, we saw residents promenading, dressed in their best, in the coolness of the darkening night. The odor and ‘feel’ of salt air were the other things I most noticed.

The twilight deepened. At last we turned into a very wide street, which I would later know by its Portuguese name, the Rua Direita or "Straight Street." Here the faces of buildings two or three stories in height marked the center of Portuguese rule.

I had to admit to the unsettling thought that I had betrayed my Aunt Bibiji's trust by separating from Raya and accompanying Monserrate on this dangerous path into Christian Goa. But I thrust the thought away. I allowed myself nothing but confidence in Monserrate's company and protection.

We slowed and came to a halt in front of the double doors of a square, two-storied building, whitewashed like the rest. Next to the building stood a second substantial one.

Monserrate took a deep breath, dismounted, and summoned a reserve of strength to address me.

"We have reached the buildings that are our Jesuit property," he said to me. "Our primary one of the College of Saint Paul. A chapel is one of its main inner constructions. The building contains also a lecture hall, a library room for scriptural study, and several classrooms."

"Standing next to the College," he went on, "is our Residence with a refectory for meals, rooms where we and our Jesuit brothers temporarily reside, and a separate set of rooms for our Novices and visiting guests. We and our Jesuit colleagues await the completion of another structure essential to our Society, our 'Professed House,' where in future we can live in the intimacy of full Brotherhood.

He gestured toward a large walled area containing an orchard that lay on the opposite side of the College. "We are engaged in laying the foundations for a substantial church in that area. The church is proving to be of major expense and can only be built over a number of years, but we have high hopes of it and will not rest until it is finished. With God's blessing it will be one of the most noble edifices in Goa."

He addressed himself even more directly to me. "I have been wondering, Aziz Khan, if you would care to stay in our Residence next to the College of Saint Paul. Let me assure you that you are welcome to stay there as my guest." But he frowned. "I know that you may prefer to stay with a Muslim family. However, I regret that I know of no such family that might take in a visitor. At best I could try to arrange lodging with one of our Christian families. In any case I would like to have you stay two or three months, until the hot weather comes. I can arrange for you to see whatever is important in Goa, and you will have time to observe our Society in action and ask the questions you desire about our faith."

Meanwhile Castro had rung a small brass bell on the door of the Residence. Two servants came and began taking our Jesuits' possessions inside. Torches were brought out on the darkening street. Our eight horses, Monserrate told me, would be led to the rear where they could be placed in stalls, fed, and groomed. I paid separately to assure that my Arabian would be well treated. I found myself thinking whether it would be better for me to have my two horses kept elsewhere. I certainly would not give them up!

As for my own place to reside, I had not considered being set up in some Christian home, but of course it would be the home of a converted Hindu or Muslim. Monserrate seemed to read my mind! "I believe the Residence would be for the best," he said, "since it is where our Novices and other members in training live and have the Refectory for their meals. If a room is available, and you do not mind following the rules for residents, I can arrange for you to stay there."

Monserrate's new supply of thought and encouragement made me realize again the strength of his personality and forces of persuasion. I had to make a choice right now, it seemed. I squared my shoulders and replied that staying at the Residence would suit me very well.

Monserrate looked me over. Our tired faces both seemed to flicker in the light of the torches. It quickly came to me that my Muslim dress and weapons were wholly unsuited to Goa-- and to a Jesuit residence!

"I regret to say that we will have to do something about your mode of dress while you are with us," said the Jesuit with careful diplomacy. "I believe," he added, "that it may be better for you to wear the attire of a Jesuit Novice while you are here among us. But if you do not desire that, you could dress as one of the Hindu day-students who regularly study with us."

I was not interested in the Hindu approach! Taking the dress of the Novice intrigued me, but I was wary of the possible results. Adopting a diplomacy equal to Monserrate's I answered that, as I was considering a stay of two or three months and realized that changes in appearance would have to be made, I would dress as a Novice if he were to arrange it. Monserrate's smile as we were escorted indoors told me that he felt pleased. For a Muslim to wear the habit of a Jesuit Novice seemed irregular, but Monserrate seemed to take it as a sign that I was positive about becoming a Convert. And it confirmed his being my patron. At this point I did not mean to convert. But… who knew? I was finding him to be a very persuasive man.

Next came introductions to the Brother in charge of the Residence and to three senior Novices. The Novices were grave of expression but pleasant enough within that limit. I decided to cultivate whatever friendships I could.

After washing myself and changing into simple clothing that was not quite Hindu and not quite Muslim, I was invited to join Monserrate, Castro, and the three Novices in the Refectory for a meal. I did not know what to expect in the food category, but I was not surprised when it turned out to be a simple soup and bread, the soup un-spiced except for a trace of salt. My Muslim palate revolted at this kind of self-denial, but I learned my first lesson-- that this was monastic Christian culture and I had better get used to it. Christian prayers, of course, punctuated each phase of our dining.

I soon realized that the three Novices at the table were all practicing their grasp of Persian. In the simplest of my Persian I asked the nearest Novice whether the food or drink this night were typical of the Refectory's meals. Oh yes, quite, he told me. And for breakfast? One egg, two slices of toasted bread, besides more tea. Sometimes cooked rice. "Our, uh, discipline," he added helpfully. And here I was, yearning for breast of pheasant or leg of lamb!

Evidently my stomach, like my brain, would be learning the Christian

Way. I sighed mournfully. One of the first truths of Jesuit life had just announced itself to me. Discipline!

And why had I thought it would be any different? This was a missionary outpost on what must seem to my hosts like the edge of the world! If the mind must suffer, so must the human flesh.

Clearly my hours in the study of Latin Christian doctrine, and Jesuit practice were not to be enlivened by thoughts of a tasty repast to follow. "Sometimes cooked rice," the Novice had said. Of curries and saffron I could only dream.

The very next morning my patron Monserrate began looking to my Christian education and the possibility of a Jesuit career. We sat in his room while a patch of morning light struck the whitewashed wall through his single window. I could see that for a few moments that triangle of sunlight would every day illumine the crucifix on the wall above his bed.

"I know," he said as a preface, "that you would like to learn as much about Goa as you can within the time you are here. Two or three months may not seem enough for that once you begin to go out on the streets and observe. I believe you will want to pick up a good understanding of the Portuguese language, and I certainly encourage that. I hope, however, that you will also study well our Christian mission and the special vows, objectives, and customs of our Jesuit brotherhood. To that end I also hope you will take up a serious study of Latin. Your ability in languages impresses me. It will be interesting to see what you make of your opportunities here."

He leaned back on the hard wooden seat of his chair and studied me. "Does all this make sense to you?"

"Yes," I said cautiously. "It fits very well with the thoughts I have had these past few days."

He adjusted himself in the uncomfortable seat.

"Were I one of the Portuguese who came here to rule," he explained, "there would be little to say of Goa except its control of these coasts and our trade upon the ocean. Our Christian missions, which include not only the Society of Jesus but also members of the Franciscan, the Dominican, and other Orders, have a different view. Many of us are not Portuguese. As I told you earlier, I and my colleague Brother Castro are Spanish. The Society of Jesus is noted for the varied origins of its members. We are united in our mission to convert the Hindu and Muslim peoples to our Christian religion, and to accomplish it not by force but by the persuasion of reason, example, and faith."

He gave me a glance as if afraid I may have taken offense. Fortunately I had the presence of mind to say that I was not in the least offended. As a Muslim, I said, I also believed in reason, example, and faith, and it was not my view that anyone should be beaten down by force.

He smiled. "Again I see that you are an honest young man," he said. "But would it not trouble you to hear our view that Jesus of Nazareth was the greatest and most true of all prophets, greater and more true than Muhammad, and that the man Jesus was in fact the Son of God?"

A force larger than either of us seemed to push me in this Jesuit's direction. Was it the force of honesty? I hedged.

"I would listen and try to judge rightly," I said.

But I was feeling trapped. I kept searching for the right words. Not wanting to blurt out that I would probably remain a Muslim, I took a long breath.

"I was raised by a father who taught me to be calm in the argument and to be ruled by reason. He did not teach me to hate Christians or their beliefs."

The Jesuit remained as calm as I, and the honesty of his gaze implied no threat. Immediately I knew that I would respectfully listen to his beliefs, and that I would be honest in finally accepting or rejecting them. At the same time I felt a kind of exhaustion creep over me. I was still tired from the preceding day's journey, and here and now, frankly, I did not want to argue.

The missionary continued. "You may feel, Aziz Khan, that I am pressing you to become a candidate for our Society. Forgive me if I am trying too hard to bring you into our circle. Naturally I would be most gratified if you were to consider conversion to our Christian Faith-- and become a member of our Society of Jesus. Thanks to our conversations on the road, I believe you may have many qualities suited to our Society. However, I do not wish to say so much that you recoil. You will have time to consider everything in the quiet of your mind, as long as it may suit you."

I respected this man, but I could not let myself just surrender to his zealous faith and determination. Slowly, carefully but truly I told him that I would listen, learn, and arrive perhaps at a decision within the next three to six months, or perhaps a year if I decided to stay longer. I would be happy to start by studying Latin. I would consider him my foremost teacher and try to learn and abide by the rules of the Society.

I could see elements of hope and doubt competing in his face, but I did not want to let his hopes rule our exchange. Again, as on the road to Goa, I found in him honesty and sincerity that were fair and honorable, even noble, and I would not deny him the hope of an eventual victory for his Faith. Already I had seen Castro, after our arrival, limp away and take no more notice of me. His scepticism of my conversion and dislike of my Muslim ways would not allow him even to attempt my conversion-- nor to welcome my goodwill. Were he my only idea of a Jesuit, I would never have come this far. Monserrate was something else, a man who could argue and disagree and still be polite and welcoming.

It was no surprise to me that sometimes, just observing this man, I thought of my father. Perhaps, I realized, he was my only chance of finding someone whose disciplined life, like his friendship, made him in truth a kind of father to me.

He abruptly turned to a discussion of the importance of my learning Latin. After all, he said, it was not only the language of the Scriptures but also the common tongue of Catholics of the 'Roman' tradition around the world, including the members of his Society. "You may find," he said, "that taking up the study of Latin, for someone who already knows Persian, is not only your doorway to our beliefs but is a good way to exercise your mind and-- of importance in your world as a Muslim-- will enable you to better translate and discuss the differences between Islam and Christianity."

I was glad to see that his mind was flexible enough to permit me a way out rather than simply pounding away at his hope of my conversion.

"Indeed," I said, "thanks to the relative ease with which I learn languages, and having made already a good start, it had occurred to me that it might be especially useful to be able to translate between Persian and Latin. I found myself thinking last evening, when your Novices were practicing their Persian at our table, that I might meet informally with a few advanced Novices and discuss some higher points of Persian rhetoric."

Monserrate smiled. "Our Novices are already studying advanced Persian under one of our Brothers who is Persian by birth, so forgive me if I suggest that you mainly concentrate on your Latin. You have convinced me already that you have great talent for languages, and it will be most important for me to see you develop a capacity to translate from Latin to Persian and the reverse. Our Society has much need for men with that skill." A new light in his eyes. "In fact, Aziz Ahmad Khan, I begin to think that the capacities of the translator will be of great use to you in any career you choose. Translation, after all, is a way of conveying truth and refuting error. Its every exercise is a test of truthfulness-- in the wrong mouth a species of falsehood. You, Aziz Ahmad, appear to have an unusual ability to make it a touchstone of truth."

He rose from his chair and extended a hand. I stood and clasped it, as I had learned was the European custom. Where talk about conversion had put us at odds, we could now more happily look into each other's eyes. The directness of our gazes, despite the contrast in our ages and experiences, had started a stream of more positive thought flowing.

Monserrate's change of subject had allowed me to return to thinking of him as the sort of generous, fatherly man who, at an age similar to my father's, could be trusted to guide me to use my own judgement rather than being subjected to one choice or viewpoint. And yes, I was already more favorably responding to his implication that I might remain Muslim yet provide services that any government or religion could value, those of a sound and reliable translator.

“So, my Muslim friend,” said my host, “we can return later to a discussion about how you might dress as a guest of our Society-- that and the program of study that may suit you best. And meanwhile, either tomorrow or the next day while the heat of the day is not too much for us, we can walk along the broad avenue of the Rua Direita and try a few other streets, and I can introduce you to the Portuguese city of Goa-- which has now grown almost as large as Lisbon!”

Chapter 12

Discovering Goa

Whether I wanted to or not, I knew I had to make a choice, or several choices, about my day to day dress and appearance-- since I could not simply dress as a Muslim with his distinctive turban! After our breakfast Monserrate apologized for counselling me, but assured me that, where my clothing was concerned, he was looking out for my interests. This time I did not fight him.

We both decided finally that I would wear the tunic of a Novice of the Society of Jesus. This was, he admitted, a major concession for a Brother of the Society-- to allow anyone who was not a Novice to appropriate that mode of dress! The Novices were generally expected already to be Christians, by conversion or birth, who had entered a special program of education. In my case, he reminded me, it expressed his confidence that I was willing to consider the option. As long as I could avow an open mind on the "possibility" of conversion, he believed he could argue his superiors and colleagues into accepting it. But his main concern was that, if I dressed as a Muslim, I might be attacked, even killed, if it were thought that I was a "Moor."

He frowned, but then broke into a smile. "After all, my dear Aziz Ahmad, we Jesuits have developed a reputation among the Holy Orders of being "pragmatic," even if it means dispensing with some Jesuit "rule" if it meant making more conversion-- here or in Europe or the Americas. I would not wish to carry this behavior too far, but there is some truth in it." He chuckled. "So, my friend-- be pragmatic!"

Hence I began to dress in the cassock of the Novitiate, going about bareheaded and in sandals. It continued to trouble me, since I was not yet either a committed Christian or a genuine Novice. How my Hindu friend Raya would have laughed at my quick "conversion" to the Christian faith! But of more import to me, in my egotism, was my laying aside the turban that I had used to disguise my burned face and stump of an ear. It was my punishment by Allah, I decided, for having assumed a false, cowardly image! But Monserrate more than once made clear that he was looking out both for my physical and spiritual interests, and we both knew that I was not ready to attract unwanted Portuguese attention.

What next bothered me most, at first, was a fact viscerally important to an arms-bearing Muslim-- that I could not carry any weapon! I felt almost naked without even a knife hidden in my shirt, tunic, or boots-- or tucked away under a sash! But I sadly placed my Muslim clothing and all my weapons in the care of Monserrate, who took the precaution of locking them in a cabinet, while my two horses he placed with a Hindu Christian stable keeper at some distance from the College of Saint Paul.

Since I had to accept Monserrate's point about dressing as a Jesuit Novice, I decided to take other precautions. Every place I went I carried some book or pamphlet of the Christian type-- especially one printed by the new Jesuit press recently installed at the College of Saint Paul. It was only another step in the same self-defensive road to begin wearing a large, plain wooden cross on a chain at my neck! How Raya would have laughed at that! But, truly, I now had at least modest protection from being accosted by a Portuguese officer or some bully swaggering up to anyone of Hindu or Muslim heritage. If the books I was carrying did not of themselves discourage questioning, I also began to practice being seemingly occupied with some philosophic puzzle that only I could understand!

Poor Raya. He was my hidden conscience! And yes, he would have laughed heartily at my shams and pretenses. But I did feel safer.

Monserrate meanwhile introduced me to Goa by walking with me up and down the wide Rua Direita-- the "Straight Street"-- and showing me the churches and other landmarks of the city.

He began by taking me inside the foundations of the great church, or "Se," of Saint Catherine, which would commemorate Afonso de Albuquerque's conquest of Goa on the 25th of November, A. D. 1510, Saint Catherine's Day-- although the Se was only now coming under construction and would not be finished for many years! Clearly an edifice of this size was intended to be something like the official church of Christian Goa.

Monserrate also pointed out that Albuquerque had originally built a chapel of Saint Catherine just next to the quay of Goa, but the cathedral on more elevated ground was destined to be the principal monument of Christian conquest.

Adjoining St. Catherine's church were the palatial residence of the Archbishop of Goa and the monastery of Saint Francis of Assisi. The monastery, Monserrate admitted, had been built after 1520 on the site of a former mosque. In any case it was the headquarters of the Franciscan Order in Asia. In some ways I found it alienating to see such a Christian institution laid on the foundations of another faith's place of worship. But what would be contradictory to Divine Will seemed to be natural to human wills. I only told Monserrate that I was deeply impressed.

I must admit that I found more interesting the nearby church called "Nossa Senhora da Serra," built by Albuquerque in 1513 as the site of his future tomb. Though I did not find him an admirable man-- nor, as I found later, did Monserrate-- it was clear that Afonso de Albuquerque had laid the symbolic foundations of everything else to be seen.

More important to Monserrate was the immense church that the Jesuits proposed to build next to the buildings of the College of Saint Paul. "There the great church will stand," said Monserrate, "Just near the House where our Jesuit brothers and our Novices live. With God's help we will have the church finished within ten, perhaps twenty years, and it will be the grandest church of all in Goa, a true basilica." He gazed toward the treetops beyond the orchard's wall. "With God's help," he repeated. He thought for a moment. "Perhaps we will call it the Basilica of Saint Paul. The name 'Bom Jesus' has also been considered, in honor of the 'Good Jesus' our Savior." Slowly and deliberately he crossed himself. He smiled at me. "We shall see."

I had noticed that a small but impressive church stood at a distance to the west on the crest of one prominent hill. "Ah yes," said Monserrate, "the 'Holy Hill'-- the Monte Santo!" The hill lay at a fair distance, but

Monserrate resolutely guided me there. The church, he explained, had architectural touches in the naval mode of Portugal's King Manoel. Probably the oldest of all churches in the city, said Monserrate, this one was called "Our Lady of the Rosary." It was located near the edge of a steep cliff where Albuquerque was said to have watched the final battle for Goa. It was on this spot, with its magnificent view of the coastal plain and north across the river Mandovi, that Saint Francis Xavier, founder of the Jesuit missions both in India and China, had often preached to large crowds. Here the shade of a large tree sheltered a stone-cut bench. I immediately saw the shaded bench as a place for me to read and relax in coming months-- especially on hot afternoons when the rooms of the College of Saint Paul stifled both study and leisure.

Monserrate and I returned to the city's center and the Rua Direita. He began identifying the chief buildings of government in Goa. One was the Viceroy's "palace" built near the Portuguese quay on the site of the palace of the Bijapuri king who had contested the Portuguese plan to make Goa-- once a proud ancient city called "Govepuri"-- into a fiercely protected Portuguese port. The older palace had disappeared except for its grand gate of entry, which the victorious Albuquerque deigned to leave unharmed-- now a symbol of Portuguese victory!

It was evident, as I looked around me, that many other Bijapuri Muslim buildings must have disappeared under Portuguese hammer and chisel, or had collapsed under the thunder of Portuguese cannon fire-- or be blown up by kegs of gunpowder!

The last large building, other than a large administrative building or two including one for public records, was the "Palace of the Inquisition." I felt moved to ask why the word "Palace," since it was basically an arm of the Roman Church! Monserrate hedged on that point, but said that the Archbishop of Goa, like many another such potentate in Europe, was said to occupy a "Palace" because of his extensive powers over the population.

As it happened, the Palace of the Inquisition stood on the square opposite the foundation of what was to be the great "Se" or "Church of Saint Catherine." Monserrate turned happily to discuss that. I however, was still puzzling over the 'princely' power of life and death which was attributed to the Grand Inquisitor of Goa. Monserrate took a deep breath. "The Inquisition was established here in the Year of our Lord 1560 as a means of examining-- and punishing-- heretics and unbelievers who refuse to repent sins against the Church and against God."

He sighed. "To my mind the Inquisition, if of some use, should not have been introduced here in all its power. It has developed a reputation in Europe for extremes of imprisonment and punishment-- and is even more questionable here, because it has made the Church of our Lord Jesus Christ seem strange and cruel. It embarrasses me especially because it was introduced to Goa after being originally requested in 1542 by of our Jesuit brother Francisco Xavier! I can say more of it later-- if you ask."

But I resolved not to embarrass him further about an institution he did not personally approve, even though I found the Jesuits routinely supported the Inquisition and its public Burnings of persons, including former Jews and many a former Hindu, judged to have fallen back into "heretical" beliefs that could not, somehow, be forgiven or extenuated by the Church and its missionary Orders!

After this introduction to the "scene" in Goa I turned to my studies in Latin and Portuguese. These, along, with studies of Scripture, especially of the Four Gospels, took up most of each day except the Sabbath. Even my lunches and dinner hours among in the Refectory at the College were not restful, as some Novices or proper Jesuits pointedly ignored me and others-- the ones who were studying Persian-- went out of their way to sit near me and question me, expecting me to speak in "my" language.

I did what I could to assist the Persian learners, and indeed three of them became friendly and helpful to me in return. They, along with Father Monserrate, were my lifelines to the better shores of the Christian world. We finally agreed that we would review our Persian together three days for their benefit and Portuguese another three days for mine! One end of a Refectory table became acknowledged "Persian and Portuguese" territory during meals, and I could relax and talk freely there.

Even then I would have been exhausted by my studies had I not taken whatever opportunity I could for excursion into the City. I would stroll the length of the Rua Direita-- all one and a half thousand paces of it, the principle street of Goa-- from the Viceregal Palace and back. Sometimes I passed the walled enclosure of the Palace and went near the docks, where I could see Portuguese carracks, naos, and smaller boats of several kinds sitting at anchor. The river Mandovi was broad here, but it broadened still more as it flowed west to sea. I hesitated to stand watching long, because Portuguese sailors and ship's officers, along with Viceregal soldiers and officials, were all around. If someone looked my way, I would turn in a leisurely way and walk back uphill, reciting my Catechism as if deeply absorbed in my Christian education.

Lesser squares and junctions of two or more streets were my favorite places for watching the life of this great port. Lines of porters, bent under their packs or head-loads, would be moving with surprising speed at their peculiar, loping walk. Next to them might be advancing two or three elephants with loads piled on their powerful backs, their mahouts prodding them as necessary to keep the beasts in line. There were a few, but not many, wagons on these cobbled streets, but strings of pack-horses or mules would pass, and sometimes a camel or two. Runners would appear with some grandee's palanquin, taking turns at the poles to carry their master through the crowd while that worthy gazed through half-parted curtains with an expression of haughtiness or boredom.

Soldiers under officers would march past keeping some semblance of order. Clusters of off-duty soldiers and sailors sauntered or pushed their way through. Portuguese officers or "Fidalgo" gentlemen on horseback, swords swaying at their stirrups, could often be seen riding among the throng, accompanied by liveried footmen. Above it all rose the hubbub of voices in more than one language, for one could see not only Portuguese soldiers and traders but Hindu, Arab, Armenian and Jewish merchants of the city. Making the stream of color and noise complete, like an undercurrent, were the shuffle of feet, the clatter of hooves, and the rumble of wagon-wheels. I heard it said, with much pride, that the city was in both size and importance equal to Lisbon!

The main course of the Rua Direita, that Straight Street, was flanked by an array of stone-fronted or whitewashed buildings of importance--palaces, churches, monasteries. The shops of merchants, goldsmiths, jewelers, stonecutters, ivory-sellers, and other artisans tended to exist in clusters that stood on streets just off the "Straight Street."

Within a month or two I was advancing rapidly in my study of Portuguese conversation. This brought an important change to my habit, especially at the College of Saint Paul and in its vicinity, of dressing as a Jesuit Novice. I had remained uncomfortable about this practice, which was made worse when I sometimes saw 'looks' and heard whispers about it--directed at me. The College and its associated Jesuit buildings stood at a distance "up" the Rua Direita from the Portuguese docks and most administrative buildings. Rather than adjusting myself to Monserrate's pragmatic reasoning, I decided that, whenever I went far from the College in any direction I would exchange my Novice's tunic for regular Portuguese clothing-- including a broad-brimmed hat with long, nodding white feather!-- and make intensive use of my new found Portuguese grammar and vocabulary. Meanwhile, under the Portuguese hat, I could wear a tightly fitted turban that covered many of my facial scars. I was beginning to spend more and more time in the hot afternoons enjoying the illusion of being a "Goan" gentleman-fidalgo of modest means-- who just incidentally happened to be studying Christian matters at the College of Saint Paul. And when Monserrate eventually found this out, he first cautioned me but then became supportive. "Just do not carry a sword!" he would say with obvious alarm, knowing how the average fidalgo generally wore one as a demonstration of status or "class!" I was, he said firmly, to "get into no quarrels"-- as the more confident fidalgo types were wont to do. I would not compromise or embarrass him that way, I told him frankly. His answer was succinct enough. "Please see to it that you never do, because there are Brothers who disagree sharply with my lenience!"

I decided that, to remove some pressure from my studies, I would continue a type of unholy "pragmatism" that I was finding especially enjoyable. In the middle of the late afternoon I would stroll out into the city, look into the merchants' shops and finally choose one-- where, with luck, I could have a cup of thick, sweetened coffee and engage in casual conversation with the owner. There I would practice my Portuguese as we as being a polite listener.

In such ventures I soon realized that I needed to invent a personality and personal history for myself as a "Turkish" Christian. It was tedious to have to remain silent or change the subject as I sat at or near the door of a shop. I found that the shape of my eyes spelled "Turk" or "Moor" to many a Hindu or "ex"-- Hindu shopkeeper. The resulting curiosity would be plainly etched on my host's face. After all, Portuguese of the "fidalgo" class usually would not deign to associate with-- let alone "talk to"-- shopkeepers except as providers of this or that commodity.

But I, with my "discussable" identity, could turn questions and comments to my advantage and enliven the conversation-- or just change to another!

I became the fictional Christian product of a Turkish family which had originally served the sultans of Turkey. My great grandfather had been made a prisoner of war by a Spanish nobleman of the early 15th century and had been enslaved and forcibly converted to Christianity. This relative of mine had proved to be an able servant of his captor and had been freed by his owner's will, whereupon he had taken service under another Spanish nobleman. His son my grandfather had moved to Portugal to escape Spanish Christian abuses of "Moors," and had taken service under Portugal's military officer attached to the household of Portugal's famed Prince Henry "the Navigator," just as Vasco da Gama was opening the direct sea route to India and its spice trade.

The plot of my story grew more complicated with the Portuguese conquest of Goa. My grandfather, I would say, used his connections to have his son, my father, attached to the squadrons of Aphonso de Albuquerque that finally wrenched Goa away from its Bijapuri sultans in 1510, and my father was one of Albuquerque's officers who settled in Goa as a member of the Fidalgo aristocracy which had emerged by the 1520's. I was born to the family and, as was its tradition, apprenticed to a Fidalgo officer. An outbreak of cholera (or, some said, the Plague) in Goa took the lives of my father, mother, and elder brother, and when my Fidalgo employer decided to retire to Portugal, I was left with a small estate and very little money, or, as I learned to say it with a shrug, "poucos Crusados." But I had invested well in the spice trade, especially at Cochin, and could afford a decent living in Goa.

With the story of all these generations and adventures, I could entertain almost any shopkeeper who chose to share his coffee with me. I could turn away more piercing questions about my family and fortunes with sad looks and solemn references to the entire generation of Portuguese Goan aristocrats destroyed by the Plague.

I should not let these excursions into a fictional existence imply that I was spending far less time in my Jesuit and Christian studies than in frequenting the streets and shops of Goa. Only in the middle or late afternoons could I afford such liberties. My mornings were entirely absorbed in my Latin and Christian studies. Also I was expected to give some attention to the Roman Church's "Offices" of traditional prayer and worship.

As a Muslim with five traditional times a day for individual or communal prayer, I found the Christian day conveniently divided into eight Offices of "Matins" between midnight and dawn, "Lauds" just before sunrise, "Prime" at sunrise, "Terce" in midmorning, "Sext" at noontime, "None" in midafternoon, "Compline" before retiring at night and "Vespers" at sunset. It was relatively easy for me to fit into this system so far as I might choose, and to coordinate it with the five Muslim prayer times-- Fajr, Zuhr, 'Asr, Maghrib, and 'Isha'-- with Fajr at dawn and Isha at sunset a slightly different schedule.

I was accustomed to the exact Muslim adherence to the communal texts of their prayers, but learned that there was a similar precision in the Christian communal prayers. Fortunately, if one were good at memorization, had a good 'ear,' and were diligent in practice, correct recitation of very long texts could become habitual. I kept my Muslim prayers much to myself, either by praying alone at convenient times or by giving only silent utterance to their texts. MY reputation for precise knowledge of long Latin texts, notably of the Four Gospels and of the 'correct' prayer texts, brought me praise in some quarters of the College of Saint Paul-- and scarcely concealed envy in others.

Of the envy I could only say, in all honesty, that the precision came as much from my long-standing Arabic and Quranic discipline as it did from hard work in my Latin and Christian studies. And when I was too hard pressed if the subject of my possible Conversion arose, I learned to smile and say that one never knew when God would decide to work a miracle!

The most stressful problem for me, though perhaps the least visible to others, was Brother Castro's unrelenting hostility. He had a dozen ways of expressing it-- or more! Often, when he passed me, or even saw me across a room, he would purse his lips critically, saying nothing but letting his disapproval show. If he were talking to some Brother Jesuit and I came into both their view, Castro would interrupt their conversation briefly and stare at me as if I were a nuisance or was rudely interrupting his conversation and peace of mind. And he passed me when we were both alone, he would often then act as if I were invisible, which is hard to do when you are passing in a narrow hall!

And, I knew, he did not like Monserrate and would find almost any excuse to avoid him, or to ask some third person if he had noticed that Monserrate was moody and hard to approach sometimes. It was just a way with Castro, I realized, of spreading doubt and ill-feeling.

Sometimes as I read my Gospels it seemed to be that the man was a Judas looking for a wedge between Jesus of Nazareth and his more intimate disciples and friends. If he overheard Monserrate praising anyone he would put on an expression of impatience, even of a certain contempt-- aimed not, of course, at Monserrate-- oh no, nothing so direct-- but at the person who was the subject! "Brother" Castro had almost perfected a skill at casting unworthy doubts and creating shadows where there were none.

I asked myself sometimes how he had ever been accepted into the Jesuit fold, unless there were more Jesuits like him! But when I occasionally saw him wearing a superb mask of pious prayer and "service" to the Jesuit cause, I knew the answer. He was a natural master of deceit, and wore it as comfortably as he wore his Jesuit robes. And I, who was not by nature inclined to suspicion or cynical observation, would do well just to stay away from him-- and yes, out of his field of vision that disturbed me.

I continued on my path of doing well at my Latin and my Christian studies, so well that even the carping and stares of a Castro could not dislodge me from the College of Saint Paul, and I had my own coterie of friends and admirers-- especially among the Novices-- if that was what I wanted. As long as I "did" well, I could stay the course.

And when the "bad" days occurred, which they sometimes continued to do, Monserrate's company and example were my restoratives.

Chapter 13

The Absent Brother

One afternoon the Rua Direita was so crowded that it was an effort just to navigate my way through the throng of tradesmen, overladen bearers, rumbling wagons, pack trains of horses, and loud clusters of Portuguese sailors. I decided it was time to leave the place.

Abruptly an elegantly attired horseman, riding as if he were the most noble of fidalgo "gentlemen," came straight at me. I resented his condescending look. Four pairs of his liveried attendants followed smartly on foot. I just managed to step aside-- tempted to slap his Arabian horse smartly on the rump!

Then I stared at one of his footmen. Raya! My brother's name almost burst from me. Dark skinned in the Tamil way, his hair short and slightly curling at the ears, the young man had an intelligent face-- a face marred by a scowl that recalled Raya's when he had fallen into one of his bad moods!

This copy of my brother Raya caught my stare. His scowl turned into an assumed fierceness. I opened my mouth as if to say something. An apology for staring?

No. He was not Raya! His gaze hardened, then shifted past me. It all happened in a rush, like seeing an unknown captain leading his men toward a battle somewhere. In an instant the feeling of recognition dissolved.

A sense of loss swept me, catching me by surprise. Raya! I had not thought of him in weeks. Ever since we parted at Dharwara I had blamed him for our separation-- for my own stubbornness! Now I felt the guilt I had been carrying on my shoulders. How long had I been in Goa? I counted backward. Two months!

So I had been the heroic, misunderstood one, had I? The big adventurer and taker of risks. I was ashamed of myself.

I had to contact Raya! Maybe not apologize, exactly-- but write to him. The trouble was, how long would it take a letter to reach Bijapur-- or reach Raya if he had gone somewhere else? He did not owe me anything. Maybe he also thought he did not owe anything to Aunt Bibiji! Instantly I thought of my aunt's walled garden and house, her well-trimmed garden, the fountain at its center, her special charbagh with its four beds of flowers and fruit trees.

Would this Hindu "brother" of mine have gone back to the Tamil country? No, not to the ruined "City of Victory!" He would have hated that. But somewhere to the south!

Somewhere-- trying to recapture a lost youth, lost city, lost… father? I bit my lip. This was not time to be feeling any guilt. Or regret. I had no time for that.

Still, I was restless.

I walked to the Holy Hill on the west of the city. I could sit on the bench in the shade of the big tree I had seen there. I could look across the city's church steeples to the river Mandovi-- watch the incoming ships. Or turn and look out across the Sea of Arabia with its scattered clouds and distant horizon. Maybe I could think up there on the "Monte Santo." Settle down a little. Or was it something else I wanted to do? Walk back and forth, back and forth, swinging my arms, making fists that wanted to hit something-- feel pain.

Because there he was-- still in my mind's eye. My brother! My partner on that crazed ride to his "City of Victory"-- city of defeat! And I had hardly bothered to show some real sympathy. I had to get out of there, too! And then we were joining the Jesuits on the road-- joining Monserrate. Yes, and riding to Goa with my new companions while my brother went riding alone, back to Bijapur with the message to my aunt.

Reaching the top of the Holy Hill, I looked around. The thick stone walls of the "Church of our Lady of the Rosary" were not welcoming. Too heavy, too impersonal. Yet the view, yes, it was grand. I sat on the stone bench in the shade. But I was finding it hard to relax. And at last I knew what I felt. I was lonely-- lonely for that dynamic, infuriating "brother" of mine with his "moods," his defects, his sharp and cynical wit. Not defects like mine, maybe. Only different!

The coming sunset found me still sitting there, my thoughts wandering. Sighing, I got up. I went back downhill. Past the Augustinian monastery, that seemed almost empty, almost forgotten in the rush of other Holy Orders to build bigger monasteries, bigger churches down in the valley. The Franciscans who wanted a big monastery, too! The Jesuits with their hopes set on a great basilica they could call their "Bom Jesus," their "Good Jesus," the Savior of Mankind.

I sat down before dinner at the Refectory of Saint Paul's. I wrote the letter I had to send to Raya. Addressed it in care of my aunt. Sealed it with wax. Two days later the letter was on its way.

I had found a convenient caravanserai on one of Goa's back streets. I made my deal with the Hindu baniya who rode back and forth with his horses and pack-laden mules, between Goa and the Muslim capitals of the Deccan-- the ones that had enriched themselves with the spoils of the Vijayanagar! Their Muslim sultans and courtiers could pay well. My letter was a minor thing. It would get delivered. The price came high, but it would serve.

After the next morning's breakfast I strode through the tall gateway of the College of Saint Paul and stood a moment in the early sunlight, feeling its heat-- the humidity of the Konkan's coast already bringing the perspiration to my face.

"Raya," I thought-- "You bastard! Answer me!"

Two months passed. Another two weeks. Another….

A letter! From my brother! Incredible. An actual letter. I loosened its wax with the tip of the small knife I always carried, hidden. I smiled to myself. At least, if someone-- on a busy street, in a shaded lane, on the docks of Goa-- wanted to kill me, I had <u>something</u> to fight with!

It was Raya's handwriting. But… in code? I studied the scrawl-- and burst out laughing. That boyish amusement we had invented-- very long ago at my aunt's house one afternoon when we were bored. A

Friday, when I had planned to spend my day at my prayers for a change. But no, the big inventors were inspired. A special Language for Two. In case we ever had to write something-- a message-- meant only for us!

I sighed. Gradually I recalled the code. Spell every word inside-out, every letter first on the right, then on the left! The letters backward, too. Right, left-- right, left. And now at last the first big result! Lines and lines of nonsense that anyone in his right mind would not bother to pore over. Especially if he were a merchant with better things to do.

Finally I unraveled the mystery-script. A little game that, when you knew the rules, might just be useful again someday.

I strolled the two thousand paces, more or less, that took me back to the Holy Hill and the Chapel of Our Lady. Far enough from the college to feel like a big distance. Back to the bench in the shadow of the tree where I could seriously concentrate on translating the screed Raya had sent. I did not enjoy the message at first, and it was surprisingly long. But it grew in interest for me as it proceeded from Raya's pen. The beggar was actually in a friendly mood!

"Brother Aziz," began Raya, "whatever else you do-- I don't much care-- do NOT convert to the Christian religion! Surely you have to know that it would literally kill our Aunt Bibiji.

"For all her efforts to convert me the black-skinned Hindu to Islam, she is too reasonable to force anything upon me. BUT, if you convert to the religion of those Christian monks you would join, I would not be surprised if the <u>least</u> you aunt did would be to disown you! And I do not think you would wish to cast aside the wealth of your parents <u>and</u> your aunt--not even for a life of Jesuit alms! Aunt Bibiji's house and grounds alone would be a great inheritance for you. And in case you think I am selfishly trying to get part of that inheritance, I would entirely waive any right to her estate. I would rather be free of encumbrances--and I mean just FREE. You can have the whole estate. I am sure your father and mother would have wanted that-- without letting some mongrel Hindu share it!

"And now, aside from a complaint or two, I come to the part where our little code does the most to protect us from unwanted readers! Since your departure I have changed my purposes in life. I am now-- shall I say it?-- dabbling in a roving merchant's career! Dabbling, I said. But in fact I am laying out my plans and starting to make contacts. I will try specializing in the more rare gemstones of the Deccan, rare woods like the sandal tree from forested regions, even some of the nuts and fruits introduced by the Portuguese into the Konkan-- things that differ from the usual trade in pepper and other spices, the cotton cloth and the imported carpets. I am considering the import, too, of Arabian horses that we have found to be such good mounts for the man with his Mongol bow and his Portuguese musket!

"Frankly I forsee an ever wider and deeper market for all forms of foreign, "Firinghi" weapons-- including muskets with the new firing devices-- the Wheel-lock, the Snaphaunce! Anything to attract serious buyers, especially the sultans and their officers in the Deccan. The "Grand Mughal" in the north is clearly thinking of subordinating or absorbing-- yes, I do mean conquering!-- our Deccan Sultanates. But if they remain strong, and become even better armed, the noble Akbar might just leave them alone awhile longer!

I am thinking not only of importing muskets-- you must understand that I intend it to be through some unusual sources!-- but also the latest, of the long-barreled pistols from Holland and Belgium and Spain and Germany that also have the new triggering devices and can kill at close quarters. And, if we are talking about self-defense for the "average" Muslim, then you might well consider acquiring at least a pair of the new muskets and pair of the new pistols yourself-- at a good brotherly price!

"Why, I might ask, should not any man of self-respect in the Deccan not arm himself with the best of weapons, including the ones that can, with practice like we have done, bring down a man at a hundred paces or more-- and the short-barreled ones that, with care, can be relied on at twenty to forty paces!? The market is there and will expand. I see no reason not to put whatever modest wealth I have into that market-- and develop a reputation for skilled but honest dealing that will increase the weight of my own pockets. The Portuguese-- or Spaniards or Dutch or English-- will not respect either Muslims or Hindus the more for sitting with out-of-fashion, unreliable matchlocks and Mongol bows of wood and bone and sinew that grow slack in the rains of our country while the rest of the world arms itself and passes us by!

"I have heard that even the Great Mughal to the north, although he is arming more and more of his elite brigades with matchlocks both imported and locally produced, will not bother himself to possess weapons better than those matchlocks-- or does he fear an army that might turn and cast him out if better armed? Is his monopoly of power so great that he can afford to ignore every Firinghi who nibbles now at the edges of his empire while he dabbles in religious debate among mullahs who know nothing beyond talk of the divine favor that radiates like the sun from the "world-conquering" Padsha! Even I, the "spiritual" Hindu, say-- Such manure!

"If I were "Padshah" and controlled his resources NOW, I would stop all senseless forays into the Afghan plateaus and Himalayan valleys that sap his power. As a man of sense I would stop toying with the idea of controlling the states of the Deccan-- which, after all, keep order where there otherwise might be a sea of troubles, with wars breaking out again and again among them. I have always wondered why these sultans allow the crops of their farmers to be again and again ridden into the ground by bands of roving horsemen, or stripped away to feed armies with bellies so numerous and hungry they barely have the strength to move and the energy to fight!

"Well, Brother, here I sit-- or actually stand, for I think best when I pace back and forth between sorties with pen in hand! You may now think <u>me</u> a madman-- a prince without a kingdom or country! But I keep thinking of these mercantile adventures. You may feel that I am a hopeless dreamer. But I would like to put more golden coin in my pockets And besides-- who knows? The time may be coming-- it may have arrived!-- when it is better to be the merchant-prince than to be a royal one!

Oh yes, I know. I speak of prospering and peace, and yet I would deal in weaponry that few can afford-- and that those few would rather keep a monopoly than chance that hungry farmers might rise to victory in waves of revolt. But I have perceived the truth that no one can long control the slow but steady spread of new means of making war and keeping 'peace'-- through strength! I will deal in luxuries, as I have said-- and am already beginning to do so. But I will *also* deal in things that men of your training and mine may find more practical and profitable.

"If you read anything here that is of value, write again to me sometime or at least think over what I have said! Continue to write in this special language of ours, so that we may engage in our twaddle without interruption! And if you ever abandon this questionable service of Firinghi masters that you seem to be cultivating, especially this religious nonsense, you may want some of my services-- whether of arms or of luxuries of gentler kinds, and live in comfort if nothing else!

"Yours in eternal friendship, Brother-- despite the frowns of my demeanor and, on occasion, the raising of my voice!

"'Raya.'"

Slowly I folded the letter and tucked it deep within the folds of my sash. It would be worthy of repeated reading.

Yes, this Hindu brother of mine was halfway to being a "'madman'," as he himself admitted. But a brilliant one!

How strange are the uses of genius. How rare to have a "brother" of such far-flung thoughts who, I could see-- I could feel it like the warmth of a hand or a gaze!-- really wished me to be his friend and who would be mine, if only I would let him.

I sat awhile looking over the city of Goa and the distant river Mandovi. My thoughts seemed to bunch before me and then flee like antelope. Raya's face, too, came and went before my inner eye. A face by turns handsome, intent, bold, laughing, serious, intense--and painfully honest!

Some of his thoughts amazed me with their perceptions. He had laid out a veritable feast of ideas for my consumption. I hoped he would become that fat merchant-prince he spoke of… well, at least become that successful one he envisioned! And surely, if I ever changed my career to be more in tune with his, I might need those weapons of which he was now making himself the merchant and princely champion.

For the present, at any rate, I was in Goa. It seemed so far from this brother of mine. And yet, I could surmise that he was considering lines upon which he could safely engage in lucrative trade through this port of Goa. He had my admiration, and certainly my respect, for his practical, inventive ways of thinking-- and for expanding his field of vision in his own way, as I was doing in mine!

Even, it occurred to me, if we were each in pursuit of a kind of dream-- both of us speculating! And I knew him well enough to see that he could accept the ups and downs of fortune-- or so it seemed-- better than I could!

What would become of us, Raya and me? We were prophets without an audience! And, like most prophets, more likely to be stoned than adulated-- if all our ideas and efforts became known!

With the sun still high, I descended the Monte Santo. I found myself thinking that here were chapels and churches and a monastery that made Albuquerque's conquest appear almost in essence a religious war, when it had been fought as a brutal, territorial, dispossessing one that might better have been celebrated by the phrase that sometimes seemed to describe Goa best. A phrase about wealth, not Christian zeal.

Here, at my feet, lay "Goa Durada"-- Golden Goa. And it was not the color or weight of the sun that had given it its hue, but the clash of steel against steel, boom of cannon, and sweet sound of gold coin ringing upon its glittering neighbor.

I sighed. Were not the Jesuits, including even my friend Monserrate, doing their part to create here an all-too-human empire even while they "fished for souls"? They would almost certainly not even be here, not in such numbers, without Portuguese conquest!

Thinking of Monserrate now-- who was my Christian friend as surely as Raya was my Hindu brother-- perhaps I did not wish to know the future of this Christian "crusade." Portuguese conquest had produced amazing wealth for Portugal. Had it really made the outcome of Jesuit crusading more certain?

Chapter 14

Jesuit, Or "Fidalgo"?

The three months I had first expected to spend in Goa had become four, then six. Any real achievement in Christian studies and Latin was not to be had in less than a year, I soon realized. Nor, as I considered it, would less than two years be adequate. At this rate of advance I would not reach Bijapur again for another three or four years! I saw that, in truth, anything like full expertise could require a decade!

I sat down at last and wrote my Aunt Bibiji "explaining" myself. She would not like the choice I told of-- not six months or a year but two or three years! At the same time I had to hope that she would see my desire to make this venture to Goa worthwhile. A difficult task but one I thought worth trying, I told my aunt. I knew she would sniff. Excuses! The best I could hope was that she would appreciate my writing at all.

As I had already contacted my brother Raya, it seemed no big problem to write my aunt at the same address. However, there being no regular mail from Goa to Bijapur, I again had find some informal means like a Hindu or Muslim caravan. But this time a friendly Hindu day-student at the College came to my rescue. His family were active in trade with the Deccan. His uncle in Ponda, informed me that my letter might be taken to Bijapur by a caravan leaving the next month! I offered to pay well, but it made no difference. A caravan was not a mail service. I resigned myself to the delay.

Aside from my studies, which occupied primarily my mornings I was beginning to make more frequent sorties into Goa's streets. in the afternoons. My progress in speaking Portuguese encouraged me to range farther into outlying parts of the city and test myself, as usual, by speaking to shopkeepers, making inquiries about their goods and prices, and taking notes on common words and phrases, especially the more colloquial ones. By the time my poor letter started its long journey to Bijapur, I had become fairly expert in navigating the streets and districts of Goa.

Fortunately I also learned where all the best shady public places were. A place I especially liked was the shade of the large tree atop the "Holy Hill" that I had first seen when Monserrate had introduced me to "Monte Santo and its Manueline church. The hill was about twice as from the Rua Direita and the College, but I did not have to worry about being bothered much by other visitors to "my" path of shade and its stone bench. And there was almost always at least a faint breeze on the Monte Santo, so I could stay and study whole afternoons. The view from "my" bench to the river Mandovi and its harbor was impressive. But most of all I enjoyed turning on the bench and looking out across the Sea of Arabia, which was truly inspiring with its small clouds drifting landward and slowly, as evening came, massing together into mountains with lightning flashing and sometimes a rumble of thunder. I remembered how as a boy I had often climbed to my parents' roof and sat under the smaller roof of the barsati while I idled the time away watching the clouds above the plain of the Deccan to the west of Bijapur. I had long ago lost count of the sunsets I watched from that barsati! Here I had a different scene of glory to watch, but there was still something to be said for each of the scenes. And oddly, I found myself becoming more reconciled with my parents' untimely deaths.

I decided that my calmness and reconciliation was mainly the result of feeling safe under the care of Monserrate whom I held to be absolutely the best of Jesuits. I could not persuade myself to ever dislike him or wish to do something that would hurt him-- so calm and reasoned was his manner, and with his quiet flashes of humor, yet thoroughly serious in his faith in God and Christ. More and more often, as I paused in my studies there in the shade, I found myself thinking that I respected Christian ideals like Monserrate's, even when I knew that most Christians, like most Muslims, seemed often to forget their ideals when the rough ways of earthly life surrounded them and thorns lay thick in their paths. And now, on this particular afternoon where these thoughts had come to me, I meditated as long as I could until the sun sank in the western sea.

Suddenly I knew I would be late arriving at the Refectory for dinner. I sighed as I got up and hurried downhill, knowing only too well the stares that would be turned my way from some predictable quarters!

An important new idea had been working in my brain, and by the time I reached the College the idea had seized upon me completely. It was time to start going out into the city now in new clothing-- Portuguese clothing! My Portuguese fluency had improved to the point where I was ready to experiment with that instead of keeping to a Jesuit Novice's tunic. I found that many Portuguese men had taken to the habit of exchanging their country's woolen pantaloons and close-fitting vests for lighter versions woven in cotton. I would emulate them as I visited merchant's shops. Truly I had begun to notice that my Jesuit tunic closed out many a topic of conversation-- and some of the more common idioms that attended it. I wanted to know and be able to use those idioms in a pinch or a corner where I did not wish the question of my religion or race to play a large role-- or my Jesuit preoccupations either!

A special advantage for me came from another fairly common habit of Portuguese men in Goa, who preferred to continue wearing wide-brimmed hats of felt-- but also, under the hat, would wear a bandanna of cotton. I would quickly adopt that practice, which allowed for the bandanna to be wrapped tight against my head so that it covered the worst of my scars!

Indeed, I began comport myself more and more in a gentlemanly "fidalgo" manner, walking in a relaxed but purposeful way. With the best of custom I could now doff my hat and languidly fan myself with it on hot afternoons.

By the end of another week I had supplied myself with my new fidalgo dress and manners. However, I lacked one option which was almost an essential-- the wearing at my side of a rapier with modest but "serious" scabbard and hangings! I knew that my patron Monserrate would disapprove of such military behavior, but I saw that I would be more and more tempted to acquire a good rapier and complete my 'fidalgo' look. Finally I surrendered to the temptation. Unfortunately I felt I had to engage in some secrecy at first. To go about armed made me, still the aristocratic Muslim at heart, feel a new self-respect. But while in the environs of the Jesuit College I must make a secret of my unaccustomed weaponry. A guilty secret would not serve me in the long run. Sooner or later, and actually "sooner," I would have to divulge my plan at least to Monserrate. But I must not try to make him an accomplice!

I would exchange my Jesuit habit and sandals for my Portuguese array in the back room of one of the shops where I was well known now, and where the owner was one of those "pragmatic" Hindus-- that word again!-- who would accept my choice without too many questions.

But one sort of question would no go away so easily, especially if I took to wearing a rapier at my side-- along with the shorter, narrower sword known to some as a "poniard."

So it began-- my "Fidalgo" transformation-- with all the risks attached. But I found afresh that I was most comfortable with myself as an aristocratic Muslim of the Deccan. A genuine, if sometimes (even to me) surprising change was to realize how little my months studying Latin and Christianity had affected my basic image of myself.

Soon I also found that I had a half-denied fascination with Portuguese fencing, since any Portuguese gentleman regarded it as in armed, self-confident importance. Knowing that my Muslim heritage of the Deccan was as good as any of these "men-at-arms," I not only craved their Portuguese weapon of choice but began wishing I could acquire the appropriate skills!

But was not I going back to a not-so-well hidden sense of a Muslim calling to be rider, huntsman, and soldier? I spent some hours thinking it all over-- and it made no difference. The best I could do was swear-- no, no, to vow!-- that whatever I learned or did would all be devoted to a capacity for self-defense, and never to be engaged in without careful reflection on its purpose, which I could explain and justify to Monserrate! All in... "due time."

I recognized, of course, that my association with the Jesuits did not allow me a place among such sword-bearers! I had to keep beating back the thought that it would be unseemly and foolish for me to place Monserrate in a more difficult position that he already occupied because of me! But, by and by, impatience wore me down. Now that I had had acquired my rapier bearing the mark of Spain's "Toledo" steel,

I could not resist wishing for places and times to experiment with the weapon!

I had more than once watched the duels between Portuguese who quarreled in the streets, and I knew it would take time to learn the arts of fencing with rapier. For awhile now I only followed Portuguese example with my eyes, but at last I purchased a small treatise on the swordman's discipline. It was time, I decided, to find time and place for practicing that discipline.

One afternoon a solution came to me. During an afternoon stroll I happened to pass an old walled estate that had suffered a disastrous fire and had been abandoned. The burned-out house and its large, walled garden stood on the slope of a low hill somewhat south and east of the College.

Turning at a rear corner of the wall, I came to a heavy wooden gate with rusted iron fittings. The door's lock had long ago disappeared, and the gate stood half open, blocked inside by weeds and bushes. Giving thought to the possibility of snakes, I decided that with my sword and high-topped boots I was wearing I could dare to enter and follow an overgrown path that presented itself.

Looking carefully around, I found that I was seeing an orchard of once-fine orange trees and a large space, more or less rectangular, that would have been a garden! And now, if it could be cleared, would not the garden make a good place to study my lessons in the shade of some tree-- and begin my swordsman's practice of his craft?

In an instant I appointed myself the discoverer and "keeper" of this ruined orchard and garden. I followed this by making discreet enquiries within the neighborhood as to the reason for the estate's ruin and abandonment. Why, indeed, had such a place for many years drawn no new owner, no purchase or restoration?

Though my enquiries remained cautious, I soon discovered the reasons. The owner of house, walls, and garden had been a Portuguese naval officer, a man who had married a Muslim woman, a "Converso," and had installed her grandly there. He and his wife had been known for their lavish entertainments with lanterns strung throughout house and gardens. But after several years a fire had broken out while the owner was at sea, and both his wife and their three children had suffocated and died! Returning, the officer began to go mad. Even though a Christian, he killed himself with heavy drinking and the taking of opium! The place seemed cursed now. Rumor had it that the ghost of the dead man haunted the ruined house and the grounds-- and could be heard on hot summer nights moaning and weeping. The slightest breeze seemed to convey strange sounds, strange odors.

And why was it, people asked, that voices would especially be heard? To all eyes the place looked forbidding, unholy-- the house a pile of burnt beams and collapsed walls, the orchard and garden a ruin of weeds and twisted tree limbs, the walls like the enclosure of an enchanted tomb. What person in his right mind would even enter that place where ghosts could be heard keening on nights when the monsoon winds blew and the rain seemed to fall with extra force on the surrounding streets and lanes-- let alone try to reoccupy the ruins?

But I was not superstitious, I told myself! Besides, I had no interest either in the burnt-out house or its supposed inhabitants-- and I would have no need even of the orchard or garden except for shade and some open space on hot afternoons! And as for fears reasonable or otherwise, I noted, too, that the elevated ground of the area, from which the river Mandovi could be seen in the distance, had continued to contain many a fine house with its splendid view. Obviously people of wealth and quality had not abandoned this hillside with its "accursed" ruin! For me, too, the walled garden raised no fears. Within the month I cleared the space almost entirely, and busily made it seem my own.

Here I resorted now almost every afternoon, dressed in my Portuguese way, armed not only with my rapier but also with mattock, shovel, an hoe-- tools that enabled me to level an extensive area of former garden for my studies and practice at fencing. The old orange trees, their shade relieved of weeds, were my shady arbor for periods of reading and recitation and moments of rest between bouts of fencing with imagined opponents!

I sometimes saw how foolish this "swordsmanship" of mine might look-- and, in truth, how awkward and inexperienced it was. But I tried to ignore the contradiction. I continued to watch every aspect of Portuguese behavior on the main streets of Goa, including the swordplay that was part of their boasting and quarrels. I was slowly learning my passes, thrusts, and parries.

Meanwhile, I rationalized, I would remain in good physical condition despite my long hours sitting immersed in books. My afternoons at practice with the rapier meant less time spent in study-- and more late reading by candlelight! Still, I persisted.

On occasion someone, perhaps a curious member of some family living nearby, or a servant sent for the same reason, would look in on me though the half open gate while I sweated and called out the name of each of a fencer's proper moves. No one, however, seemed officious enough to complain to the authorities-- or sufficiently brave, given the place's reputation, to come inside the gate! I fancied myself the master of this, "my" domain.

One day, however, an event occurred that put in question all my fencing efforts-- though purely 'defensive' in their intent, as I like to believe!

I was walking near the upper end of the "Straight Street," the broad Rua Direita, where the public Pillory stood and where crowds of off-duty sailors often raised their voices amid the sounds of hawkers of cheap wares shouting the praises of their merchandise. This day there was a crowd, too, but for a different reason.

A Portuguese carrack had, the day before, arrived from Lisbon with its crew and some paying passengers. Among the passengers, two had brought with them a quarrel. This was no ordinary matter of a half-playful challenge by casual acquaintances, but a deadly encounter in the making. As it was my habit, I quietly made inquiries about the cause of the quarrel. It happened, I was told, that the ship now at anchor had been becalmed for two weeks off the western coast of Africa-- a not infrequent occurrence, and one fraught with tensions. The two men, both "gentlemen" by reputation of birth, had developed a quarrel over a gambling debt and had moved from insulting each other to defaming each other's families in Lisbon. During the ship's becalmed days, the two men had twice drawn their rapiers, but had been restrained by the ship's first mate and then its captain. And now on this hot, still afternoon under a burning sun, these fidalgo "gentlemen" were resorting again to their swords.

I warned myself not to linger with the crowd, but to watch swordsmen in a deadly match was a temptation more than I could resist. Besides, the crowd was big and pressing closer around me. The two men were already circling each other, snarling insults of the vilest kind, not excluding the character of sisters and mothers. Glancing around, I saw faces in the crowd almost slavering in obscene fascination and glee. This was no piece of "play." There had to be blood. Even I, with no stake in all this, felt my heart beating fast.

The two men made small circles with the tips of their swords, reaching out as if to touch in a sort of dance. Now they rushed upon one another other, thrusting and parrying in a clangor of steel. They passed each other, changing places. Again the dance of feet seeking advantage, the fierceness of probing gazes. Another pass and clash of steel. A surge of blood from the upper arm of the fighter who seemed the younger. A sneer from the lips of the other man, the older. His eyes bored into the other's face. "I spit on your mother," he said calmly. The wounded man reddened, his eyes almost bursting from his head. Fear seized me, and I felt cold. The wounded man, I saw, had become a raging elephant-- taunted by a tiger. He would charge. The tiger was patient, half crouching, making small circles with the tip of his rapier, making little thrusts with it. He was smiling. I grew colder, contracting inside. The younger man plunged, thrusting again and again, seeking the clash of steel again. The tiger retreated a few steps, still poised, drawing the elephant toward him. There was a flurry of feet, then a silence.

The elder's sword had passed completely through the younger's body, between two ribs, finding his heart. The younger man was staring, but at nothing. His sword had only pierced the edge of the older man's shirt, leaving a small wound at the waist. It was as if, now, the older held up the younger man by the main force of his rapier, face to face, inches apart. The tiger was watching his enemy die. No one spoke. The two men, the crowd, the earth and sky-- all silent. The older man's muscles strained with the weight of the younger's body that slowly sagged against him. He spat in the younger's face, a face with eyes already dim and bleary. Slowly the victor withdrew his rapier, shoving at his victim's chest with the left hand until the steel came free. Blood gushed from the dying man's wound, soaking the clothing of both enemies. The younger man fell at the other's feet.

There was a slow gush of air-- from the crowd. They had seen an execution. So had I. Almost physically sick, still I watched the victor. His face seemed to be locked in a demeanor of hatred. He had killed and did not care. A little smile twitched at the corners of his tiger's mouth. He was exulting.

Suddenly a shout. But not from the crowd that lingered. The King's authorities were coming. A detachment of soldiers, running on the double. The crowd surged back, caught between fascination and a wish to escape. A captain appeared at the head of the detachment, followed by a sergeant, a corporal-- three officers with swords drawn. I saw the pistol neatly contained by the captain's sash. The captain brought his men to a halt a dozen paces from the victor in the fight. Loudly, for everyone in hearing distance, the captain announced that this was an unlicensed gathering, that it would immediately disperse-- except for the survivor of the duel!

The victorious "gentleman" had used the hem of his shirt to wipe his rapier's blade with quick fingertips and had half sheathed the weapon. He stared back at the captain. His anger had become cold, but hard, like his steel. "Your name!" bellowed the captain. The victor was still silent, staring back. His mind seemed to be locked within what had happened. Again the captain's voice. "That scabbard with your weapon-- place it on the ground!"

The crowd had begun slowly, silently to back away, to creep away, wanting to run, afraid to run. I, too, wanted to run-- but could not move. The captain repeated his order for the swordsman to lay down his scabbard with its weapon. I heard a low voice. The swordsman's. Almost too low to be heard. But the words were an insult. They were a refusal. Unthinkable.

The captain slowly drew his pistol, cocking it. My mind said to me that the pistol was the new "wheel-lock" type that had recently started appearing in the possession of Portuguese officers, but.... I was not able to finish my thought. There was an explosion. Fire spit from the pistol. The rebellious swordsman dropped to his knees, astonishment in his gaze. He pitched forward. The captain had shot him dead.

By such events, on land or sea, is authority enforced-- and mutinies and disorders ended. The crowd quickly dispersed. Faces were pale. So was mine. I walked away fast like the others. I was afraid to touch again my weapon in its scabbard. I, who had thought I could work a miracle and make myself a Portuguese swordsman, the master of a rapier. Now I saw it was not to be. I had not enough time for either 'lessons' or practice.

All I had to do was to meet was one man more experienced than I with a rapier, more efficient, more… murderous. He would kill me and feel no awe, have no regret. Everything that I had gained in Goa-- all the ways as a scholar that I was restoring the honor of my family, all the fatherly care bestowed on me by Monserrate my teacher and friend, I would have squandered!

For two weeks I did not return to "my" garden, or even go into the streets. I was diligent in my studies-- and possessed by fear, and by that death I had seen.

I had wrapped the rapier and its appointments in tight wound cotton cloth and hidden them away. I would regain my composure, I knew, and return to "my" garden-- but only to study now.

However, I was not quite ready to give up my pretensions-- my hard won "fidalgo" identity! I began to go out again, but only with the short-bladed 'poniard' at my side. That and a sturdy cane would serve to some degree for defense if I were desperate.

If by some chance I came upon a fidalgo quarrel on the street, I now would stiffly walk away from the situation, leaving the impression as far as possible that, as a gentleman, I felt myself to be 'above' public brawling.

Chapter 15

A Mission To The Mughals?

Two weeks of serious study, on the other hand, had again convinced me that I was acquitting myself well as a Jesuit scholar. The irony was that, during those same weeks and the month that followed, I was also shaping and disciplining myself in the image of the fidalgo-- the Portuguese gentleman and man at arms-- while my Jesuit studies were bringing me closer to Monserrate again!

I had continued wearing my Novice's clothing at the College of Saint Paul, and was still combining my Latin studies with my Portuguese language progress. At meals I and my closest friends of the Novitiate continued our alternating days of conversation in Latin and then in Portuguese. Almost every day Monserrate would stop me after prayers or studies or meals and speak to me first in Latin and then in Portuguese, examining me with a smile, a little challenge, and an affable correction if I needed it. Perhaps that made him simply a mentor to me rather than a father. But it was what I had yearned for from a father, too.

Without my realizing it, Monserrate had begun to feel more pride in me, like a father might of a son. It was exactly the relationship that I had been wanting-- and strange that I was not aware of it at first.

I fully realized his growing sense of closeness the day he stopped me outside the Refectory after lunch and told me he was hearing good news from my teachers-- especially from the Brother who was my Latin instructor. "He tells me," said Monserrate, "that you are making remarkable progress again after a period of slackness." He might have asked about the 'slackness,' but he was kind-- and I decided not to enlighten him as to the reasons!

He added quickly, "I am proud of you, Aziz Ahmad, and glad to see your great abilities given such play. It reminds me of an idea-- and a proposal-- I had meant to discuss with you."

As usual when he was serious, he had me come with him to his small room at the hostel. He motioned me to take one of his two chairs. It was becoming a little ritual between us.

"I believe you know," he said, "that there is talk among Jesuits about the "Great Mogor's" empire to the north, and how its reigning sultan, Akbar, has begun to question the ideas of Islam and to invite argument and debate. Some have thought that this event is due to the emperor's having married a woman of a leading Rajput family-- indeed, a woman of one of the highest and most distinguished of Rajput dynasties. Would it not, then, be in the great Akbar's interest to turn his Muslim court's thoughts toward accommodating his Rajput marriage and tolerating the Hindu faith? And might the emperor not consider other religions in his domains, or in neighboring states, to be worthy also of his serious consideration? Why not, then, Christianity? And-- though it might seem miraculous-- might this Muslim sultan, by far the most powerful in the whole of the country, decide to convert to the Christian faith and, at one stroke, either to bring the rest of his Muslim countrymen with him, or at least to impose a more tolerant regime on the land?"

Logical yet more and more fired with zeal as he delivered himself of these ideas, he was watching me more closely-- filled with a hope that I would agree. "These," he said excitedly, are the kind of thoughts that are now circulating among my Jesuit colleagues." And next a note of triumph. "And Akbar the Mughal sovereign, their "Padshah," has recently been asking of a visiting Jesuit at his court a variety of questions about the Christian Faith and our Society's mission here! A wonderful opportunity seems to be taking shape, as if by God's Will."

He paused to observe my response. I was not reacting, however, with quite the enthusiasm that he had expected. I did not wish to discourage him, feeling like a respectful son faced with a father's grand ambitions. Yet I must have shown that I was somewhat sceptical. How could I support his enthusiasm without wholly submerging some doubts that were bothering me?

I took refuge first in a somewhat long, drawn-out breath that implied 'Well, let us see now…." I knew he would catch the inflection of that less than thrilled response! Meaning only to pause, he had come to a total stop. He waited, trying to be patient.

Next I tried an apology. "It does seem a wonderful chance to advance the Society's hopes. And I do not wonder that the Padshah would be impressed by Jesuit zeal and discipline. He must have heard good things about Jesuit performance in Goa, along the coast of the Konkan from Goa to Cochin, and elsewhere!"

But then I paused, too, and took a deep breath. "I do wonder, though, what the result would be if this emperor, the greatest Muslim ruler in the land, converted to the Christian Faith and tried to change also the beliefs of all or more Muslims-- and especially the orthodox Sunnis who are the majority! Such an event might well be-- I am inclined to think it would be!-- a great source of tension and upheaval-- and bring, perhaps, a violent end to this great sultan's reign and his dynasty!"

The effect on my mentor was not what I could have wished. I did not fail to see his face redden just a little. I began to hate myself, truly, for speaking bluntly and giving such a direct and undiplomatic answer to his array of hopes.

Monserrate gazed at me a long moment. "But," he said, in an effort to restore his initiative, "if this great and powerful emperor were to invite a group of Christian scholars, perhaps Jesuit, to come and argue the advantages of their religion, would not the invitation be a worthwhile opportunity for us to at least explore avenues toward his conversion?"

I sighed reluctantly and studied my fingers awhile. "Yes, in principle. But 'worthwhile,' as you know, does not quite mean 'inevitable.' Muslims are a powerful, armed people who have often fought "Unbelievers" rather than tolerate their existence. I do believe, dear Monserrate, that this emperor's conversion-- or even a serious attempt to secure it-- might end in the martyrdom of those, and I regretfully mean the Jesuits, who sought it-- and, besides, result in the displacement of the sultan who welcomed them!"

I watched my friend and mentor move uncomfortably in his seat. It embarrassed me again to see him attempting to control his feelings, in view of his intense faith, and not to dispute my contradictions. I also hated myself for daring to speak thus to a man I regarded as father! For if this were a dream, this conversion of the great Akbar, still it was honorable. And if this or any other Jesuit were willing to be martyred....

But my mentor did not try to press the issue. He had, indeed presented it as a series of suppositions-- and he could, if he wished, retreat to safer ground.

At last Monserrate smiled. "I have raised all these questions, because I wondered, like you Aziz Ahmad, whether I am merely indulging in fantasies. Some of my Jesuit friends have already shared with me some doubts similar to yours." He sighed. "It may be that I should not have raised these issues at all."

I could see that he still wanted me to take a more favorable position-- and at least allow him some fragments of value in his assumptions. "Forgive me," I said. "I was too quick to cast doubt on the venture. And I do know it is only being discussed, not concluded."

He smiled again, though ruefully, and sat straighter. "You are diplomatic, Aziz Ahmad. I know and appreciate that. But-- you are dealing with a Jesuit, and we men of the Society of Jesus are stubborn, always willing to take the risks of death. However legitimate your objections, you know that I, with the others, are here to spread the Holy Words of God and Christ, even if it entails great risk and possible death by martyrdom."

I nodded, but without enthusiasm. I was against my purpose to push Monserrate-- or any other Jesuit-- into the jaws of death. But while I sat in silence he raised a hand. "Far better, young man, that you are willing to speak a hard truth rather than an easy lie. I would be a poor friend and teacher if I wished you only to give happy answers even if they are untrue!

"But," he added, "let me tell you the rest of what is in my mind-- especially as it affects your own future." I kept to my silence as he sat opposite me. For awhile, indeed, we were both as silent and motionless as two crows waiting for a cricket to alight in the grass on a dry hillside. It was not the best figure of speech I could devise in the silence, but....

Monserrate came to my rescue. "I did not mean to say that the Society might send a mission to the Mughal unasked, my dear Aziz. Everything would depend upon a friendly invitation from Akbar himself, with assurances of our welcome to his court at Agra or Fathpur. And while we would go in expectation of his protection, we would not begin by some raw attempt to refute his or his officers' belief in Islam. We would have to be guided by his manner of receiving us and his way of speaking to his courtiers about the purposes of his discussions, and indeed any resulting debate-- to listen carefully before speaking, and to respond in a manner that would not embarrass the emperor nor provoke resentment among the Muslims around him."

I was glad to hear his newly cautious theme, and I quietly told him so. He smiled, relaxed a little, and proceeded.

"We know, of course, that Persian is the language of this ruler's court and government. If we Jesuits were to display a fitting knowledge of Persian, and have expert translators with us to make certain that we are understood, it seems to me that we may be able to lay a peaceable and persuasive groundwork for discussions with the emperor-- possibly in private-- for persuading him to consider, not simply the advantages of Christianity over Islam, but the advantages of his Conversion-- then we will have achieved a great deal. Perhaps, on the other hand, he will agree with the first part of the proposal but not the second, and we will know that we still have presented our Christian faith well. Who knows what achievements we may rightly claim? But if we have not made grave troubles for the emperor we may yet, upon some future occasion, win him personally to our faith. And meanwhile we may have laid grounds for the conversion of others in his realm, will have served God and Christ, and will have made our mission in some ways, if not all, the success we envision.

The logic of this faithful Christian made me admire him all the more. He was both rational and realistic. Yet, while, I trusted Monserrate to carry out such a plan and accept its results, I remembered that he would not be the only Jesuit on such a mission, and that other members of the mission might not share his caution or restraint. A disagreeable member like Brother Castro could ruin Jesuit chances from the very outset! Almost as bad, if the Jesuit to be appointed leader were not Monserrate but someone sent from Portugal, Spain, or Italy to achieve 'success' at any cost-- even on pain of alienating many men of importance in Akbar's court-- the antagonism might in the end destroy the success of the mission and leave the friendly Mughal isolated and his reign endangered!

But was I only to repeat to Monserrate what I had already warned? I decided to remain silent and try to nod agreeably!

"All this is the reason," said Monserrate, "that I am proposing, even this far in advance, that-- if you desire, Aziz Ahmad, and if you continue to progress in your Latin and your knowledge of the Christian faith-- and if I am a member of the proposed mission-- that you would accompany me to Hindustan and act as my personal secretary! If you meanwhile have seen fit to convert to the Christian faith, that would be excellent. But even if you remain Muslim it would remain my wish. It would have, either way, the advantage that, with your knowledge of both Persian and Latin, you could act as a bridge between the members of our mission and the Muslims of the emperor's court-- a voice of independent reason and-- shall I say it?-- and more persuasive, even-handed interpretation of both Christianity and Islam!"

With that kind of offer, fired as if a salvo in a running sea battle, Monserrate actually blushed.

I had to admit that the offer excited and almost overwhelmed me. My age and situation made it a daunting challenge. And I had to restrain myself because I was, after all, only sitting at Monserrate's feet and still far from qualified in the ways I would have to be. To say yes to his proposition would be a commitment to a good deal more study both of languages and of the Christian-- and Muslim!-- scriptures and traditions. And it was no certain thing that either Monserrate of I would be available and ready when-- and if-- the mission were appointed and sent on its way. If he were sure of being chosen, then probably there would be no obstacle for me. But when I thought of the Society of Jesus as a whole-- and of a member like Castro in particular-- I was deeply concerned.

I was incredibly honored. But it was not the time to leap about like a grateful puppy!

Something of my pleasure must have crept out, however. For Monserrate was gazing at me with a restrained but happy smile. I quickly realized that he had thought this through and was quite sincere. It was simply not in his nature to play with someone's hopes.

Finally I leaned forward. "You are both my teacher and my friend, dear Monserrate. All I can say us that I would gladly accept-- and qualify for-- this challenge and your confidence in me. I would join you in such a mission with complete dedication. I would try to serve the mission in a wholly honest way-- and, as you say, an even handed one. I would do whatever I could to make it a success-- a true and honorable success in all the ways you eloquently suggested."

Here I felt myself reddening because of some of the contradictions that my part in the mission might confront-- a Muslim speaking in behalf of a Christian mission!

"I know… I have to say… that I remain Muslim, but fortunately you have anticipated that possibility. You have nevertheless given me your confidence. Such generosity I… how shall I say it? I both respect and treasure it." And I recalled an earlier statement he had made. "I will remember, as you said, that it is better" 'to speak a hard truth rather than an easy lie.'" And I found myself laughing. "Harder, I am afraid-- but better!"

We could both relax now. "Now, back to your studies," he said, rising with me. "But if you find that after all this you cannot study today, then indulge your afternoon habit of going into the city and finding a patch of shade in which to take your ease. Just for today!" And he grinned as I went out.

The next several days were happy ones for me. I did go out and 'take my ease' that first afternoon, but it was an 'ease' full of thoughts, hopes, grandiose ambitions, and just an occasional piece of self-doubt. The rest of those days I worked at my Latin-- but also, to ease the stress, my Portuguese.

I felt a certain ease at heart, because I had reassured myself of my ability to reason clearly and well-- even if I had not convinced Monserrate of my position. And now, living in Goa as an already hot spring was slowly unfolding itself into a dry summer, I would make my studies pay. And I had Monserrate's confidence and support-- and his proposal, a commitment A vow!

I knew, of course that the talked-of mission to the "great Mogor" would not unfold for several years, if at all. And there would be obstacles, opponents, and possible failure, as both Monserrate and I knew.

But there would be time in plenty to give more thought to all that. Just now I glowed in the warmth of Monserrate's trust in me.

Chapter 16

Arguing The Inquisition

I basked awhile in the warmth of Monserrate's invitation to go with him as his personal secretary in the event of a Jesuit mission to the Mughal emperor. The offer gave me a new sense of identity and purpose. It drew me closer to Monserrate and, as he must have hoped, made me more inclined to become Christian and a member of the Society of Jesus! It seemed to justify me in not merely wearing the tunic of a Jesuit Novice but in actually qualifying myself for the Novitiate.

Yet dreams and ambitions of this kind could be a poor guide to real success. Monserrate was my sponsor, and I admired him. But he was not able, alone, to make a Novice of me. I would need the general support of members of the Society, and there would always be members such as Castro to deal with. Castro represented other strands within the Christian world, men who despised Hindus, Muslims, Jews and members of other faiths and races. Anyone who was not "European." even if devoutly Christian, was not thought reliable enough to be a Novice or "Brother" of the Society of Jesus. Jesuits like Castro felt this way also about former Jews, fearing and mistrusting them. Certainly, upon this view, a Muslim and a Turk like myself would not qualify.

But there was another problem, one which lay like a dark cloud on the horizon of the Society-- and had lain there long before my arrival. It was the Inquisition. Established at Goa in the year A. D. 1560, it was very visible and-- in my opinion-- dangerous institution. It was supposed to "purify" the Church, but first in Europe and now in Goa it had become an instrument of terror.

The sight of long lines of "Penitents" condemned as "heretics". Hindu Conversos-- men and women who had converted to Christianity-- now were often thought to be guilty of falling back into evil, un-Christian way beliefs or practices. Most of the accused in Goa were former Hindus. It was not an everyday event, but it happened often enough to throw fear even into the heart of a Muslim like myself who was considering Conversion and undergoing the Jesuit program of training in that direction. And because the Jesuits cooperated in the public Auto-da-Fe at the site, where the worst of the "heretics" were to be burned at the stake, the role of the Society of Jesus was visible, too. It would have been shocking enough to have seen the Portuguese accusing and executing other Portuguese, but to see them proceeding in the same way with a conquered and dark-skinned people seemed to me a cruel injustice. It was true that all the governments I had ever known punished rebels and ordinary criminals, often putting them to torture and death. But to know, as I did, the message of Jesus of Nasareth, Son of God-- who had taught compassion, forgiveness, and mercy!-- made the Inquisition a terrible contradiction.

It was to the higher truth of Jesus the Christ that I was being called by my admired teacher Monserrate, as well as by the Christian Gospels. I covered my ears sometimes when I heard the church bells announcing another Auto-da-Fe and the burnings that followed. It was all too cruel, too cruel. I had heard someone say that it was the Church in Spain that especially embraced the methods and message of the Inquisition. But Goa was not Spain, and the people of Goa were not Spanish. It especially chilled me that the Society of Jesus, with its zeal for converting the whole people of Goa and of India, tolerated the Inquisition and co-operated with it. A conspiracy of silence? Was that the best Jesuits could manage?

I had bccn brought up to bclicvc in honor. I had known in all its bitterness the injustice done to my father, and the hideousness of his death. Now my faith in Christianity was at stake-- my faith in the Society of Jesus, my faith even in a good man like Monserrate! And I was faltering. I thought back to the Qur'an in which I had been educated. The message of Christ was of mercy and forgiveness. Now I remembered the first principles of the Qur'an. The message of Jesus the Christ was the same, at heart, as that of Muhammad. It was Truth to which the Qur'an summoned Muslims-- to have faith in God, in Allah, "the Merciful, the Compassionate!" I saw it like a light that suddenly blinded me. If God, whatever the name or mode of existence or powers attributed to Him, were compassionate in very essence, how could any mere man claim that God was "his" and yet forget or betray these principles-- and twist them into violent shapes of terror and death, or hatred and meanness?

But I did not come to these ideas only in the privacy of my thoughts or by calm "philosophy." The subject sprang up one night at the tables on the Refectory of the College of Saint Paul. That evening, following a major Auto-da-Fe and many burnings, the Inquisition was on everyone's conscience. And though I considered excusing myself from the table and seeking my own way to hide behind the Jesuit conspiracy of silence, I stayed at the table-- and spoke not once during the discussion that broke out among the Novices around me. For once I, the Muslim, set courage aside!

Several of the dozen Novices around the long table looked embarrassed and unwilling to speak. Finally a senior Novice said, reluctantly but truthfully, that the Inquisition was meant to "persuade" converts not to break the Christian vows they had taken. He added that the institution had been developed in Spain to keep Jews and "Moors" in line, because many had converted after the Conquest, but mainly to keep their wealth and property safe. The question was, were they "sincere" in their Christian vows? The Inquisition, because it held the powers of life and death over converts of this type, could bring many to maintain their vows-- or renew them!

Again glances passed around. A third Novice sighed. "We of course apply the same goals in India to former Hindus, Muslims, and anyone else who converts but return to some part of their old ways." He flashed a look at me, knowing I was a Muslim! "As with the Moors and Jews in Spain," he said, "there are always some who convert mainly to save their lives and properties."

There was a long silence. One or two Novices could not resist a glance my way. Most of them seemed to be studying some object in the table in front of them.

But the eyes mainly came to rest on the most advanced Novice, whom everybody knew to be one of the more daring. His name was Afonso, and everyone knew that not only was he Portuguese on both sides but also that his family was a distinguished one and that he, of all present, was the most protected from harsh discipline if he made a statement that was bold.

He took his time contemplating, but at last cleared his throat. I was encouraged to think he would be reasonable, because he had shown an especially friendly manner toward me and some of the Hindu "lay" students!

"To tell the truth," he said, "and to consider the whole truth about the Inquisition, I am afraid to say, is complicated. I know that we who are from Portugal feel that the institution is more Spanish than Portuguese. But there it stands, even in Goa, a fact throughout the Roman faith and accepted by the Church."

He looked carefully around the table while his words took effect. "I myself," he said, "have humbly tried to understand the necessity of such an institution, and I have had private doubts. Every Christian, but especially in the Holy Orders like ours, owes it to himself to consult his conscience in the matter-- and attempt to arrive at an acceptance of the Inquisition based on both reason and faith."

Again he looked carefully around the table. "Upon examining my own conscience, I must admit that, because of the violence with which Converts are often treated, and because it is sometimes-- I might say often-- done in a public and terrifying way, I would rather that the "Rigour of Mercy" had been left in Europe and not imposed on the people of India. For, after all, the population around us has been long accustomed to the beliefs and practices of the Hindu and Muslim religions-- which are hard for them to abandon, even as it has been hard for Muslims and Jews in Europe to abandon their faiths! The fact remains, however confident we Christians are of our religion," he said, "that many a person in India, would find it difficult-- and in some cases impossible-- to reject everything of their past and their society and culture had taught them to respect."

Seeing that not all his listeners were of his mind on the subject, he surprised me with his next statement. "I cannot resist the thought that we, devout Christians that we are, might also be tempted to fall back sometimes on something familiar if placed in their position."

Immediately there was a stir. The last speaker had apparently asked too much of some consciences around the table.

He raised a hand. "Do not misunderstand me. We believe that Satan is our enemy, always stirring up rebellion within our Christian faith. Ours is the True Faith. I only hold that we should exercise the very highest caution and uphold Christian mercy before engaging in judgements calling for a sentence of death. We should work very hard to reconfirm the faith of persons who have come to us-- who have come to Jesus Christ and to His Church!-- by offering the mercy of Christian love rather than the terrors of Christian punishment. Would not that have been the way of Jesus Christ our Savior?"

I could see that he was rushing to complete the daring excursion upon which he had embarked. Because a quick look told him that one of the Jesuit Brothers was hastening our way with a frown. What had the Brother overheard? Or was he merely acting on an expectation of some seriously wrong at our Refectory table?

But what made my blood run cold was that I immediately recognized the approaching Brother of the Jesuit Order! It was my old enemy Castro.

In an instant Castro was at the table. His voice was more than firm. He was angry. His frown of disapproval settled first on Afonso, the Novice who had last spoken. But then he swept the group with his eyes. I was not surprised that the furious gaze rested a moment on me! But his words were for everyone.

"It should not be necessary," he grated, "for a Novice of the Society of Jesus to realize that the Holy Inquisition-- an arm of the Church-- should not be a topic of speculation or ill-informed debate!" Again his gaze swept us. I noticed, however, that it seemed to fly past the last speaker, Afonso, without taking notice of him. Castro was speaking to the rest of us. "A Novice of our Order," Castro went on-- "and any aspirant to membership in the Society of Jesus-- should follow the principle, the rule, that the Holy Inquisition is a subject beyond both his competency and his position!"

Castro looked pointedly from face to face again after this salvo. "I suggest that the Novices here retire to your studies now-- and your prayers for greater wisdom."

The group, including a frowning Afonso, promptly dissolved. This time there were no words or glances exchanged. Brother Castro remained standing like a hostile sentinel at the head of the table.

When enough backs had turned and moved away, the Jesuit's stare settled upon me. I was not surprised-- and had remained standing at my place.

"You, Aziz Ahmad Khan in particular," he said, "are not, as you well know, in reality either a Novice or Lay Brother. In future I will expect you to forego the discussion of questions for which you are not suited. Do I make myself clear?"

"Why, yes!" I said, adopting a steady stare in return. "I would certainly not wish to ask 'unsuitable' questions about so important a Christian office as the Inquisition! And in this case, if you would ask the Novices at the table tonight, and they are honest, they will tell you that I did not either ask any questions or engage in any discussion whatever! I was perfectly aware that I would not be held 'competent' to discuss the Inquisition!"

I waited for "Brother" Castro to contemplate this truth. He was silent, his mouth almost writhing in frustration.

And then I decided to end this miserable confrontation with another statement to my interrogator-- for so, after all, he was. "I would only add, respected Brother Castro, that in all honesty our conversation at the table was restrained, reasonable, and innocent-- although perhaps against some Rule. I thank-you, Brother Castro, for clarifying the "error" into which we had fallen!"

I bowed deeply. With that I turned and left the Refectory. I knew Brother Castro all too well. He was not finished with me. I would not give him the dignity of lecturing me further!

I knew, too, that I would hear from Monserrate about this. Any action of anyone on Jesuit premises always seemed to sprout wings and become the next day's subject matter of rumour and commentary. But I did not owe it to Brother Castro to grovel. I would save my humility for the Jesuit I respected.

And yes, the following day Monserrate did join me as I was returning from lunch at the Refectory. "Please, Aziz Ahmad," he said when we were alone, "I can guess that you were honestly offended by Brother Castro. But you had to know, before he interrupted, that the Inquisition is a topic of a restricted sort that is forbidden to members of the Monastic Orders. It is simply too sensitive a matter. Brother Castro-- though seldom as restrained or diplomatic as I would like-- was in principle quite right not to let the discussion continue, however innocent your part-- or lack of a part."

Suddenly my mentor dropped his voice and became more intense. "I am in no way enamored of the Inquisition or its introduction in Goa. I had already told you that! It is, to say the least, an embarrassing contradiction to the Supreme love of our Savior-- and, I believe, not in the interests of our Jesuit reputation, in which we try to make our Christian Love visible and spread it with humanity in our hearts."

I could not let that pass. "But that was precisely the point being made by Afonso, the Novice who was speaking!"

Monserrate sighed. "Yes, and it accords with my own private view-- and obviously with yours. But dear Aziz, we of the Society must live with that institution and its contradictions. Please try not to talk more about the Inquisition among your friends of the Novitiate. You will avoid further clashes with Brother Castro, and meanwhile, when there is some time for the two of us to talk privately, I will try to answer any questions you have."

It was my sign to express gratitude for Monserrate's attempt to help me. "I am sorry to have placed you in a difficult situation, Father Monserrate. You are my best friend and counsellor. I want you always to be proud of my behavior." and with that I and Monserrate, whom I always thought of as "Father"-- as with a priest-- instead of his technical standing as a monastic "Brother" of the Jesuit Order, were reconciled again.

Yet it depressed me that even Monserrate has, in his way, imposed a sentence of silence on me. And now, every time I saw the Inquisition's "Palace," the building chilled and shocked me. I also let Afonso-- who was my particular, boldest friend among the Novices at the table!-- know that I shared his view of the Inquisition-- and appreciated his honesty among colleagues who might disapprove of it. And I asked him that, if statement were made against me either by a Novice or by Brother Castro, Afonso would point out the truth-- that I said nothing and taken no part in the discussion! I only asked that he and other would honor my restraint-- even though I now saw that without my speaking up as he had dared, I had not honored his honest courage, and I was profoundly ashamed.

What I did not tell him was, though I know it must have occurred to Monserrate, that things of the nature of the Inquisition-- like Jesuits of the nature of Brother Castro-- were not destined to make my own acceptance of Christianity any the easier!

From this point onward I did not raise any debatable questions whatever among my novice comrades, and I dug deeper into my studies of languages. To anyone who questioned me I explained that I could not afford to neglect my Latin or my Scriptural studies. But without saying it I also vowed that I would focus harder on my Portuguese language study-- and try to spend more time moving about in Goa in the broad daylight of reality.

In the long run I might be less inclined to Convert, but now that was a subject that I did not propose to discuss with anyone-- even Monserrate. He had done too much for me that I did not wish to bring into doubt, and as much as possible I thrust the Inquisition out of my thoughts. The irony was that, like Monserrate, I found it such an unhappy subject that I became entirely silent about it, putting off until some indefinite future the need to grapple, in good conscience, with either its mission or its effects. And now I know, to my sorrow, that I had been a coward.

It would be years, too, before I could look at my own Faith, Islam, with any view of reconciling its inadequacies or internal contradictions. It was not, I felt, that I was immoral-- or that the Muslim religion was-- any more than its Christian competitor.

But we often hide from ourselves what lies in plain view. Thus I had become, and so had Monserrate, a "Believer" who would not, or could not, bring himself to face the contradictions in his Faith-- even if they often led to untruth, meanness, and violence.

Meanwhile how easy it was to judge others and exempt ourselves! The whole subject of the Inquisition had indeed become a conspiracy of silence. And somehow, neither I the conscientious Muslim nor Monserrate the best of Christians-- for so I would always feel him to be-- ever discussed these things again.

But as I read onward in the Gospels I was studying, I came to the eighth chapter of the Gospel of John where Jesus of Nasareth said that no one sinful himself should cast the first stone at another found in sin or error, especially if it were a matter of taking that person's life.

I began to think more and more about what was shared by the Christian Gospels and Muslim Qur'an-- the belief that among the essential qualities of God were Compassion and Mercy!

It was too bad that human beings, thinking themselves rational and virtuous, often lacked those qualities of compassion and the bestowal of mercy-- and that often their religious leaders would close their eyes to the truth also.

Chapter 17

Doubts And Diversions

My discouragement over the argument about the Inquisition had been more than a passing sentiment. I began seriously to question making any decision in favor of Conversion. Following upon that had been my depression over my misbegotten attempt at becoming a master of the rapier!

The impact of what I called "The Night of the Inquisition" remained heavy. Why was I keeping up with all these Christian studies? Except for Monserrate's offer of my being his personal secretary on any Jesuit mission to the Mughal court, which still was not fully decided upon, I felt a general decline in incentive. The one area of my studies that still moved me highly was the Portuguese language, my main key to the life of the Portuguese Goa.

The matter of dressing like a Jesuit Novice had continued to concern me, because I knew that was one mark of being eligible for the Novitiate. And that question was precisely the one that Castro had referred to when he chastised the Novices for discussing the Inquisition. The way Castro had done this had stunned the Novices into silence, and he had attacked me in the bargain. Certainly I did not wish to embarrass Monserrate, my friend and mentor, by speaking out. Yet I knew that any anger or resentful display on my part would weaken and hurt this one Jesuit who had befriended and sponsored me. Better that I should sink myself deeper in my studies and keep quiet!

Yet, as days became a week, then another week, I grew more and more tired of the atmosphere of constraint and prejudice around me. Monserrate might tolerate it, including Castro's recent behavior. In dealing with a colleague like Castro, I decided, only a highly devout Jesuit, maintaining his faith and the rigors of his "calling," could have much sense of dignity and purpose. For myself, I began to see the goal of the Novitiate fading, and to feel that I would do best my remaining a Muslim and not trying to mask my doubts. Yet I could not bring myself to disappoint Monserrate.

The issue remained-- did I seriously care any more about converting? For if not, I might as well, in such privacy as I had at the College, maintain my connection with the Qur'an and its teachings-- and return to greater care with a life of Muslim prayer and custom. If I continued with modest study of Latin and the Christian scriptures and was present at all required worship and prayer sessions, there was little I had to fear even from the hostility of Brother Castro and his like. Or so I hoped.

On my conscience for some time had been the question of keeping up my Muslim prayers. I had realized recently that I had become slack about my Muslim five prayer-times a day. I had tried to retain all five in the privacy of my room at the College, including the kneelings and prostration. But now in fact I had begun to maintain only the dawn and evening prayers instead of the traditional five, and I was not faithfully observing all the ritual observances of the Shahada. Now, with my renewed doubts about Conversion, I began again to practice all five prayer hours, even though it interfered with my practices of Christian prayer. But I proceeded to lay out my little-used prayer rug again at least three or four times a day and be serious in my recitations, kneelings, and prostrations. The discipline felt right again.

Still, I continued to respect Monserrate as a serious Christian, and I was drawn to the Christian ideals of love and generosity, peace and humility-- even while Jesuits like Castro drew my distaste. I would keep trying to find a middle way between these and other extremes. Indeed, my daily prayers in both the Muslim and the Christian manner found me beginning to respect freshly the best in both the Islamic and Christian faiths, concentrating in each what most persuaded me, what I needed most in my life and my soul.

As for wearing the tunic of the Novitiate, I could not simply stop that while on the premises of the College of Saint Paul-- out of respect for Monserrate if nothing else. But I could continue to go into the streets in the afternoon wearing my Portuguese "fidalgo's" clothing without feeling serious offense to my mentor.

I could continue going to my garden-- or to the Holy Hill-- to read the Scriptures and recite my Latin lessons dressed as a fidalgo, and to perform my Muslim prayer appropriate to the time of day. I knew it was an attitude of compromise that many a Muslim-- and many a Christian-- might reject. But while in Goa I could not please everyone, any more than I would mock anyone's beliefs or practices. I could also practice my Portuguese aloud, and give it the same fluency that I had once dedicated to Persian. And last-- a practical and selfish matter. Whenever I went out from the College walls I could hide most of my childhood scars by wearing the accustomed tight cloth around my head under my broad-brimmed Portuguese hat!

Finally I found myself wishing to return to the practice I had begun of locating shops where I could practice my Portuguese speech and hold commonplace conversation with the shopkeepers. Dressed in my Portuguese fashion I could now happily spend an hour or two striking up acquaintances with Hindu or Christian merchants-- and accepting offers of the thick, sweetened Arab, Syrian, or Egyptian coffee that made the conversations a pleasure.

As it happened, I soon found the shop of an elderly Armenian Christian who, together with his grown son, was deep into the selling of cotton goods. In fact the Armenian's Portuguese was not as fluent as mine, and I could put him at his ease by adopting the role of a good listener, with many expressions of interest in the niceties of cotton cloth manufacture, weaving, and sale. Soon I learned much about the cloth trade of Goa, Cochin, and other Portuguese ports along the Sea of Arabia.

I would not have stopped at the Armenian shop so often-- sipping thick, sweet coffee until I almost tired of it-- if, besides the merchant and his son, a third person had not appeared one day-- "just a serving girl," said the merchant when I asked. While the merchant and I talked, however, I could not resist glancing at the activities of the servant in the back of the shop, then watching them more closely. The "girl," indeed, seemed to be about my own age. She followed the Indian-- and Portuguese-- custom of keeping her head mainly covered by a length of cloth, in her case a Portuguese shawl it seemed. And I was concluding two things. She really was quite pretty, or would have been if her dark hair were not so covered and confined by the shawl. And her listless movements and emotionless face told me, even though she was half shadowed in the interior of ship, that she was not happy with her work.

Suddenly I realized that a silence had fallen over my conversation with the Armenian merchant her employer. And I saw that, lest I feel I should apologize, the merchant was following her with his own gaze-- and was not happy with her work either!

"Has she been long at the shop?" I asked.

He gave me the flicker of a smile. "Not long." He allowed his gaze to drift to the face of his grown son, who was sitting on a stool just inside the shop's doorway and going over the week's receipts. I followed his gaze. The son was keeping at his work without any show of interest in either our conversation or in the girl. But the young man was near to my age. How could he not be interested in a girl-- a pretty, Portuguese girl-- working as their servant? If anything, he appeared to have the habit of a kind of truculence. What he might be hiding behind the sourness I could not guess.

I could not avoid stealing another look at the girl in her shadowed environs. Then she stepped into the late afternoon sunlight falling through a window. The glow of her eyes seemed to reflect the glow of her half-turned face, and I was certain that she was looking back at me. She frowned, compressed her lips slightly, and turned back into the shadows. Besides that sudden flash of annoyance, the one thing that struck me was her beauty. It left me stunned a moment.

I glanced aside to see if the merchant were watching me, assessing my reaction. Was it a smile I saw again under the scraggle of his beard, or a mocking look-- or both? It was as if he said "Pretty, isn't she? Just the sort for a young man like you." Or like his son, I thought to add. The son who, by his expression, might just have been drinking vinegar-- or some of the bad coconut "feni" they sold in the streets! And abruptly I sensed that the son was studying me, too. His… rival? I let my gaze drift indolently across his and settle, with a smile on his father's face. I could not resist adding a shrug, as one man might join two others in judging a prize camel that none of them owned but all, each in his way, might wish he did.

It was time to go. I knew that. I thanked the old merchant for his generosity. In that I could be entirely sincere. Fortunately it was not necessary to thank his son for anything!

The two of us exchanged affable words and a goodbye. The merchant added the conventional wish that I would return at my convenience. The son gave me a quick, inscrutable look and went back to his receipts.

As I walked away it seemed to me that the serving girl, when she turned my way that moment in the shaft of sunlight, had let the scarf slip back a little-- without meaning to, of course-- and had revealed strands of lustrous black hair, a beautifully pale Portuguese face, and lips that.... I quenched the last part of the thought and focused on the rest of that faultless, pale face.

I scanned the street, the shadows of buildings, and the sky and judged that it was still only mid-afternoon. Since I had brought with me the Latin textbook recently printed on the College of Saint Paul's printing-press, small but efficient and newly imported from Portugal, I had intended to go to my garden and study awhile. But now it was getting late. I turned toward the College of Saint Paul again.

The face of the "serving girl" kept coming back to astonish me. Yes, she definitely could be either Portuguese or Persian....

I had hardly reached the College gate when I met Monserrate. Surveying my Portuguese clothing and poniard at my side, he smiled and asked if I had had a good afternoon walking and reciting. The comment startled me-- as if he had seen me at the merchant's shop. But I caught myself. "Yes," I said, smiling back, "I have a favorite garden spot, quiet and spacious. Perhaps you knew that I almost always go there, either to study awhile or simply to relax." It was as close as I dared to come to honesty as a best policy.

Monserrate said no more about "walking and reciting," but told me that my Latin teacher was highly impressed with the way I had settled back into my studies after the unfortunate incident of the Inquisition. The teacher, he added, was expressing high hopes for me as a Christian scholar! I thanked him politely, adding that, yes, I had again attended to my studies-- especially the Latin.

"You seem to be flourishing in Goa's climate," said my fatherly patron and friend. "It is nice to see you looking fit and, I might say, 'animar!'" How odd, I thought to myself. I had just been thinking of the "serving girl" and the Armenian shop! But "animar"? Exhilarated? That seemed a little strong for the mood I felt.

But both of us could play at opening a subject and then gliding away from it. "Do you think the monsoon will be upon us soon?" I asked.

Monserrate shrugged. It would come soon enough, he said.

What an idiotic conversation, I told myself! It was almost as if father and son had long ago earned each other's secrets, and it was more useful to engage in banalities than get serious about anything that could lead to an argument.

I was grateful when my mentor wished me a good evening and went his way to dinner at Saint Paul's. For a moment I was happy, because the face of the serving girl had again come to my mind. But then, when I tried to focus on her, she disappeared! What was this all about, I asked myself, when the image of a certain person would knock at the door of one's mind and then disappear when the door was half open?

When I reached the Refectory my friends among the Novices were noisy in welcoming me to "our" table. It was to be the evening of Persian conversation we had planned. And the girl-- suddenly her face was as clear as in a mirror! I launched an effort to devise a silent Persian quatrain.

"'God has provided me a glimpse of you

My mind cannot be still, and plays its part."

By the time I ended the second line she had disappeared once more. But her departure prompted my last two lines.

"Yet He has sent an angel's message, too,

That urges patience on a rash, unruly heart.'"

Chapter 18

That Girl Again, And A Song

My curiosity did not diminish after I left the Armenian shop, and I found myself remembering that the "servant" girl, when she bent over some reels of calico, seemed very pretty indeed. Like women everywhere in the Muslim world-- but also in Christian Europe, I understood-- she had kept a scarf or another length of cloth over her head, for such were the demands of Muslim purdah. It was a habit that I had also seen among the Portuguese women on Goa's streets.

It was not easy in Goa to see any woman's face clearly, I would have to say. Shawls or head scarves obscured or entirely hid almost all. I did not see the serving girl at first. The old man's son was at the door this time, and I did not find his son so congenial a companion. He seemed to be reluctant to offer me any coffee, and his father had gone out. At length, nevertheless, he relented, and we sat sipping together in the canopy's shade.

Then, suddenly, the serving girl returned from some errand or other. She had pulled a Portuguese shawl-- a rather faded one-- over her head and shoulders while walking, and did not see me at first because she had been keeping her eyes downcast in what took to be her private thoughts. I noticed that her dress was not new and showed considerable wear. Her Portuguese cotton blouse with its ruffled edges at the neck and wrists seemed clean but thin of fabric. Her sandals, which could barely be seen beneath a long skirt, were shabby and almost worn out. The thought came to me that it was both inconsiderate and not likely to help the shop's business to allow a servant to go about in such clothes. It would be wise of the merchant to make her look better provided for! But I cautioned myself not to leap at conclusions.

Seeing me, the girl abruptly changed directions went around to a rear door of the shop. I was taken aback when the merchant's son raised his voice and shouted, "Girl!" I heard no response, but after a moment she came to the front of the shop. Though pretty even with her face half hidden by her threadbare shawl, I did not expect her to look happy. And she didn't. Also it did not surprise me that she looked only at the rude young Armenian next to me, since he was also her employer, and never at me.

"Yes?" she asked in proper Portuguese. That by itself pleased me more than she could have realized, because it revealed her identity almosty without doubt. A pretty Portuguese "servant" in an Armenian shop!? The inconsistency made my eyes open wider. I had to resist staring.

"You brought what I asked for?" said the merchant's son in the same abrupt way as before.

"Yes," she repeated. "I placed it on the counter as you told me." I could hardly blame her for saying it with taut restraint, given the way her interrogator had shouted and was sourly regarding her.

"Obrigado!" was his only answer. He dismissed her with a wave of the hand. Without a glance my way that I could detect, she turned and disappeared into the shadows of the shop.

The merchant's son gave me a contrived frown. "You see how well this "servant" behaves. My father must have told you what a wonderful purchase he made of her." He smirked. "Now even he begins to regret it. She knows little of obedience-- or even how to do a day's work. But…" he shrugged, "we feed her."

"And," I put in, "you discipline her?" He shrugged again. "I would like to! But my father-- you know that he is old. He tolerates her nonsense, If she were <u>my</u> purchase, she would give me satisfaction-- or else!"

I considered a moment what a wonderful son this father had. The old man had "purchased her"-- I remembered that phrase exactly-- and the son was determined to get "satisfaction-- or else." She was being treated like a slave.

Since the son seemed now to be without further interest in my presence, I proceeded to excuse myself-- politely-- and depart. I left the shop for the walk of half an hour to my walled garden. At least I could relax awhile in the shade of the orange-trees that I was trying to revive.

Yet I was full of thoughts as I walked. I would see that girl again, I vowed. I would make inquiries-- bit of the Armenian father, not the son! The questions would be reserved, but I would learn more.

I turned my steps unconsciously into the Rua Direita and toward the docks. Finding that I had almost reached the rising walls of Saint Catherine's Cathedral to me left my left, and not wanting to approach the "Palacio" if the Inquisition on my right, I turned into the street that led to the "Archway of Conception" and the "Church of our Lady of the Mount" a distance east of it.

As I reached the Archway I slowed. A beggar was sitting in the monument's shade. Playing a battered three-stringed rabab, he was singing in a rough but surprisingly tuneful voice. A glance at his beggar's bowl, empty of all but a few trivial coins, struck me as evidence of the disappointments of most men's lives, but his face, turned upward with blind eyes, was glowing with devotion to his song. It was a song about a lady named "Catarina."

It was enough to make me stop and listen. At first I had thought of the sainted Catarina, that "Saint Catherine" to whom Albuquerque had pledged his conquest of this Muslim town Now I was confused. What "Catarina" could it be?

I bent and dropped a silverpiece into the beggar's bowl. Both song and the voice that sang it appealed to me. The man stopped playing and gave me an oddly beatific smile. "I thank you, stranger, for your gift," he said. His speaking voice was as rough, as "old," as his song, but clear enough.

I cleared my throat. "This song you sing of "Catarina"-- it is not the saint, but who?"

"You have not heard of her?" he asked with genuine surprise. "She was the first woman of Portugal-- of Europe, some say-- to set foot in this town after its conquest by the great Afonso de Albuquerque. At least you know of him!"."

He waited, building up his little store of surprises. Getting no answer, he went on. "She is the beauteous Catarina a Piro I sing of. She, and the song, too, are famed in Goa. You must not have been here long!"

To that I admitted, eager to have him continue. "Would you repeat it? I have another coin to follow it."

He chuckled. "I was singing in the Dakkhini tongue," he said. "You know that one?" A little, I told him. He turned his face toward mine again and seemed to study me. "Then you are a Turk," he said-- "and of the Deccan. I hear it in your voice!" I laughed partly in genuine surprise at his alert ears. Sing on, I told him. And he repeated. The exact words but with more drama, more fervor... "Catarina, oh Catarina..." To the end.

My second silver-piece clinked into his bowl. "That is all you know of this song-- this woman?" I asked.

He fingered few chords on the rabab. "She came by the same caravel that brought her lover Garcia da Sa. Lovers, yet she was a commoner and he a noble lord.In those days-- even now!-- the lower classes of Portugal are expected to marry within their own ranks. But if the two of them were indeed lovers and came to escape scandal, it followed them! He knew that he would become Governor of Goa That, besides his noble heritage, should have separated them forever. But he set her up well, giving her a grand house, a palacio. It was said he often visited her there-- even after he became Governor. They would go out together in the late twilight of summer evening, seated as discreetly as they might in a two-seated sedan chair, the 'cadeirinha,' borne on the shoulders of her servants. And sometimes, it is said, he would go in with her afterward and spend the night in her arms."

He paused for effect. "Does it surprise you, my friend?"

I snorted in derision. "That they were lovers-- or that people took a great interest in their doings?"

He chuckled back. "It may have been some servant who told people that her mistress had won the favor of this great man. It was also said that he wanted to marry her, but the Church would not permit it!"

This time I kept silent. But it reminded me of something I had heard, and then read, about Jesus of Nasareth and how he was too close to a certain woman who who washed his feet with her hair! People thought that Jesus should rebuke her, keep her away-- that he was too tolerant and forgiving of her behavior-- even though it was clearly based on love and respect for him. Even some of his disciples wanted him to repudiate her.

But the beggar was continuing. "And the years passed, and they both grew older. But she remained in the house he had given her, and each Sunday attended the church of Franciscans in Goa and was generous with her tithes and many other gifts to Christian charity, and she remained humble and silent when voices lashed out at her or whispered their rumors. But then came the sickness in her lungs that was the fate of many in Goa during the long, rainy seasons. Slowly, slowly she sank. And now, silent and remote in his elevation-- though he sometimes saw her still-- the noble Governor da Sa sent medicine and some said even attended at her bedside! Yet she was still treated as a woman of bad repute by those who had for so many years been critics and detractors." He paused again to ask what I thought.

"About human tolerance and cruelty?" I asked. I sighed. I suppose they let her die and go to Hell-- they wished and <u>wanted</u> her to go to Hell!"

"But a strange thing happened!" he said. Almost a miracle! For as she lay dying, the great and saintly Francisco Xavier, the Jesuit whom no one could criticize, spoke in the ears of certain men of the Church, and he told them that not one Christian soul should be lost to Redemption and sent downward to Satan that could be found willing at last to make Confessions of his or her sins! And these great men were stunned and ashamed. And the eloquent Xavier caused those great men to send the message to Catarina a Piro and to Garcia da Sa that she might marry him on her deathbed if she-- and he-- were willing to confess to all sin! And then the noblemen and the commoner did make Confession of their sin, and the priest who took their confessions -- some said it was Xavier himself!-- gave them the Sacrament of Marriage as she lay in

Articulo Mortis, while the noble Governor sat beside her holding her thin, white hands."

The beggar sat silent. His face was glowing again. His dead eyes, too, seemed to have a glint of light in them. And for a while I think of nothing to say. But I added the rest of my purse of coins to his bowl.

As I turned and walked away toward the gates of the College of Saint Paul, I heard the man tune his rabab and sing again. And his song was the same.

"Catarina, oh Catarina, do not leave me like this.

Call me to your doorway again. Lay on me the blessing

of your soft white hands, the scent of your raven hair,

the loveliness of your eyes, those lips I would kiss

a thousand times. Oh Catarina, Catarina my love...."

Two days I lingered at the College, unable to remove from my mind that afternoon when the beggar sang for me of Catarina a Piro. And I asked around about her, and was told that the song was essentially true-- and she and Governor da Sa were real, and that her tomb lay in the church of our Lady of the Rosary on the Monte Santo, the Holy Hill-- and his tomb, too.

On the third day, as I was going to my garden to study, I did return to the Armenian shop. There again I found the merchant on his porch in the canopy's shade.

I had hardly arrived when the serving girl, not realizing this visitor was sitting in front of the shop, appeared at the door with a message for the merchant.

Wearing the usual scarf over her head, but having pushed it back because of the heat inside the shop, she started to speak in broken Armenian-- but stopped abruptly when she saw me. The merchant proceeded to answer her in his Armenian tongue and ask for more information. She changed color, more pale than blushing, and tried to answer in Armenian. The merchant smiled and told her to speak Portuguese, since she spoke that language better!

With a quick glance at me, she spoke in the low but clear, accented voice that reminded me she was Portuguese-- and did not take further notice of me while she talked with the old man.

He queried her further about the piece goods she had referred to. She seemed annoyed both with him and with herself-- and with my gaze in her direction.

I had not realized that I was studying her face there, even half hidden by the cloth she kept over her head, and that I was especially watching her mouth to follow her Portuguese phrases. I tried a little nod and a pleasant smile, but she returned a reticent, retiring look, now with a frown of genuine annoyance. She had to know that I spoke Portuguese as I had used it often while at coffee on the terrace. Did she think I was some prying busybody-- or someone, not different from her in age, who recognized her beauty and was entirely too interested? I could not tell.

The conversation about cloth ended, and she quickly went inside again. The merchant turned to me with a smile. "You see that her Portuguese is much better than her Armenian-- and, indeed, as good as your own!"

I shrugged. "After such few phrases," I said, "I am in no position to judge."

The merchant sighed and stroked his grey-flecked beard thoughtfully. "Perhaps I made a bad bargain in acquiring this girl," he said, "for she does not like the work I give her. She wastes my time."

"Wastes your time?" I echoed. His smile had faded. "She does not take orders well. And my son, he complains that she is impertinent."

I studied him. "Do you think she may resent her having been purchased?"

He stirred and sat looking glum. "I do not see that she had a choice. The fidalgo who sold her-- I mean to say, who sold me her services! It was a contract, you understand-- made the claim he had acquired her in a fair bargain."

I wondered what kind of "bargain" that was! The merchant looked at me sourly. "I did not inquire closely enough, it appears. She is not used to work! That is my feeling."

I tried a smile. "Perhaps she does not like to think that she has been bought and sold."

His gaze hardened. "She was not given a choice!" he said bluntly.

Being aware that the Portuguese had servants of several kinds, including African slaves, I could see the man's point. But this girl, she was too pretty and too… Portuguese! There was something wrong here.

I had to admit to myself, in honesty, that she interested me. No doubt she 'interested' the merchant's son, too! Especially I disliked the feeling I had about the merchant's son.

I followed that lead. "And," I said casually, looking for neutral words, "your son does not like her."

The Armenian raised an eyebrow. Then he laughed. "Oh, he 'likes' her!" He eyed me, since I was very near his son's age. "And you," he queried lightly, "you 'like' her also?"

I must have reddened, but I kept my reserve. "She is very pretty," I admitted. "I would not surprise me if your son liked her."

I saw distinct raillery in the merchant's eyes. "You are perceptive, my dear young man."

It was time to go!

"So," I thought as I strolled away, "this 'servant' is not to everyone's liking. And for one person, apparently, too much to his 'liking' in ways not disclosed.

I made my way quickly back to the College. "Study!"-- I told myself. After dining in the Refectory, I did try.

But somehow a particular face, beautiful and severe together, kept appearing to me sometimes by day, sometimes in my dreams."

That girl again! A mere "servant"?

What I kept hearing in my mind were pieces of a song I had heard the beggar sing.

None of it made sense to me at first. But I thought it over. Was I a kind of noble Da Sa-- albeit it a Muslim one-- who might well be allowing to pass unrecognized a human fate that I might have rescued from despair, from men's cruelty?

But it seemed fatuous of me to make such an issue of this serving girl's fortunes and hardships.

I was beginning to find life full of disappointments and puzzles. The story I had just heard was only one more small piece of the picture of human frailty.

I had to study my Latin now. I started in with rare fixity of attention-- even for me. But for the rest of that evening, and several to follow, my Latin lessons made even less sense than a serving girl or a beggar's song.

Chapter 19

Complications, And A Duel

Another week had passed. After late morning prayers at the College, I decided that I would go out into the city again. As usual now I changed into the cotton pantaloons and open-necked shirt of the fidalgo, along with the black hat with its white feather, and at my belt the poniard. And, rather than my rapier, I carried the sturdy cane I had acquired.

Thus apparelled I could go anywhere in the city. First I would stop at the Armenian shop and have a fresh look at the situation there-- and, I hoped, see the Portuguese girl. My second stop would be my walled garden, where I could read my latest assignments in the letters of Saint Paul to the Corinthians and Ephesians!

I went straight to the Armenian shop, and was grateful to find the merchant sitting outside under his awning, without his son's disturbing presence. And as for the girl, luck seemed also to be with me from the start. I had no sooner arrived than the girl appeared at the door with a stack of blousing she had brought for the old man's inspection.

Quickly welcoming me, the Armenian turned to the serving girl and started thumbing through the stack of cotton blousing. I stared at the girl. She compressed her lips and returned my stare with a frown. She had already been in the act of pulling her shawl more fully over her head, and now she jerked the fabric farther over her head and face and gave me a look of outright distaste. But in astonishment at seeing the beauty of that tight pale face and dark hair, I had forgotten all decorum. I simply stared. It did not help her mood, which had started in boredom but had now turned to annoyance. And she had a right to be angry! My attempted smile had a totally wrong effect.

If the merchant noticed any of this little drama, he did not seem to care, but continued fingering the goods the girl had brought him. I waited-- turning my gaze strictly to the cotton pieces in question. I guess that he prolonged his inspection to make it clear that the girl was his servant.

At last the Armenian finished his inspection of the layers of cloth. Grunting, he waved the girl back into the shop. This was not, I concluded, going to be an afternoon of polite conversation over small cups of coffee.

But it seemed that I was wrong. The Armenian suddenly raised his voice and called the serving girl back. "Mira!" he called. Her name! At last her name!

"Mira," I repeated to myself. Kept repeating it. I would find myself repeating it silently, yet hearing its echo in my mind. While she was still absent a moment, I asked the merchant of he knew her last name. Was it on the contract he had signed? Her married name? Family name? Did he know those, perhaps?

Abruptly I realized that I was becoming a little too, well, 'obvious' in my interest in her. I tried to sit back and relax, pay no attention to her.

The merchant smiled at me. In fact, it was a grin. "You young men are all of the same cloth and cut." He looked down, preoccupied a moment-- was remembering something, someone. He twisted a finger in his beard. Scratched his neck. "No point my being critical," he said. And laughed to himself.

"I was just like you when I was, say, twenty or twenty-two! Like everybody else you get over it a little. Get to be a little more careful what you say-- what your eyes say, too! A pretty girl does that to us-- even sometimes when we get old-- almost forget how it was. We work, marry, have children. Get too busy-- or just bored. And our wives, too. They go through the same thing-- or something like it. No more moonlight in the garden. Eat fast at the kitchen table. But then, maybe once in a year, we see what we used to see-- a pretty girl, maybe our wife-- the way she was then. Seemed like a lifetime ago. But still longing, sort of. The way it goes. Doesn't last too long. But sort of nice. Have a dream or two. Talk to the girl. Be old and funny. Then back to 'now'"

He stirred and craned his neck toward the rear of the shop. "She should have that coffee ready. Ah, she's coming now."

He gave me a quick look. "I have it! Married name-- Bardez. Wife of Jonathan Bardez! Bad name. Don't like it now, didn't like it then. But-- family name? I have to think! "Something really Portuguese, like "Bar.... Bartolomeo!"

But the girl Mira was about to reach the little table between us with the coffee in its tall, narrow-necked pot and two cups on the tray. He thanked her. So did I-- but she paid me no attention and didn't seem to care. I could barely see even her forehead and eyes.

Still, it didn't stop me from thinking about her. "Mira. Mira... Bartolomeo. So much better than...what was it? Bardez. Mira Bardez? Wife of Jonathan Bardez? Truly ugly. "Mira." She should be... just Mira!

The girl returned. She was carrying more sugar and hot milk in separate little containers. "The coffee seems a little strong," she said. "More milk and sugar may help." She was only looking at the merchant when she said this. Me she ignored, and disappeared again toward the rear of the shop.

Now I knew it was she who had made the pots of coffee I had been enjoying in my three or four earlier visits. And I had never thought who had prepared them, or praised them as they deserved. The effect now was to make me feel like an ass!

The merchant bade me sit. I tried to get back in the mood for casual talk. I asked how his son was doing. "Oh," said he, "he is very good, especially at accounts and making sure things balance. But he is restless these days. I think I will send him down to Cochin to manage one or both of my shops there. If he does well I can let him stay and hire a cousin of his here."

I found myself thinking, "Now that would be good riddance!" Why I thought it I was not quite sure-- except that he was of such a sour disposition-- and unkind to Mira!

The Armenian and I drank coffee in silence awhile. At last he sighed. He gazed at me over the small, thick lenses of his eye-glasses, which were now more commonly in use. “That girl, she was not worth the money at first. But as I told you, she learns fast when she wants to, and I am seriously training her. Pretty women are a bore, usually. Unless trained for a job, they go on thinking only of themselves.”

I decided to go straight to the point I had intended before my arrival. “She is working under a contract, I believe you said. Can you not just void the contract or sell her services to someone else?”

“Oh,” he responded, “but I am training her, as I just told you. She is beginning to listen to me. In another month, I feel sure, she will have become a worthwhile investment!

Now it came to me that I really had not been listening. He intended to keep her! I had hoped he might wish so badly to get rid of her that he would let me buy out her “contract!”

I tried another gamble. “I believe you said that her husband had sold her “services” to you. Couldn’t you sell her again and regain the cost of those services? Perhaps by now her husband would agree to take her back and return your money!”

The Armenian studied his fingers. “Her husband has left Goa. He sailed for Lisbon some months ago! His last words I remember: ‘Consider her all yours, my friend!”

“He said that?” I asked, astonished. “He was ‘selling’ his wife as well as her “services?” She might as well be a piece of property! Or a slave!”

The merchant frowned. “You place too much importance on this girl, I have to say! I do not treat her as a piece of property-- or a slave. With care I am beginning to make something of her. A proper servant!” His comments reduced me to silence at last.

We had finished the coffee. I had better be going, I told him. He did not object. And with that I rose, saluted with stiff grace, and launched myself back into the street.

I was completely at a loss now. I had wanted to see if I could 'free" the girl, and I had misjudged. I would go up to my garden and try to accept realities. In fact the girl did not care for me. I had alienated her with my rude stares. If I had 'lost' this chance to help her, it was my own fault! And it seriously hurt that, if I had just had eyes to see, she now viewed me as another pretended "fidalgo" like her husband, or worse, an importuning "gentleman" with the eyes and visage of a Turk, who was just trying to buy her for himself!

I kept walking rapidly toward my garden on the hillside. Thinking of it always seemed to relieve me of my burdens. Not this time. The girl-- "servant," slave, and now "investment"-- was beyond my reach. I almost wanted to shout--"Let the merchant have her!" But I knew in my heart that I did not believe it.

I reached the garden with my mind in turmoil, unlocked the heavy lock in its still heavier chain, and went in. I left the gate ajar.

Not having brought my rapier, I had at least brought the sturdy cane I owned. The cane had some advantages as a means of dealing with snakes or scorpions that might challenge me or slip away to their holes. Dressed in my Portuguese fashion with leather boots, and carrying my poniard, I was confident about dealing with most surprises. But I was supremely unhappy. I began by stamping my feet and swinging my cane in vigorous arcs. I opened the Latin text I had been studying, set it open on a tree-stump, and marched back and forth shouting Latin declensions. The stamping and shouting felt good.

While my back was turned toward the garden's entrance, I did not see the trio of Portuguese soldiers stop just inside the gate. They were observing me with amusement. I saw them and abruptly stopped my exercises, cane in hand! I could think of nothing to do but lean on the cane while I caught my breath. My shabby audience nudged each other and grinned.

So this, I realized, was my reward for not being aware of my surroundings-- and that God-forsaken open gate! Immediately I realized, too, that the gate was my only convenient exit. The only other was an entrance that lay beyond the overgrown ruins of the original owner's house, and I recalled that the only exit though the house, which I had once explored, was blocked by three or four fallen, half-burnt beams. And the garden walls around me were encrusted with sharp pieces of broken glass and seashell!

But most of all, I know that looking those directions would convey to my little audience of three a combination of panic, fear, and desperation-- not messages I wished to send. My best strategy was to seem cool and unconcerned. Not easy. But with the odds of one ill-armed man against three experienced attackers, I had no other real alternative.

I looked back at the three men who were watching me. Two seemed to be accomplices. The third, a little better dressed, appeared to be their leader. Smiling, the three slowly advanced, keeping the manner seemingly casual and conveying no threat. My best move was-- to do nothing, except estimate how I might discourage them from getting within the length of a sword's blade.

I saw the leader, in the middle of the trio, as my main opponent. He would make any big decisions, like whether they would either wound or kill me. I would try to keep my gaze locked on his-- and to address only him.

The three were a raffish little crowd, unshaven and looking as if they might not have been paid for several months. A surly and ill-kempt lot, not badly clothed, but sturdy, with the strong wrists of swordsmen, and with steel at their sides-- not only swords but daggers. And more, one of them-- the one I had identified as their leader-- carried a pistol thrust into the sash of his sword-belt!

Faced by these 'gentlemen' I wondered especially about the pistol, the long, curving handle of which was inlaid with ivory, the barrel ornamented with inlay of silver. The pistol was of the latest wheel-lock kind. This was no ordinary weapon! And immediately it struck me. It had either been stolen-- or taken-- from some Portuguese officer, an officer who may have paid with his life for being drawn into a duel with this man. What chance then did I stand? My poniard would be useless against him and his two accomplices. And my cane? Absurd.

And I knew the truth. I was about to die.

Well, I could make it a heroic death. I might beat down one of these brigands! But would that be a "hero's "death-- to die alone in a deserted garden? There was no consolation in it.

I almost shuddered. I was going to die at the wrong time, in the wrong place, and only Monserrate might care enough to seek me out and have buried whatever remains he found of the Muslim who had followed him to this "Christian" town, wandered unwisely into a trap, and wasted all the hopes he had invested in me as my friend....

But the three soldiers were not being impressed with these thoughts that gripped me. They were here to enjoy an hour's or half hour's entertainment, and I could do nothing to stop it.

But... nothing? I would have to try something. Anything.

The three of them stopped just beyond sword's reach. Three smiles glittered where teeth still remained. There were not too many gaps in the teeth except in the smallest of the three men who appeared the least formidable in height but had the broadest shoulders and most strongly muscled right arm. The leader, who was tallest, might have been handsome were it not for an old scar running from his chin to the edge of an eye. The man I judged to be his "second" was of middling height, swarthy-- with a smile that was the most evil of the three. I was not sure which of them had been the instigator of this confrontation. It was clear, however, that they would advance and gradually force me back if I gave the slightest sign of retreat. I had only one choice. I would have to face them down.

I looked at them calmly, mastering my fear, masking it in desperation-- and held my ground.

The three men kept their gazes level with my eyes, assessing me. I returned the compliment. But it was clear that the leader and perhaps all three, were looking at my face and eyes-- and seeing a Turk.

"A Mussalman, by my Faith!" said the leader in a corrupted Portuguese accent. His forebears had been farmers, I supposed, and he a son with soldiering for his fortune. I looked back still calmly, coldly, silently holding his gaze. He surveyed me with a kind of curiosity, as one might study a horse he might ride.

The man I judged to be his main companion tried a different mode of address. “You,” he said, “are Mussulman, or I am no Christian.” I doubted the thickness of his Christian convictions, but there was no doubt of his hostility. I still said nothing, giving all my thought and strength to showing no fear. It was the third, smaller man who most tested my fear. Fingering the basket-hilt of his rapier to make me see it, he very slowly withdrew the blade, trying to capture and hold my gaze with it.

I determinedly shifted my gaze to the scarred captain of this little brigade, and smiled a little twist of a smile-- as if I would not sully myself to be challenged thus.

The smallest man suddenly drew his blade fully out and leveled it at my chest. I had constrained myself not to ‘start’ or step back. Slowly the steel approached my heart.

The three of them were all smiles again. Not friendly smiles. “He don’t fall back before betters, I see.” It was the second’s comment. Always, I thought, a man on the alert to read his leader’s thoughts and create some incident for their sport. I kepy my gaze on the leader’s.

“If I do not fall back,” I said in precise Portuguese, “it is because I have only this cane to lean on, and because I am not the Turk you make me out to be.” The phrases confused them, as my determined bearing did. The leader and his second glanced at each other. The third man’s sword point wavered ever so faintly.

It was the shortest who recovered first. “A Mussulman,” he scowled, “but he’s bold to use our language!”

I regarded the man a moment, not changing expression. “I am bold to use your language because I am a Turk in blood, but a Christian by birth. I am neither Muslim nor convert! And I proceeded to tell them my fictional story about my family history-- all the way down to how my father had served with Albuquerque in “bringing these Mussalmans to heel." It had the effect I needed-- keeping my attackers listening, motionless, and distracted. They were silent until I had finished my little myth. And I kept my gaze fixed on the leader's.

"So," said he, "let's see the chain on your neck, Christian-- and the Cross of Christ the Savior!" I looked back, my gaze flickering only a moment. I slowly opened my Portuguese shirt! And yes, there was the cross I always wore now, both at the College and in the street! Even Monserrate had advised it.

"This is my Cross," I said, showing it but keeping my left hand firm on my cane, to pay witness to my Faith!" It had been deceitful of me to keep the Cross at my neck. Now it made the deception a lie that might save my life.

Yet I was quailing inside. In another moment I could be lying in a pool of heart's blood, writhing in the dust of a deserted orchard, far from help. I would be dying. However, I was not dead. I had taken the initiative. It was time to play my high cards. The highest.

I kept my gaze firmly on the leader's. "You are to go," I said firmly, "and leave me to the purpose for which I came here. I came to study-- and to meditate. To pray without disruption. I do not need to have my peace distributed by soldiers or sailors."

All three stared, slightly uncertain. I persisted. "You have my leave to go." And I waited, still eyeing the leader. The leader's gaze shifted to my shoulders, my throat, the Cross. I remained as I was. Cold and imperious. Confident.

The leader flashed a look at the other two men, giving them a little jerk of the chin toward the gate behind him. They stared at him a moment. Then the sword of the third returned to its scabbard. A reluctant return, but complete.

The three of them gazed at me, waiting for some move on my part. I did not accommodate them. They turned almost as one and stalked back the way they had come.

I had won, I had won! I wanted to shout for joy. But I did nothing of the kind. The jackals might turn on me! I leaned on my cane, following the three with my eyes in a pretense of boredom as they reached the gate. The second and third man stopped at the gate and stared at me coldly. Their leader turned also and stared. He was studying me-- closely. I did not change expression. At a word from him the three disappeared.

I turned slowly and walked into the shade of a tree. I paused. Walked farther. My ears seemed to turn like an animal's, expecting the sound of feet, expecting a sword's point through my bowels-- or a pistol ball through the heart. But nothing happened. The three men had gone.

I sagged against the trunk of an old orange tree, feeling it's smooth trunk and little nodes and striations and its own kind of roughness and age. I turned again to look toward the entry. No one. I had 'won' this little game-- and faced them down. It was good to draw breath, just to be alive. Later I would pray. First I just wanted just to walk, lock the gate behind me, feel the ground under my feet.

It was not long before I thought of the Portuguese girl. "Mira!" That wonderful name. Might she still be within my reach? With a twinge I knew that I had not wished to end my life and lose her. Yet I had *not* lost my life-- and I *had* lost her!

Forget the Armenians and the girl, I told myself. Complete what studies at Goa bring you satisfaction. Then pay your respects to Monserrate and go back to Bijapur.

Chapter 20

Discovering Mira

It was a week later. I had kept to my studies, but I felt more and more like a hermit clinging to his rock or his cave. Whatever my goals, I had to have diversion. Why not give the merchant's shop another try? It would be a relief to exchange my Jesuit Novice's tunic for my Portuguese clothing again. Since the attack by the three soldiers I had returned to wearing both poniard and rapier, but I had no desire to use the latter.

Should I try the Armenian shop again? No, I decided, there was nothing I could accomplish. And the girl? Either she would resent my arrival, or the merchant and his son would feel defensive. I turned my steps instead toward the hill where stood the heavy-set stone walls of the Church of our Lady of the Rosary. The day was sultry, and the hill promised a faint breeze and a good view of the city.

Why, I asked myself, would anyone want to live on this sweltering coast with its jungle, even granted the shade of its coconut palms? What but commerce-- and the vision of profits-- could a man want here!? I smiled to realize that I was not thinking like a merchant, Muslim or Christian, but as a Muslim horseman and noble of the Deccan plateau, with its distant horizons and near absence of forest. Wasn't I practical enough? Evidently not. Wasn't wealth important? Of course it was!

I shook my head and took the road which led to the Holy Hill. It would be a walk of some half an hour by the main road, and the early afternoon sun was already hot. My Portuguese hat and cape were rather warm, and I decided to take the better shaded combination of roads that led to the Holy Hill past the impressive Augustinian monastery which had been founded in the Christian year 1572 and had a fine, large bell-tower. The monastery also had a cloister into which, by a postern gate, I had often slipped into their gardens and enjoyed the shade of their trees and covered walks. But today, seeking the afternoon breeze off the Sea of Arabia, I would pass by the monastery and go on to the smaller road that led to the top of the Monte Santo. I was already glad that I had supplied myself with the usual leather flask of water, a piece of cheese, and some small loaves of bread that would provide me a lunch atop the Holy Hill!

As I took the street that would pass the monastery, I looked ahead and happened to see a lone woman, clearly Portuguese in her long grey skirt and her wide shawl covering her head and shoulders and reaching her waist. Even at my casual saunter I kept gaining on her, and soon I realized that, although apparently young, she was limping and looking worn out. Slowly I came even with her and cast a glance at her half covered face.

I almost cried out in surprise-- and so did she. She was the Armenian merchant's servant girl, Mira! We stared wordlessly at each other. Abruptly she tried to turn aside and flee into a narrow lane in the shadows between two houses. "Mira!" I shouted, "Don't run-- I will not hurt you! But she was not running, only limping as fast as she could, and in an instant I caught her by the voluminous white sleeve of her cotton blouse.

She tried to wrench away, but I was stronger-- and just as determined as she was. In three or four steps I had pulled her to a halt in the narrow lane. "Come back to the road," I said. This lane is no place to be!"

She glared at me. "Leave me alone!" I shook my head, and started pulling her back toward the street by her sleeve.

"You really must come out of this lane," I said feelingly. "I have an apology to make. Please, you must listen and hear me out. I will not hurt you at all. Not at all!"

Slowly-- I could see that her ankle was really hurting now-- she followed me, almost stumbling. At last, standing at the shaded corner of the main street, she stared at me with a face full of alarm.

"You are some kind of brute," she said, tears coming to her eyes. "Please-- kindly release my sleeve. I will not listen to your 'apology.' I will not accept it!"

"You mistake me!" I said in desperation-- not daring to relax my grip on her sleeve. "I am a candidate for the Novitiate. At the Jesuit college, the College of Saint Paul. I would never hurt you or any other woman. Never, if I can help it-- if you will just listen and not try to run away. If I stared at you too hard in the merchant's shop, I am terribly sorry. I did not mean to. But you were so sad when I went there. My heart went out to you. It is true!" And so I crossed myself awkwardly with my free hand "You were so… so beautiful, and you looked so sad… and well… weary of the world. I just wanted to see you, talk to you! But instead I annoyed you. Frightened you. And all for nothing.

"You were another man's abandoned wife-- another man's serving-woman, contracted to him, I had no power over you. None!

"Yet I… I kept wondering about you-- kept staring at you. And the more you tried to cover your head and face with your shawl, the more I tried to see, and kept staring. If I could but be there again-- and not stare, not frighten you! God forgive me, but I frightened away the one person I most wanted to see, to know! And until almost the last time I came there, I did not even know your name. But Mira…! I could not stand it. I could not stop wanting to see you, to have you look back at me, smiling not frowning, just accepting my presence, not angry, not hiding from me, running from me!"

I suddenly went to my knees right there in the street, and saw that I was still gripping her sleeve, making her a captive. "I am so sorry, Mira. Even if you run now. Even if you do not forgive me. I am so sorry!" And I opened my fingers and let them fall from her sleeve.

She was staring down at me strangely, like someone seeing a strange bird and seeing its broken wing-- my damaged face-- and not knowing quite what to do. He eyes were large and dark. But she did not run.

Her face softened the slightest amount. I could still see the fear lurking at the edges of her eyes, and in their depths. And yet I fascinated her now. I had broken through the highest walls -- perhaps one gateway-- of her mistrust.

"Tell me your name again," she asked cautiously. "I had forgotten it." And I did tell her. The whole of it.

A touch of strangeness came back into her look. "Aziz-- Ahmad-- Khan," she intoned. "A Muslim. And a Turk! I had guessed right." It was not triumphant-- or a challenge. Just a fact being stated.

My eyes still implored her, but I said nothing. For now I was the one in fear. The fear that she would still spurn me and turn away. That I would never see this beautiful face again, this girl that was a dream, my desperate dream.

But she did not turn away. Something in her mind had changed, almost like the wind that had buffeted a headland and had now dropped away."

And yes," she said quietly, "I am Mira. My whole name is Miralindo Bartolomeo. I will not run away now."

I was in shock. For suddenly I wanted to have her look down at me like that forever. Or up at me with brighter eyes! It did not matter. So long as she would not spurn me and turn her face away.

She looked to the left and right. "Please stand with me," she said. "For my ankle is badly hurt, and I am afraid. And I am tired-- and so hungry! I have not eaten in two days-- a night and a day. And all I wanted to do was to go and see my priest, my Confessor, at the little Franciscan church at the foot of the Holy Hill. And now I am standing here with… with you, Aziz Ahmad Khan… and I need your help. Your help! Please."

I wanted to reach up and take one of her hands with the strong work-hardened sinews that I had begun to notice. "Strong hands," I thought-- and slender but strong fingers. Strong like her inner self? And I began to have an epiphany. A goddess of hunt, perhaps… when she was not hurting. A clear-eyed archer whose invisible shafts had pierced my heart.

"Please, Aziz Ahmad Khan," she begged, and reached down with both her hands for both of mine. "Stand and go with me-- to the small

Franciscan church where I may see my Confessor, I feel such a sudden weight of misjudgement and sin upon me, and I must confess it or fall crying somewhere, until nightfall comes again and wraps me in its darkness."

And then as if waking from still another dream, another nightmare following hard upon the last, she smiled and took my hands, and I let her pull me up-- I helped her!-- and we stood, as if by a miracle, face to face. And neither of us had fear in our eyes now, or a determination to be angry, or anything but a kind of calm acceptance.

"I will take you to your priest," I said, looking into the depths of her eyes as she was looking into mine. We were "estimating" each other, yes, but we had joined hands-- in this dream, or bythis miracle, I could not say-- and something inside if us had already joined hands, too, even if we could not say exactly what it was.

"But," I said, as we go on to your church and priest, let me find a better place-- the cloister of the Augustinian monastery ahead-- where you can have some of the bread and water and cheese I have brought, and you will feel rested and more able to walk when we go on to your Franciscan church."

And before she could reply or show new fear, I said, "Never be afraid of me again, Mira. In your whole life, whether we are together or far from each other, never fear to trust me and what is happening in my heart. I do not feel wise-- or superior, or whatever people believe will give them power. To fight for power more often separates then unites, To have life is not to have control over life but to find friendship in it, and joy in it. And I am now your friend and your-- and I hesitated and saw her eyes tremble, just faintly-- and I changed the words and said, "and may be your love someday."

Then I turned from holding both her hands that close and gave her a little space, and a little more. And she looked up at me now, since I was taller, and gave me a winsome smile that said to me it was all right to be with me, and that she was ready almost to have me woo her, and yet she did not impose anything upon me, and I felt a rush of happiness.

We went ahead now, her right hand holding my left, and I steadied her as we went. In a little while we reached the walls, and the little postern gate, of the Augustinian monastery, and went in while my eyes assured her the security I had promised on the road. She sat near me on a bench beneath a tree, just close enough, and had the bread and water I had brought and a few bites of cheese, and her smile of gratefulness would have illuminated a thousand monasteries-- but warmed and consoled one heart, which was mine.

"The merchant," she told me, "was hard on me at first, and wanted to get rid of me. But he had that contract-- with my abusive monster of a husband, who sailed away as soon as he could. I do not know what happened to him--if he lived or died, if he ever reached Lisbon or never did. But here I was, still in Goa-- and now another man's servant. And the Armenian old man did not like me, did not want me. So I served him badly, resenting him.

"But at last, I am not quite sure why, he decided to keep me-- keep and train me. He became kinder. He gave me better food again, and clothing. He let me go out in the city. And I tried to learn his business. I did learn. I served him better.

"But there was also his son to satisfy, and he was a young man with a tongue like a whip. He reminded me of the husband who had abandoned me, and I began to hate him. And-- can you guess what happened?-- he began to make advances to me. Advances in nice language, but not with a good heart. He wanted me for his mistress-- that was all. And I resisted. I became tense, nervous, angry all day.

"Then one day the old man left for a week to look after his-- his 'investments,' he called them. Then I was at his son's mercy. But the son had no mercy, no honor. He wanted me, and he would try to persuade me, then hold me down with his strength. He said he would tie me up next if he had to! So I ran away when he was careless. I ran into the night with just these clothes. No cloak, no blanket. No money even to buy food. Perhaps I was foolish. I should have planned better how and when to leave. But I didn't. I just fled. And here I am today. Tired and hurt, with this terrible ankle. A burden to myself. And now a burden to you."

And while we sat she told me that she felt she could never go back to the merchant's shop again, even if she had to starve and die to be free. And then how I came-- and almost frightened her out of her wits! But I kept talking to her, talking good sense. And I apologized, and it was a real apology, she felt, not just a contrived one. And now she was learning to trust me-- another man she thought she could never trust! And I was saving her from her despair-- and from her false judgment about me, from her mistake to think every man was a liar and cheat, that there was no honor among them.

But now a fresh day seemed to have dawned. Suddenly she saw new light, new light everywhere to guide her, and it was all right to be wooed by an honest man-- a man named Aziz Ahmad Khan, who was a Muslim and a Turk-- and that, too, was all right now! She said the last with a little laugh even, and we both could laugh now. And suddenly the day was a really bright day. A very bright, wonderful day.

In that mood we went on to the Franciscan church and to her Confessor, Father Jerome, who had been the only man she had ever known before this day, she told me, who had learned how she really felt inside-- and tried to understand.

Chapter 21

The Franciscan Priest

Mira and I eventually reached the little Franciscan church nestled near the eastern foot of the Holy Hill. Her limp was even more pronounced now, and I kept holding her nearest hand to steady her. Neither of us said much, but I apologized about seizing her arm at one point when she almost fell.

She told me more about Father Jerome, the church's priest. He was Italian, she said, with great warmth of personality and much sympathy for the difficulties of his flock of Hindu Converso parishioners who sometimes had difficulties with the Universal Church's family values and its condemnation of the slightest compromise with Hindu theism, even in its monotheistic forms which admitted of certain triads and divine incarnations. Jerome bore the weight, as a dedicated Christian and Christian monotheism--with its seemingly contradictory doctrines of the Holy Trinity and of Holy Mary, Mother of God! No wonder, I thought, that it was so easy to accuse Hindu Converos of backsliding into "heresies." But the Italian priest also was much loved, and his numbers of parishioners had grown until he held two masses each Sunday in a full church! Mira thought it helped that he was a musician as well, and that his elegant little organ delivered from Italy drew many Conversos to his hymn performances on weekday evenings.

Thus Mira seemed quite comfortable having me meet the priest. He had been her Confessor for four years and knew all about her past and present situation. she said, but if I hesitated to meet him I could just take her to the church and slip away. I replied that I would do no such cowardly thing! We went to a side door of the church, and she rang the handbell beside the door.

The man who answered the bell was in fact the priest's deacon, himself a Converso. His look first at Mira and then at me conveyed warmth toward her and serious doubts about me! But he hurried to bring the priest. Mira saw my grim mouth. "Oh please, you should not worry!" she soothed. But I shifted uneasily, and did worry.

The door reopened. With the deacon was the Franciscan priest. The priest gave me a cursory inspection. But he quickly turned to Mira with a smile that showed no concern.

Mira's presence of mind seemed complete. "I had turned my ankle, Father, and this gentleman came to my rescue. He is Aziz Ahmad Khan, a Muslim from the Deccan who is studying our Faith under Brother Anthony Monserrate, one of his Jesuit teachers at the College of Saint Paul." Her voice was so confident that the Franciscan smiled and promptly shook my hand.

Now I found myself being studied both by the priest and by the girl I had accosted and, after a fashion, rescued. My head was full of confusion. If I wanted to separate myself from the situation all I had to do now was beg the favor of being excused, then either turn my steps back to the Holy Hill or return straight to the Jesuit College. But I did not really wish to do either. I wanted to find a way to keep seeing Mira now that I had discovered her! But it was now in the hands of the priest or Mira to dismiss me politely if that were their choice.

Fortunately it was Father Jerome who came up with an offer I would accept. "Why not rest awhile, Aziz Ahmad Khan, while I take Mira's Confession? I will also arrange for her to wash up, change into clean clothes, and Mira can rest and you and I can talk awhile. Does that suit you?"

I may have reddened a little, but I was happy to say yes.

"So, Mira," he said turning to her, "let us us go first and take your Confession, and then you will have time to make yourself more comfortable while I speak to this young man who came to your rescue."

In other circumstances I would have thought that Mira and I were being addressed by a Muslim matchmaker! Father Jerome was that skilled at bringing potential-- or actual-- lovers together.

He promptly disappeared with Mira in tow, leaving his deacon, who had the improbable title "Deacon John-Paul," to guide me to a bench in the hallway where I could sit and contemplate my future!

As I waited I tried not to speculate, but my mind would not keep cool or still. Every thought and feeling in me concentrated itself on Mira now-- and told me that I was falling in love with her! I wanted to shield her, protect her. If the priest could help me it would be easier. If not, I was contemplating independent moves I could make.

Abruptly it hit me that one of the first things the Armenian or his son might do would be to contact the Franciscan priest, guessing that he might take Mira in! How could he resist their demands? Would he just have to turn her back over to them?

Almost immediately I thought, "No! Before that I will take her with me to Bijapur! I would just leave Goa-- take her by force if I had to! Then I saw how foolish that was, and unworthy of me. Mira and I were not lovers. She had only begun even to tolerate me, let alone flee Goa with me! And the authorities would probably punish Father Jerome if they could not seize me! And my friend Monserrate-- they could punish him, too, for permitting me to wander as I had been doing! Where could I turn, if not to Father Jerome?

The time for Mira to Confess seemed like an hour. What could they be discussing? My character and intentions? The chances that the priest could keep the Armenians at arm's length? Whether or not Mira could trust my word-- or could trust to my taking her away from Goa, by her choice not just mine? Could she, a devout Christian, see her way to marring a Muslim-- to face his bigoted society in its views and treatment of women, however tolerant and generous he might personally be?

I was miserably reviewing these questions when, after a full hour, Father Jerome reappeared-- without Mira's coming, too.

I rose to greet him, but he made me sit back down. I steeled myself for the worst. But he was smiling! He sat down comfortably.

"I will be direct and honest with you, Aziz Ahmad Khan-- just as I have been with Mira. After circling around the subject, I finally asked how she felt about you-- if both of you felt only tentative, if her feelings about you were positive, if she might find herself falling in love-- whether she wanted to take the chance on falling in love! We discussed what might happen if the Armenian merchant and his son decided to pursue your return. Suppose they proceeded to thrust me the priest aside as unqualified to offer you my protection! These questions she answered-- and many more-- with surprising directness and practicality."

He sighed. "I incline not to be drawn to the idea of sudden affection, sudden love, Aziz Ahmad Khan. But I found that you had almost miraculously broken through Mira's despondency of the last three or four years, that you made her feel you wanted her but wanted her in an honorable way! I tried to caution her, telling her that she needed more time to see you, be with you, and decide if her first impressions had been correct. She was willing to take somet time, get to know you better, and then decide what she most wanted herself. But it was the first time since she had left Portugal that she really felt so sure about anyone. And how was I to answer that?"

He shifted his position. "So, if you feel as strongly about her as she does about you, my suggestion has to be that the two of you keep seeing each other, use some reasonable restraint, and ready yourselves to make some very important decisions. And I will also remain in touch with both of you." And he fell silent, looking directly into my eyes, and retained the pleasant smile with which he had begun.

I looked back at him gratefully. "You have my pledge, Father Jerome, that I will honor Mira and do whatever I can to make her future more pleasant and hopeful." I took a deep breath. "The words may seem easy to say, but they are not. And I can promise that I will not do anything, in the next weeks and months, to frighten or disappoint Mira." I adjusted my seat. "And yes, it is not to much to say already that I am in love with her but do not wish to do anything that would ever frighten or disappoint her. Maybe that is not enough to vow-- but nevertheless I will honor it, and honor Mira."

"Thank-you for that honesty, Aziz Ahmad Khan-- and that pledge," he said quietly. He sat back, visibly relaxing. "And now I will tell you, as I told Mira, that I have a temporary measure in mind that you both may like. I have already sent Deacon John-Paul to make an enquiry and an offer to a Converso family that I know and trust-- I mean converts from Hinduism in their case. I am offering to pay Mira's lodging for a three month period, renegotiable to six months, so that she may have a secure and, shall I say, comfortable place to live while the three of us-- you, Mira, and I-- decide how you feel about each other and whether a second three months would be useful."

I thanked him enthusiastically, and promised to make the first three months a successful enough testing period, so that his expenses would not be excessive. Meanwhile, I told him, I would continue to see Mira, especially in the afternoons, and try to make sure that she was happy with all the arrangements. We shook hands on the bargain.

When Mira returned to meet in the presence of Father Jerome as our guarantor, it was not long before the priest's Deacon returned with the Converso husband's signature. According to plan Mira would first stay two nights at the little Franciscan church, then meet the Converso family and move into her room.

I looked delightedly at Mira. What I saw in her eyes had more caution than I felt. She was still facing a brave, uncertain future. But I returned exulting to the College of Saint Paul.

Chapter 22

The 'Converso' House

I woke up at the College the next morning feeling an immense freshness-- and relief. I was even calm enough to hear a bulbul's melodious little voice in a a hedgerow beside the Refectory next door. And this would be my first day of really going to 'visit' Mira. We would go from her sanctuary at the Franciscan church to the 'secret' house that had been arranged!

Father Jerome had done a miraculous job of determining the fate of Mira's former husband. Now Mira and I could be married without any reasonable challenge. If we married soon-- and went promptly to Bijapur-- we might avoid any further question at all!

Now I only needed to think constructively, I told myself. For one thing, Mira and I would go with Deacon John-Paul to meet the Converso husband and wife who had contracted to have provide Mira a rented room. Their house, though I had not seen it, was said to be on a quiet street comfortably distant from both the Armenian shop and the busy Rua Direita where she might be seen, identified, and arrested. Father Jerome was truly being a friend to Mira.

I had also thought of finding another set of Portuguese clothing for Mira at the shop where I had bought the first two. I had fortunately come close to her size, but now I knew it for sure. I also had convinced myself that she really liked what I had already found, and I would find something else that could be mixed nicely with anything she had. And I could do it just after the noonday prayers at the College, or even slip out of a rear prayer stall early. The thought should have made me fill guilty, but now it did not. Mira was beginning to be first for me.

I finally did stay for the communal prayers, but when finished I quickly slipped back to my room, put on my Portuguese finery, and headed out the gate for the clothing shop I wanted. As luck would have it, I saw Monserrate at a distance-- and he saw me. Looking me over, he raised a hand and waved. I waved back. But I could avoid talking-- and did. There was something sad in the way he gazed after me as I hurried on. More than our steps were diverging now.

When I arrived at the Franciscan church with my new box of dress wares for Mira, she was already dressed in one set I had given her-- and Deacon John-Paul was eager to go and introduce her to her new landlords. I felt rather childishly disappointed at not having time to see Mira immediately open her new things. But-- we went immediately to the Converso Christian house.

Like the houses neighboring it, it was of a comfortable well-off "Goan" style with red-tiled roof and windows with almost paper-thin seashells set in them instad of glass. We knocked with the brass knocker, were invited in by the man of the house and met his wife in a decently but not ostentatiously furnished reception room. The only "art" we saw was a pairing of religious paintings, both in European style-- the Madonna with the baby Jesus in her arms, and a seated Jesus teaching his followers on the Mount of Olives. I had seen a crucifix with with Christ Crucified hanging over the room's doorway. Other than that there was no art Christian or otherwise on display. "Right Here, the Perfect Converso Home," silently I dubbed it. We sat having tea in the usual "Goan" blue-and-white tea-wares imported from China.

The man of the family excused his haste to leave, because he had two shops each in Calicut and Cochin that he needed to give a two-months' visit, including the difficult travel times. This startled me, because it meant that essentially he was assigning all responsibility for Mira to his wife-- and I remembered that only he, not she, had signed to the lodging arrangements! At the moment I could only take a deep breath and resign myself to a weak smile. But I promised myself to be on the alert for problems with his wife now that she would be effectively in charge.

Also I made a mental note that she spoke fairly good, though Konkani-accented Portuguese and therefore would understand just about everything said to her or in her presence. I did not like the direction I could see this taking. It depended a great deal on whether she liked

Mira, or considered her an annoyance. And I would have to trim my comings and goings accordingly.

The room set aside for Mira told me immediately, as we viewed it, that there was trouble ahead. It was a darkish room that might once have been set aside for a grandmother-- or simply for storage! I had no door but only a curtain hanging on thin brass rings. It's window were three, small and set high on the outer wall, with iron grills intended to keep predators out-- primarily snakes and crows. The amount of natural light, I thought, was more like that of a dungeon than a room in which to sleep, wash or read comfortably. For furnishings it had a rope-bed that would normally have been assigned to a servant, the bed having only the thinnest of mattresses-- if it could be dignified to that extent-- and a thin blanket with worn edges. To improve the 'look' of the bed, a four-foot wooden bedstead had been added against the wall, and there was a wooden peg centered above it as if for a framed picture-- or a Crucifix? Other, sturdier wooden pegs adorned the wall, for clothing no doubt, and there was a large chest at the end of the bed for folded clothing and valuables, though I saw no evidence of a lock. In one corner of the room was a chest on long, thin legs, with latched doors and, under the legs, cheap ceramic bowls for water. Ah yes, food storage! In the opposite corner was a small table with its center cut out to hold a fairly large wash basin, and inside the ceramic toureen stood a tallish, mismatched brass pot for storing and pouring water. Any hot water would have to be procured elsewhere, putting the landlady and her single servant, a sour-faced woman, "in charge." So much for dignified washing or bathing! And, no doubt, forget any cooking! The rest was empty space-- and walls plastered white. Mira stared, turning in a circle.

After leading us to the room, the Deacon and Mira's new landlady had excused themselves. Their voices filtered in now from the front balcony which they had mounted by stairs at the end of the house. Did the Deacon like what he had seen of Mira's room. Or did he care?

"Am I really supposed to live here-- sit, eat, bathe, and sleep?" asked Mira flatly. I was silent. "And I am to fold and lock up my nice, new clothing here?"

I sighed. "No doubt. Unless you complain to Father Jerome about it. Assuming that <u>he</u> cares." But that was unfair.

Mira was silent a long time, but used te silence to look at and touch a variety of items-- including, at last, trying to pat and plump up the very flat mattress that lay limply on the knotted ropes that supported it.

"I will find you a much better mattress," I told her.

She looked up sharply. "I thought I understood that" 'good quality bedding'" would be provided, including freshly washed sheets and towels every week!"

"I have the same memory," I said in sceptical tones. "It looks like you will have to complain-- in fact, make a habit of complaining."

She gazed helplessly back. "Surely you are joking, Aziz my dear." I gave her a grim look and shrugged.

"And as I complain I can make an enemy of this woman-- while her husband is eternally, conveniently absent?"

"I will see to the bedding and towels," I said firmly, and added another mental resolution. I was going to acquire for Mira a small writing-table and matching chair, and oil-lamp with enough light to read and write by, and a nice vase for which I would give Mira fresh-cut flowers every day!

She deserved all that, at the very least, for putting up with this poor treatment-- and "Christian" hypocrisy!

Mira gazed at me even more hopelessly. "My little hole at the Armenian shop was smaller but better than this. And I had at least warm water from the store's stove! She looked upward at the three small, iron-grilled windows. "And it was better lighted! And had a real door that I could close and latch from inside as well as out-- instead of that wretched piece of drapery hanging on its rings." She turned in a woeful circle. "Can I sit down on this cot-- it barely pretends to be a bed-- and just cry?"

I had bad news for her. "I think if you sit on that so-called bed you <u>will</u> cry. The mattress is one thing that <u>I</u> will immediately replace!

We heard a tinkle of laughter from the Christian landlady on her balcony. I wanted to go and break up that pleasant conversation-- and direct a few, choice words to the Deacon, too.

"Then may I just cry in your arms?" asked my despairing lady. I opened them and patted her quaking shoulders while the tears flowed.

And that was how we were introduced to Mira's fine, new landlords and fine, new room.

Before we left the house I did, in the Deacon's presence prevail on the lady of the house to provide the fresh-washed sheets and towels that had been contracted for. And, to spare myself the trouble of asking for anything "extra," I bought a small writing-table and matching chair and a decent oil-lamp to brighten Mira's nights. Oh yes, and purchased a sturdy lock and key for the clothing chest-- and, from the nearest bazaar, the thickest possible new mattress!

But all in all, I found that my best course was to get Mira away from this place as often, and for as long, as possible. Which, fortunately, I could do by having her spend every morning at Father Jerome's church, where she could mend old clothes-- especially his none too new Franciscan priest's brown Franciscan tunics and robes!-- along with the church's none too new draperies. And because, whether anyone liked it or not, I would come every weekday just after noon prayers-- and either meet Mira at the head of the sloping street where she was staying, or meet her at the church.

Clearly there was going to be no truce between Mira-- or me-- and the Converso merchant's wife. We were adversaries from the first moment.

Chapter 23

Asking And Answering

It was not very long, though, before something at the Converso house did go "really wrong." The third week.

Mira and I had decided to go up the Holy Hill and sit in the shade of "our" tree awhile, just to chat where there was a breeze off the Sea of Arabia. This time Mira broke down in tears when we sat down together. "That woman," she said, "I hate her! I am afraid of her! You know, Aziz, how I told you that she stands outside my doorway in the evenings and watches me, peeking around the corner of that cloth hanging there. Recently she has begun doing it every single night. I can actually see her smiling there, enjoying my discomfort. Twice I have spoken to her about it, asking her what pleasure she gets from it! But she silently disappears before I can reach the doorway, and the hallway outside is black as midnight. I fall asleep only before dawn. When my three little windows tell me that morning has come, I sit up feeling exhausted. And then, when I dress and start out for the little church, I can see her eyes at a crevice at the front door, her eyes mocking me. It opens, then it closes. I look up and down the street. Other doors are slightly open. Quickly they close. I am being watched by everyone on the street! Aziz,I swear it. She is like some kind of demon-- bewitching me. I begin to think that all the women on that street are demons following me with their eyes. How much longer can I take this, Aziz? Can you speak to Father Jerome about it? He could talk to her, tell her to stop. Or I can tell him all this in Confession, ask him what to do. I can ask him today, beg him to make her stop, or move me to some other place!

Mira was clutching both my hands by now. Her touch was not warm as usual, but cold and damp. My worst fears were suddenly being proved right-- that this "Christian" woman had hated being intruded upon, and now she herself had become the intruder. With her husband gone she could do whatever she wished. She could terrorize Mira-- try to unsettle her mind. Yes, to drive her into madness. The woman was like

Iblis, the Muslim Satan, making trouble in the world, spreading fear, seeking every weakness to exploit.

So I said yes to Mira's telling Father Jerome what she had told me, asking him to help. And then, after she had given her Confession, I went to him myself.

But I had another plan, too- or rather, a firm resolve. Leaving Mira in this inconstant state, where she lived in a dream world, was not helping her. It was not helping me either! I, too, was walking in a kind of dreamlike state, neither dedicated any longer to my Christian studies nor being able to complete my dedication to Mira's good. We could marry now without concern of her former husband. Monserrate sensed already that I was wavering in my devotion to the road that led to Conversion. I felt already that my time in Goa was coming to an end-- that sooner or later it had to. Why let this drag on until someone was hurt-- or Mira and I were cruelly separated? I would have to seize the initiative sometime. Ask Mira to marry me, ask Father Jerome to perform the ceremony, become fully and gladly responsible for both her future and mine. I would ask the priest today!

But when I went to the church and tried my idea on Jerome, he surprised me. He did not want me to rush into something that was fraught with complexities. I was Muslim and Indian. Mira was Christian and Portuguese. We might think that we could bravely overcome all the religious and cultural differences, but could we? Certainly we were aware-- or at least I should be, given the studies I had undertaken--that on many subjects Muslim and Christian ideas were quite different. Even by itself, Muslim marriage was more restrictive, its customs bearing harder on the woman. Could I expect Mira to give up such Christian customs of independence that women had-- even if in return, she might profit, perhaps, by certain forms of security and the mutual support of the large family"? What of the many language barriers that would exist for her but, thanks to my my early training and now my greatly expanded range, I did not feel and would not experience? What of the entirely different set of scriptures and religious customs that had shaped my life as an adult man, when she the adult woman would have to begin to understand them almost as a child, with my help and through my eyes? Marriage might seem simple to me, but for her as a woman it would mean many more changes of subtle kinds, such as the way our children were to be raised. Could she just raise them in the Christian way, yet do so in a larger Muslim family? Would they not be shaped by both cultures and perhaps respond much differently than expected?

On and on Jerome lectured and questioned me, until I was as much in confusion, and felt myself almost as unready to marry as I had been a year ago, or two or three years ago. And now I saw that I was unready to ask Mira to understand it all in one large dose! Was I justified in asking her just to have faith in me, faith in my wisdom, and to plunge in over her head, then wait to see how it would all turn out? The whole set of questions stunned and depressed me. How could we deal with the obstructions that sullen "reasoning" and truculent "reality" placed in our paths to marriage and fulfilment? Were we no better than ignorant babies, or fools bent on mutual destruction?Then I did something that I would not ordinarily have done.

First I prayed for divine wisdom-- both Muslim and Christian. Then I asked Mira!

She looked thoughtful for awhile before answering."This seems to me as much about feelings as it is about reason and logic! I know how I feel about you, and I believe I know how you feel about me!

"We have talked many hours up on this Holy Hill where we are sitting. We know that each other's childhoods were, what big changes came to our lives and changed our views of ourselves. How it is, especially, to be an orphan in a world meant for families, and yet how such independence strengthens our ability to make choices. How we have both been scarred, literally scarred, and how we have learned to carry these scars and overcome the doubts we may have about our acceptance, and to find that we are perhaps wiser and stronger for it. We have talked about the doubts and uncertainties we face, that we are not 'just normal' but have gained special insights into ourselves. We know that neither of us will just run into the crowd, or float on every wind that blows, but that we take confidence in being the individuals we are. We have sympathies for those left out, left behind, or just less fortunate, and cannot just ignore them.

"Yes, Aziz Ahmad my love, this has been-- for me as for you--- to talk about factual things, real things, opportunities and losses, boundaries and the way people surmount them. But, as you are asking, where are the "feelings" in all this?

"They are right here, in your heart and mine, and the resonances are there, the sympathetic responses like one string resounding to another, "answering" it. We have been in the realm of "feeling" all this time!

"And what are the results? What can we feel now? Call it the desire to keep these resonances going, keep "answering" the pitch of each other's strings, and feel a strange but real warmth in our hearts-- and with that warmth in our hearts a lingering sense of meanings beyond meanings beyond meanings, like the resonance of strings echoing away, away, away.... To me it is like having a special world just for the two of us, some sort of harmonic Eden!"

She paused in this amazing outburst of thought "You may think I am foolish or maybe have lost my senses in a whirl of talk, Aziz Ahmad, but my experience of pain over so many years have made me a kind of philosopher-- if women can be philosophers!-- and when I try to give a name to this almost musical experience, this resounding of inner strings, well.... I call it Love! Yes, it is love. A true and pure love that seldom finds itself a place in this discordant world.

"Tell me that I am a dreamer, Aziz Ahmad. Maybe you don't 'feel' it this way! But I have to say again, it is Feeling. And it goes beyond anything you can call Reason or the practical thoughts of our ordinary days! That's what we have found in each other, I believe-- this feeling I call Love-- if you can forgive all this strange 'talk' of mine. "Reason" tells us what we can "know." "Feeling" tells us what is our heart's desire-- to what we can aspire! It is the essence of love that goes "beyond" naming what is mysterious and wonderful, "right" and ennobling, true and wise, celebration and sadness, the urge to explore the "feeling" of two strings sounding, two voices singing, and the purest pleasure of harmony. It is what we mean by transcendent Beauty, be it form or meaning. There is no exact word for an essence.

"Oh, I do wish I could say it better. But sometimes the words elude and beggar me. Try to describe the bulbul's song, even the sparrow's twitter. I listen sometimes, and I cannot. We have 'near' words, approaching words, but not <u>the word</u>. We can only say, "How that pleases me!-- or makes me cry, or laugh! But of course, this is only a woman's raving, something for men to shake their heads and smile at. But I don't relent, or care. For we women can be "philosophic, too. It is our born right also."

Suddenly I, the man, realized that I was staring at this Philosopher in a woman's form-- this "Oracle"of mine who dared to "think" like a Philosopher! And it stunned me, almost stunned me out of my wits. Because when I thought it through I found it as wise and logical as anything that a Saint Thomas might have written to "explain" Truth or to offer as "proof" of God's Existence. Such talk as this from Mira might be full of metaphor, yes, and metaphor is a "likeness," not the Thing Itself, but when faced with the great mysteries, where no commonplace word will do, no description of "fact," it is the metaphor that can come closest to the reality-- whether of resounding strings or reverberating hearts or souls swaying together in the wind, we must turn to the poet-- and to his and her metaphors, for what comes nearest to what we <u>feel</u> and what we want to say.

And to Mira I said at last, when she had fallen silent, "That was a true gift of your thoughts <u>and</u> feelings. Yes, dear girl of my heart, I have learned to listen to you well. For your thoughts <u>and</u> feelings is what I was trying to have from you-- not as "woman" only,but as woman <u>and</u> poet, woman <u>and</u> philosopher. And now I know, again and better, that you and I are well launched on the sea of Love, the mighty flow of it-- lifting and inspiring us both. We are <u>helping</u> it flow through us and slowly,slowly carry its seeds of Understanding, watching them settle and take root and grow in new and amazing ways. This is the normal "love" we have when we are ordinary lovers-- though we are that, too! It is the pure Love that rises into a different sky and leads us toward the most inscrutable of mysteries, the highest yearnings we can have. And though we never quite arrive, because that is why mystery IS. And now we know better what it is we "feel" when there is not single word for it, but only the heights and depths we reach because we let it flow through us, and sometimes are least aware of it.

"Let us plant beautiful flowers of feeling-- and watch them grow, and be there watching when they blossom into mysterious fragrances. And if there are strings we play or words we say, let them sound, too, in beauty and harmony, letting us come as close as breath to what each other feels.

Mira looked back at me a long time. "It is a strange, new poetry for me. But I am beginning to think now for myself-- in poetic, abstract ways that I had never dared. And now I can be brave, not just weaving and nodding and trying not to say anything too boldly for fear that someone will mock it-- or misunderstand. Now I can speak up and say "I love you, I long for you, Aziz Ahmad Khan! I do not see how I can live without you"-- and why would I want to? I can say it all out loud and not be afraid, worst of all, that you would belittle me or laugh at me. Now I can really live to the fullest and be filled with joy sometimes-- even in the midst of vast changes and becomings, the 'comings and goings' of life's adventure, the small changes and becomings that we often hardly sense at all.

"That love is how I feel, Aziz Ahmad. And it will embrace you and care for you, and laugh with you and weep 'over' you, for as long as my body and soul both live-- and perhaps yet longer when only our souls can speak to one another."

And so we continued to talk in this way whenever we felt the urge, or needed to explore a mystery or even just a misunderstanding, petty or important. Because, altogether, it put us in better communion with each other, and deeper understanding even of the petty, unpoetic things that were part of every day.

And this time, when we had let our thoughts flow as far as they could find a course, I ended by saying the most simple, factual thing I could-- and still use the language of poetry between us invented.

"Thank-you, my dear love," I said. "Thanks to these moments that so mysteriously flow, I would marry you tomorrow if Fate permitted-- or Father Jerome agreed. And sooner or later it may be that both of these events come together and resonate one day."

"We can wait," added Mira,"until all the strings of love resound together in some powerful, strange moment and then there is no obstacle that man or God would put between us."

I would have said more, but Mira calmly put a finger on my lips and said, "Let me speak from the heart, dear love, and try a poem of my own this time."

"Though this might be the last

We ever thought or knew

Still would our love be true,

And our two souls would fly

To God's pure realm above

This earth, beyond this sky"

Chapter 24

Love In The Rain

Mira and I were finding our way into growing confidence and warmth. We were falling in love, deeper and deeper each day. It should have been obvious to the most casual by-passer, let alone any thoughtful observer. But Father Jerome had asked us-- instructed us really-- not be hasty about becoming complete lovers or rushing into marriage, and we were trying to satisfy him.

Yet it should have been obvious, too, that a passion for each other should also begin to develop. It did grow steadily-- I almost said stealthily-- as we opened ourselves to each other's feelings and ways of thinking. The Holy Hill had become the place for us to sit and talk almost every afternoon. With the monsoon seriously approaching now, we also looked closely at the big clouds massing above the coast more impressively each week.

One day we discovered that we had slipped into a habit of holding hands. Exploring with a fingertip the strength of my wrists from long practice of archery, Mira frankly asked me what I thought about Father Jerome's having placed a kind of vow upon us, that we should be "cautious" in our relationship. I told her that at first I had sometimes resented his advice, but how I had concluded that it had provided us with a kind of open-paled fence through which feeling and thought could smoothly pass rather than becoming a stone wall that forced us to leap over it.

"I hope," I said, "that you won't take me as too cautious a lover, Mira. In fact, I find that in a strange way I have enjoyed our slow awakening and opening to each other."

She laughed. "Well spoken, my philosophic lover. But forgive me if there are days when I think it a hard discipline, and would really like to kiss you very thoroughly."

I laughed. "Maybe we should put kissing on a schedule. Treat it like hakim's prescription! Imagine the label. 'This medicine to be taken once a day. Please report if untoward side effects occur.'"

Mira caught the mood. "So, my dear man, you think my kisses would have 'untoward side effects"?

"Certainly," I chided her. "Like palpitations, trembling, and possible failure of the heart."

"Hmmmph!" she came back, and folded my fingers under hers on her knee. It was how we dealt with many a subject that could easily become too serious. Because without suitable caution we might be holding hands too violently!

We did talk seriously many a time. Much of our conversation was meant, however, to just pleasantly while away the time on long, hot afternoons. I told Mira how Raya and I had learned horsemanship, archery, and musketry from old Qarah Khan, and the tough discipline he insisted upon. She told me how the nuns found her wandering the streets after her parents died and took her in gently without fuss and taught her the discipline of their lives and worship. I made a kind of epic of Raya's hopes of seeing the ruined wonders of Vijayanagar and how he reacted when he found the ruins so complete.

Mira asked me to explain how Raya and I met the the two Jesuits, Monserrate and Castro, on the road to Goa. I added how we succeeded in rescuing them from the betrayal by members of their Hindu caravan guards. I explained more about my respect for Monserrate, who could do hard things in a graceful way and make discipline of mind and manners a thing for admiration instead of harshness-- while a man like Castro, though trained in Christian "charity," understood nothing of it and had erected around himself a fortification of coldness and suspicion which chilled the better instincts of others. Mira in turn told me how the Superior of her nunnery resembled Monserrate in the genuine warmth of her faith, so that she could issue criticism and preserve discipline without harming the other nuns' morale or weakening their faith.

Usually, though, we kept to less controversial subjects like flowering trees that were native to the Konkan or were imported and planted by the Portuguese-- and the nuts and fruits they bore, and how the Goan fiery drink of feni was most often made from the toddi sap of the coconut tree, and how the fruit of the "caja" tree from Brazil was processed into the popular cashew nut. But we were not trying to be experts, but simply exchanged casually what we knew of things. For instance, we both enjoyed the country's birds and liked identifying those we saw in the trees, fields, swamps, and brackens of the coast. Often we laughed at the antics of the common mynah and crow and the way herons perched upon the backs of plodding water-buffalo and used them as a movable supply system for stirring up winged insects.

Even more casually we talked about what we had experienced in the different parts of the world where we had grown up-- the north of Portugal for her, the center of the Deccan for me. She spoke of the Basque seafaring men and the risks they took in fishing the cold Atlantic. I told of India's farmers walking to their fields with their wooden ploughs over their shoulders at the first light of day, and how their work-songs upheld their spirits.

Mira would often say, when we talked like this that it was strange how little we knew of the least-- and yet most common-- of each other's countries and cultures, and how wonderful it was to have this new freedom to explore our two worlds together-- and how, when I sat listening with a smile to her stories of Europe, she wished that we could spend a whole lifetime traveling and sharing these different things, not spreading suspicion and war and hardship wherever our peoples met. She thrilled at how much that we discussed seemed like a dream to her-- but more, how it seemed very like a dream just to sit pleasantly together and to talk at all, lightly or heavily as the mood persuaded us!

And I would sit with her in the shade as we did talk, or walk next to her through the less frequented streets and lanes of Goa, and reflect on how like a miracle it was that we had 'found' each other, and that we were becoming friends even as we felt our way into becoming lovers. I began to think Father Jerome had been right, that we should take this time to 'discover' each other more fully while the opportunity was-- or it seemed-- so promising and peaceful.

But of course I knew-- as Mira did-- that this could only be a short, passing phase in our lives in Goa. For she remained the runaway living in an unsympathetic house under the reluctant forbearance of a "Converso" woman. And I? I was the student of Christianity who had recently realized that my pleasant time in Goa under Monserrate's patronage was likely, and soon, to come to an end, especially when-- as I now thought it more right and necessary every every week, every day-- I would have to reveal to Monserrate that I wished to leave! What would be the breaking point? I kept having to ask myself that. There were too many contradictions revealing themselves! Soon, very soon, I could afford to wait no longer to follow my heart's course, to marry Mira if she would have me-- this Muslim man-- for her husband, and to take her with me to Bijapur.

It was an afternoon, a week later, when the monsoon Rains threatened ever more cunningly to arrive-- first in sudden downpours that could drench you completely if you were sitting on a hill like the Monte Santo, the Holy Hill, or if you were walking on what a few minutes before had been a sunny street in the late afternoon, And here we were, Mira and I, sitting and talking atop the Holy Hill while the clouds massed over the surface of the Sea of Arabia, and the heat from the air and water kept pushing the clouds higher and higher, farther and wider.

And finally I said to Mira, "Have you been thinking, as I have, of the real possibility of a storm-- perhaps a quick but strong one-- could could come rushing in and burst upon us? We could certainly get a complete drenching!"

Mira seized the opportunity to turn where she sat and lean back against me. She had never done that before! "Isn't it strange?" she asked. "But somehow as long as I am with you, dear Aziz Ahmad Khan, it does not matter."

Instinctively I put an arm around her waist. The perfume of her hair had begin to do its magic-- as she intended?-- on my poor wits. "Well," I said lazily, "maybe it won't rain. We might just get a little wind. Or... a lot!" But with Mira's fragrant hair, along with the fabric of her scarf which seemed to have acquired that fragrance, and her slender body leaning against mine, I could not find the will, somehow, to make her get up and go down the hill with me.

We just kept watching the storm. Or at least we pretended to. And it did begin to take a more imminent shape, with rumbles of thunder in the caverns of clouds where lightning could be seen flashing sometimes.

The air around us was taking on a lighter, fresher quality as small pieces of a breeze seemed to advance from the storm-front and find our sitting place under the suddenly restless branches of the tree overhead. I sighed, trying not to sound alarmist. "That breeze is going to become a gale, I'm afraid. And when the clouds send their grey tentacles ahead to find us, and the real wind begins, we and our hilltop could be in the direct path of thunder and lightning like nothing we have ever seen or expected!"

"I understand, dear Aziz," said Mira, "and if it is a time chosen by God to strike us, this most wonderful dream-time of ours together would just…end."

"No," I said, feeling sudden alarm. "For I could lose you Mira. And even if we lived, we could be burned and crippled and still alive-- alive in an endless nightmare!"

Mira sat up straight and gave me a concerned look. "You are a terrible man, Aziz Ahmad Khan, scaring me that way!" She harshly straightened her skirt. "And I will be very angry if you do not follow your bad little speech, now that you have made it, by seizing my hand and pulling me down the path from this beautiful spot like some kind of captive!"

I reached, grabbed her nearest hand with a grin, and pulled her roughly against me. "See how cruel I can be?" I retorted.

She let her weight, such as it was, remain leaning there an instant. "Take me, cruel man, down this hill, before I kiss you with a violence you will not soon forget." I caught her mood.

"Then," I growled, "give me one violent kiss of yours right now, so that I will know the fullness of your enmity!"

She twisted, leaned against me a third time, and gave me the 'fullness of her enmity." It was oddly like Heaven! The flames of Hell could not have been more terrible when she broke away.

But the wind, too, had come to buffet us as we stood still exposed atop the Holy Hill. And with it I heard the rain coming. "We are in for it now!" I said, and started pulling her faster. We must have gone about thirty steps when an instant burst of lightning and thunder came together, and the lightning struck-- and split!-- the tree we had been sitting under! We both fell as if struck by some blunt force, and lay staring at the tree. In that fiery moment, with the smell of lightning around us mixed with the smoke from the burning tree. I thought for a moment that we would die now! But then I thought, "God have mercy, but our 'time' has not yet come!" And I turned to Mira-- my soaked and now frightened lover lying on the ground beside me-- and folded her in my arms, and kissed her hard and long.

When we sat up we were so wet-- and still so stunned-- that we looked like fish that had drowned in their own element! I smiled, trying to pull Mira back into the fantasy world where we had so shortly ago resided, so that perhaps the shock of the lightning, which was certainly real, would be less. Mira looked up at me with eyes and face shining and said-- "God did not want to punish us. He only warned us. Or was it His celebration of our love, that did not deserve to be ended? He has given us another chance!"

"Let us go quickly, dear Aziz, before I begin to tremble and faint for fear of how close we came to… death. But were we not both warned and reassured by God in the same moment? Isn't it so?" And I pulled her along with me, holding her around the shoulders awhile, then just holding one of her hands as I drew her after me.

Where would we go now? Which direction? Toward the little Franciscan church? But we had already arrived there that first day we really met, looking like two refugees. I did not feel better about taking Mira back to the house where she lived-- also like a refugee-- where she was supposed to have a safe haven.

But the woman recently had surprised both of us by taking a more pleasant way with Mira, and-- although I remained suspicious of the woman's intentions-- Mira had been somewhat pacified and was trying to think more positively about the woman and not be alarmed by her unpleasant moodiness. In any case I did not expect the woman to have changed her basic attitude, which was hostile, but I did not want to keep Mira feeling uncertain. Better to just keep quiet, I told myself, and hope for the best.

On this wet afternoon, in any case, it seemed all right to arrive early at the woman's house and give Mira the chance to dry herself and re-dress.

We were struggling along the cobbled streets like two drunken sailors, but our moods, despite some wild swings as we remembered the lightning bolt, had been given time to recover. I told jokes, made silly statements, and generally tried to revive Mira's sense of balance. And I was succeeding.

The rain had stopped awhile, and the sun was trying to peer around the corner of the great mass of clouds overhead. I thought to myself that more rain could fall and drench us worse that we already were.

I knew Mira had fully revived when she grinned and said she was glad we had broken through that idea that we could never kiss because we had not had the time yet to become absolutely sure of Father Jerome's approval! I assured her that I had decided that we needed now to become our own guides and "rule-setters." Jerome, too, was obviously weakening, I told her.

"Good!" she announced. And made me slow down for a thoughtful-- and less violent-- kiss. Which meant that, as we didn't stop walking, our hips kept bumping and she started giggling. "Talk about breaking through!" she said.

But then I felt a shift in the air around us-- and that breeze that had started blowing when the rain first came. True, we were getting close to the Converso woman's house, but not close enough to avoid getting wet again. I looked up. Dark clouds were rolling overhead again. Sure enough, here came the rain.

I pulled Mira closer to me again and moved to tighten her shawl over her drying hair. She gave me a quick smile and squeezed my hand. And the waters gushed from the sky.

Mira reacted gaily. "Let it pour!" she exulted. "Maybe it will remind me to give my lover another of those fearsome kisses I had promised him-- if he will just stop dragging me along so fast!

I decided that slowing down for the threatened kiss would be worth the intense pain of it. "Let the Heavens open!" I decreed, and stopped just short of the street where the woman's house was.

It was a good idea, because this kiss was the best yet-- though I of course declared it, rather breathlessly, to have been the worst! And Mira's eyes were shining afterward, too.

"We can now finish this journey," she declared-- "unless, dear lover, you wish to return that meeting and conversation of lips in the same spirit!"

I returned the compliment, although more gently than I had received it. Mira clung to me awhile after that one, swaying with me. I smiled down at her. "Enough now, I suppose?"

"Well," she sighed, looking at the sky, "I do believe the sun is returning to its natural sovereignty. Or at least it's peeking around the clouds again."

"Very well," I said. "To the house!"

And around the corner and down the street we went. And to the doorstep, where I raised a hand to ring the bell beside the door. Until a hand of Mira's came up and stopped me in mid-ring. "Just one more!" she pleaded. "And this time," she allowed with a grin, "embrace me like you mean it! I am tired of playing pussycat around this lady and walking tiptoe so she will not be disturbed, poor thing!"

Something told me this was not a good time to be throwing our "relationship" in the lady's face, but… we embraced. And Mira lifted her chin and kissed me 'thoroughly.'

The door opened. The woman's eyes, which had started to see us with the usual dullness, came alive. With rage! And I knew as our eyes met-- mine over Mira's ardent shoulders-- that someone, Mira or I or we, would have to pay for this! Maybe not immediately. But after the shock wore off a little and the woman's natural serpent's way of thinking-- as I had once identified it-- came into play, there would be consequences. Maybe…Karma? Or at least she would study how to pay us back, and in particular to pay Mira back somehow….

And then the door slammed. Mira still did not relent. "Again!" she said, "Please, my love!"-- enjoying this moment no matter how angry the woman might be. And I let her kiss me as long as she wanted, and tried to kiss her back with the same force even if Icould not manage the same zeal at this moment!

And then, slowly, the door opened again, and Mira turned to the stone-faced woman and said, quite prettily-- "So sorry. Rain drenched lovers sometimes forget where they are. But we meant no harm."

"'Meant no harm'?" No, I was afraid not. For the woman would conclude that at least one of us-- and probably both-- had planned it exactly as it happened.

And my love turned to me in the same mode, smiling as if nothing whatever had happened that could be objected to, even if it WAS right here on he front step in full view of any of the lady's neighbors who had cared to watch-- and I found myself betting that they did. Maybe the penalty would come at a time a little removed.

And Mira turned back to me and gave me another light, bright kiss-- and looked at me without relenting one small amount-- and said, "I will see you tomorrow, my love," and went inside, while the woman stepped back, still stone-faced, and let her in. And I bowed slightly in my usual way and excused myself. And the lady, without change of expression, closed the door in my face before I had even finished the excuse.

I waited to see if there would be shouts or blows. But there were none I could detect. Mira had faced the woman down.

I waited longer. Still no angry events that I could hear.

I turned and walked back toward the College of Saint Paul. Slowly. Feeling exhausted now. And-- I had to admit as I touched my lips-- extremely well and thoroughly kissed!

The sun was going to set, I observed. As mysteriously as they had come, the clouds had departed. The storm was over.

Well, <u>that</u> storm anyway.

Chapter 25

Dreamtime And Rescue

As I approached the Jesuit buildings I found myself yearning to be in a mood of victory. Mira loved me! We had shown the woman at the house that she could not control us! Yet more than anything I was anxious. The uneasiness would keep creeping over me as I dined at our Jesuit tables.

The last moments at the dark doorway of that evil woman's house left me concerned. Mira's glance had assured me she would be all right. Then she would have gone down a dark hallway and turned into a still darker room-- a room with no door but only a curtain attached to its rod by brass rings.

I could not shake from my head the image of the woman's sudden anger at the front door when we stood kissing in our half dry clothes after the rain had stopped. Strange, but I suddenly imagined that the woman's clenched teeth had become fangs, and she had been transformed into an image of the Hindu dark goddess Kali, render of souls.

I found myself reluctant to go to bed after my last prayers! Was that hostile woman, unable to reach me with her spite, plotting some kind of revenge upon Mira? And when? Tonight?

It had troubled me that the woman's husband had not yet returned from his month's business in Cochin. Christian he might be, and I wanted to believe that he exercised some restraint on his wife's behavior. But if he were not at home? The whole atmosphere of that "home" seemed stifling and dangerous. I went to bed in unrest of mind. Fitfully I dreamed, though I did not realize it. I saw the woman coming like Kali from her lair. She passed through Mira's thin curtain like a ghost, creeping toward my sleeping love in her dark room. I wanted to warn Mira-- to shout, to get between her and the fanged creature advancing with staring eyes and a cadaver's limbs. My sword! I reached for it, groping with hands that had no strength. The demoness turned my way, fixing me with her unchanging stare. Slowly a long tongue extended itself from her mouth, red with fresh blood. Mira's blood, still warm!! She had already killed Mira, had drunk her blood!! I tried to thrust out my arms, my fingers splayed in horror. I could not move. The woman's fangs were searching for another throat now. Mine! They….

I woke up shouting, flinging my arms out in the heat of the summer night. Sweat had sprung from every pore. Mira!!!

Suddenly, ashamedly, I knew I was in my darkened room alone. Had I wakened everyone in the hostel?? But only one man stirred in the room opposite mine. Now he snored again. Slowly the snoring lulled me back toward sleep. Yet I fought against the sleep. I could only think of Mira lying alone in that black room of hers!! Had she been dreaming, too? Had the woman come, standing at the curtain, listening to Mira's uneasy, innocent breath? Had she waited there, then walked softly away again? Or had she… done what?

It was daylight when I woke again. I leaped out of bed. It was late I would be late to breakfast! I dressed fast, badly, and rushed into the refectory. I ate fast, thinking only of Mira and that woman.

Abruptly I saw my companions of the Novitiate moving already toward the chapel. I had forgotten! This was supposed to be a day of special prayer. The prayers would be many-- and long. In charge of the prayer service would a Jesuit brother known for his great zeal-- known also for his boring sermons.

But more. Monserrate would be there. He would notice me. He would smile in welcome. I would be trapped, unable to slip out as I wanted to. But Mira! I had to get to Mira!

I ducked onto a bench in a rear corner of the chapel. With luck I would see Monserrate come. I was torn between loyalty and despair. I must try to go unnoticed. I buried my face in a Missal. I felt disheveled and dishonorable, unworthy of my teacher's trust. But I stuck to my seat.

Luck was with me when Monserrate and sat to the front this time, his back to me! I tried to concentrate on the prayers, the collective Responses. I coughed. Coughed again. That was the key, I realized.

Coughing with more purpose the next time, I desperately mumbled an excuse and left by the rear door, barely remembering to turn, genuflect, and cross myself. What a fool and hypocrite I was! If ever anyone deserved disciplining....

But I went back to my room, still dressed as I was in my Novice's cassock, and changed to my Portuguese clothes. At the last moment I remembered to snatch up my sword in its scabbard, then sneaked out of the hostel like a thief-- and ran! I ran almost the entire distance to the lane and the house where Mira should just be rising.

Out of breath, almost staggering, I stopped at the head of the lane to see if there were people in view. One elderly lady and her servant were going into a house. Then no one.

My heart sank. Mira would have no idea I was coming. It was the wrong time of day. She would think I was an idiot. She would be right!

I reached the door of the woman's house at a walk, trying to look calm and self-sure. I knocked. Knocked again. What a fool I was, I thought!

The door opened-- just a crack. Standing there was the female servant whom I had seen before. She almost jumped back!

Why in the world was I here? Running until my legs were in torture, my heart pounding. I had almost collapsed!

But then I realized there was something strange. The servant just stared. The woman of the house did not come to the door. The servant nervously said something about her mistress not being at home, and would I be pleased to come again later? I persisted. "Now!" I said. I would see Mira now! The servant blanched. Mira? Yes, Mira. More fumbling for words by the servant. Mira? No, Mira was not here. Mira was...elsewhere!

I brushed past the servant and went straight to Mira's dark room. The two small, high windows cast a grey light on the room.

The room was in chaos. The cot, Mira's "bed," stood twisted at an angle, its one sheet and blanket half on the floor. Clothing lay scattered in heaps. The wash-basin lay upturned, its cup broken in a corner. The writing table lay on its side, one leg broken. The pen I had given Mira lay on the floor with several pages from the desk, with the vial of ink, still fortunately stoppered, nearby. The lamp I had bought for Mira lay broken at a distance, its oil spilling out in the grey light of morning coming from the three high, grilled windows

I heard a noise behind me and froze. The woman, that damned woman! But it was the maidservant. She had coughed and was "explaining." Mira was not here. She had gone…"out." Of course, I thought-- out! But not because she wished to. Then I remembered it. My God! The dream!

I had been right. The dream-- it was crazy, but an omen. An omen! And yet, this chaos was no dream. Someone had done this, had seized and taken Mira somewhere. But where?

I turned on the servant, forced her out of the room, her back against the wall. Towering over her, I brought my face down to hers. "Where!?" I grated. "Where is she!" I knew the servant was perfectly familiar with the Dakkhini words. She quailed. "Mira!!" I said with a snap. "Where is she!?"

The servant would have run away, but a I grabbed and twisted an arm. "Tell me!" I snapped again. It was a shout this time. It should have wakened anyone in the house-- brought someone-- the woman?-- to confront me. Silence. No one came.

"Do you wish to die!?" I shouted, whipping out the knife I kept under the sash at my waist. I held the keen Arab blade at her throat. She gargled something and tried to point…where? To another room in the house? To the rear? Rear of the house??

Using a door I found at the rear of the house, I dragged the woman outside with me. "Here?" I demanded. "Where!"" The maid twisted in my grip, feeling the blade of my knife against her throat. I planned if necessary to wound her, not kill her She pointed still unable to speak, continuing to choke on her words. I looked. There was nowhere o hide someone, except maybe-- that! A crude shed for storing wood and charcoal. A tiny, filthy shed.

I dragged the woman to the shed, my knife still at her throat. I could not afford to release her. And then the shed's rough walls shook. Someone lay there, had been stuffed there. I saw a pale white foot-- two feet, bound with rope. ran the few steps to the shed. The rough walls seemed to shake-- did shake! Inside the door, a woman's pale white feet tied with strong sizal rope. How could she, Mira-- anyone!-- be crammed into that tiny, filthy space?

Re-sheathing the knife, I kept a grip in the servant's wrist. I started throwing pieces of charcoal aside, furiously littering the small space behind the house. Mira's arms had been bound to her body. Forced into her mouth was a gag of wadded up cloth. She had almost suffocated! Her nightgown had been torn half away, and she lay muffled up in her grey cloak now sooty and streaked with charcoal, her eyes red from crying, her tears straggling through the charcoal dust. She looked so pitiably at me that I wanted to cry myself. But the rage in me was greater.

I wanted to embrace her, hold her, let her cry or wail. Whatever! But first I had to remove the gag that was choking her and the dirty rope binding her arms against her sides. Last I slashed the rope that bound her feet.

"Oh, Aziz!" Mira cried, and wept against my shoulder, clinging to me even as I kept my grip on the servant's wrist. I held the two women that way as long as I dared, letting Mira cry, half embracing her.

Why in the world had she been stuffed here?-- if not to hide her from me!? The sizal strands of rope were not thick but quite strong, wrapped around and around Mira-- around her cloak and arms and torn nightgown together, tying her like a goat or a sheep. I would have cursed, but tried not to alarm her. Yet all the while I was thinking hard. Where was that woman?? Had she gone to the Armenian merchant or his son? But no, she probably would not have known about them-- or where their shop was. But she must have gone somewhere for help. The truth flashed upon me! She had gone to find police or soldiers and have them come and take Mira away. Mira was to be delivered over bound and gagged like an animal, a goat for the slaughter!

I had to get Mira out of this place right now! No time to find everything, pick up and save things, talk things over. "Mira," I begged her, "Can you get up? Can you walk? We have to go. We have to leave. Now!"

She stared at me, but nodded. "Yes.... Now. I will try!" I helped her to her feet. She almost fell twice. I started walking with her, holding her steady.

I looked around. The serving woman had broken free from my grip. Where was she!? Nowhere to be seen. Maybe...going already to find her mistress? To find that "Christian woman, that employer of hers, who was probably, right now, coming back with two or three men to finish her dirty, low work for her and bring this Portuguese girl to "justice"-- this orphan who was some man's wife, his property, his slave, his plaything-- 'til death did them part! I almost laughed at the absurdity. Mira looked up at me. I shook my head and quenched any thought of a smile-- even a cynical smile. We had to go and keep going!

"My skirt!" said Mira suddenly as we passed her room. "I need my skirt, my sandals-- my crucifix!" Of course, I thought, her crucifix that had been hung on the peg above her cot. What wonderful Christians, I thought of the Converso man and wife! I found the crucifix where it had fallen also-- in a corner, on its face, the face of the Savior. I tucked the crucifix in a large pocket of my Portuguese pantaloons. Fortunately Mira still had her key to the trunk that held most of her clothing, and she stripped the remaining items from the pegs along the wall-- and wisely, before I could say anything rolled the clothes and some other valuables into her bed-sheet and tied its corners hard. I myself retrieved the pen and scattered sheets of paper from her broken desk and put them in my deep pocket with the crucifix and other small items. At the last moment I remembered to have Mira put on her sturdy Portuguese shoes to help her walk the long distance to Father Jerome's church. I glanced around, picked up her bundled clothing, and took her by the arm. "Let's go. Now!" I said. We went quickly together. I admit I was almost dragging her.

Briefly I stopped with Mira at the head of the street, where we could look back half hidden by the corner of a house. I looked down the street, but saw no evidence of anyone's coming, and turned to lead us onward. Just then I heard a sounds and stepped back to peer around the corner.

A woman-- that cruel woman who called herself Christian-- came with two uniformed men, walking fast, into the lower end of the lane. With them was the servant urging them toward her mistress's house, the house that might have been the end of Mira's freedom! I did not let myself think of other consequences for Mira or me. She and I simply, silently started walking away as fast as we could. In time, if we did not sprain an ankle or twist a knee, we could reach the Franciscan church-- the temporary safety of its walls. But that safety would be enough. Because now I would persuade Father Jerome to marry us-- if not for my welfare, then for Mira's sake. And we would go to Bijapur.

It was the first time I understood completely what it meant to Christians to have the four walls of a church as a sanctuary not to be rudely breached by civil authorities, even if the person was a criminal or any other person in flight. But in the Islamic world there were refuges, too-- including the houses of peasants or townsman, that were considered places of sacred safety for anyone who entered and cast himself upon their residents' mercy and protection.

Truly it was a long march Mira and I had undertaken, and I had to have us rest sometimes. But at last we reached the Franciscan church's side door, where we could enter without too much chance of observation

Father Jerome stared at us in shock. The Franciscan wavered a monent at the Church's side doorway. Quickly he ushered us in and had his deacon arrange privacy for Mira to bathe and do the best she could with her clothes. I gave him a hasty summation of what had happened at the Christian woman's house. How Mira had been bound for delivery over to Goa's authorities. How I had realized that only here, in his church, could I find a place of safety for Mira.

We stood now in the foyer, looking at each other seriously. "Father," I said, "for a month I have been wanting to ask you to consider marrying

Mira and me. But I had to be sure that the right time had come-- perhaps a time made necessary by the chances-- the imminence-- of Mira's capture." I took a deep breath. "The time has come, Father. Mira and I barely escaped unnoticed when the Christian woman brought soldiers to her door take Mira away. It is time for me to take Mira to Bijapur, if she will accept that-- as my Christian wife by your act of grace!"

I calmed myself and became more determined. "Father Jerome, I pleaded, "I need to have your blessing on Mira and on me-- the blessing of marriage. Christian marriage, yes, but I the Muslim will honor it absolutely, And it needs to be done today and now, if you can agree. You have to know that I will protect Mira with my life."

The priest held up a hand. "You need not say more, young man. I will do whatever I can to help you."

He gazed at me again in silence. Perhaps it was only a brief silence, but to me it seemed a year.

"Yes, Aziz Ahmad, I will join the two of you in Christian marriage." He paused. "I only have to ask that you will allow Mira to remain Christian if she wishes." He gave me another long look.

"I do desire it," I said-- "and have already assured Mira. In what had just happened this morning, God, be He Christian or Muslim, has spoken too loudly to be ignored."

I followed these hurried words with a deep breath. "Call it Destiny, Fate, Karma, or the Will of God. I love Mira and I am afraid for her. If you will marry us now, please arrange also for Mira to remain in your church for one or two nights, before the woman can bring Goan authorities to the church's door. Since it is the Christian woman who has breached the agreement she and her husband made with you, I think that for those one or two days, at least, she will hesitate to do anything rash."

He considered a moment. "Do I understand that, in view of the insecure position for you both in Goa, you plan to take Mira with you to Bijapur?"

I smiled back. "Yes, Father. Mira needs not just a husband she can trust, but a new life. I can arrange that new life in Bijapur. It may require two or three days to make all the preparations and be gone. I might even have my belongings and two or more horses ready by noon tomorrow-- or at least in readiness for a departure from Goa at first light the day after tomorrow."

Jerome followed my plans with a knowing eye. "I will go now and speak with Mira," he said. "And I do understand the need to move with deliberate quickness. If both you and Mira are satisfied, I will join the two of you in marriage within this same hour." And his kindly gaze was all the other balm I needed.

Except one. Mira provided that with her own, glowing smile.

It was tremendous to be able to sit on the bench in he church's foyer-- that familiar bench where I had so often sat waiting to see Father Jerome, or waiting for Mira to finish her Confession. My mind raced ahead. Before the day was over I would be Mira's Muslim husband-- which Islamic tradition sanctioned among "People of the Book"--and she my Christian wife as the Church's traditions-- though reluctantly-- did not contest. And one more compromise would be mine to offer, though Muslim authorities and families normally disapproved it. I would vow and certify that, if Mira so decided, any child of ours could be raised in the Christian faith if it was her desire. In that, her will would be my will!

Even though I did not expect Father Jerome or Mira to be cloistered too long in discussion, I recognized that he might still caution her not to be rushed into this marriage without considering the cultural differences to which she would have to adjust. But, I knew, Mira and I had often talked of such matters, and I knew-- so much had happened and been said-- that she was ready to take this leap of "faith, hope, and charity" as Saint Paul might have said! And this particular Muslim husband had had an unusually deep introduction to Christian ideas and customs before asking her hand in marriage!

Thus, rather than debating cultural differences at this last moment, I was already thinking of the practical side of readying ourselves to leave Goa and cross the Ghats. Perhaps even before nightfall this same day I could recover my Arabian horse and my armor, weapons, and Muslim clothing for the ascent of the Ghats. And, God willing, the next morning I would acquire for Mira a smaller Arabian horse, a little mare, for her to ride in comfort. I would find for her either a side-saddle or a regular one of the type that more experienced riders, Muslim or Christian, man or woman, might prefer. We would pack everything we could in bundles on three or four Indian pack-horses. I would arm myself not only with an archer's weaponry but muskets loaded and primed that I had learned to trust.

And finally, Mira, dressed as a Muslim woman I planned, for her protection on the long journey to Bijapur, would wear the shalwar and kamiz that would cover her from ankles to wrists, the duppata over her black tresses, and wear over these, whenever she was in public, the burqa. That last thing I knew, would offend many a Christian, but it would give Mira an anonymity that she might very well be glad of because it would mask her Portuguese features and relieve her from too much scrutiny by strangers and authorities who might block or delay our progress.

One problem only I saw as remaining-- to inform Monserrate of all these changes and gain, for me, his very important blessing.

Chapter 26

A Christian Marriage

Alone with my thoughts, I was almost frightened now. I knew enough about the Church's views, customs, and vows of marriage to know that I was asking for a very deep decision from the Franciscan priest-- and from Mira and me.

The vows of marriage were meant to last a lifetime, "'as long as you both shall live.'" Because priests understood this even better than a husband and wife, Mira and I would have to be fully serious and committed. And, unlike the practice among Muslims, no taking of a second, third, or fourth wife was to be contemplated-- not at the same time! Nor, among Christians at any rate, was a mistress or a variety of partners authorized. I was facing a truly decisive moment.

Meanwhile, already, I was making a range of decision about what needed to be arranged before Mira and I left Goa. And foremost would be the necessity-- both practical and moral-- of notifying Monserrate of my main decision and trying, in all good conscience, to receive his approval and blessing. That last would be, in many ways, the greatest demand that I would have to meet-- a moral dilemma almost-- given that he was the reason I was in Goa at all, had devoted myself to Latin and the Scriptures, and had so far been proof against an enemy like Castro! And now, not just standing here in a Franciscan church but walking back and forth in my unease, I could truthfully say that my greatest challenge would be to gain Monserrate's blessing.

And the priest returned-- with Mira. If I had any doubts about her agreement to this immediate marriage, they suddenly fled before the light in Mira's eyes and the glow in her cheeks. Even though, selfishly, I had expected her to say yes, I had not expected this marvel. I was all I could do to just smile and bask in her radiance, the more because she had had to borrow a rather plain woman's dress that was in no way a model of the bride's genuine love, if not a fine raiment. And be joined in marriage by a priest who as her Confessor knew her well-- and who, though no Muslim, had become my friend.

Jerome came straight to the matter. He began by having us stand on separate sides of him, while he held one of our hands in his.

"Aziz Ahmad Khan, you will not find in this world anyone who loves you more than this Christian woman," he said, "and who could be more grateful for what you have just done. I also assure you that I know your great love for this woman who has come into your life. May you always honor her and be kind, gracious, and quick to give and its corollary, which is to forgive. Do not marry her in order for her to serve you or for you to be critical and demanding. Remember that many an error and fault are what life brings to our paths, not something that was intended to wound or is the error or fault within your partner. Speak gently one to the other, not in anger, spite, or harshness. Do not let jealousy harden your heart, but think on winning trust yourself. Always speak the language of love and caring, and think of the other's needs before you consult your own. Live in peace with your wife and, if you can, with the world."

It was a noble speech, though not a part of the church's liturgy, and the food for thought in it amazed me. It also revealed the amount of understanding and love in the priest's heart that he wished to make his legacy, whether toward a man or woman brought up in the Christian heritage, or toward one brought up in any other tradition. As a Muslim, I vowed in silence that I would always gratefully remember this kindly man, Father Jerome.

When he spoke to Mira, it was in the same manner and in words and thoughts hardly differing. And when I looked over at Mira during some of the same phrases, I could see that she was absorbing his message, too. The glow in her face made evident the same warmth and gratitude that I had felt. Would she remember these words, as I was determined to do? I felt sure of it. Father Jerome's heart seemed to have reached out and embraced Mira's heart as it had encircled mine.

The good man led us to a railing at an altar in one of the church's alcoves, below a leaded window that showed Jesus of Nasareth leading his flock of sheep. Somehow that window, which was just catching the rays of the late-morning sun, was like a reassurance to anyone who knelt below it during the wedding vows that followed.

The priest stood calmly smiling before us and began the Sacrament of Marriage. I had found, upon reading the Latin text of the marriage earlier, that Saint Paul's instruction on "Caritas" were in fact perfect for the bride and groom as they were for the congregation to which he had written his letter known as "First Corinthians." For caritas could be translated as "charity" but here had the meaning of love as a deeply "caring" commitment between man and wife. I thought it wonderful to be united this way in the glow of a "love," a caring, that had already taken deep root in our hearts.

And when Mira looked up at me at the end of the ceremony I saw in her face a radiance that almost brought tears to my eyes.

After what she had experienced this morning, I felt chastened to remember how I had almost lost her forever to the world's cruelty and betrayals. But now, as if by a miracle, I had made myself truly her life's partner and defender. And there on her finger gleamed the golden ring that I had carried almost a month and thought she might never wear.

As we stood hand in hand for the priest's final blessing, Mira was still looking up at me with a glorious smile. I found myself humbled again by the fact that the day's events, strange and violent as they were, had brought about this miracle.

Yet already I was thinking of another event that seemed almost miraculous if I could carry it out. I must speak honestly to Monserrate now, not try to escape that task. To have his blessing would be difficult, I assumed. But I had no choice.

I had to take Mira away from Goa. Too many humiliating events had occurred here. There were too many bad memories. Mira had now broken a "contract" and would always be under the threat of arrest, imprisonment, deportation, or worse. Meanwhile my welcome at the Society of Jesus was wearing thin. It could not be good for either me or Monserrate if it became known that I would not become a Christian after all the favors given me, It was time to leave, and I now had a wonderful wife to take with me I could only hope that Monserrate would understand.

I was meditating on such thoughts when the Franciscan stood with is at he rear of the church and discussed our departure. He trusted me, I could see, to carry out my part of our bargain. Even though Mira and I were safely married, my self-imposed deadline for leaving Goa was still a desperate measure and much needed. But this Franciscan priest's confidence in me gave warmth and determination to my heart.

I had no doubt that this honorable man would keep Mira safely here at the church while I arranged our departure. Together and separately, the Franciscan priest and I had a bargain to be carried out, and we must not fail.

I hesitated a moment, realizing that I should give the priest a proper payment for his great service to our need. Another moment's thought and I realized that within the seams of my innermost garment I had diamond of quality that I had long reserved for some important exchange. Now surely was such a time. I cut open a seam and brought out the diamond, hiding it in my right hand until the time was right. As the priest led us to the rear door of the church, from which I could leave as usual without attracting any great attention, I placed the diamond in his palm.

"For alms," I said, "and to reward you for wedding us immediately and for protecting Mira these next two days."

Father Jerome stared at the stone. "Oh no, it has too much value!" As he turned it over in his fingers I could see that Mira was also staring at it. I had never tried to have it assayed, but I could guess that it was worth at least a year of substantial charities. I watched him put the diamond in an inner pocket.

If he had been anyone else-- with the exception of Monserrate-- I might already be regretting my gift and feeling perhaps that I had been a fool to part with so rich a stone.

But the good man seemed to have read my mind. "I know," he said, "that I seem presumptuous to accept this jewel. But I also know the importance of alms in both my religion and yours Aziz Ahmad Khan. It will therefore be my first care that a generous two-fifths of its value go in equal division to our two religions. The remaining three-fifths I will hold in trust for Mira, who at any time after a separation from you may receive her share. And this day I will put my hand to a document confirming these terms. Is it our agreement?" Mira and I, both in a state of shock, agreed.

"Now," he said, "prepare for your journey as man and wife. Mira will remain in my protection-- and my prayers. Move quickly, Aziz Ahmad Khan, and I believe you will find that your friend Monserrate will understand your need." And he turned to Mira.

"You, my dear Mira, will need to remain tonight, perhaps two or three nights, here at the church. I share your disappointment, as it may be, that you and your husband must be absent from each other these nights, but at least you will be safe."

Somehow the expectation of a first marital kiss had been ignored by both Mira and me for these few moments! But before either of us could frown or blush, the priest our friend turned and propelled me to the rear door.

"Get you gone, my dear young Muslim," he said with a smile. "You have been generous twice today. Generously you rescued the lady who is now your wife. Generously you have employed me to be your friend. Permit me to remain your parish priest in Goa-- and the lien-holder of your wife's dowry. Go to Brother Monserrate. I feel sure that he will understand the importance of this day and will forgive your desire to leave immediately for Bijapur."

He saw me glance Mira's way and hesitate to go, and he said, "I also gladly permit you to give your wife a brief kiss as you depart." I turned, yearning instantly for Mira. The priest's smile broadened as our embrace threatened to prolong itself.

"Very well. Out the door with you, Aziz Khan. Go, and return with good news from Brother Monserrate!" I stumbled out upon the street's paving stones with the pressure of Mira's kiss still lingering on my lips.

There could be no question of the challenge I would have tomorrow in showing Monserrate my gratitude but being firm in my decision to take Mira immediately away from Goa. And I knew that I would also have to tell him honestly that I could not see my way clear to Conversion.

I had to be prepared to give him this disturbing news after all he had done for me! But yes, I would take Mira to Bijapur.

I hitched up the belt on which my rapier still hung in its scabbard. Without the weapon at my side, even if I did not use it, the streets of "Golden Goa" would suddenly have appeared a great deal more threatening.

I could not resist thinking of four lines of verse that might construct a Persian quatrain, though not a ghazal. The "lines" I stitched together were as close as I could get.

"The setting sun seemed eager to embrace

The moon and plunge into the sea's delight.

Alas, but I the man could not behold

My bride nor fold her in my arms this night."

But the priest was right. I would do better to concentrate on what I was going to say to Monserrate!

Chapter 27

Confessing To Monserrate

My marriage that afternoon to Mira had left me happy and excited. Here we were. Mira and I, well and properly married-- by a Franciscan priest. Now, I told myself, I could truly rescue her from the claws and confines of Goa.

I searched my feelings. I knew three things, and would defend them to the last. I loved Mira, this Christian girl, with a pure and holy love. I had taken the most serious vows, trusting in God's justice and mercy. I had given my sincere acceptance of her right to remain within her Faith!

And now it was time to find Monserrate and 'confess' to him what I had done-- and why-- in the hope of his understanding.

The prospects did not look good. I had already made one big mistake, I had agreed earlier to "report" to my mentor and patron each week-- and now it had been two weeks since I had really spoken with him at all!

Besides, this night after dinner seemed the wrong time. Monserrate would be tired after his usual long day of study and teaching. Definitely the wrong time for me to walk in with the messages that I now had to give him!

I sat down at the Refectory table and tried to look preoccupied-- which with Mira I <u>was</u>. And maybe my mentor would just not see me here at all! And then, of course, when I least expected it, Monserrate appeared-- and did see me, and politely asked me to drop by his room after dinner. I really had no choice but to agree-- and let Monserrate have the initiative!

I quickly finished my meal and went to Monserrate's room. Something about his demeanor had warned me that this might not be a pleasant conversation.

When he opened the door and gestured toward my usual chair, the feeling strengthened. Was he for some reason playing cat and mouse with me? I was seized by a sense of alarm.

Monserrate sat in silence a moment. He cleared his throat and gave me a hesitant look. In the name of God, I thought, let him say what he had to say!

"I have to apologize, Aziz Ahmad," he began, "but an unpleasant subject has come up, and I am afraid you are at the center of it. I do not do this willingly, but the Provincial of our Order has taken me aside and asked me to discuss this with you." Then silence again.

"If it is that serious," I said, trying to measure his demeanor, "then it must mean that I have offended someone, and now you, dear Monserrate, are being held to account."

He shifted uncomfortably in his chair, then looked at me straight. "No, Aziz Ahmad, this is a different matter."

I studied his face. "We have known each other a long time, and you are my friend," I said. "Just tell me."

Again he cleared his throat. "Very well. It has come to the attention of the Provincial that you have been seeing a young woman, Aziz Ahmad. He reminds me that the behavior, while probably quite innocent, is against the rules of the Society, and that-- while you are not formally a Novice of the Society, nor yet a Christian convert-- it does complicate your living in our midst and engaging in studies toward the Novitiate."

His hands twisted in the little pyramid he made of them. "I am not overly concerned that you might "see" a woman, Aziz Ahmad, especially if it is a passing thing that had not involved you in an intimate relationship or become a matter of mutual ardor-- I am sorry, I should just say it-- or finds you falling in love!

He tried to smile. "I know how such things can happen. I also know how they can be blown out of perspective and become matters of rumor and innuendo. But I am not sure what to do in this case. You have too good a mind, are too devoted to your studies, and are not one usually to take risks of being noised about in such a way. But, Aziz Ahmad, it would help me a great deal if you would tell me honestly what is going on, If there are false charges or misleading statements-- indeed, misleading appearances-- then I can gladly defend you to the Provincial and, if need be, to our entire Society."

My mentor and friend regarded me hopefully. My mind, however, was already afire with anger and moving in several directions at once. One direction was to find out, if I could, who exactly had gone to the Provincial with these accusations. Instantly the name of dear Brother Castro had come to me. It was so like him! He knew as well as anyone that I was not in truth a Jesuit Novice-- nor was I a Christian convert! He also had reason deep in that devious, jealous mind of his to be rid of me and to hit at Monserrate in the bargain.

"So," I asked, "who was the conveyor of these insinuations to your Provincial? Could it by chance have been Brother Castro?"

But I had taken up too hostile a posture, and thinking twice, I should have realized that Monserrate would now feel he had to defend, not me, but his Jesuit Brother! But he was also truthful.

He reddened. "I am always sorry you have such a hostility to to Brother Castro," he said-- 'but yes, it was he."

I settled back hard. "Thank you for the truth, my dear Monserrate. I only wish Brother Castro were so truthful-- and so concerned with spreading accusations that could hurt me, you, and the morale of the Brothers-- and the Novices!"

But of course I knew that I had been 'seeing a woman'-- and had indeed fallen in love with her! And I should have been more aware that my nemesis Castro would find out. But find out what? Just that I was "seeing a woman"?? In any case, my relationship with Mira, even if her name was not yet known and bandied about, had reached a crisis point of which I had not been aware. This, I saw, was the beginning of collapse of my relationship with the Society-- and with Monserrate if I were not careful! For yes, this very night I would have to tell Monserrate about Mira. Even if I did not use her name I would have to admit our marriage-- and take the chance of embarrassing and terribly disappointing him.

But I did not want Castro to have too easy a victory over me. It would also be a kind of triumph over Monserrate! And Castro, unfortunately, was not above telling a useful lie-- or at least insinuating one.

I decided to go on the attack.

"As usual," I snapped, "Brother Castro condemns people he envies or does not like. True or false, his accusations disturb and upset people. And he walks virtuously away, presuming to be of great use to the Society of Jesus. Even if I forget about myself, and leave you in an innocent position, he has besmirched both of us somehow. I hope the Provincial will realize this and not let Castro's "story" became common talk or cause for some grand decision' by the Provincial-- that I must leave, which certainly I can do, and am now even more prepared to do-- and that you must be faced with remonstration because of your liberality and kindness toward me. Fie on Castro! Let him take his innuendo and insinuations elsewhere! I will be leaving in any case-- for reasons he does not have the imagination to fathom. I must let him have his big victory for the cause of obedience and decorum!"

I was out of breath, and stopped the tirade. Much more, and I would be savaging Castro again. The point was-- what more did I need to tell Monserrate? How much,especially did I need to tell him about Mira and me-- this "relationship" that Castro had so happily discovered?

But Monserrate was looking at me now in a different frame of mind. He must have realized that I was not denying the 'relationship' Castro had exposed!

Monserrate was my friend. He was trying to help me! And that left only one alternative, here in the privacy of his room. I would tell him everything!

"Please trust me and be patient," I said. "I will tell you all that you need to know."

I began with having seen Mira at the Armenian shop-- and guessing that something was wrong about the picture, and then finding that in essence she had been sold into a kind of slavery by her profligate husband. I told how the man had abused and abandoned Mira. And yes, I told him Mira's name-- though I asked him feelingly to keep it confidential and "in trust" for me. I told of going back again and again to the shop as I found out more about Mira's history and the humiliations she kept suffering- and seeing that Mira was really a good person who had been severely abused, was at her wits' end, and was desperate for some kind of relief. Then I told how the merchant's son had tried to seize her and how she had fled in the night, and that quite by chance-- and it was true-- I found her two days later walking in a strange street, and 'accosted' her, and made her realize that I was not an attacker and could be regarded as a friend.

I next told of Father Jerome and his small Franciscan church, where he ministered faithfully to a Hindu Converso congregation-- and was also Mira's Confessor and friend. From there I passed to the arrangement for Mira's "secret" lodging at a Converso house, and how the husband's wide and frequent travel left his wife in charge of the conditions in which Mira had to live-- like a prisoner, almost, and certainly like an unwanted burden! I told how I began to "see" Mira almost every afternoon when I could get away from the College of Saint Paul, and how we began to fall in love, and how after a few weeks we knew we were in love. But how, also, we had promised Father Jerome not to engage in serious intimacies but to get to know each other as friends first, and that, though it was difficult sometimes to resist the 'intimacies,' other than a few kisses, we did fulfill our promise.

And then came the afternoon of "Love in the Rain" as we later called it, when we were almost killed by a lightning bolt, and we knew now that our love could not be hidden any more. And then the night when I dreamed of Mira's being attacked by the Converso woman, and how I rushed the next morning and found that the woman had seized and bound Mira and was in the process of betraying her to the Goan authorities! But how I rescued Mira and took her to Father Jerome, and how he married us that same day in order to protect Mira and give me a chance to take her away from Goa and go to Bijapur.

To clear Mira of any charge of being married still to the man who had abandoned her and "sold" her services to the Armenian merchants, I then told Monserrate the whole story about the sinking of the great ship "Navidad" when rounding the Cape of Africa and how the so-called 'fidalgo" husband must have gone down with the ship, for he was manifested on it, and it never made landfall in Portugal-- and therefore how Father Jerome felt free at last to give Mira and me a proper Christian marriage.

And last I told how here I was, feeling guilty for not having informed my Jesuit friend and mentor of the whole business of marrying Mira, but wished devoutly to have his blessing on me and, yes, and on Mira and our wedding, and that I had planned to see him decisively the next morning, 'confess' all, and seek his forgiveness for waiting so long and leaving him in ignorance.

I had tried not to rush to a conclusion-- but there it was! Nothing more could be done but to await Monserrate's pleasure, and have hope of his understanding!

Slowly, awkwardly Monserrate got to his feet. He gave me a little glance that I could not interpret, and stood thinking. Then, after he had paced a few, slow steps back and forth in the crowded little room, he turned seriously to me.

"So," he said quietly, "I see that you will want to leave Goa now and return to Bijapur with your new wife. Frankly I do not doubt that you are much in love with her, your Mira-- and that you felt, I think rightly, that she had no future here in Goa. With you in Bijapur, she can have a whole new life. I may not be saying this well, but I doubt that your wife will find that adapting to Muslim culture will be as easy as you hope or as she imagines. Yet I still must give you credit for a decision that was a responsible and practical one in your circumstances in Goa. I hope the decision will be best for your wife's future and for your futures together."

I could see that he still was not happy with me for giving up my Christian studies in order to marry Mira and return forthwith to Bijapur, and that the pain of my not having confided earlier in him was strong. But

I could do nothing just now to reduce that pain. There was an ache around my heart, too.

I replied that everything he said made me respect and love him more--and to see him all the more clearly as my symbolic father, who had always been a source of instruction and practical wisdom to me. "Thanks to you," I said, "I will be proud to tell the world of the inspiration you have given me to become a scholar and translator rather than only a professional soldier like my deceased father-- may his soul rest in peace. And I intend, with the help of God, to become the kind of scholar and translator who, over the years, would be the friend of what was best in both Islam and Christianity."

Then I saw that it might be a poor consolation to Monserrate that the best claim he had made on me, with all these Christian studies and his hope of my Conversion, would be that I would hold Islam and Christianity equal or in some kind of balance in my mind. But I could not resist that thought of a balance, and we must go our ways with that much difference in our views.

No, Monserrate's faith could not be mine, nor mine his. But we did share a mutual respect as scholars and men of religion and, I felt, simply as human beings who must often "get on" together and sometimes work together as well. It would always be happier for me to feel that, for every Castro in human affairs, there might also be two Monserrates--or a thousand! But how I might convey those thoughts to Monserrate just now as my friend, just my friend, I did not know. I hoped it would be easier another time.

All in all though, now I felt a sudden calm after all the stresses of the day. As calm as the oarsman of a small boat that had almost been swamped and borne down by a great ship, but an oarsman who with desperate rowing had narrowly escaped. With my lone passenger, now my wife, I had slipped astern of the gigantic hull, endangered less and less as its wake diminished. Poor in wealth, perhaps, but rich in each other, we might still reach a safe landing. We might, as Mira and I would do a little later, look on this day-- indeed the last two days!--as the strangest yet most fortunate of our lives.

And Monserrate, too, suddenly surprised me with a smile. He stepped to me and hugged me! "Instead of wallowing in gloom I should be happy for you, Aziz Ahmad. I am happy for you!"

Then he held me at arm's length, observing me freshly. "Go with your wife Mira. Return to Bijapur! I may never see her. But from your own good qualities, I know you will take care of her and be kind to her." He was silent for a moment, then brightened again.

"Would you tell me about your Mira-- describe her if you can?" An odd request, I thought. But I would do it because I wanted him to feel he knew her!

"Mira," I began, is to me the most beautiful woman I have ever seen-- and is yet a girl of barely twenty-four years. I know that when I say beautiful" you will think, "Of course! That would be true in any new husband's eyes, no doubt!" And I laughed-- "I would wager a great diamond on the truth of my observation! She has, I would say, a special kind of beauty, as much internal as of her face and form. I would call it a "thoughtful" beauty, not a vivid, laughing one. She has suffered too much in life-- orphaned in childhood, sent off to Goa with half a dozen other young girls to become the wives, mistresses, or playthings of "fidalgo" worthies who would scorn a mere Goan Converso bride, married against her will to a fidalgo gambler and idler who used his whip on her back when she would not 'cooperate' with his drunken urges, then put out by 'contract' to an Armenian shopkeeper when her husband contrived to abandon her and sail for Lisbon, and finally forced to run into the night to escape the advances of the Armenian merchant's son. She was hiding, destitute, until I found her and took her to her Franciscan Confessor at his church!"

"Even now," I went on, "she seems to meditate sadly during many a conversation. She…reads much. She wishes to study Persian! But she is no sit-in-the-corner scholar or pedant. All the beauties of the world seem to delight her-- birds and flowering trees, fields of rice, broad beaches, setting suns above the Sea of Arabia, clouds that remind her of elephants or camels, dragons or sea creatures…." I came to a stop because Monserrate was laughing at me!

"In sum," he said, "you love her dearly! You must have waited eagerly every day to flee our College confines and be with her again-- perhaps atop the Monte Santo, the "Holy Hill," where we were told by Castro you had been seen deep in conversation with her." "Yes!" I said, exasperated, "dear Castro!"

"But," said Monserrate, holding up a hand to calm me-- "Now that I know the rest, I cannot blame you. She was charming, Aziz Ahmad, and young-- as you are. The rest of us are perhaps too old to remember such days when they were ours! And now I know, too, why you had rescued her and why you wished to marry her. In many ways she was so like you. Both of you orphaned in childhood, your face and neck disfigured by hot oil in a sweet-maker's shop, her shoulders marred by the cruel blows of a whip, both of you trying to find charity, love, and honor in a cruel world, and-- how shall I say it?--both of you intelligent, curious, eager to learn! Have I spoken truly?"

I sat silent, feeling mellowed in the warmth and glow of his new enthusiasm-- how he had spoken so few words, captured so many essences. The man was truly my friend.

"But one thing more," he said, "and the most important. I see that I was jealous of your Father Jerome, who was so fortunate to bring you and this girl together in the Sacrament of marriage. May God forgive me, but for a moment I wished that I had been that Franciscan priest! If I had known then what I do now, I would gladly have joined the two of you in marriage myself."

In the silence that followed his admission, Monserrate and I were reconciled.

"Remember," he said, "that I have promised you a place as my personal secretary if I am ever to accompany a mission of the Society of Jesus to the great Akbar of Hindustan. I will inform you if and when that mission is decided upon, and you may confirm to me what your decision it. But I will ever hold you in respect, regardless of your choice."

He studied me awhile. "You had said you wanted my blessing. Aziz Ahmad. I am thoroughly happy to give it. But it can be a sinple thing and does not need formality. If you will kneel here in the presence of God and Our Savior Jesus Christ I will give it now."

I knelt gratefully, and he placed a palm gently on my head as he made the Sign of the Cross above me.

"Wherever you go in this world, Aziz Ahmad Khan," he prayed, "I wish you the joys of true and mutual love with your beautiful Mira. Keep that love always shining and bright. If you are blessed with children, bring them up lovingly and well. Give of yourself generously to them all so that they may have trust, confidence, and contentment. Let honor and learning remain your inspirations. Be compassionate to the poor and neeedy. Be always honest and trustworthy in your dealings. Offer to God your the daily worship, gratitude, and praise owing to your Creator. Blessed be you now Aziz Ahmad, and your Mira also, with long life and happiness. All this I pray in the name of God, His Son, and the Holy Spirit."

And again he made the Sign of the Cross over me.

I stood up relieved and happy at last. Monserrate took both my hands in his.

"Though it is to my pain," he said, "I would have you leave me and leave Goa now. I will give you a message to show to any authorities you may meet. You will be named my message bearer, under my signed name as a Brother of the Society of Jesus. That should be enough if you are dressed as a Portuguese gentleman accompanied by your wife in the raiment of a discreet Portuguese lady, properly cloaked and veiled. Once you reach the peak the Ghats you will, of course, use your wisdom about all matters of dress and decorum, including having both Mira and yourself appareled in the Muslim way, she wearing the burqa. As you can see, I would not have anything go wrong with your journey to Bijapur. I trust as always to your careful judgement, my friend!"

"Now," he said, "Get you gone! Retrieve your Muslim belongings, your horse, your weapons, your clothing. Provide for Mira. Leave at earliest light one day after tomorrow." He chuckled. "Has your spiritual father now given you all the advice, and more, that you have stomach for?" I laughed and assured him that his advice was sound.

I was turning to go when he said, "Just one thing more!" He studied me a long moment, his face softening. Then he won my everlasting gratitude.

"Go with God, my son."

Chapter 28

Ghats And A Tiger

Two days later, at first light, Mira and I departed Goa. I rode Dandivan, my fine old Arabian, and had found a little Arabian mare for Mira. We led two pack-horses apiece, heaped with our belongings.

For the first period of the ride, extending from Goa to the nearby foothills of the Ghats, I followed Monserrate's advice that Mira and I should both dress in the Portuguese traveling style, with Mira's face almost completely hidden by a shawl. We would only change to Muslim dress, including an all-covering burqa for Mira, when we reached the crest of the Ghats.

Monserrate's final blessing I kept in my heart and prayers that morning. "'Go with God.'" We certainly needed that blessing. I had never ridden anywhere with Mira, and the journey though the jungled passes of the Ghats would not be an easy one.

Monserrate had also given me the promised letter identifying me as his "messenger" to certain Muslims in Belgaon-- which, by chance were my uncle and two assistants at their Sufi Khanaqah, in case we needed to have the signed letter when we reached the Portuguese checkpoint where Monserrate, Castro, and I had stopped almost four years ago.

As we rode, however, I felt wiser to avoid that checkpoint, whose captain and half-breed troops I remembered. I had questioned some persons in Goa whom I felt I could trust, and they had suggested a less well-known pass that, while rougher, would take us up the Ghats in fact more quickly.

As I rode ahead on my stallion and Mira determinedly followed close behind on her mare, I found the turning point we needed. Soon, as fast as sultry midday and a rougher path allowed, we were ascending the Ghats. I worried now that I had not been careful enough to think through the prospect of a night amid the Ghats.

Also, as the sun began its decline from the zenith, I saw clouds banking themselves in masses of white above the jungled valleys and ridges ahead. I had brought some lengths of heavy cotton cloth to make a kind of tent if we needed it. Now I was reassured that the lengths of cloth would keep us dry!

One thing I was not sure about was how Mira would react to the coming of darkness or the forest denizens we might face-- panther or tiger, to name only two. I knew how unwanted animals might be driven away by the sight of fire, noisy shouting, and varied weapons, for I had several times asked about it before and after that first experience of the Ghats.

I had expanded my range of weapons for the journey. Thanks to the newer muskets in Europe, especially in Germany and the Low Countries, for this adventure I had provided myself not only with my well-tried old matchlock musket but also with two "wheel-lock" muskets of the newer kind with the "match" replaced by a spring-loaded trigger and a key-wound wheel that would strike fire to primer in a small steel "pan." I had spent considerable sums, too, to acquire two of the newer wheel-lock pistols with their long barrels! I also carried my excellent old Mongol bow, a supply of arrows, and my trusted scimitar.

The rugged nature of our trail was as serious a problem as any. Mira tired quickly while she rode, even with a saddle cushioned by extra blankets. And I had forgotten how traveling a rising path among rock outcroppings and overarching trees would weary an inexperienced rider. Brave as Mira was about coming with accompanying me on this venture, she had to ask me more than once to help her dismount and stretch her legs.

In the first shadows of the late afternoon the Ghats began to assert more fully their mystery among long, sloping ravines and canopies of great trees. Mira looked at me more than once in a questioning but silent way, and I began looking for open forest spaces with enough level ground to make a good stopping-place.

I also considered again the piles of cloud that I had seen massing ahead. Rain would be another sort of obstacle-- and challenge. I only could hope that I had brought enough of those lengths of double-thick cotton awning for a makeshift tent. Of equal import, I had laid in some wood for starting an all-night campfire, and I would cut additional dry wood with my small but sharp hand-axe. If together we collected and cut wood, starting well before dusk, we could make a bigger fire for our protection.

I was beginning to be nervous when I heard the cheering sound of water-- as from a waterfall over rocky ledges and stone channels. Intermittent rain already had fallen on the top slopes of the Ghats, enhancing whatever falls already existed. The rush of water made me think it a good place to spend the night.

Approaching a stony ridge, we found a half-overgrown path. Evidently we were not the first visitors as we left behind the main upward trail! Soon we came to a substantial set of falls. In fact, there were several levels of ledges of water-smoothed rock that could be adapted as a campsite. After the main time of the Rains there must be roaring falls here! Best of all, we found a shallow cave of rock and, to our surprise, piled-up lengths of wood left there from large fires built on more than one occasion-- and, on a flat area within easy reach, enough space to hobble our animals. We gazed at what seemed like a direct gift from God!

As soon as we could unload our pack horses and relieve our Arabians of their saddles and gear, Mira started collecting light brances for easier fire-starting, while I cut up some of the thicker lengths of wood to build our fire high and keep it that way. It we slept alternate hours, we also could both keep watch. I also explained to Mira that, while we and the horses were fairly safe here, I also had the advantage of an open field of fire for my muskets in case of danger.

I tried not to specify the exact danger, but Mira's eyes widened. "You mean, like tigers?" I gave her a smile meant to be a casual admission.

But now I noticed that a light mist was sometimes stirred by the wind among the falls on both our left and right. Another "problem," something told me, especially if anything but the lightest breeze sprang up! But I reassured myself that we could keep fairly warm and dry, thanks to the cotton 'awning' I set up and some warm clothes we had brought-- even if wind-blown spray from the falls made the area a little damp. But with a pair of light woolen tunics for the shoulders and main part of the body, we could be happy. As the daylight began to fade, I kept using my hand-ax to bring handy lengths of firewood.

In less than an hour, when the sun had set beyond the surrounding ridges, we still had a kind of grey light around us, the effect heightened by the fine mist that also seemed to prevail now. Fortunately the coming of dusk cooled the air above, and the masses of rain-cloud subsided and wasted away. On the other hand, the mist around us continued to keep the air damp close to the ground. All that mist now bothered me. But there was an overhanging ledge at one place which could be turned into a comfortable place to sleep if we kept a good-sized fire going through the night. I soon had a decent fire laid and burning there-- although it would take a lot of tending to keep it alive in the mist-damp circumstances. We dragged together the packs that we had taken from horses' backs and piled the packs around our cave-space to keep us more warm and dry. We also piled on enough clothing to help keep the night's chill away.

Mira had opened some brass containers of food, especially cooked rice and supply of idlis. We warmed hands, faces, bodies, and stomachs together. But the mist still made for a bad night's sleep and a poor atmosphere for the lovemaking I had half counted on. Frankly I was feeling sorry for myself, which made for being a poor lovemaker anyway. Mira consoled me with a hug and a kiss-- but she, too, was cold and damp. We tried to settle down among our packs, while I worried about keeping dry my three muskets and two pistols. That concern, at least, was a a good, manly subject for the great Protector I was supposed to be!

Mira seemed satisfied that we had enough wood for the night. I tried doing most of the wondering and worrying. I also built up the fire a little, feeling better as we watched the flames. Sitting side by side, our bodies warmth under their layers of clothing provided a little more comfort after our long day and the hard climb on horseback.

But we had added a quick hour of working together to set up campsite and firewood, and I soon realized that Mira was sleepy already. So I volunteered to take the first "watch" of the several that we had agreed on. We assumed that keeping the fire burning with visible flames would be enough exercise to keep the watcher awake!

I could see and hear the horses stir occasionally as the mist wetted their coats where they stood hobbled in a small circle. I had covered their backs, especially those of my stallion and Mira's mare, with cuts of the awning we had brought, but I knew they were cold, and it bothered me to know they were stamping their hooves sometimes and shuddering the way horses did. At last I separated myself from Mira's warmth and went out to try drying them a little and rubbing them down. When I returned to Mira's side, I had just enough energy left to focus on keeping the fire going.

After a while I started nodding off, of course. I had to use more of our valuable wood to re-stoke the fire. Now I was really cursing myself for the mistake of choosing this place, and I used the old Mongol trick of cutting parts of my hands with small, shallow, but reasonably painful knife-cuts to keep myself awake. Somehow I managed to keep the fire crackling until midnight. But I did drift off to sleep now and then. I delayed waking Mira for her turn as fire-keeper, but finally had to surrender. Mira already had a pile of sticks ready at hand. Soon I drifted off with my head on her nearest knee.

It must have been two hours later when I came awake with a start-- and found that we had both been sleeping peacefully while the fire had turned to coals and almost guttered out.

But I said nothing to Mira and, after building up the fire again, tried to keep her propped comfortably against me. I wanted to see the horses and do something for them, but instead I could only listen to their stamping and occasional snorts. And soon I was asleep again-- until I woke, startled, an hour later.

I heard a horse's snort, much louder than before. Then another snort. Then another! There was alarm in those sounds. Soon it was seconded by stamping and whinnying. Somewhere out there in the night, beyond out little circle of safety-conferring packs, was a threat to the horses.

I quickly started rousing the few coals that had not gone out. Chips of wood by the handful restored some flames. I stared into the shadows. The horses, all of them, were noisy and restless now. I needed a firebrand!

Somewhere out there was an animal. It didn't take me long to guess what kind of animal! The horses kept up their sounds of alarm. Two or three whinnied. Slowly, by reflex, I found the cold steel of a musket with one hand and dragged it into my lap. I checked the primer. The whole weapon felt cold. Under my breath I cursed the mist.

A horse neighed. No, it shrieked! There was a struggle. I fanned up the low flames in front of me. The horses were drawn back into a huddle, except for one. That one had fallen to its haunches. With fangs sunk into its neck and great claws sunk in its foreparts an immense tiger was bearing it down, its blood streaming, its eyes wide with terror and approaching death. The horse was Mira's mare.

Without pause or thought I raised and would have fired the musket I held. There was a click, then silence. The primer had gone damp! Mira was awake now, staring at her little horse, at me, at the horse again, at me.... Shouldering poor Mira aside, I snatched up another musket and leapt to my feet in the half-light. And then I hesitated. Mira was straining to see in the flickering shadows.

Perhaps I was fortunate. I might have misfired and only wounded the tiger and drawn the animal's attention to myself and Mira! What might have happened then I did not dare contemplate. In any case I needed to reload powder and primer in all three of my weapons rather than daring to do anything rash. I could not save the mare from dying, and with luck the monstrous tiger would slowly drag it away into the darkness to be consumed!

The worst of it was that, while somewhat safe ourselves, the crunching of bones and other sounds of the tiger consuming its prey made a low but almost unbearable noise. I so wanted to kill that tiger! Mira sat stiff and anguished, watching the tiger, then my efforts to reload all our muskets and pistols. I could not bear to think that Mira and I were helpless. But in all honesty we were safer that way. I prayed to

Allah that he would bring the grey light of dawn sooner and dispel this maddening mist, so that I could better defend us.

Mira's fingers were locked on my shoulder, interfering with it, but I had not the heart to criticize her. She was staring with me at the huge beast that was devouring her little horse-- even while she repeatedly tried to look away. The tiger's muzzle and paws were bloody from mangling the poor horse's body, but its own coat and mighty forepaws had a terrible beauty that I could not deny. And I could not deny it its unlucky prey.

Quickly snatching from our declining stock of wood, I was at least able to build up the fire until the four pack-horses were well within its light. The tiger, too, saw the flames-- and began to labor at dragging the dead mare into the darkness where he best parts of its body could be devoured in peace. My thoughts raced. I found myself saying under my breath "Peace be upon you, gentle mare. Peace also to you, lord of tigers!" My words were like a mantra, for I was really begging that I and Mira could remain safe. I kept building up the fire, reckless about the small pile of wood left. I could not endure the darkness.

For her part, Mira could not bear the sight and sounds-- and with them the odors-- any longer. "Maybe you could… I mean… do something about the tiger," she whispered desperately. You reloaded and prepared your weapons, didn't you?" she asked. And then she buried her face in my sleeve. Her warm breath soon turned to tears. I sighed, glad to see that she was still so calm, though so distressed.

I had not just reloaded but had put my bow and arrows in readiness also. Now we would not sleep, but remain sentries though the night. And the tiger would have its meal by either light or darkness. The whole thing was just too terrifying and beginning to be sickening. For now the tiger lay sated next to the mare's carcass and, like any member of the cat tribe, was licking its paws. There in the half light of our little fire it was tidying itself! The pads of its big paws looked huge now. Mira had stopped crying but kept her eyes and nose buried in my convenient sleeve. Gently I cradled her head more comfortablyu against my arm. Other than that there was little I could do but hope she would fall gradually asleep.

Suddenly I felt a startled jerk and a little cry from Mira. I had fallen asleep again after an hour's alertness!

She shook me cautiously and pointed, her eyes wide and finger trembling. The tiger was not looking at the other horses-- or at us!-- but was slowly dragging away the bloody remains of its meal. It had already dragged the mangled horse a dozen paces away, down the slope of the shelf of rock. The remaining horses-- and we two, perhaps, had been saved by the meal that had assuaged the tiger's hunger! At least for this time, until dawn.

I checked the three muskets. I almost stood and raised one. But Mira pulled me down. "Can't we just wait and see if that monster slinks away-- or falls asleep?" asked my sensible wife.

I grimly studied her face in the dim light. "Perhaps you are right," I finally said. "We might do better, once the tiger has disappeared or stopped at a distance, to rouse ourselves and proceed to re-saddle two horses and re-pack the other three while I keep a close eye on the beast." I thought awhile longer, watching the tiger at work still dragging the dead horse farther away. Only if the striped beast turned to approach us would I have to kill it-- or fire a shot or two to discourage it! But then to reload!? Would I have enough time-- or the steadiness?

I gave Mira a look that I meant to be encouraging, but still hesitated. If we could just get through the night, maybe with daylight we could at least make noise enough to persuade the tiger to remove its prey farther-- or simply to retreat. A couple of pistol shots in the air might have the effect. But just banging brass items together might achieve as much and not waste any pistol shots! The pistols, in any case, were too lightweight to do much damage to the tiger. I sighed. Every move was a risk. All I knew was that, with the daylight, we would have a chance to re-saddle and re-pack. Then, with the tiger still digesting its meal, we might move slowly, safely away.

I gave Mira a look-- and managed a little excuse of a smile. "We had better wait until sunrise. Maybe pray a lot!" She gazed back in sudden misery. She was almost too fearful-- and exhausted-- to talk. But I took her hands in mine and started to pray-- in Portuguese, so she could join me! I cannot say that God "heard" us and gave any sign of approval or pity. But somehow we felt better. And now, with light creeping into the lower edges of the sky, we saw the dawn coming.

Perhaps it was God who heard us praying-- or the tiger! In any case the animal, now near a stand of trees, lifted its head to gaze at us-- and moved off along the trees.

"Rattle some things!" I urged Mira. "Metal against metal! I will do the same. Animals in the wild are said to feel more fearful than annoyed when they hear busy sounds! And if the tiger starts to return, well-- make a bigger din!" And we began to strike metal upon metal, gun-barrel upon gun-barrel! And I stared into the cluster of trees, and could not see the tiger. I gained courage. "Keep banging!" I said mindlessly.

While Mira did that I quietly began pulling our things together and reloading our horses. Especially I reprimed my weapons and placed them where I could snatch them up. I peered into the grey light before sunrise, and looked for the tiger. I still did not see it anywhere!

Half an hour later we were ready to leave. "Insha'allah!" I said under my breath. "God Willing!"

Still no tiger! We slowly mounted, looked around one more time, and slowly but decisively-- both in silence-- returned to the main trail we had left. Several times either I or Mira looked back, our gazes sweeping the trail and the forest. The tiger, by the mercy of God-- or Allah-- had allowed us to go our way!

An hour later, as the sun crested the ridges eastward, we were still moving swiftly. Only one sacrifice we had made to the god of tigers, if there was such a god. Mira's little Arabian mare.

I stole a glance at Mira. She was pale and tense, keeping her thoughts to herself. I knew she had loved that little horse which without the slightest complaint had carried her so far, only to die.

I reined back to console Mira. "It was almost," she said in a small voice, "as if it were God's punishment of me when our wonderful tree was destroyed, now to kill my little mare because of my presumption in loving you."

Bringing our horses to a stop, I leaned and kissed her. "When I have come close to death I have also wondered if it were God's will," I said gently, "But when I am reasonable I do not think so."

She sighed. "No doubt you are right, dear husband. But still it seemed…a strange coincidence."

"But not because of your love for me," I insisted, "or mine for you."

I kissed her more lingeringly and held a finger under her chin until she smiled back at me.

My Arabian, Dandivan, seemed grateful for the touch of my spur that allowed him to pick up the pace again.

Chapter 29

Deccan Day, Monsoon Night

With each hour, and the rising sun, we progressed eastward. Traveling at last on more and more level ground, surrounded now by smaller trees and lighter growth, we were approaching the end of our crossing the Ghats. We had survived that terrifying night and found ourselves riding in the glow of a clear day's sunlight.

Like Mira I had kept thinking about the tiger. But now it was a kind of bad dream, a nightmare that the tides of life and change would slowly wash away. I forced the lingering visions from my mind-- at least for the present.

Sent by some cruel miracle, or frightening us only by chance, the tiger had worked its magic and gone away. Yet, even a month later I would find Mira in tears one evening. She was crying over the death of her little Arabian mare. I gently held her until she could again banish the images of horse and tiger from her dreams.

The morning just now was fortunately bright and cloudless, and I tried to change the mood. "I am always thinking," I said, that Allah, in His mercy and compassion, has led me to you. Now I know that it is true."

She silent awhile. "Thank-you, Aziz Ahmad. You have a way of making me feel better even in dark moments. I promise to be cheerful now."

I decided to focus our thoughts on the Deccan. "A fairly large village lies between us and Belgaon," I said. "It is the same village where I first, almost four years ago, began my journey down the Ghats with Father Monserrate and an annoyed Brother Castro. Perhaps we can stay in the village tonight."

I paused. "The sky is clear now, but the monsoon with its thunderclouds will probably return in the later afternoon or night. I am sure our Deccani farmers will be glad for the downpour, even if we are not."

Mira sighed. "It is all right about the Rains. I am used to them. And everything seems to be very dry around us. If the stands of trees around us could talk, I am sure they would agree with the farmers!"

For myself, I had just seen a flight of green parrots settle into the tops of a stand of sal trees. They reminded me that since I had left the Deccan I had not seen many birds I recognized, other than the commonplace mynahs and crows. Now I would be on the lookout for the plump rollers and long-tailed flycatchers with their aerial displays and the low-voiced koels that celebrated the coming of the Rains. And as the stands of trees thinned, the rough country above the ghats became more and more an open plain. I told Mira how the countryside would change, and how memories were coming back to me.

Soon, as we passed through a good stand of trees along the course of a small stream, Mira asked if we could stop and rest in the shade. "You know," she said, "I really feel the need of a bath, and there are enough small trees and bushes trailing along the stream to give us some privacy."

I listened to the stream splashing among some rocks and saw tracks where deer had come to drink. The sunlight glittering here and there in the water made me think that a bath was not a bad idea. Soon we had hobbled the horses a little way from the stream. Tigers, fortunately, we could forget about in these environs.

I proceeded to tell Mira about the ways that ordinary farmers and laborers, both men and women, often provided for some extra personal privacy. I explained to her that bathers would go into the water, or even bring it up from a well and pour it over themselves while dressed in the day's clothing, but would meet the need for decency by slipping a dry garment over the wet ones, then remove the wet clothes and dry them without dislodging the fresh, dry ones-- the drying done, if the farmers or laborers were men, often by wrapping all or part of the wet clothes into a large turban to guard against midday sun.

Mira announced with an accusing grin that if I thought the two of us would be "more decent" that way, she would certainly comply. With our backs turned to each other in mock seriousness, we proceeded into the water a little distance apart, draped dry garments over some convenient limbs that hung over the stream, splashed about awhile, and then drew a dry piece or two over our wet things. I had noticed, without comment, that Mira had added to her dry pieces a large Portuguese shawl of fairly heavy, opaque fabric. Thus we performed our ritualized "privacy."

Amid laughter and some fumbling we succeeded. "See," said Mira, turning to face me with the Portuguese shawl fetchingly displayed, "all clean and decent!"

I looked her up and down, and cast judgement. "I do like the shawl." Which brought forth an instant blush. Then a grin.

Standing at the water's edge we embraced, laughing. I kissed her face, shoulders, arms, and hands in turn. She took my hands in hers to keep them from wandering farther, and planted a firm but lingering kiss on my lips-- then giggled, slapping my chest, and pushed me away.

"No more of that!" she said, "if we are ever to reach this village you talked about." She added, however, a conspirator's gaze. "I shall reward you later."

"You had better keep that promise," I retorted, "or I will have to demand satisfaction! "And" I said, looking around at the stream, the trees, and our horses-- "you are fortunate that I did not insist on my conjugal rights here in front of our animal companions, give or take birds and monkeys!"

"Oh yes," laughed Mira, "we certainly would not wish to embarrass any birds or monkeys!" And with this and other banter we soon remounted and rode onward.

Our bathing, in any event, had put us in a better mood and helped us put the affair of the tiger in a less distressing frame of mind. We could look forward again, not backward.

The day was becoming hotter, the air heavy and moist. First came white mounds of cloud, then darker hues that massed behind us and spread inland. Fewer and fewer clumps of trees provided their shade. I picked up our pace, but only so much that it would not be too tiring if we rode steadily.

Cloud towers were massing overhead by mid-afternoon. With Mira still riding behind me on Dandivan, I pushed our horses harder toward the village where I knew we could spend the night. The monsoon rain could start seriously at any time. Being in the open on horseback would not be a good time to arrive at the village-- drenched, tired, and strangers to the place.

I tried to remember the location of the banyan grove where I had stayed overnight with Monserrate and Castro before our early morning departure-- so many months ago-- for the Ghats and Goa. The semi-darkness of the banyan grove and our efforts to pack our horses and be gone before sunrise now lingered with me as distant memories.

Now, with Mira as my company, I worried about the lack of structures giving protection against the sun, wind, or rain-- except for a handful of rickety stalls for horses. Merchant riders and their attendants were expected to erect tents and provide for their own protection, if they were not to sleep merely rolled up in blankets on the ground!

The sun was sinking toward the horizon behind us. It seemed to be weighed down by the massed weight of the clouds above it. Meanwhile the clouds issued rumbles of thunder while they expanded overhead, hoarding their rain for the moment when there was to be no holding of it longer.

Mira half turned behind me to watch the lightning play within the cloud-caverns before each rumble of thunder sounded. She leaned against me from her side-saddle position just behind me. She put her arms around me and squeezed. "You are thinking, my silent husband that we will be caught in a pouring rain, and there is no convenient rooftop awaiting us!"

I laughed. "Exactly, dear wife. Soon I will not even have to think for myself-- let alone finish my mental sentences!"

"Consider it a boon," said Mira. "Thinking can be a hard business. Better to share the burden with someone more talkative, like me!"

I moaned. "Very well, smart one. So tell me-- what am I thinking at just this moment?"

She assumed a mock-judicial gravity. "You assume that we will most likely get very wet before we reach this village ahead, but, whatever our lodging, we will quickly fall asleep exhausted."

"I am thinking of having to put us up, wet to the bone," I countered, "and lie awake in some horse-stall with a leaky roof!"

"What a charming tale!" she replied with a laugh. "As if we were Joseph and Mary, finding that Bethlehem in those days had no room left in an inn, and we would have to summon up a stable!"

I picked up the lead. "At least you will not be some pregnant lady about to give birth under your leaking roof!" But I hesitated to take the figure of speech too far. "Let me just see if I can find us any sort of room at all!"

"And not being either the Holy Mother Mary or a pregnant lady," said Mira, "I have at least married a husband who, if he finds us a room, with or without leaks, I will have to thank him in a manner most grateful."

"That," I said, "is a thought well worth the challenge!" I rode forward more jauntily, tolerating the storm-clouds.

Then I remembered that Mira would need to arrive in the Muslim fashion, covered from head to foot as Muslim custom required. I sighed to think how a Muslim man was expected to ensure that his wife would arrive in all places covered like a secret, contraband possession. Wet or dry, we would have to arrive in the village in such a style!

I gave a glance over my shoulder. "Well, dear mind reader, would you care to have another sortie into what I am thinking?"

She looked back studiously. "About?"

I grinned. "See. You do not know everything I think!"

"Something serious, I suppose," she said, mulling it over. "Oh! You mean that I am to arrive as a proper Muslim wife! Or at least," she added, "as a proper Muslim's wife!" She mused longer. "And I had better, very soon, cover myself completely so that you, master, may not be embarrassed or humiliated!"

"Exactly," I said. But I really did not want to make fun of her. She would tire soon enough of this essential Muslim routine, the hiding of a proper wife behind either a house's walls or a head-covering fabric!

"I am sorry," I added, meaning it. There simply was no alternative, once in the Deccan, to be as Muslims of the Deccan. And the more so if we were also to be married by Muslim rites!

"I am sorry, too," said Mira seriously- "because I was half complaining. It was still my Christian way of thinking! And yet, as you, dear Aziz, have more than once explained, it serves many a good purpose of securing a woman's honor-- yes, and her real virtue-- in a world dominated by men! Why, even in Portugal and Spain, 'decent' women and especially wives are taught to cover their heads and lower their eyes and show proper respect for almost any man-- and bare-headed boys are allowed more openness than any woman!"

I saw her warming to the subject of a woman's subordination-- in either a Muslim or Christian world. She caught herself and relaxed. "But really, I apologize," said Mira. "You did not make these customs or rules, dear Aziz, and you do not defend them." And she touched my arm, then leaned and gave me a kiss on the neck.

"I will swathe myself in cowl and burqa," she added-- "the better to show that I love you, Aziz Ahmad, and care for your feelings as a Muslim-- and your reputation. Do not worry more about it."

And I said nothing, but smiled at this woman who, if she had given up much to be with me, had also earned my love.

A breeze had sprung up like the one the night before. With clouds gathering close behind us, their tops roiling upward, we paused by the roadside while Mira found, readied, and put on her cloak with the cowl-- and over that the burqa. We re-mounted in silence. The late afternoon breeze was becoming a brisk wind.

"Let the rain come or not!" announced Mira. "If either of us is wet through our garments, we both will be."

After another half-hour's ride, as I saw the mud-and-straw walls of the village ahead, the sun was sinking toward the horizon. But this was to be no ordinary sunset. The disk of the sun was about to be hidden by monsoon clouds. The wind had risen and was gusting around us. Disturbed birds were fleeing before the rain!

In a few moments we and the horses were caught in the storm. Soon we would be completely soaked.

But we had luckily reached the walls of the village, where a row of farmers were returning at a trot from their fields. Half naked in their tucked-up lungis and their turbans, the farmers were doing a surprising thing. They were loudly chanting a song to their Hindu gods in celebration of the rain! And Mira and I in our wet clothing? We were miserably bowing our heads and pushing forward as quickly as possible toward the caravanserai I had told Mira about.

My main objective was to reach the wide, roofed verandah that I remembered at the front of the caravanserai owner's sturdy house. The verandah would give us a chance to dry ourselves a little, while our horses stood hobbled in the rain. From my momentarily dry refuge I gave a hard look at the horse stalls set around three sides of the caravan-serai. Already I was wondering which of the stalls we would find ourselves occupying as we spent the night!

I quickly introduced myself to the Hindu owner of the caravan-serai. I knew I was not expected to introduce my wife! Besides, only one communication was important. It did not take me long to agree to the man's price for the use of a horse's roofed stall for the night.

As I turned again to Mira, I remembered our earlier banter on the road. "Joseph and Mary after all!" I announced. I only hoped that Mira, still not entirely wet enough through and through her layers of cloth, could appreciate the humor.

Our "lodging" for the night was, in fact, a set of two horses' stalls. Beholding them, Mira laughed. "At least we may not have three "Wise Men" disturb us in the middle of the night!"

We did our best to tether our horses outside. Then we used all the dry, fairly clean straw thatwe could find in the adjoining stall to make a bed of sorts for ourselves in what appeared to be the best protected, dry area-- a wooden platform at the back of the stall where some large bags of grain were stored.

Torrents of rain kept breaking forth and drumming on the thin roof of our none too grand sleeping quarters. Though we removed our wettest outer clothing, we were still damp and worried about leaks that might suddenly spring over our heads.

In a few moments we had replaced our wet clothing with dry items laid down fully clothed under a slightly damp layer of three blankets which I had had the sense to cover tightly! By this time I felt thoroughly tired, but gave Mira a smile as we lay on our backs and interwove our nearest fingers. Thunder rumbled somewhere overhead, and a new burst of rain came.

The night of intimacies that I had originally hoped for now seemed distant. "What a wonderful way to spend our first 'civilized' night together!" I said to Mira-- trying not to grumble, and failing.

Mira moved closer and held my hand tighter. My fingers squeezed back. But I had decided I would not press her for anything. I was regarding myself now as a noble protector instead of an impatient lover.

"You are thinking again. I can tell," said my bride.

I rose on an elbow. "And you can guess-- what?" I asked, feeling suddenly a little annoyed. Annoyed at whom or what I was not sure.

"That you are not any more relaxed that I am. Very likely we will wake up drenched, even under our blankets!"

My will to be noble had weakened. I was remembering how she had looked that morning wrapped in a wet shawl.

Mira was silent awhile. Then she pulled me down and kissed me long and gently. "Lie close to me, dear husband," she said.

Her natural perfume seemed to rise, surround me, and help me forget my annoyance with the rain and the odors of the stalls and hay and sacks of grain. I realized, almost with a start, that I could feel her heart beating.

She kissed me again, sighed, and edged closer.

Suddenly there was a huge flash of lightning and a crash of thunder that seemed to come directly over our heads!

We both jumped and lay startled.

Next came a rush of rain that pounded on our fragile roof. The roof started leaking in one corner, then in another. "Let's hope our elegant bedding stays fairly dry," I growled. "The horses will have a hard night tethered in the rain."

Another flash, another roar from the sky.

Mira responded this time with a distinct giggle. "God seemed to be making sure that we do not take our dignity too seriously!"

I turned on my side facing her, intent on giving her a goodnight kiss. Just…one…kiss!

A flash of lightning was followed instantly, as before, by a massive explosion of thunder! Mira could not suppress another giggle. She proceeded to kiss me very firmly. The rain continued pounding-- and dripping.

But it no longer mattered. The kisses I was receiving were more astonishing than any barrage of thunder. I surrendered to the delight I felt in this wife of mine.

The next morning I could not recall when the rain stopped. I was only certain that Mira and I had fallen asleep in each other's arms.

It was another day that began with bright sun in a clear blue sky. But somehow it was a brighter, more miraculous sunlight than any I could remember.

Chapter 30

Belgaon At Last

By leaving the village as soon as possible the same morning, we should be able to reach Belgaon before dark. I could only hope that my Sufi uncle, after a little surprise, would arrange a Muslim marriage for us on the following day. I would have to be very persuasive! But I had been entirely serious about having not one marriage rite but two, first Christian and now Muslim. I felt equal to any terms my uncle would set.

As we neared Belgaon my spirits kept rising. I told Mira as much as I could remember about my uncle and his Sufi khanaqah.

Mira tried to understand Sufism. It proved hard to explain. I had to use Christian words-- to explain how a formless God could entertain love for mankind and respond to human love in return. How, like Sufis, Christian men of discipline, learning and love would wish to worship God in deep sincerity. How Sufis went further than most Christians by assigning God qualities worthy of mankind's admiration and emulation-- even to the recitation of these qualities by Sufis as a set of ninety-nine "Names" of God, to be memorized and repeated in group prayer.

I explained how Sufis were not simply monks, withdrawn into communities that tried to stay away from all temptations of the normal world, but that they were known to travel from place to place seeking to spread the word about their enthusiasm and love for God. Some practiced their Sufi rituals only among themselves, but others sometimes "witnessed" to kings, giving rulers a holier and higher view of the Creator and advising them how to rule more justly and with more compassion.

Mira kept asking questions, convincing me that she really wanted to know how these men contemplated and worshipped God-- that "Allah" which in essential ways was but another name for the "God" also of

Jews and Christians. I could see that she wanted to understand my uncle and be able to appreciate his religion. She made me feel more and more proud of her and convinced that she would move deeper and deeper into the world of Islam, perhaps that she would actually convert at some point.

She was fired with enthusiasm now, as I was, to go straight to the Sufi khanaqah and meet my uncle. Everything seemed logical and in its place. While she would have to remain silent, her face fully veiled in the presence of men other than myself, she would know that I was explaining our presence to my uncle and asking him to arrange a Muslim wedding ceremony for us.

As I had hoped, my uncle came to meet us in the inner courtyard of the khanaqah. I greeted him respectfully, thanking him for whatever he could provide for us. With the palms and fingers of my hands together before my face I bowed to him. Receiving my bow with the same gesture he welcomed me.

But did he welcome Mira? That was, I suddenly found, a different matter. He tried not to look at her where she stood slightly behind and to one side of me, but he did steal a glance and then another. Then he grew blunt.

"The woman," he said, "is she Muslim?"

The bluntness took me by surprise, and I tried to stall. "Well, she… is considering it. I mean, becoming fully Muslim."

"But you say you have already married her in the Christian way? In a church. In Goa. A priest performed this… wedding?"

"Yes," I said, "but I feel-- we both feel-- that marrying in the Muslim way would bring us even closer together and give strength to our bond."

My uncle merely looked sceptical. He gave Mira's veiled face another look, this one more searching, as if he expected her to understand everything we were saying.

I quickly explained that she did not yet understand Persian-- or Arabic! But she was trusting me to teach her in Persian. "At the moment we speak to each other only in Portuguese. In Bijapur I will find her a teacher and…."

My uncle's face twitched slightly behind his flowing beard. His assessment of Mira, I felt, was entirely negative. Here stood this Christian woman married by Christian rites to a Muslim-- but no Muslim herself, and whatever she might believe, think, or feel only God knew!

Suddenly I wanted to protect Mira. I felt like a child confronted by some strange holy man. The holy man hardly understood my intentions-- and, to the extent he understood them, frankly disagreed. Mira was a mongrel, he seemed to be thinking, a person out of place and not especially desirable to have standing here in this Muslim place.

"I might tell you more about the reasons for our Christian marriage," I said, trying to think of some approach my uncle would understand and approve.

His gaze swerved back to me. "You spent some long time in this feringhi city of Goa," he said, making clear that the Portuguese did not particularly belong on our shores, "How long, did you say?"

"About four years," I stammered-- "just over three and a half."

"And you were doing…what?"

"I was studying Christianity under a Jesuit teacher. He helped me gain a knowledge of the Latin language in which the Christian "Bible" is written. I also learned a good deal of the Portuguese language. I learned much about the Europeans. I also came to the conclusion that…."

My uncle sniffed. "Yet your father's and forefathers' religion was Islam. You were not proud of our Muslim faith?"

I was feeling more and more foolish. And angry. Why was I being interrogated like this-- while Mira had to stand there like a dumb animal while its groom was being flogged!??

I explained, keeping the Persian words as simple, direct, and calm as I could, that of course I had pride in the religion of my father! But I wished to understand Islam better, and to do that I chose to study and compare it with Christianity!

What I got for my effort to explain was more of the same scepticism.

"And you spent three and one-half years doing this?"

I roused myself and stood taller. "Yes."

I had decided that if the rest of the conversation-- not to mention our relationship as nephew and uncle-- was to be on this level and in this tone, I might as well just be blunt. And by now I was determined not to apologize for Mira or for my intent to marry her by Muslim rites!

"And now you wish me to arrange for a Muslim wedding between you and this Christian woman?"

I started to take a deep, antagonistic breath-- but checked myself. "Yes," I said firmly, "that is what I wish."

My uncle smiled. "I see you have become more assertive-- and may I perhaps say, bold?-- since you and your friend… what was his name 'Raya?' … first came to Belgaon and spoke with me."

"Yes," I repeated-- not returning the smile. "I suppose that is so."

My uncle meditated a moment, holding my new "'bold'" gaze with his own. Then he surprised me a second time with a twist of a smile on his lips. "I see that my sister has conveyed something of her character to you."

I surmised that he meant Aunt Bibiji's tendency to keep her own counsel and even 'talk back' if it pleased her!

My uncle cast another glance at Mira. A long glance. He smiled again and shifted the look back to me. There was no point, I guessed, in his talking "to" a woman, Christian or otherwise.

"Very well," he said, "I will arrange this Muslim marriage for you and your Christian wife. How long do you plan to remain here? Have you a week? Two weeks?

The statements were a kind of challenge, but they did not find me unready now. "Thank you for the arrangements. But as to the length of our stay, I need to have the wedding as soon as possible. If not today, which is half over, then tomorrow. We-- my newly Muslim wife and I-- will then stay for a week. We will need some private rooms, or indeed a small house for that, because my wife is very tired after our long ride from Goa. I realize that you may not care to know more about her, but that is all right-- so long as she is given the respect due to Muslim man's wife. I did not wish to impose her presence for long on you or your companions of the khanaqah. The wedding simply needs to be soon!"

I waited. He was silent-- as though thinking what a burden and a bore that all this was going to be.

I decided to take the risk of pressing him-- and offer a material reward. "I really would like to have the wedding planned for tomorrow morning or, at the latest, tomorrow afternoon," I said. "Meanwhile, if you will discuss with your companions what lodging may be available for a week in the town-- somewhere respectable of course-- then I will be happy to pay whatever is necessary for that week's stay. And, of course, I will be happy to pay whatever fee the presiding mullah asks, if it is within reason, and to provide some payment also for the two required witnesses to the wedding. And you especially will have my sincere gratitude, Uncle-- besides a substantial gift of alms from me to advance the work of the khanaqah."

I could see that my uncle's mind was that of a perfectly good account-keeper and of a man who, however deep his spiritual commitment, understood the uses of money. But I had better stop before I had promised too much of that commodity!

"There is a seat here in the garden, just near the fountain," said my uncle almost cordially. "If you and your Christian lady are willing to wait here awhile, I may be able to return with answers about your ceremony-- and about the lodgings."

I thanked him with a precise salaam. He returned the salaam with newly dignified reserve and departed without further excess of words.

I turned finally to Mira. To speak ordinary Portuguese again, rather than my uncle's stilted Persian-- with the vocabulary that constantly tested my internal dictionary of that language-- was a great relief. The relief was almost as great as that attending my uncle's departure to consult with his friends.

Without worrying over the reactions any of the Sufi gentlemen who might observe us, I reached out and took Mira's nearest hand. Giving the hand a squeeze and searching out the questioning look in her eyes, I drew her across the garden with me to the fountain at its center shaded by the branches of a very large tree. I pulled her down to sit next to me on the ledge surrounding the fountain.

"Thank God that is over," I said, meaning it. "Perhaps tomorrow we will be wed-- God willing!" It was time to smile. "Tomorrow," I told her, taking both hands, "We will be man and wife-- both Christian and Muslim.!"

"I am sorry, Aziz Ahmad," answered Mira. "I could see your uncle questioning and lecturing you, and I could almost feel you stiffening and then becoming cool and resolved." She paused. "Do you want to go and look after our horses and goods, which we left with the watchman at the khanaqa's gate-house?"

I shook my head. "I just need to relax with your hand in mine-- and wish that I could see your face and have you lean your head on my shoulder." I, too, paused.

She calmly reached up, released her veil where it covered her entire face, and refastened it at one side that I could see her eyes. Her gaze first met mine, then flicked briefly left and right around the courtyard. "If anyone is staring," she said, "let them. I think, if my woman's thought interests anyone, that you have just endured much for my sake-- <u>our</u> sake! And if indeed your uncle has gone to rally his forces and meet our needs, which surely you must have asked in that calm but forceful way of yours, I believe we will have what we need and can soon enough be on our way to Bijapur."

She looked up, her graceful lips smiling, and added, "And I can soon enough give you a number of the many kisses I owe you."

I wanted to collect some of them immediately-- but remembered my severe uncle. I compromised by holding her fingers in mine while we waited-- and waited-- for my uncle or some messenger to put in an appearance.!

Eventually, to my surprise, my uncle and two Sufi colleagues appeared. I sighed. Mira put her veil back up. The three men stopped four or five paces away, trying only to look at me, not Mira-- who had freshly restored her veil to her whole face. The men looked me over and stole a few furtive glances in Mira's direction. It was not a convivial scene.

My uncle, however, without a smile or waste of breath, surprised me with a positive answer to my request for a wedding and a house! Probably I guessed, his ingratiating smile did not reflect his thoughts. No doubt he felt that my requests were at the lower depths of impertinence!

But yes, he said, rooms had been found for us-- for a week. Indeed, an entire small house not far away. The two men with him had friends who could arrange it. Then the best news. A local mullah who sometimes led the members of their mosque in prayer had been contacted, and he announced himself to be happy, given the fee arranged for his services, to wed us the next day after the noontime prayers! And yes, with my uncle were the two Sufis who would be our required witnesses. They, too, expressed gratification with the retainers they had been offered! My uncle's faint smile as we salaamed upon the three men's departure told me that he had counted up "alms" for the khanaqah besides, and that the sum would allow a small fee for his own services.

In fact I had anticipated the agreement on costs by arranging the sale of two more small gems in my possession-- gems as usual sewn into the hem of my Portuguese waistcoat. I took Mira immediately to see the house my uncle had arranged for. We quickly decided it would be fine. It had the privacy we needed after so many days in which privacy hardly existed.

It had been a chore to negotiate with my uncle, but at last, after the Muslim rites tomorrow, Mira and I could have a relaxed week-- Christian wife and Muslim husband-- without having to be put to further tests.

Chapter 31

A Wedding In Belgaon

It was already the night before the wedding I had demanded. But now-- crisis! Abruptly I realized that I had forgotten a very important part of the ceremony. Mira would need to be attired in the red-silk wedding clothes expected of all Muslim brides! Fortunately the next morning was not a holy day of some sort, so I had us rise early and betake ourselves to a shop specializing in such dress.

Mira thought it was very amusing that I had given no thought to her Christian wedding attire, so that she had taken care of it all herself! But Muslim wedding dress was more complex. It involved red shalwar-kameez pants and blouse matched with a flowing silk veil of red-- and several items of gold jewelry! Besides which there was always a lot of work for a "dresser,' or several of them! In the normal case there had to be at least one important female relative-- the mother! In fact I knew, though imperfectly, that several such female relatives-- grandmother, aunts, adult sisters-- as well as the mother would be expected to participate! And then there would be some necessary seamstress skills with needle and thread-- perhaps a family servant or two! And there would be women and girls required to apply henna patterns to feet and hands-- an expert task in itself! I ended the evening with a strong prayer to Allah, with more than the usual petitions and prostrations, and repeated the beggings and pleas in the usual prayer at dawn!

Poor Mira. Either she would have to be the one 'dresser,' or I would have to be that 'one!' With the jewelry I would do my best, but the henna I would have to foreswear. I almost went into a panic, and Mira had to smooth my fevered brow when I confessed-- while I conveyed us in a rented rickshaw with a driver who 'understood' my problem! Thus in desperation, I took us to a Muslim wedding shop in the main bazaar where at least the minimum of dressing could be managed. I hoped.

When we arrived at the shop in mid-morning, with Mira in her burqa, I tried to cover a fresh outburst of panic. The owner and clerks were all men! But the owner, after gazing at me as one would look at an idiot, went to the rear and came forth with-- his mother!-- who was distinctly not in purdah due to her age and family authority! The dear woman shook her head sadly, directed me to sit down in a corner, and took Mira to a back room that served as storage and alterations space. Mira threw me a sympathetic smile as she disappeared. I must have blushed several colors of red as the male staff-- all of whom, it turned out, were the lady's sons!-- gazed at me with barely hidden amusement.

About half an hour later the owner's mother returned. Where was Mira? But lo, she followed in a sort of grand entry, dressed all in elegant red <u>and</u> the necessary' jewelry that might-- no, that would!-- come near ruining me financially. She did lack the henna decorations, but displayed eyelids adorned with a liberal application of black kohl powder. When her gaze flashed its beauty at me, even under the red-silk veil, I could swear that everybody saw it and was reduced to silence. How was I to thank the owner's mother, who was wearing a very self-important smile? <u>She</u> did not require a veil and was too much an authority to care, because all the men in the shop, other than myself, were her sons! Only one problem remained-- or two. What would I need to pay? And clearly Mira would have to wear her burqa as she returned through public streets, beautiful as a princess, to the Sufi khanaqa-- and would have to continue wearing her finery, under her burqa, until the afternoon's marriage had been accomplished!

And then the largest blow to my male prestige. The commanding lady, fixing me with a frown, asked me why I had not discussed "Mahr" with my wife to be! Suddenly I felt sick and must have looked it. "Mahr" was a husband's pre-agreed gift to his bride, usually a fairly substantial sum of money, as a kind of assurance that, if he set her aside-- divorced her-- she would have basic funds to live on-- not perhaps to live well, but to maintain her dignity, especially if she had little or no support from her natal family! Needless to say, I froze. "You had better decide and promise it to her <u>now</u>," said my fierce questioner, "or I will send my eldest son to your wedding to inform your mullah of your neglect! Trusting the lady to do exactly what she threatened, I took Mira aside, explained Mahr, and gave her a figure that made her gasp. In no way would she expect or accept that much, she told me! Then she asked to have some time to contemplate the subject. Since we were speaking Portuguese, I turned and told the closely watching lady, in Persian, that we had settled upon the sum I had proposed. She shook her head at my incompetence, and seeming wealth, and announced the price of her dressing services. Needless to say, I paid. And as the lady helped Mira into her burqa, I had to endure her continued smile of victory-- or was it, of natural feminine superiority? Though I managed to get us back to the khanaqah with an hour to spare, I was near to collapse!

As they had promised, my uncle and the other Sufis at the khanaqah arrived in an agreed-upon room. The men paid no particular attention to Mira, whose burqa and demeanor would have discouraged it in any case. I made small talk with them as we awaited the arrival of the mullah who would preside over the wedding. Meanwhile these men of religion seemed to be more interested in my survival in the fabled city of Goa, and to hear a tale of my experiences there, than to discuss my marriage!

I wanted to review what Mira was to say as her part of the marriage rites. But she was already sitting apart from me and my uncle and his Sufi companions who had agreed to be our two required Witnesses. Finally I decided just to go and talk to her, since she was sitting, though within hearing distance, quite alone. Mira held up a slender hand and touched my face, making me realize how steady and cool the hand was. A sudden calmness returned to me. Mira's love pierced the cloth of her burqa as if it were the lightest of cotton, silk, or spiderweb! I felt humbled. And she began to repeat in a low voice, as I had explained twice earlier, how the wedding was to proceed!

"'Ijaab' is the basic groom's statement," she intoned, "when he proposes marriage to the bride-- three times. 'Qobul' is how the bride says 'I accept', which is her response three times. Two formal Muslim witnesses are required to hear each occurrence of Ijaab and Qobul before the 'Nikah', or written Agreement, can be signed by the groom and bride. The mullah recites certain Surahs of the Qur'an relating marriage, and he instructs groom and bride to provide Ijaab and Qobul. The bride may add to "Qobul" some word or phrase, such as the often heard

'Insha'allah' meaning 'God Willing' or 'As God Wills.'" And I knew Mira was smiling now, because she had mastered my tutoring!

In fact, she had gone beyond it. "Do you terribly mind if I ask about one more thing? Of course I nobly agreed in my male egotism. "Do I have to specify a Mahr?" I sighed. "No. It is a custom not often observed. But I have made the promise separately to you, and I won't go back on it." She was still thinking over a response when the mullah arrived. I returned to my seat directly facing the mullah.

The gentleman wasted no time getting to the substance of the marriage. He had Mira and me sit a distance apart but close enough that we could hear each other's words, make prompt proposal and response three times, and be clearly heard by the two witnesses. Then and only then, he reminded us, could we sign the written Agreement or Nikah and be not only acceptable to Allah as man and wife but be recognized as such throughout the Muslim community, the Umma.

Mira had assumed a proper dignity from the first. The slight adjustments in the angle of her head told me that she was listening intently to the verses of the Qur'an recited by the mullah, and her three responses in Arabic to my three times repeated proposal she pronounced carefully, clearly, and with nice precision. I felt extremely proud of her, especially when I saw that the mullah, after her third response of "Qobul" gave Mira a glance that showed her performance had impressed him.

He had not asked about an agreement on Mahr.

The ceremony was everything I could have asked, especially as Mira in her burqa was more than a little isolated and had to listen very intently in this strange environment. But she had done brilliantly with the few phrases she needed, and I was immensely proud of her.

When the ceremony was finished I expressed thanks to the mullah, my uncle, and the witnesses. I could then excuse us.

I helped Mira put on her burqa again, although I hated to cover her beautiful wedding-wear-- or the loveliness of her face and form-- so soon after her marriage. Quietly, however, almost whispering it, I told her feelingly how well she had done.

We returned to our rented house in quiet satisfaction. Fortunately the little house was very near, and Mira was not bothered by the glances of many strangers. But I still felt some uneasiness because the bareness of the house now disappointed me.

However, I did have a present for her, which was a small but elegant gold casket for her wedding jewelry and any other valuables or choice keepsakes. After helping her remove the burqa, which at least had the advantage of being new and of good quality, I led her by the hand to sit on the edge of our marital bed, which I had supplied with a new mattress of more than the usual thickness and softness, as well as a coverlet with abstractly woven floral designs. And though she had seen me lay out these new things, she now looked at them with fresh pleasure while we sat together.

But what I myself saw when I looked at her-- with beauty contained and made greater by her red wedding apparel, her wonderfully woven tresses, her golden wedding jewelry, her kohl-darkened eyelids, and the glossy red of her lips and fingernails-- was a heavenly Peri come down to earth just for my enjoyment, my admiration! She was now twice mine, by both Christian and Muslim rites-- and so framed in my love's vision, that I could do nothing for several moments but sit in astonishment.

And now the two of us, who had already shared so much, and thought that we knew each other so well, could explore all the wonder of it again-- those parts of our experiences together that had surprised and pleased us from the start, and those that now in greater wisdom and intimacy we could remember even though they had been painful or difficult! But I had no doubt, from these few moments forward, that we had been blessed by God, call Him also Allah or by any other name of worship-- and that, Insha'allah, we would continue to deserve and have His blessing and live by His Truth.

Then, suddenly, I realized that Mira was studying my face as I had been studying hers, and something like my thoughts must have been flowing through her. For her smile, silent awhile as was mine, had in it a gratitude and admiration that seemed to match and rival my own. And I took a deep breath at last and said calmly "I love you, Mira," and she, without seeming to need breath at all, said "I love you, Aziz Ahmad Khan."

Have I said that I also bought and secreted away a variety of edible things I knew she liked? These small but fragrant gifts included dried fruits and nuts and elegant small rice-cakes and other sugared confections! All these I now felt that I could offer her, or display to be later enjoyed. And when she saw them, Mira's eyes widened and she said in awe, "I did not expect this elegance, even from such a wise husband as you, dear Aziz!" I had twice come close to making her marriage a farce, and did not feel wise at all. But I was happy to bask in her gratitude.

Then she said, "I have my own gifts for you, dear one. Some will be spiced or unspiced foods, because I know of your love for curries and saffron. Some will gently light up our nights for a week with wicks dipped in essence of sandalwood or champa flower. Some will be other simple things that make a lovers' bedroom a place of comfort and rest. But best of all my gifts for you, my love, is one that will inform you specially about the depth of my desire for you and the long-constrained passion in which I have yearned to embrace you!" To the last of which she added both a smile and one of those unspoken messages of the eyes that told me more than needed to be said-- or, perhaps, could be. And I did not ask for enlightenment but only regarded her with delight.

What lovers say and do is not, really, what they would eagerly lay out before the world to be read or seen. These special things are for them to enjoy in privacy and contentment. And so it would be with me and with Mira this particular afternoon and for the several days and nights that followed.

Still, we did not rush into embraces, but tried this or that item from the array of foods and sweets that I had chosen for us. Meanwhile I could see that Mira was as reluctant to remove her wedding garments as I was regretful to see them folded and laid away for the purposes of memory. Then, too, we were waiting for the shadows of evening when our intimacy would be made the more elegant by fabrics that hid as much as they revealed and by the perfumed candlelight of Mira's promised sandlewood and champa flower.

Fortunately we had a small table that was not too badly proportioned, together with two chairs with fabric-woven seats that I had found for us in a nearby bazaar. These and a vase of cut flowers added just the aura of homely pleasures that our wedding justified. With one slightly taller candle to light both our faces and the contents of the table, we could dine both this night and the several to follow with some show of the grand manner! And we both laughed to think that, were this in Goa, we might even have had some performance of the Portuguese viol or flute to entertain us-- or, I offered, the pungent voice of the three-stringed rabab.

Then, when complete darkness had descended from sky to earth, except perhaps for glimpses of a three-quarter moon among the nightclouds-- or, said Mira, if the monsoon were not to drum so hard on our roof that we feared its leakage and collapse!-- we could follow our desires and spend our night in a husband's and wife's forgetfulness of what the rest of the world might either do or care!

We were also anticipating the baths we were going to in our small place, but with the privacy now to enjoy them-- as Mira reminded me of our joke when we bathed at ths stream in the open a few days earlier-- "without the birds and monkeys watching us." And now were going to enjoy having even a small kitchen area with a charcoal-burning, clay-walled stove that occupied a corner, because that small stove would heat the water for the baths we would take using water from a well outside that served ours and several other houses.

"How nice," said Mira as we built up a fire in our highly inadequate stove-- "A servant's kitchen, with which I am already familiar from my former employments!"

I smiled back indulgently from our table with its single candle. "And I am the servant to match you, as it was I who brought in our week's supply of charcoal with which you have built your servantly fire!"

"And," I added grandly before Mira could retort, "I promise baths for two every night for a week!"

Mira laughed. "And for morning, and for possibly noon, too!"

"At least," I added, "until our supply of charcoal ceases."

And it was not long before our water was warm enough. Soon, with the help of a large copper basin and some smaller and larger towels, our fatigue from the long day was washed away.

Clad now in light robes of softest cotton that I had chosen one day when I was in a mood for simplicity, we began to woo each other.

"Imagine it is a palace," Mira advised, "and we can pretend to live a few days like traveling royalty."

I grabbed the Portuguese hat with the feather that I had brought from Goa, added the rapier in its scabbard, and struck a ridiculous pose. "The power of imagination conquers all!"

Mira turned laughing and kissed me, pretending to swoon in my arms. I returned the kiss with one more grand.

The shadows from the tiny candles that Mira had brought kept dancing on the walls.

Slowly this first night of our Muslim marriage our lovemaking became a wondrous thing. We were both still feeling a little subdued and hesitant at first. I was especially gentled and awed by this woman who had accepted so much to be with me.

But soon, facing each other in honest readiness that searched each other's eyes and found a home there, we moved from gentle overtures to delighted kisses and embraces. Spurred by a longing that no longer felt hesitation or limit, our excitement reached its peak together. Sighing and murmuring, we lay subsiding together a long time, our faces close as breath.

And I said, finally, "You are now truly my wife."

"I did not lie," I added, "when I told you I have never known another woman. You are wonderful." And I told her that even now she was a mystery to me, and that I hoped she would forever remain somehow mysterious so that I would never want to stop unraveling the delight I felt in her.

"Even if I were the most masterful of poets," I said, "I would never be able to give full meaning to my feelings in this unpoetic world."

She seemed to mirror my mood. "In no day of my life had I ever known a man like you, Aziz Ahmad Khan. You rescued me not simply from a forced servitude but from despair. I am so much changed, so awed by my good fortune-- your kindness, your gentleness, your passion-- that I almost do not know myself."

"Be patient with me," she amended, "while I find myself again, shape myself to my new life with you, blend into the currents of this new world. Finally my old self will be another person, a tiny fragment of my memories."

We gazed at each other awhile in silence, this wife and her husband. Drowsily lying close to her, I found myself thinking that even if the whole world were to dissolve and we, too, were annihilated, I would count it all worth the price as long as we had shared the many beauties of the life we had already had with each other

I could only think to say as I felt sleep coming, "I love you, Mira," and her responding kiss lay softly lingering.

Chapter 32

On To Bijapur

Our first three days as Muslim man and wife were three days of Paradise. Unlike most newly married Muslims we did not have to begin dealing immediately with relatives, especially the intruding sort. We blissfully enjoyed each other's company alone.

The first evening and the next morning we had no interest in going out at all. The second morning, which began with clear skies, we went out in the early afternoon and strolled among the shops of the nearest bazaar, returning with foodstuffs we wanted, and I had a second supply of charcoal brought to our door by the charcoal-seller. We felt as if the idyll could go on forever.

The third morning, however, the sky quickly clouded over, and by midday we were treated to the pounding of heavy rain on our rooftop. Fortunately the roof did not leak, and we spent the rest of the day indoors. At first that was no misfortune for a pair of lovers, but as day became night and squalls of rain continued to fall, we both became a little restless. We could make a few jokes about a renewal of our Goan afternoon as lovers in the rain, but eventually we were sobered by the fact that we could become stranded in Belgaon-- when what we needed was to go on to Bijapur!

We awakened from a long afternoon's pleasures to find that the sunset had been short and we were being pitched into a new round of thunder, lightning, wind, and rain. Mira sighed. "Do you think, dear lover, that some demon is trying to end our sojourn in Heaven?"

I laughed. "Or, if I were some sour-faced mullah, I might conclude that it was Allah Himself who was telling us that He had had enough of our pleasures, when gratitude to Him was due for allowing us these few days of withdrawal from a sinful world!" Mira, quick-witted as usual, observed that God might be pleased because we were carrying out the normal prerogatives of marriage!

"It may also be true," I said, trying to be funny, "that Allah is disturbed because, although I have prayed to Him each day at least once to bless our love, I have unfortunately reduced the customary five prayer-times daily to a single one! It is commonly held that someone in the he midst of a grave crisis might dispense with all but one of the five prayers. But this is no 'crisis'!"

For a long moment Mira looked at me seriously. Abruptly I saw that I could be making her feel guilty for causing a crisis of conscience on my part. "I am sorry!" I blurted. "I did not mean to bring up a question like that!"

Mira still gazed at me in discomfort, as if she had "made" me deviate from the five orthodox Sunni prayer-times. I quickly moved close to her, face to face, and gave her a stern look. "As your Muslim husband I order you not to feel guilty my love! And if you will now, instantly, allow me to kiss you, I will show you that I mean what I say!"

Another long moment ensued before I could get the required kiss, but at last I did-- punctuated by a new, thunderous crash and downpour of rain! Then although Mira yielded not only that one kiss but several others to follow, I sensed that she would not forget my unorthodox 'error.' And I was right, because from that evening onward she would often remind me when each of the five formal Sunni prayer-times arrived. Mira had resolved, as she sometimes expressed it with a little smile, that she had married a whole Muslim husband-- not one-half or one-fifth of one!

To honor her in return, I undertook to kneel with her whenever she felt the need herself for a prayer to God. Perhaps I should have thought that strange, because there was no particular hour or ritual involved, except for her to cross herself before and after her prayer. Foremost was the Christian sincerity of the moment! There were formal prayer-times and texts within the Church, I knew, but Mira had chosen to marry a Muslim and faithfully support him in his faith. In future my Muslim prayers would express gratitude to Allah for allowing me to marry this wonderful Christian girl!

Early the next morning we made ready to set out for Bijapur. By noon we had departed. Storm clouds were already banked on the western horizon, and I found that Mira, as usual, could be very sensible when it came to making practical decisions. We left Belgaon trusting to the fact that the Rains might leave us a little space to depart-- and because I had told her of a town not too far away where, God Willing, we might be able to spend a dry night! Mira's reply, with a mild correction-- "Insha'allah!"

In truth, we did get wet in sudden downpours more than once on both days of the journey. Wet or dry, however, we could reach Bijapur and my Aunt's house before too late the evening of the second day, and we both remained cheerful. I was learning that a true and honorable love is what makes unwelcome things bearable.

We rode together, I on my reliable Dandivan, Mira on a new Arabian that I had found to make her riding more comfortable. I did not mind that that I was almost without resources after purchasing the new horse, but I knew I could restore my finances after arriving in Bijapur. Mira meanwhile was happy with her new Arabian mount, which enabled her to ride steadily for long periods at the swift, loping gait typical of these horses.

With two pack-horses apiece, it was not always easy going. Mira, though, had become an experienced rider by now, so I was intent on reaching the city of Bijapur by sunset.

The closer we came to the city of my upbringing, the more excited I felt. The atmosphere of Goa had been alien, often dangerous. I could not identify with that place, hard as I tried. Now I felt a lightening of spirit, a freedom to be my true self and return to my heritage. I felt more relaxed than I had for many months, less confined by a need to learn foreign customs and speak an unfamiliar tongue. I was coming home.

Here we were on the open road, crossing the undulating fields and plains of the Deccan plateau, a plain cross-cut sometimes with gullies and dark outcroppings of rock. Mira seemed to feel more freedom herself. I could banter with her, be more ready to describe or explain what we were seeing. She could correct my Portuguese grammar more precisely and supply my vocabulary with new words. We were more and more confident of each other, exploring our feelings, more eager to exchange our thoughts. Even our stay in Belgaon had included tense moments, especially those relating to the details of a Muslim wedding. Now nearing Bijapur it had become a tranquil journey again.

On this high plateau we were farther from the monsoon's frontal assault, and although afternoon clouds were beginning to mass and swell even here, the sun still stood clear and ruddy above the horizon. Yet there was already a cooling of the air, and the shadows grew longer. Flights of herons rose from irrigated fields. Pairs of mynahs strutted beside the road with their usual fuss and mimicry. Bullocks plodded toward village compounds, urged on by the sticks of pestering boys. Farmers, thin but wiry in strength, walked with wooden plows slung across their shoulders. It was the scene I had loved as a boy growing up. Now I enjoyed it as a man returning from a different world.

Here there were few hills high enough to erect an easily defensible fortress or a city that, except for royal tombs or tall minarets, could be seen at a great distance. When I caught my first sight of Bijapur, it lay low and obscure on the horizon. The stone of its buildings and walls was a grey schist of the Deccan that was sturdy but could be cut into convenient blocks. That made it all the more important to search the horizon for Muslim minarets, towers, and domes that had been inlaid with colourful tiles-- like those, Aunt Bibiji had often told me, in distant Persia.

When at last I could point out the city to Mira, it came as a surprise to me that the citadel, the Arqa Qila, "Fortress of the Sun," only made a low profile on its hill. The fortress was large and strong enough, however, that the citadel seemed to extend a protective benediction all across the walled expanse of the city.

More and more impressive as we approached the city was the fact that really had two sets of walls, those of the citadel with its compact array of royal buildings and its wide moat on the lower sides, and those of the city itself. The city walls were strong in themselves. They spanned more than six stadia as the Portuguese might measure them. These walls were eight times the height of a man, with over a hundred bastions and four great gates oriented north, east, south, and west. The walls constituted a huge ellipse within which the several districts of the city were embraced.

And I knew, moreover, that most of the citadel and the city walls had been the creations of one man, Ali Adil Shah, the Sultan of the Ali'id dynasty that had reigned for many years now. He was the sultan, suspicious by nature, who had executed my father on charges trumped up by jealous rivals! This only demonstrated, of course, that although the sultan had Councils large and small in which he conferred with his ministers of state, his rule was absolute-- in which respect, as I would later learn, he resembled Akbar, "emperor" of the Mughal dynasty.

It was the usual custom for the Muslim ruler to acquire the title of Sultan or Shah-- either being the nearest equivalent of "King." The more powerful the Muslim ruler, the more likely he was to claim the title of Shahinshah ("Ruler of Rulers") or, as in the case of the Mughal ruler of Hindustan, Padshah ("Ruler of All"), each of which was near in sense to Emperor.

It was common knowledge that, whatever the country or realm, rulers took their titles with great seriousness and often to deadly effect if challenged. As Mira observed, "In every country of Europe, however small, the current ruler would style himself King, Prince, Count, Duke or the like, be he ever so powerless in fact, and it would be a truly stupid subject who called the title 'just a word' and treated it with disrespect!"

Mira and I proceeded to amuse ourselves for the better part of an hour by discussing all the titles that some ruler might lay claim to. If Europe had its Kings and Dukes and the rest, my country had its titles like Rai and Raya and Raja-- and among Hindu rulers even "Rajadiraja," King of Kings. And while Muslim monarchs might lay a claim to be Sultan or Shah, those with Turkish or Mongol blood could as well take the title "Khan." It followed that those claiming the highest and broadest power could dare to call themselves Emperor, Shahinshah, Padshah, Great Khan, "Khan of Khans," or whatever title lay within human ingenuity! Thus power dignified itself in every country and clime.

With this kind of small-talk, we soon found ourselves approaching the southerly district where my Aunt Bibiji lived. "The district," I observed, "happens to be called "Shahpura" or "The Shah's Town." And I thought to say, in humor, that my aunt 'ruled' within her house and her walled compound "like some Shahinshah of Persia!"

Unfortunately this last statement of mine did not get a laugh or even a smile from Mira. And as we rode through the crowded streets just before sunset, I abruptly realized that a chill had settled on Mira's mood.

I pulled my thoughts together. "Mira," I asked, "is something wrong?"

She sighed. "Aziz Ahmad, I am sorry, but suddenly I am afraid your aunt may not like me! After all, I am this Portuguese orphan you have acquired, and our Muslim marriage a few days ago does not make me a Muslim! She… she could tell you to go away and take me some other place to stay."

Her flash of fear went straight to my soul. It shamed me. Here I had idealized my aunt and had assumed a simple, warm welcome. And yet I was arriving here unannounced-- and yes, bringing with me a new wife who was not even Muslim! And now Mira was afraid.

I turned in the saddle and reined my Arabian back next to hers. "I am the one who should apologize," I told her. "I am putting you in what could be a very difficult situation. I had been feeling certain that my aunt would admit and welcome us, and now I realize how you would not be sure at all."

"It is all right," she said. "I am just confused, I suppose. I had been so wanting your aunt to like me, but now I see how she could really dislike the idea of this 'foreign' woman you have brought home!"

But here we were, almost within view of my aunt's gate! "Do you," I stammered, "…do you want me to find some other place to stay for a few days? Or at least wait until tomorrow, when we have rested and can start a fresh day in a fresh mood?"

Frowning, she paused to think. "Well, tomorrow might be better. But

I suppose that would only delay any objection your aunt may have." She paused. "I should not be so fearful. If your aunt is everything you say she is, then she will welcome us both. Your aunt may be angry with you, of course, since you have been away so long. But after all, I belong with you now-- by not one marriage but two!"

"Well, in any case it is about to rain again," I said, gloomily surveying the clouds overhead."

Mira grinned at me. "So. You would prefer to ride somewhere else in the rain, and be even more wet and unreasonable by the time we find another caravanserai with a leaking roof?"

"All right!" I almost shouted, "so you're the reasonable one and I'm being a…."

"Big fat Fidalgo," she offered.

We rode the rest of the short way to my Aunt Bibiji's gate.

The rain had not started-- yet.

Chapter 33

A Mixed Reception

And now we were at Aunt Bibiji's gate, and I had begun to have my own doubts about Mira's having to meet my aunt tonight!

"One alternative," I said, "is just to leave a message for my aunt tonight and then go and find lodging somewhere. We cannot just turn and ride away! I laid a hand on one Mira's. "I can leave the message for Aunt Bibiji with our old gatekeeper Riaz Bahadur, who is a born diplomat and will surely present it with whatever care it needs. Riaz Bahadur will do doubt answer the bell at the gate. I can say we have just arrived, and need a night to rest and recover ourselves, and then…."

But Mira shook her head "Here, help me down now. If I could out-face those people in Goa, I can face a few moments of uncertainty here! Why don't we just assume that your aunt, however surprised she is, will really want to see you. And you and I are attached by invisible cords now. She will open her arms and her heart to you-- and not send either of us away!"

I dismounted and helped Mira down. "I am so stiff!" she moaned. But she tried smiling again-- and adjusted her burqa. "Were we not saying, just today, how brave we were?"

Frankly my faith in my 'bravery' was at a very low ebb. But I had to keep a confident look-- if only for Mira's sake.

I rang the bell at the heavy wooden door. There was no sound within. I rang again-- harder. Now I heard a voice. Voices? The sounds of our old gateman-- and maybe his wife? And a boy's voice, too. Another servant? His son!?

I rang again. The boy must be fourteen now-- since the old man had lost one wife but married another. Working here for Aunt Bibiji, he had needed the help! Yes, definitely his son.

Chains rattled. A big key turned in a big lock. The solid wooden door of the gate opened just a crack. Two pairs of eyes, a man's and a boy's, stared through the crack. Abruptly the gate swung open.

"Master Aziz! You! You have come!" The elderly servant-- actually he was only in his late fifties-- was good old Riaz Bahadur, a wrinkled, grinning prince of a man whom I knew as well as the house itself. We embraced.

"And…?" He gazed at Mira in her burqa.

"My wife!" I exclaimed. "My wife Mira!"

Skinny old Riaz Bahadur bowed low, touching his forehead with a reverential hand.

Dear old Riaz. He was quick to pull me inside the gate, bow and beckon to Mira, and have his son lead in our six horses. Then it would be too late to retreat!

By the time I got through these thoughts, Riaz Bahadur had done exactly as I guessed. We were inside. Politely trapped.

But I had invented a message for my aunt already, so I gave it.

"Riaz Bahadur, please go and tell my aunt that I a here with my new wife, Mira, and I would like to speak briefly with Aunt Bibiji this evening. In the meantime I will have found a place for Mira and myself to stay the night, and it will not require Riaz Bahadur and his wife to make my rooms ready on such short notice. Mira and I will be more rested by tomorrow morning, and then I will happily present her to you at your convenience."

I asked Riaz Bahadur to convey the message right away while Mira and I waited at the gate, and to return with an answer as soon as possible.

He was gone awhile, and I was having fresh doubts. Evidently my aunt had heard voices at the gate and guessed it might be her "Prodigal" nephew returning. Riaz Bahadur returned with a sad face, almost avoiding my eyes. He took a deep breath.

"Your aunt says that this is a big surprise, Aziz Ahmad, due to your long absence and almost complete lack of communication, and it is rather thoughtless of you not to have told of your marriage and to arrive now without any notice!" That left me suitably humbled! But he next tried a smile. "'However," she says, "'I am not a landlord, I am your aunt, and I will not have the dishonor, now that you are here, of allowing you and your wife to go somewhere else for the night!'" His smile brightened. "She says that I and my wife are immediately to prepare your rooms for you. And you are to make no excuses!"

After wading through all this rhetoric, Riaz Bahadur gulped air to catch his breath. He continued. "As for her meeting your wife Mira tomorrow, your aunt says she will be delighted. She does not ask you to rush. Please bring your wife to her sitting-room during the hour before noon, and remain in attendance on her. Meanwhile, this night, your aunt does expect you to come and speak briefly with her while your wife is getting settled in your rooms! He sighed. "'And remember,'" she says, "'No excuses!'"

I glanced at Mira. I could almost see her smiling behind the veil of her burqa. Her eyes were saying, "'See, I was right. She took us in!'" But my eyes kept responding, "'Of course. With your husband properly humiliated and embarrassed!'"

But I knew I wasting time in self-abasement. Of course my aunt would be stiff toward me. It was my own fault! Only Allah could know what she would have said and done if I had not had Mira along for 'protection!' I took a very deep breath.

"I do not suppose my aunt expected a reply?" I asked Riaz Bahadur. "No, Shaikh-ji. She did not seem to!"

So I shrugged, gave Mira a quick look accepting the inevitable, and gestured to Riaz Bahadur to lead the way.

The old servant, wearing a smile again, escorted us across my aunt's immaculate walled compound, through her special version of a charbagh with its fourfold irrigation channels watered by a central fountain, and immediately up the stone steps to my two old rooms. Fortunately, I thought, my rooms-- now Mira's and mine-- were at the opposite end of the house from my aunt's rooms!

Riaz Bahadur's son meanwhile had gone to inform his wife. We had hardly arrived with and started unpacking the things most essential for this one, "first" night when the wife and son hurriedly arrived, started laying out bedding, and lighted some lamp-wicks. As the light rose the rooms proved to be perfectly clean and neat-- although with their grey stone walls rather barren looking!

I commented on the place's cleanliness after almost these four years. Riaz Bahadur grinned broadly. "Did you think, Shaikh-ji, that your aunt would have allowed anything different?"

We both had a laugh at that one! He then told me he would arrange some items from foodshops in the bazaar for our breakfast, and that he hoped my wife and I would sleep comfortably until the morning's noise of crows and mynahs became too much to ignore. He also reminded me that my aunt expected a short visit from me already this night! Smiling, he excused himself to go and finish bringing up our packs and getting our horses settled in stalls near the gate.

I loved this man. Always busy at something, he and his wife were never to be found whining or obsequious. They lived in their sparely furnished little quarters near the gate not as mere servants but as friends of the family. "Riaz" meant a man of austerity, discipline, and devotion. Riaz Bahadur had that kind of character.

A simple-seeming but profound Muslim, he neglected none of the five required daily prayers, and, though not formally a Sufi, made a daily practice of personal Dhikr, the recitation of the Ninety-Nine Names of God. If I needed a model of our Muslim faith, Riaz Bahadur was that model. It was the special grace added to his service and faithfulness.

""Shaikh-ji?'" I heard Mira say as she laid her clothing in order. "A strange name for my husband."

"It means something like 'Master' or 'Learned One,'" I said. "Aunt Bibiji started informally calling me that back when I was about ten and was studying the Qur'an."

"Somehow it still seems appropriate," said Mira with a grin. "Shaikh-ji," she repeated. "My literate and wise husband."

I laughed. "It sounds pretentious. You can better keep calling me "Aziz Ahmad."

She laughed, too. "Maybe I will just call you "Shaikh-ji" when you <u>are</u> pretentious."

"Watch yourself, woman," I came back. And I was about to kiss her thoroughly and somewhat violently, when she reminded me about seeing my aunt first. I moderated the kiss and embrace!

"I will still be awake when you come back, dear husband. Just don't be too long about it!"

I washed up quickly and went to my aunt's sleeping room.

Aunt Bibiji was sitting propped against a huge pillow on her bed. She gazed at me a moment. I did a dignified salaam, knelt by the bed a moment, and pressed my forehead against her folded fingers. The fingers slowly unfolded and caressed my hair, then moved and caressed the textures of my child's wounds, then lifted me by the chin for further inspection. Only after that did I sit back on my knees to converse with her.

"You know why I had to be fierce with you, Aziz Ahmad, don't you?" she asked. "You would have spirited your wife away for the night and dishonored me for not accommodating you here at the house. You are indeed, nephew, a kind of Prodigal Son!"

"Did you, Auntie, ever sense that I was coming back?"

"Oh, I dreamed it several times, but it never happened. So I stopped hoping. Then the other night I had another premonition. It woke me in the middle of the night!"

Her eyes developed a twinkle. "So I called for a favorite astrologer and had him come and see your rooms and make some calculations. He predicted that you would return alive, unhurt-- and asking a favor!"

So I told her the outlines of Mira's life, her natural grace, and beauty, her quickness of mind, and how I had wooed and married her-- even though, in the circumstances I could not remain with her in Goa. And now, I told my aunt, I "hoped" that Aunt Bibiji would agree to teach Mira Persian-- with my "assistance!"

My aunt was observing me with some scepticism. "So you have given up all your efforts, including your study of Latin, without regret?" She shifted against her pillows. "This Portuguese Christian girl-- no I will say "lady," for that seems to describe her character!-- has changed your life so fully?" My aunt smiled, and I realized she was now thinking of other days, perhaps in her own life, that I was not acquainted with. "And you have married her and brought her to Bijapur." A statement, but implying a question.

"Yes," I said, trying to look-- and sound-- innocent! But I saw that she would gradually wring the rest of the truth out of me. So I would give her part of it. "Actually, I have married her according to not one but two rites-- Christian and Muslim. I wished to be as honorable as possible, allowing her to remain Christian if she wishes, but opening her the gates of Islam."

My aunt stared. "And she accepts this and will try to adapt, perhaps even convert to Islam?" The words did not carry much weight of expectation. Still I repeated, "Yes, and… I think that when you meet her… you will see why."

Aunt Bibiji shook her head at my simple-minded confidence. "And," she said, "I am to teach her Persian so that she may prepare to spend her life with you, her Muslim husband." Another statement implying some answer.

I decided to be even more bold. "It may be, I feel, that she will go with me someday north to the empire of Hindustan, the Mughal empire, where her knowledge of Persian will be necessary to her, in view perhaps of my taking employment there-- possibly in the employment of the great Padshah, Akbar!"

But if I had thought this would impress my aunt, I was wrong! She shook her head slowly again. "This you say although you have not even explored the possibilities of taking employment with the house of our own ruling dynasty, the Ali'id monarchs? It seems-- how shall I say it?-- somethat far-fetched, not to say presumptuous" She paused. I kept silent.

Foolishly, I had almost told her about Monserrate and the proposed Jesuit mission to Akbar's court in the north! That, I saw now, would have awakened my aunt to a good deal more questioning and head-shaking! We might have been up the whole night!

"Well," said Aunt Bibiji tiredly-- but also politely-- you and I can talk about this later." I gave silent thanks to Allah that I not opened any new avenues to argument!

My aunt sighed. "Meanwhile your new wife awaits you, and if you wish to present her tomorrow, I had better not keep the two of you up late." And I received a smile. There were more sides to that smile than I wanted to consider just now!

"Gird your loins!" I thought, using that Christian phrase. Because I could see that there were rough waters ahead. And one subject I had better avoid-- would it ever be safe to introduce?-- would be the possibility that I might return to Goa and take up Monserrate's patronage again in order to join a certain Jesuit mission to the "Grand Mogor," as members of the Society of Jesus were inclined to call Akbar!

Slowly I rose from my knees, feeling stiff throughout legs and body, and stood, and tried to smile.

I stepped forward, bent to touch my aunt's nearest, elegantly sandaled foot, stood straight again and gave her my salaam with the best dignity I could manage. I kept my smile appropriately grateful-- and in place.

"Thank-you, Aunt Bibiji," I said, "for considering these ideas of mine. They are not even, exactly 'plans,' only thoughts I wanted to share. Tomorrow, at any rate, you will meet Mira. I will 'present' her, if it pleases you, an hour before noon, giving you time enough to ask the questions you wish before the midday. You can judge her for yourself. I think that she will satisfy you that she is... wonderful. That she is as bright as she is beautiful, and that marriage of mine-- or rather these 'two' marriages-- were no mistake. But...." I trailed off.

My aunt surprised me. She gave me a genuine, relaxed smile. "It is good to see you safe and well, Aziz Ahmad. You have ambition and set your aims upon great objects. You have also stepped into marriage-- and with a Portuguese Christian woman! I find it daring, even courageous of you. You have your father's spirit! You will take risks-- yes, and sometimes make mistakes-- but you will not just sit and wait for the fruits of life to fall in your lap. I would not admire you or continue to support you if I thought you were doomed to failure. I admire you because you will not give up easily-- and because your heart is good."

She continued to look at me in a friendly way. "Bring your new wife to me in the morning. I am sure you will have prepared her well, and that neither she nor I will be disappointed."

With a strange feeling of relief I touched my brow and gave her my salaam again. She was still watching me fondly when I departed. And Mira would be waiting.

Chapter 34

The Presentation

We awoke suddenly to the raucous cry of a peacock that had alighted on the rooftop above us. Crows and mynas had sharp calls, but the cries of the peafowl family were all the more penetrating. Was this awakening an omen of good fortune, as many of my countrymen assumed, or a mere accident? In any case the peacock's mate answered loudly from the branches of a nearby tree, and the male flew off to the tree.

Mira smiled against my cheek and would have fallen back asleep. But the imminence of Mira's presentation to Aunt Bibiji had weighed on my dreams, and now I was wide awake. It took me awhile to realize that we had plenty of time before the presentation. We could afford to lounge comfortably on our terrace, which nicely caught the morning sun.

Mira had saved back some wheat-bread puris and two or three pieces of fruit that Riaz Bahadur's wife had kindly provided for us the night before, but as I was pulling back the curtains that closed off our sitting-room from the sunlight already bright on the terrace, I saw Riaz Bahadur hurrying our way with a cloth covered tray. He was bringing an array of hot, fresh puris and cups of steaming tea. Strong as the tea was, I was glad that Riaz Bahadur's wife and remembered to add a good deal of milk-- which with its extra richness was likely to be the produce not of a cow but of a bullock.

Riaz Bahadur also brought an array of fruit, with grated coconut as a side dish. I made much of our appreciation, but he modestly insisted that it was all his wife's doing. He had kept a low table with its folding legs standing against our wall, and we were soon relaxing at the table with our breakfast.

Mira asked whether I would always expect to have such wonderful servants at hand when we set up our own household. "Of course," I said, joking, "unless you prefer to do all the shopping, cooking, and cleaning yourself!"

She laughed and gave me a look reserved for people who are idiots. "If I am to be a great Persian lady like your aunt, would not a complete staff of servants be more correct?"

"Well," I said, "let us just hope we can find any as intelligent, attentive, and polite-- oh yes, and honest!-- as Riaz Bahadur and his wife. But I will try."

"I'm sure you will, dear man. Else you may not eat so well or have a presentable house!"

Mira anticipated me. She sighed. "Well, I had better get ready for this 'Grand Event.' I only hope your aunt will not see me as one of those "Feringhi Portuguese' in need of a good lecture and plenty of discipline!"

I begged her not to worry. "You will do fine," I said. I did not tell her I expected to do enough worrying for both of us!

In Belgaon I had provided for Muslim clothing that Mira might like to wear. Now, once she had slipped back into our sleeping-room and started her toilette, I could contemplate, while having another cup of Riaz Bahadur's blend of tea and milk, how my slender wife would look in Muslim salwaar and kamiz. The delicate but feminine pantaloons of the salwaar would cover her from waist to ankles, and the loose-fitting tunic of the kamiz would provide a cool extra privacy from the neck to her knees. Her footwear would be slippers or sandals.

I reflected that a Muslim woman of decency or rank, if going out into a public place, would be wearing also a long cotton chador from head to foot, to be certain that her face was covered. Or at the very least, the lady would wear over her head a wide scarf that would allow for a veil to be attached in public places or whenever she was among persons unrelated or unknown to her. After all, I thought, even the Portuguese women wore a large scarf over their heads when going into the streets and shops, or going otherwise to places where men not of the family would be present.

I had decided that it would be better to have Mira wear over her head and shoulders a scarf of fine silk and to attach a veil for this first meeting. Mira was used to veiling herself during our travel from Goa, so I did not worry about her knowing what to do. In any case, when meeting an older person like my aunt the added reserve and dignity would not be out of place.

At last Mira emerged, with everything in place except the veil which she would add later to the scarf over her head. She was wearing now, too, the jewelry which I had made a gift to her for our second marriage, including not only gold bangles for each wrist but also a delicately golden Persian symbol of the pomegranate adorning her forehead at the center, with matching large earrings, and all this set off by a golden ring artfully attached to a septum of her nose. She was so achingly beautiful in this transformation that I could only stare for the moment. Was it thus that a man had his first vision of a goddess!?

Mira did not wait for further encouragement, as if she felt that I might stare at this transformation forever and not know what to say. She turned slightly to one side and then to the other. "Do you like it?"

I… I like it very much!" I breathed.

Mira smiled and became even more gorgeous-- and, in a way, ethereal. Perhaps not a goddess, but an excellent incarnation of one! And here I was, a Muslim whom the compassionate Allah had just rewarded with the gift of a lovely wife-- a lady who was in all things the most beauteous temptation to idolatry!

"Are you really Mira?" I asked reverently.

She looked back at me as I suppose most goddesses would have regarded a human being-- with reluctance and a trace of amusement. "Now don't talk nonsense," she said.

I tried to stop myself from staring and return to the casual, witty manner that I imagined I normally possessed. "Then I can worship you!"

She laughed. "Well, yes, if you must. But not too long! This appearance is mainly intended for your Aunt Bibiji's appreciation."

I grinned and collected my wits at last. "Or more likely her astonishment!"

I was still staring at Mira's face. Her already beautiful lips, that had first been one thing to captivate me, had been given a deep red color etched at the edges in a very delicate line of dark kohl. How skillful the fingertips that had made that line!

Slowly now, like a miraculous lotus with red petals floating on the waters of an oasis where a traveler had come to drink, the red lips were obscured by the blue veil that Mira drew across her face and fastened to her scarf. She was smiling at her little flash of humor.

"Alas," I moaned,

"Here stands the love-drunk fool

Who chased this vision to a pool

Where he might drink of it.

And now in abject fear he perishes

To think he'll never see again

These soft red petals that he cherishes."

And then, as if to punish me for my weakness, the goddess I saw, in a mysterious urge to seduce me, pulled aside the veil and released it from her fingers. And she laughed!

"Before you decide to die for love of this goddess you think I have become," said the goddess, "let me just be Mira again. And get up and come and kiss me! And then we will call Riaz Bahadur, and ask him to convey to your aunt the message that we are ready."

How does one describe a kiss asked for by a goddess? How, even more, could one describe her kiss felt in return?

Had it been another occasion, as of an evening when wine and song had carried me to the point of desiring this woman more than anything in the world, I might have shamed myself by embracing her too roughly.

Fortunately I did not try to embrace the goddess at all! I merely let my lips linger on hers. And why? Because a taste of Paradise is something to linger over, and you may never, truly, reach Paradise again.

And the lady, who had become Mira again, whispered to me-- "Thank you." It was as simple as that. "Thank you." But it said a large number of things.

Quickly then, while Mira added some finishing touches to her hair, I dressed myself in my best set of Muslim pyjama and kurta. Then I called for Riaz Bahadur, who as it happened had already come to the steps leading up to the terrace, and had decided to sit on his haunches at the foot of the steps until he heard me call. Instantly he saluted with his best salaam, called me "Shaikh-ji," and went to deliver my message to Aunt Bibiji.

A hundred heartbeats later he returned. My aunt, he announced, was ready.

Mira and I descended the terrace steps and took the garden path to my aunt's sitting-room. Wearing a freshly wound turban, I took the lead-- the man's role. Mira came several steps behind. I felt somewhat like a pompous ass who hangs at the doors of the great and says "Yes, Bahadur-ji. Of course, Bahadur-ji," and does whatever is expected.

Mira on the contrary, walking her dignified four steps behind me, seemed to me to stroll with the most steady but relaxed gait in the world. But then, I supposed, goddesses did walk that way!

And almost before I knew it, as if we had floated there, I was standing before my aunt, having given her my salaam, and Mira wearing her scarf and veil had stopped the same, precise four steps behind me-- and a little to one side.

Suddenly I was intensely proud of my new wife. Overnight this Portuguese girl had become a Persian woman conscious of her dignity. Even in subordination, lodged in the house of her husband's aunt, she seemed to radiate the sense of a Muslim man's first of wives, dutiful but secure.

If not really a goddess, which would have scandalized every Muslim in the world, since they were strict monotheists, she was a wife I could be proud to call my equal in intelligence, honor, sensitivity, and-- oh yes-- humor.

Here in my aunt's sitting-room, however, the outcome of my presentation was entirely in my aunt's hands. Aunt Bibiji looked more than usually impressive this morning, as if immersed in the gravity of thoughts that had concerned her ever since my abrupt arrival and our conversation the evening before.

With a show of unconcern but a slight tilt of the head, my aunt gazed at me and my female companion in turn. Mira continued to stand behind me, her head and face covered, her eyes downcast.

Advancing, I knelt as I had the night before, touched my forehead to my aunt's slippered feet, bowed in formal salaam, then stepped back and knelt again. My head must not be higher than my aunt's, as befitted her age and status.

Acknowleding my salaam, my aunt gazed at Mira with ontinued equipoise. Fortunately I could rely on Mira to keep her eyes lowered and return even a direct inspection without flinching. I sank to rest on my heels near my aunt's dais and waited.

"Tell your wife she may come forward now," said my aunt calmly. As yet she had indulged in neither a smile nor a frown.

I bowed again respectfully and turned to Mira. "My aunt asks you to approach," I said in the usual Portuguese, trying to reduce the tension with a smile. With the smallest flicker of eyes Mira acknowledged my translation of my aunt's Persian.

Mira stepped forward as I had, but more slowly and gracefully, and went through the same brief ceremony of kneeling and salaam that I had. Then she knelt and sat, too, on her heels, resting her hands in her lap. Again I felt proud of her decorum under my aunt's austere gaze.

I addressed my aunt quietly but firmly. I had rehearsed carefully my introduction of Mira, as any respectful son or nephew would do.

"Relying on the mercy of Allah, and in hope of your own benediction," I said, "may I present Mira, daughter of the honorable Francisco Bartolomeo of Portugal. Recently, according to both Christian and Muslim rites, she has become the wife of my heart. I take the utmost pride in having acquired a wife who will be respectful of our religion and a credit to our family."

My aunt carefully pronounced the name "Mira." I could see a sincere welcome taking shape in my aunt's eyes as she added a small but cordial smile. "Come just a little closer, my dear," she added. "Let me see you."

Mira rose enough from her knees to move forward, coming to the very edge of the dais. It astonished and pleased me again to see her bow gracefully and kneel again, as if every sinew of her body had become Persian.

"Please lift back your veil," said my aunt in kindly tones. "I wish to see you as you fully are."

Mira complied, keeping her chin low, her eyes downcast. She rested her hands again in her lap. My aunt studied her. How like, I thought, the lady would have studied a new gem or a book of poems presented for her approval!

"Your wife is very lovely," said Aunt Bibiji with the flicker of a glance in my direction. Then she raised her voice to become more dramatic and address Mira. "You are as beautiful as my nephew has described you, my dear Mira. His judgement appears to be most trustworthy."

Even without understanding exactly what was being said, Mira could understand the drift. Her eyes slowly lifted to meet my aunt's. The two women suddenly seemed intimate, as if each could now estimate the other freely. Neither of them seemed to take notice of me now. It struck me that there was no condescension in my aunt's eyes, nor any sign of fear or conceit in Mira's returning gaze.

Aunt Bibiji continued to look at Mira now, not allowing me to interrupt. "If you are as devoted to your husband as I think, wife of Aziz, and are as good a student of our language as you are of our manners, you will find favor in my household."

I translated for Mira only enough to make the main point. "My aunt says she is already finding many good qualities in you."

Now, in a move that I had warned Mira of, my aunt curled a forefinger under Mira's chin and studied her face more carefully.

With a glance in my direction she kept talking. "I see here, if Allah is merciful to my eyesight, not merely a girl but a woman."

If she stopped there, I would have concluded that my aunt was the soul of welcome. But she did not stop.

She turned her head slightly my way. "If your wife is Christian now, dear Aziz, I do not propose to make it a concern, but I have the hope that she will convert to our Muslim faith in time, freely and because it, like her own, is an honorable religion." Aunt Bibiji gave Mira's face another approving look and gently removed the finger from Mira's chin.

And my aunt gazed directly at me now. "Are we not all, dear nephew, 'People of the Book,' both Muslim and Christian?"

I smiled but said nothing. The conversation was not taking a direction I liked or expected! I had already told Mira that she was free to remain a Christian if she wished. I had made it a vow. Now I was grateful for the thought that Mira did not understand what my aunt had just said!

Fortunately Mira kept kneeling calmly, however uncomfortable the position, and was willing to be talked "around" without having to respond. For the rest she was the very image of the devoted Muslim wife. In that I could be glad.

"She will do well," announced Aunt Bibiji firmly. "I can see it." She looked more directly at me and said cheerfully, "The two of you may rise and step back if you wish."

I conveyed the idea to Mira. My wise wife took a moment to return her gaze to Aunt Bibiji's and raise her hands to join the palms at the level of her eyes with a look of gratitude before she stepped back and joined me. I could see my aunt's eyes widen slightly in happy surprise at the good manners Mira kept showing.

Happy as that made me also, I was grateful that my aunt did not insist on a lot of conversation to follow. She merely thanked us both for reassuring her that our marriage would be a success and that she and Mira seemed likely to get along very well. And then, while the three of us were all smiling in a mood of relief and satisfaction, Aunt Bibiji dismissed us.

The "Presentation" fortunately had not become some kind of interrogation. There had been no questions expecting even a spoken reply from Mira! She had not been pressured, either, to display some knowledge of Persian-- and was not treated as the "Feringhi Portuguese" that Mira had feared.

As Mira and I were returning to my rooms I told her she had done wonderfully. The little look of triumph she gave me, and the smile that followed it while she still walked four steps behind, keeping up the formalities awhile longer, informed me that I had not been wrong to marry this lady and that, with due appreciation to Allah, I could now give an internal whoop of joy!

As I offered Mira my hand in ascending the two steps to our terrace, I let a little of the joy communicate itself. "You succeeded, dear wife, far beyond expectations-- Aunt Bibiji's or mine!"

The bright smile I received was a rival to the sunlight around us. I thought I spied just the smallest trace of the goddess still granting me the vision of a red lotus in bloom.

Chapter 35

Educating Mira

After the worries surrounding the Presentation, I had hoped that Mira and I could spend a day or two just relaxing, enjoying breakfasts on our terrace, strolling at leisure in my aunt's garden, and perhaps going out to see the great city of Bijapur. The very next morning, however, Aunt Bibiji beckoned me to her sitting-room.

I had asked my aunt to set aside an hour when we could discuss Mira's 'education' in the Persian language and Persian ideas, emphasizing my desire that Mira would become an educated Muslim's proper wife, able to read, write, and think in a sophisticated way! But I did not expect a discussion so soon.

However, Mira had begun the day by putting our rooms in order better suited to our differing needs. I had no excuse to put off seeing my aunt.

Aunt Bibiji had surprised me that first evening in Bijapur by agreeing immediately to help Mira learn Persian. Now my aunt began by saying that she had been impressed with Mira's intelligence and desire to learn. With my help, considering that Aunt Bibiji and Mira had no common language to be used as a bridge, and that my knowledge of both Persian and Portuguese would be the keystone, Aunt Bibiji seemed to be moving directly to a discussion of a teaching method.

But I had not anticipated some more important thoughts, from my aunt's viewpoint, about my overall plans for my life and Mira's. That proved to be the real topic that my subtle aunt wanted to discuss!

She worried, Aunt Bibiji said, because she still saw no evidence that my hopes of returning to Goa had in any way diminished! In fact, she added, she had spent an almost sleepless night worrying about the selfishness in my attitude.

"I cannot overcome the feeling," she announced, "that you will push

Mira's Persian studies too hard because they are your gateway back to Goa, Monserrate, and a Jesuit mission to Akbar."

"Do not misunderstand me," my aunt added. "I actually like your new wife. I expect even to become fond of her. Thanks to Allah she is devoted to you. But think! Insha'allah, there will be children coming. A husband and father's life is not like a single man's. For one thing you have as yet no employment you can turn to. Will I always be here to support you? If Allah wills it, I have a few more years to live, and I will help you as much as I can, whether it be in maintaining you here or in teaching Mira the language of Persian. But you must think far beyond that!"

She frowned. "But if you are already planning to return to Goa, imagine that it can be done in two or three months' time from now, it means you do not see the trouble in my taking full responsibility not only for housing your lovely wife, who no doubt will comport herself quite well, but for teaching her a difficult language and doing so without your presence and assistance!"

We sat in silence a few moments. She waited for me to reply, and I knew I had nothing that would satisfy her. I could not deny that I hoped to have Mira's studies so well in hand that in three months, at most, I would be ready to return to Goa.

I expressed my genuine willingness to help with Mira's lessons. I had less confidence in my being able to secure a job. I asserted that I would do my best in both arenas facing me.

However, after discussing things back and forth for the better part of an hour, I could see that Aunt Bibiji still was not satisfied with my rationalizations and "excuses." Finally, despite all my explanations and defenses, Aunt Bibiji told me that she was going to propose a solution--and that she would expect me to honor it. When she put the matter that way, I had little choice but to agree!

"Let this be the end of all argument," she said. "As I respect you, dear nephew, I will respect your charming wife. And if she is as good a student as I guess, she will learn quickly not only the Persian language but the customs and beliefs that go with her new residence in a Muslim house and Muslim society. But you yourself must come to an agreement with me."

Suddenly I could almost see it written on the plastered wall behind my aunt's head-- that I would be fortunate ever to get out of Bijapur again!

Aunt Bibiji cleared her throat. "It is now the beginning of the summer Monsoon, and already the Rains have begun. Your wife needs you just now, needs your company and your help in making what is for her a giant step into our Islamic culture and society. And, you have told me so casually, the two of you are married by both Christian and Muslim rites-- when either set of beliefs and expectations would be a huge demand." She shook her head. "Really, Nephew, you have dared to complicate your life-- and your Portuguese wife's-- almost to a breaking point. But I suppose I must get used to such complications. I will try to understand-- yes, and help to "educate" Mira as much as I can."

"So," she said, "now to my point. You will stay here with your wife through this three month season of the rains, and not only that but through the two or three months that follow. To be more precise, I mean that you will stay at least through the celebration of Muharram in the first month of our Muslim new year! That will allow time for you not only to help bring Mira's education to a fairly advanced point but also to determine what career will be open to you here in Bijapur-- and to know more certainly if you still wish to return to Goa. Am I right?"

To refuse after all this would seem shockingly ungrateful. It bothered me to "have" to say yes, but I was not yet ready to challenge this aunt of mine.

Aunt Bibiji was quick to accept silence as consent!

She nailed home a last point. "And equally you owe it to your wife to stay with her in the event that she becomes pregnant and needs your presence and support all the more!"

Seeing my blank face, which conveyed the fact that I had not really considered Mira's becoming pregnant right away, my aunt put on a look of finality.

"Honestly, Nephew, I do not see how you could even consider returning to Goa before the year is out, and perhaps another full year, to be sure that you support your wife and undergo a bonding with your child that may come. Men-- ambitious men-- can be so thoughtless and cruel where their wives are concerned! And they miss the best years of enjoying their children, teaching them, and being a model for them. You must not be that kind of father, nephew!

My aunt gave me a calculated stare. "Of course, if you wish to place all your future in the hands of a Jesuit missionary or a Mughal emperor, just be certain that you would be choosing the right patrons to impress by your abilities and your honor."

I had not seen my aunt's eyes flash like that in a long time. The power of her will, too, was still greater than mine. I could see that I would have to be careful and more diplomatic!

"I am sorry, Aunt Bibiji," I said. "Perhaps I do tend to be selfish. You have been a mother to me, truly, as much as an aunt, and have done much for my welfare. And now you have given me even more to think over."

My aunt looked at me thoughtfully a moment-- then suddenly smiled. "Ah, yes. I had forgotten, nephew. You are a master of rhetorical grace when you sense the need. But I will accept it as a genuine apology." She waited, but I had emptied my arsenal of diplomacy for the moment.

"So we are agreed?" she asked-- showing a sound store of tactics herself! "You will stay on as long as you can, or at least to the next midwinter months, helping your beautiful Mira, and helping me. And, I beg of you, you will make the best efforts you can to gain lucrative and honorable employment here in Bijapur. And while you are trying to find some suitable position, you will bend every effort to see to the education of your wife and support the needs of her heart as well as those of her mind."

And my aunt smiled at last. "Forgive me, please, if I have been too harsh with you, Aziz Ahmad. I have yearned so long to see you again and learn what has happened to you. And if you have truly won from the Jesuit Monserrate his blessings on your marriage and his offer of a position as his secretary upon a mission to the Great Mughal, then I also congratulate you. Whether you remain in Bijapur finally, or return to Goa, you will have my blessing, because will have given your beautiful wife the best of your love and attention. And you will continue to have many chances, if Allah be willing, of distinguishing yourself."

Now she remembered that we had talked a long time, and Mira might think I had abandoned her!

"Go to your new wife, dear nephew, and bear her my kindest greetings. Meanwhile I have only one more thing to expect of you. You will tell her about our agreement on the length of your stay-- and arrange to come with her to my sitting-room again tomorrow morning-- let us make it one hour before noonday, to have her first lesson in the great Persian language."

Since she offered no alternative, I returned to me best diplomatic manner.

"By all means," I agreed, and gave her a courteous salaam.

As we parted, she wore a newly satisfied look. She had won a difficult victory over the length of my stay-- more difficult than she might realize. But I could be grateful, too, because she had shown that she cared not about me only but about Mira.

I also knew that Monserrate had said it would be about a year before a Jesuit mission would be mounted. If I cooperated with my aunt here, I might still be able to accept Monserrate's offer in time to actually join the mission north to Hindustan. I could afford the patience to help my aunt with Mira's Persian studies!

By the time I had crossed my aunt's gardens again, I was full of good feeling about this girl that my aunt had herself called "your beautiful Mira." In the months to come I hope to be able to reside in a slow whirl of days in which study side by side with Mira would be my delight. And each day would mark the course of the earth around the sun, as Greek and Arab astronomers had long ago determined. And the sun would be Mira, and she would be in the constant circle of my love.

But to start Mira's new 'education' tomorrow? How would Mira react to the sudden beginning of her Persian lessons?

I need not have worried. It was Mira, in fact, who was ready and eager to launch those lessons-- even if it meant tomorrow! "Do I have a Persian lesson to be ready for!?" she asked.

I tried to pull her back into the circle of my arms, but failed. She was quickly up washing her face and starting to comb her hair, on the chance that she might see my aunt this same day and thank her for the early start. And now I remembered that I would have to get ready, too, for this joint lesson!

Mira next demanded that I gived her some sample sentences to memorize and translate. "Even if just one or two!"

By the time she had "prepared" her short lesson, Mira was in the best of moods. And I could see that I was going to spend a lot of time making up lists of words and phrases, questions and answers-- Persian and Portuguese.

The next morning, which fortunately was a clear and sunny one, went very well. Aunt Bibiji was duly impressed, especially with Mira's pronunciation of Persian words, some of which were modified forms of Arabic words. I could see that Mira was going to thrive on this diet!

But something else occurred, even more rewarding. Mira and Aunt Bibiji entered into a pact that for every Persian word and phrase Mira would teach my aunt the Portuguese equivalent. Soon I realized that they were their own best teachers. I could expect to see them every morning spending an hour or two deep in study and mutual approval.

I was happy to be relieved of some of the pressure of playing the Great Teacher. When they wanted or needed my help, they took it. If not, they went blithely on their way.

Meanwhile I fell into a period of restlessness, looking for things to do-- especially things that gave me an excuse to go out into the city! Better yet, I went outside the city walls where I could gallop my Arabian on the maidan and spend hours at a time on the surrounding plain where I could practice my shooting and restore the fine points of my archery.

Mira's wisdom eventually came to my rescue. One day she proposed that I teach her to ride and shoot, as a Persian nobleman's wife might do! After a variety of excuses I finally agreed. Only light riding, though, I insisted. Mira thanked me for caring.

Again she rode side by side with me, feeling the wind on our faces, her hair unbound sometimes and flying free. Our Arabians picked up the sense of freedom, too, and showed some of the spirit and fire for which their breed was so well known.

Then I introduced Mira to my second best matchlock musket, together with a tripod to help her with the weight of the weapon's long barrel. Kneeling on one knee, she was soon ready to fire at the targets I set up for her. Very soon she proved herself an excellent student in this exacting discipline. Shooting at fixed targets became a favorite sport for her, thanks to a good "eye." But I knew she needed also to learn the loading and priming routine, and this also she was soon hard at work practicing. When I saw her proficiency there, too, I took a proud step-- and rewarded her by making a formal gift of the matchlock

Meanwhile I glowed at see how quickly Mira was learning Persian. Thanks to her Persian and Portuguese exchanges with Aunt Bibiji, who was also a natural linguist, their friendship grew rapidly.

I must admit I realized that the faster Mira progressed in Persian, the sooner I might return to Goa. But I carefully kept that idea out of our conversations, and as much as possible out of my thoughts. Goa-- and even Monserrate-- were becoming less vivid memories. Frankly I was enjoying my outings on the maidan with this fresh-faced wife of mine.

Nothing, though, long remains outside a wife's or aunt's field of vision. This time it was Aunt Bibiji again who took the initiative. I needed, she said boldly, to find out if there could be employment for me in Bijapur-- especially a chance of being received at court and granted some office with the proper salary.

Knowing how my father had been treated, I was in no mood to play the courtier-- let alone the sycophant. I put my aunt aside with a "maybe" and tried to forget the whole of that suggestion. But I had reckoned without my aunt's determination, and she was soon back at the business of my settling down with a steady job and trying to find it by attending the Adil Shah's court. When I tried to remind her that it was this same Shah who had been taken in by false charges against my father, she thought it over but then shrugged.

"Years have passed," she said. "You should wait no longer."

At last I yielded and applied to be "received" at Court. Time passed without response. I was angry. Then the message came. I would be received by a high official of the realm. It would be necessary for me to demonstrate that I was wholly loyal to the Shah! Now I was angrier. Someone wished to make a fool of me-- probably with some embarrassing scene at Court. I discussed the matter with Aunt Bibiji. She admitted there was some "problem" but did not wish me to refuse the reception.

I went-- honestly trying not to seem unrealistic and too demanding. It was just my luck that the official I was to see turned out to be one of the ministers of state whom I knew to have abandoned my father's cause. And he knew who I was! The meeting, of course, was a failure.

After that I did not hear any further pressure from my aunt. "You will do better later. This Sultan is old and ill. Perhaps we will soon have a new Sultan, and your chances will be better."

Reconciled on this point, we agreed that for the present I would just concentrate on helping with Mira's Persian lessons. And, I thought, Mira and I would be able to spend more time riding on the maidan-- riding and shooting!-- and having "other" private time with me.

I began making new efforts to encourage Mira about her learning Persian. I found copies of the brilliant Persian writings of Hafiz and started having Mira learn from me how to recite passages-- and use those to begin some more advanced Persian vocabulary and speaking styles. Mira found, fortunately, that she liked this approach. She also liked the thought and style of Hafiz, which speeded her learning and her own rhetorical style. I was overjoyed to see her in a longer view--that she was on the path, though as yet an early one, to becoming a Persian writer, poet, and essayist in her own right!

To give my aunt some rest, I also brought in a native Persian speaker--an old man of reputation-- who once a week helped Mira improve her listening and practice her accent with an outsider. It helped me feel useful again.

Now I was having more conversations in Persian-- and Portuguese--with Aunt Bibiji and Mira both! For that purpose we would sometimes sit in a circle during the evening, and I would pick up my long unplayed rabab, which I had started learning as a boy, and would tune its strings and play. Finding that my voice had matured well, I began to accompany myself in snatches of old songs. Aunt Bibiji soon joined in, and Mira sang, too, picking up what words she could manage--whether in Persian or in the Dakkhini tongue of the Deccan!

With a renewed mood of enthusiasm and confidence, I decided to make another effort at finding a job in the Ali'id Sultan's government--except that I would not expect a high place or even a really good job! I would take what I could get. And this time I would make sure not to find myself conversing with some old official who had too good a memory of my father's time or the events surrounding his death.

At last I secured another interview. This time the Ali-id officer was a much different sort of man-- easy with himself, down to earth, and practical. And I discovered that, by luck, I had provided him with the kind of summary statement about my life that he found entertaining. He looked over the summary I had written-- in Persian, but this time also in Dakkhini-- and then read it again. I had told of being in Goa for several years and returning recently, but this time leaving out all reference to studying Christianity or marrying a Portuguese Christian girl. I wrote of travel, of the trading networks I had learned about, of crossing the Ghats, of dealing in Arabian horses, of confronting a tiger, of acquiring some of the latest muskets of Portuguese importation!

The official looked up at me thoughtfully-- with a grin. "You have done too many things to make my job easy!" he said. He was silent awhile.

"It just happens," he said at last, "that one of our departments is losing some staff, and a deputy's position is about to open! I do not know if you will like something that other ambitious young men might refuse, but there is room for you to rise in this post. It is in our kharkana that deals with the import and training of Arabian horses for the use of our higher officers of the cavalry and, especially, the uses of our royal house! The chief officer of this department, which is titled "The Royal Stables," deals not only with horses but with camels and elephants. As a deputy you would work especially with horses!"

He grinned again. "You do not have a delicate nose that rejects the presence of horses, camels, and elephants?" I laughed. "Well, if the post is one of 'deputy' to your chief officer, perhaps I could overlook the 'nose' problem!" He then laughed, too. "Good! I will recommend you! And because you will see that even the chief of the Royal Stables is an elderly man and may have to retire soon, your deputy's post will give your nose even less offense!"

And that was how I became an officer of the Ali'id court. Not a very fine smelling officer, in view of my days spent with horses, camels, and elephants-- but better than nothing! I must admit that I rather enjoyed informing my Aunt Bibiji of this on the day, two weeks later, that I was enrolled in the Sultan's administration! Her nose actually wrinkled! But there was no other job available-- and I would have a salary!

So, next, I informed Mira-- whose nose did not wrinkle, but who burst out laughing and clapped her hands. She had become a little depressed, too, about my chances of employment, and she knew how my aunt must have reacted.

"Deputy of the Royal Stables," intoned Mira with mock grandeur. "At least you now can support me!"

And so it turned out that not just Mira, but both of us, were going to get an education. And when it became evident that I would be doing more paperwork than stable-work-- and would not really return from work every day smelling like a horse– or, God forbid, a camel– I found myself no longer having to listen to daily sermons from Aunt Bibijij about my lack of career in government!

Chapter 36

Raya Arrives

Mira and I had been in Bijapur just over a month when Raya arrived. My aunt had told me that he was devoting himself to a merchant's career now, having given up hopes of reviving his life as a prince of the Vijayanagar kingdom. I thought it strange that this Hindu "cousin" of mine would go into trade, but Aunt Bibiji smiled mysteriously and said she would let Raya explain it the next time he visited.

"Well," I asked my aunt, "when he arrived last night did you tell him about Mira?"

"No. I wanted to leave that to you-- and to let you introduce him to her."

I countered that when he arrived Mira and I were already asleep. I was going to tell him this morning-- and introduce him to her-- but he had already left and gone into the city.

"It surprises me," I said, "that he has gone into trade and given up his princely ambitions."

I had in fact given little thought to Raya the past two years, and now I realized that I had felt guilt about parting from him so abruptly when I joined the Jesuits in their descent of the Ghats to Goa. I must have suppressed the guilt by just not thinking of him!

And now here he was, arriving at my aunt's gate in the middle of the night, without knowing Mira and I were there, and going straight to Aunt Bibiji to present himself. For a moment I felt a twinge of jealousy that he could come and go casually like that. But as my aunt often stayed up late reading Persian tomes, she no doubt found it perfectly all right.

I dwelled a moment on the fact that it was my aunt's little reading glasses that made her late-night reading possible. The small, polished lenses had given Aunt Bibiji the pleasure of scholarship even in her sixty-sixth year. Such little pairs of lenses had been developed in Isfahan or Baghdad, or according to some authorities in Istanbul in Turkey. While expensive, the lenses in their tiny gold frames were becoming common among elderly scholars and writers throughout the Muslim world, and an entire generation now used them. It was good to think that Aunt Bibiji was not behind the times.

In any case I supposed that my aunt, or Riaz Bahadur our gatekeeper, would have told Raya about my presence-- and my wife's!

And then this morning, when Mira's next Persian lesson was due, I found that Raya had already risen and had left, as my aunt said, to "finish some business in the city." So, if he were avoiding me, why should I care? Let him return when he wished. I could introduce Mira at my convenience, not his!

Besides, there was no time to think about Raya when Mira was dressing to meet my aunt and was again reviewing the short Persian "conversation" she had been assigned the previous morning. Mira's lessons in Persian had been going quite smoothly. It was just as well, I thought, that Raya was not there to interrupt her recitation-- or mock it!

And then I realized that I was still angry at this "brother" of mine for dropping out of my life at Dharwara-- as if HE were the one at fault, when it was I who had rudely insisted ongoing on with Monserrate instead of completing our joint venture to Vijayanagar-- and leaving Raya to ride back to Bijapur alone.

When Mira and I sat down with Aunt Bibiji this morning I kept pushing Raya out of my mind. Fortunately things went well for Mira, and she and my aunt continued to adjust happily and, after each exchange of a few words of Persian, give each other the looks of appreciation that marked a deepening affection.

The time for noontime prayers came, and our little party of three broke up. Mira, I felt, certainly deserved a rest after concentrating so long. We returned to my rooms, where she rested awhile. I set out my prayer rug on our terrace. As I went through the routines of prayer to Allah,

I asked His benedictions upon all Muslims-- but meanly 'forgot to include Raya in the thought.

But Raya did creep back into my thoughts, and I could only concentrate on my prayers for a few moments. I knew that he would soon return and be full of curiosity about Mira. I found myself resenting it. Yes, I would have to introduce him to Mira, but I would be in no hurry.

In fact I had already told Mira about this "brother" who had arrived during the night, and she was already as curious about him as he would be of her. Mira was trying to be in a welcoming mood. I didn't know how he would respond, I told her. It had been well over three years since I had seen him, I said-- and omitted mention of my exchange of letters with him! I could gather from Mira's expression that she thought I was being a little less than charitable. I sighed.

"It is my fault, really," I admitted. "We parted on poor terms when I first went with the Jesuits to Goa, and I never gave much more thought to Raya's doings."

"But," said Mira, "he is your brother!"

"Not a real one. My aunt 'adopted' him, but not formally."

"Yet you grew up together for several years, and learned to ride and shoot together. You told me yourself that the two of you had been like brothers! And he and you were just returning from Vijayanagar when you met the two Jesuits on the road! Would it not be better just to think of him as your brother-- or at least welcome him that way?

I had turned slowly away and was silent awhile. Yes, I was being "difficult" about this-- and churlish, too. I resolved to act better, even if in my heart I continued to resent him!

"Just be nice," appealed Mira.

And still Raya had not come back from his venture into the city's mercantile affairs.

Now a call came from Aunt Bibiji by way of Riaz Bahadur. I could not ignore that, so I left Mira to wash up, and I went.

My aunt was waiting for me, but not in a good mood. "I think I know what is wrong," she said without ceremony. "You don't want to see your brother, because the two of you parted in anger several years ago. How can you continue harboring a resentment like that? You have worked hard and achieved several successes-- your grasp of Latin and Christendom, your marriage to a lovely woman, your return safely to Bijapur. Raya has worked hard, too, and launched a whole new career. From what he tells me he is becoming a master trader, with connections across the entire peninsula-- some on both coasts, some in the Deccan. You should be proud of yourself, and proud of him! Put away any truculence you seem to feel, and welcome him. If he cannot be polite, that is his problem and he will hear from me about it You be polite!

While I was absorbing this wisdom, I did not know that, at the very moment, Raya was meeting Mira.

Perhaps you should say that he was "encountering" her. I heard about it afterward from Mira. She thought it strange but "interesting." It annoyed me to see her blush when she came to the word "interesting." I felt a twinge of jealousy! Anyway, I listened to her account.

As Mira told it she had awakened and dressed again, this time in a lighter but elegant sari-and-choli combination that I had bought for her on a "Try it for variety!" basis, as it was really Hindu raiment-- and quite lively. She was just stepping out on our terrace, where she thought I would be, and she came upon Raya instead! He had come halfway up the steps to the terrace-- and called my name.

Suddenly he backed off the terrace, and stopped in a patch of drying mud from the morning's rain. Oblivious of the mud on his riding boots, he stared. "And you are?" he asked-- more in shock than being rude, avowed Mira.

"I am Mira," she had said, making it sound more formal that she intended.

His jaw dropped. "For a moment we were both staring. I recovered first!" she said, laughing "I am Aziz Ahmad's wife. We were married just recently," she added. "In Goa."

She now related it all to me in Portuguese. "My heart had almost stopped," she said. "He was such a dark-skinned man, but one of the most handsome men I had ever seen! Dear Aziz, you never told me how handsome and engaging he was! And there he stood, like an apparition, still staring. But I straightened myself and tried to look confident. "'You are Raya?'"

"'I am Raya,'" he breathed. He was still staring. And slowly, to my embarrassment, he joined his palms in front of him at the level of his forehead. And didn't say more!

"I could not quite think," she told me. "He was so worshipful! Yet I finally got something out. "'I am not a goddess, though!'" It was all I could think to say.

"And then he smiled this radiant smile, still beholding me like a worshipper. "'You are Sita,'" he said-- "'or Maha-Lakshmi!'"

She looked at me doubtfully. "Who is Maha-Laksmi?"

"The Hindu goddess of Wealth and Beauty."

"And," she asked, still puzzled, "'Sita'?'"

"The wife and divine consort of the Hindu hero-god Rama." I managed to get it out in one long breath. And she, like my wife, was beautiful, too! That much I knew from stories Raya had told me. I had been getting annoyed, but now I was enjoying this. I could imagine Raya's 'worshipful' face while he was standing there in the mud!!

Then I realized that Mira was waiting to hear more about Rama's wife! "Sita," I said knowingly, "is a more difficult case. She is-- was-- the heroine of an old Hindu epic, the 'Ramayana,' and all I know is that Raya was tried to enlighten me on Hindu tradition, and told me it was one of the two great Hindu epics dating from centuries ago. "But I think she was the wife of the warrior-prince Rama who for some reason was exiled to the deep forest south of the river Ganga, and he took with him his wife Sita and his brother Lakshmana. As luck would have it, Sita was abducted by Ravana, the many-armed demon ruler of Shri Lanka, and Rama and his brother promptly headed south to rescue the loyal Sita. They should have failed, but it seemed they made an alliance with a troup of monkeys-- my mind was clearing now-- whose ruler, if you can believe that, was I think Sugriva and one of whose warriors was Hanuman."

I could see that Mira was still ignorant of the epic and its heroes and villains, but I scratched around in my brain to remember what the monkey Hanuman did that was so heroic. And since Mira was listening with a small, patient smile, I told the rest I could remember.

"So-- it seems to me that Hanuman was this bold monkey-soldier who goes to the demon Ravana's fortress in Sri Lanka, and he manages to get to Sita who is still guarding her chastity-- or, well, the part of it that still belongs to her husband Rama!-- and Hanuman tells her not to worry, that Rama and Lakshmana are coming and will defeat the demon-king and will rescue her-- and then he runs along the tops of the fortress's roofs and walls, leaving fire and destruction behind him, and reports back to Rama. And the "Lord Rama," who is really divine, attacks with his human and monkey allies-- oh, yes, and some bears-- though this by now is really getting farfetched!-- and kills Ravana and defeats his huge demon hosts and gets Sita back.

"And if I am not entirely wrong in what I remember, he tests Sita to see if she really is chaste-- you know, dear, the typical man-wife problem of 'trust' after saving her, and she calls on the Earth as her witness, and it opens and swallows her! Now, I think, Sita returns to him later, after he berates himself for being an un-loving fool, and they live happily ever with Hanuman as their attendant abut also their worshipper forever-- and very often, when Hanuman is sculpted or painted, Raya tells me-- the monkey is still standing or kneeling with his palms lifted and joined in worship. So, now you can see why your new admirer was acting so strange!"

My wife ignored the sting of the scorpion's tail in that last, bad-humored comment. "How sweet," she said. "Your brother was being metaphorical!"

I laughed unkindly. “Maybe. But, being really Hindu, more likely he couldn’t help himself after seeing this divine vision!”

Mira glared at me. “I hope you will live, dear sceptic, to regret that smart banter of yours. And now you have made me feel sorry for your brother-- and not think him strange at all!”

“Ah yes,” I said meanly, “love at first sight!”

She made as if to slap me, but missed. “And you, dear husband, may have to eat your dinner alone!”

I bowed to the depth of my Portuguese best, sweeping low between us an imaginary hat with its long, white feather.

Just then a call came from Riaz Bahadur. We were being invited to my aunt’s terrace for lunch! And yes, Raya was there when Mira and I arrived. And there, after the introduction so long delayed, the four of us-- Aunt Bibiji, Raya, Mira, and I-- sat at my aunt’s low table together.

So I did not eat alone, as Mira had threatened-- and I had an aunt glaring at me throughout lunch. And I had a wife smiling at her new admirer Raya-- who kept stealing glances at her with worship written all over him. And I was sitting there in gloom.

It was no wonder that, later that evening, my aunt took me aside and told me to stop acting like a jilted husband-- or else she would openly declare me a sore loser with a bad disposition!

We had an even more elaborate banquet that evening, with Raya as my aunt’s chosen guest of honor! Mira for her part tried to lure me into a better mood while Raya told stories about his travels that made everyone laugh.

Mira was the one who laughed with most approval. As for me, I continued to be jealous of my brother and his successful ‘homecoming.’. Later that night Mira set me straight with a single, short comment. “One of us had to be nice!”

The next morning as we were still lying abed, Mira turned to me and propped herself on an elbow. “I have news for you, my dear.” She waited until I was concentrating. “Would you believe I am pregnant?” The news took its time sinking into my male brain. My inevitable dumb question followed. “You are certain?”

“Yes.” And her smile made grey morning bright as sunlight. The smile and the sunlight-- and the news of Mira’s pregnancy-- were able to push Raya into the background again.

Chapter 37

New Prospects, New Plans

Once the word was out that Mira was pregnant, it was no wonder that Aunt Bibiji began to lean on me again to stay in Bijapur. If not forever, I should certainly stay during the first year—or two—of my child's life, so that I would become a constantly present and doting father.

Fortunately Mira had already committed herself to my return to Goa if and when Monserrate summoned me to accompany him as personal secretary on any Jesuit mission to the court of Akbar. But my aunt was not done with her persuasive reminders that I "really" belonged with Mira in Bijapur.

I was caught in a diplomatic vise between my wife and my aunt! And I had to admit –though not openly—that my feelings about leaving Mira and our son or daughter thrust a sword of guilt into me. What does a man do when his wife and aunt—my mother surrogate in truth—are at odds about his future? He becomes moody, sullen at times, and inclined to keep his views to himself—unless they are wrung out of him.

In my family's traditions on both the Turkish and Persian sides—the Turkish father's and the Persian mother's—one's parents desires and dispositions are primary. The wife—or wives if any—lives in her husband's family home or at least within its family circle. Honor requires that the wife genuflects to her husband's parents and "serves" them.

Of course the wife is expected to yield to her husband's wishes—where they do not come into obvious conflict with his parents' needs and desires!

Since it happened that my parents had both died early, their views could only be speculated on—or were variously remembered and weighed. And if the wife had ideas of her own, she was expected to yield to the joint pressure of whatever major part of the surviving family remained.

So there it was. My parents had long gone, and Aunt Bibiji—partly because of the strong force of her character, partly because she had in fact taken their joint place, was my Family! I admit I was not much concerned over my uncle, who had long ago withdrawn from the family circle. But my aunt? A force to be placated or very carefully treated. My unexpected return to Bijapur and my placement of Mira in my aunt's hands for her education meant extra burdens for Aunt Bibiji. As a Muslim lady, my aunt could reasonably have objected to having my Christian wife-- strange in customs and speaking a language she did not know-- imposed on her this way.

Much, truly, would depend on any "diplomatic" and persuasive qualities I could command. It also was becoming evident that Mira's characters and intentions—and diplomatic powers—were my best and only armor in a conflict where Aunt Bibiji held all the high cards of custom and tradition—and of "natural" loyalties, debts, and honor.

I had been fortunate, as it turned out, to have Raya as a competitive friend and "brother." Like him I quickly recognized injustice—and often prepared myself for danger, could make up my own mind and act decisively. Mira especially had seen these active sides of my nature. I knew how to be polite, since I instinctively felt that it serves men best. But I also learned—perhaps most from Castro, my enemy and Monserrate's—how to blunt the force of wrath or deception. Perhaps I was often too innocent-minded, but I could return a blow if it were clearly aimed at me.

I wondered sometimes if my Aunt Bibiji thought me weak or indecisive. A parent often fears these things in a son or daughter. Perhaps it is because—and I sigh at this—we hate to see our child behave too innocently or be abused. We yearn, I had learned from my aunt, to make our children a success and to achieve what we perhaps cannot-especially if we are the mothers of sons. I had learned that, in Islam as in Christianity, it is men for whom are reserved the chief fruits of power and victory—for, thanks to Aunt Bibiji, I had always studied women's lives and aspirations as much as men's. In this last, I suppose, I was not altogether a "man's" man, but I had learned that my aunt's ambitions, not only for me but for herself, were of a wise and practical quality, and that in intellectual matters she was the rival of many a man.

I remember the day when aunt Bibiji said to me, "Aziz Ahmad, you often anger me—and you often make me proud. Can you guess why?" I kept a judicious silence, knowing that I did not want to anger her. "Because," she said with a smile, "I find you largely innocent of guile or ill-intent, even when you disappoint me. You are so much like your father! I would that he had lived longer to share his strengths with you. You both have a strong sense of honor.

She sighed. "Of course you, like your father, are adventurous—sometimes too much so—and you take foolish risks. But—you are men for all that. Often, even when I am angry at some foolish thing you do, I admire your bravery." She gazed at me thoughtfully for a long moment. "Now do two things for me. Get back to your wife and help her with her Persian. And stop being rude to your brother Raya. He cares more about you than you know."

I told Mira the essence of what Aunt Bibiji had said. She smiled and considered, as I expected her to do, before answering. (How like my mother, I suddenly realized!) "Your aunt is a very observant and wise woman," she said—"and she loves you like a parent. "Her gaze focused tighter on my eyes. "We are both orphaned, Aziz, and we both know, deep down, what a parent's love is—what it should be! How fortunate that we can always share this, the world's instruction of us, if we only listen and feel it.

I wavered. I had not expected this wisdom too. And from a wife whom I often took too much for granted. How easily, I thought, that we forget what once brought us together and sealed a bond between us.

But she went on. "I know what your Aunt Bibiji is chiefly thinking these days. It is about our child to be. She does not wish you to go to Goa again—even at Monserrate's urging. And more, she wants me to waver in my support of your vow to Monserrate.

"But I know how often you call him "Father"—more than any mere churchman. It is how I feel—exactly how I feel—when I think of dear Father Jerome—this deep urgency of my many debts to pay!

"You and that Franciscan comforter of mine—so like Saint Francis with his credo of love and peace-making!—are my ideals of manliness. You almost surely saved my life and my sanity in Goa. Father Jerome knew, even more than you, how I had suffered as a cruel and abusive man's wife. He knew how the "Church"—and here she crossed herself—"betrayed its trust when it sent innocent girls to Goa's wretchedness and almost sure death of disease and poverty! That is how the Church—with its Inquisition—betrays the trust of so many former Hindus, now its Converts who committed their souls to its care!"

She caught herself, though, and tried a smile. "We owe so much, dear husband, to anyone who helps us and does not willingly hurt us! It is the Cross carried by the Meek, be they men or women, boys or girls, or mere children. Though I know you did not suffer, it would seem, as much as I, yet I know you suffered. It is in your eyes sometimes. And most of all, I know how you turned your care my way."

Her smile came back and tried to be cheerful. "And you desired me! Honestly I thought no one would ever desire me again in that honorable way. You rescued me from a creeping dishonor and death—even like that poor "Catarina a Piro" that you sometimes speak of. You are a far better man than that Governor—that fine ruler, that gentleman-fidalgo—who had the cruelty to make her a beggar and a laughing-stock all her life, and left it to a fine Jesuit priest to give her Supreme Unction. She was already half a corpse!"

And with this, tears burst from Mira's eyes, and she had to bury her face in my shoulder. The terror and shame of it made my heart burn, and I kissed and hugged her and stroked her hair, saying whatever calming words I could.

I was not surprised when, afterward, she reassured me that she would always owe me the courage in herself, her own behavior, that I had shown her that night in the forest amid the Ghats. And she had lived—we had lived—to see the sun again and be married in the Muslim way, as she herself had wanted. And now, if Monserrate my "Father" called, how could she say selfishly, "I won't have it. You cannot go!?" To marry me had been her vow. To rejoin Monserrate if he needed and wanted me—had been my vow. And now, whatever effort it took to persuade Aunt Bibiji of the need, Mira would make that effort. But yes, of course, she hoped I could spend at least the first year with our newborn child, sharing and teaching her as a father. It would root our own love more deeply than ever.

In the silence that followed I was shamed more than by anything my aunt could say. This wife of mine—Christian, Muslim, both—had assured me of her love and support, her courage if I needed it. Yes, she had a passionate nature that any man, any husband might love. But I had seen it, had tested it, and I knew its quality. And the passion in my own nature, that had been aroused by this tender wife, I would never cease to employ for her good as well as mine.

Mira's honor—like her love—I would never forget or betray. To my prayers now and for weeks afterward I added this vow. In all my prayers to Allah I swore this along with my Muslim's devotion to His Mercy, Compassion, and charitableness.

Mira and I began to pray much together. And I did not forget to ask for Divine Mercy upon my friends the Jesuit Monserrate and the Franciscan Father Jerome, upon Aunt Bibiji, and upon Raya who after all was my brother.

With all of these prospects, the days began to pass quickly. It was time for Raya, in particular, to leave with his caravan to Tamilnadu. He was more self-absorbed, more serious, less talkative now. Armed against all comers, if such they were, he had forty armed men to lead. It was a daunting task in wild country, this career as a merchant prince that he had begun. I did not envy him the life. But I knew that, in his own way, he was as ambitious as I—and would have to be even stronger, more careful, more alert than I.

The life he proposed excited him and he told me much about it. Finally, amid comings and goings, he told me that it was one of his greatest purposes to link up the Deccan and Tamilnadu by regular, reliable trade routes—yes, caravan routes for men, horses, mules, and camels—and to create long routes for the exchange of business papers, contracts, and personal messages of all kinds.

He laughed. "Why, even messages for you, brother Aziz! For it seems that from time to time you are going to wander and adventure some more—be absent from your lovely wife and growing children—take the risks of imprisonment and death! Am I not right? And will you not need a reliable delivery of messages to your Mira and your Aunt Bibiji. Remember them both, and reat them well, I say to you. For whatever others may do or say, these two women love you—and will pray that, whether suffering from wounds, disease, chains, or dungeon walls you will live to return to them!

He laughed again at my disbelieving—or was it merely awed—expression and added. "Oh yes, it is true! But is not that the essence, brother, of Faith and Fate?"

But he changed the subject again. "Be kind to your dear wife, my friend. Were she not yours, I could wish that she were mine. But—oh yes—I perceive your jealous husband's heart! You will want to keep me away from her, keep me too busy with my merchant's life to hover at her door. And yes, I will be true to you. Because you are my Brother. Because she is my Sister, and her secret name is that of Goddess Saraswati—our Hindu goddess of learning and wisdom. And like the Goddess her spirit is as pure as she is beautiful. And I will worship her from afar, but in true faith. Because I am Hindu—not some Muslim who must forswear all beauteous goddesses, or some Christian who must make Saints of them! And he laughed and chuckled until I had to laugh myself.

He clapped me on the shoulder. "It is very funny. Because Mira told me of how you regaled her with the story of Sita and her husband Rama and how Sita was rescued from the evil Ravana by some monkey named Hanuman, and how that Hanuman remained their devotee forever. And I found myself thinking—"How well I have taught this Muslim friend of mine! If he keeps this up, and commits to memory also the Bhagavad Gita, I will have to award him a Sanskrit diploma! Yes? And he broke down laughing again.

But I could not hate him. For Raya did have the soul of a teacher—a Guru, I decided. And he sealed it when he clapped me on the shoulder again and said. "Just do one thing for me, Brother. Do not worship that good wife of yours! She cannot be a Goddess—except to Hindus like me. No Muslims allowed! But I will love and serve her forever."

And now, the next day, it was time for Raya to set forth with his caravan and ride to the Tamil country. Would I see him again? I was sure of it. And yes, we would laugh and banter again while we indulged in our respective Muslim and Hindu ways of devotion to a Christian girl named Mira!

I could laugh easily—smile easily now. And I wished well this brother of mine. Partly since, I am shamed to admit, I did believe he would deliver my letters—and Mira's—according to plan!

The next morning, after farewells to Mira and Aunt Bibiji on the terrace, Raya went to the gate and met three well-armed men. Altogether, with their Arabian horses, they made a formidable array—to which would soon be added another forty riders!

Raya had dressed to the hilt in armor—steel helmet, two layers of chain-mail, breastplate, and tunic, with a tough little Mongol shield slung on his back. All these, besides the usual Mongol bow and arrows at his side. And he was armed with a Turkish sword and dagger and carried two muskets beside his stirrups—and, I saw, a long-barreled pistol thrust in his sash.

I have to admit I almost laughed. Good old Qarah Khan, the Turk, had taught us well! Somewhere his spirit must be smiling, too.

Chapter 38

A Present Happiness

I turned to walk back from the gate after Raya's departure. Here came Mira, smiling because we could be close again. She turned and walked with me through Aunt Bibiji's garden. I yearned to put an arm around Mira's waist as she moved smoothly next to me. But old Riaz Bahadur and his son, who had closed and secured the gate, were not far behind.

When we reached the center of Aunt Bibiji's four-fold garden, leaving the gatekeeper and his boy to go to their quarters, we stopped at the fountain and sat on a convenient bench I had put there in the shade of a sapling. As we sat Mira slipped her hand down to rest in mine. "Did your brother say anything yesterday, in that long conversation you had, about me?—about us?" It came as a quaint, hesitant question.

I did not want to say what was in my mind—that Raya had fallen in love with her—or at least that I thought so! But now that he was gone I could forgive him. I offered her a very loose transition of one of his comments. "He said that wherever I might go in the world, I was to keep you safe within my heart."

"How sweet," she murmured.

I pulled her close and smiled down at her when she laid her head on my shoulder. "It is a vow I will keep wherever we go, wherever we may be," I said, "here in Bijapur, in Goa with Monserrate, or wherever fortune may take us."

Mira looked back fondly but with a touch of raillery. "Even if we are separated, and you are in a faraway Hindustan?" I knew she had promised to support my decision to return to Goa if Monserrate asked, so I had to look back at her, remaining calm and confident.

I smiled. "Even if, for a time, I remain in Hindustan and you in Bijapur. But I will unite us again as soon as I can. Didn't I promise that?

She cocked her head at me. “Well, I am your first wife and about to be the mother of your first child. And don’t you know how men are about their vows?” But there was laughter in the question now.

“You,” I said, kissing the end of her nose, “are a temptress!” Then I gave her a tug that pulled her closer. “My vow is one you can trust me to keep—wherever we may be in the whole world!”

“Forever and ever?” she asked, keeping up the game. I knew that in a moment I was going to have to kiss her soundly. “I believe I said that already.” I said in her ear.

She laughed. I bent to the ear again. “Forever and ever, If Allah is kind.”

But almost immediately I thought, “Nothing is ‘forever,’ except God!” All the poets and sages knew that. Mira and I would also have to yield to its truth.

I kept thinking along that line. Builders might build, kings might conquer, lovers might be faithful. But always the old saying attributed by Muslims to Isa, or Jesus, spoke true.

“Life is a bridge. Build no house upon it.”

We could cross over that bridge but could not stay. The best hopes could falter and fail.

I thought again of Hindustan. The Jesuits for all their zeal might fail to convert Akbar, Emperor of Hindustan. Yet, if I could, I would go north in the grand attempt.

Even as Mira and I walked farther toward the steps of our terrace, I silently constructed a poem.

“Dwell not on your future, however great.
Tomorrow will come. Look to this day.
Forget all your works, your wisdom. Fate
And the Will of God will have their way.”

But I reflected a moment. The poem was too pessimistic. True, but too obvious. Allah simply was all-powerful.

Mira and I had just arrived at our terrace.

My wife turned to me. "A poem just took shape in my mind!" she said—looking surprised, then confident. "Persian verses have been churning around in my head all day. Let me have the honor!"

> "We cannot see into the future," she declared,
> "though we twine around each other's fate…"

She stopped and blushed. "I can't make another two lines fit!" I kissed her gently on the cheek. Suddenly my thoughts cleared. She would have the honor of capping her own lines!

Mira drew me into our sitting room. At its center, as usual, was the beautiful Tashkent carpet we had bought, and in the middle of the carpet lay the large, single cushion that we liked to sit together against in the evenings.

I pulled her down to the cushion.

Soon we were laughing over the Persian lines we were coming up with. I kept thinking, however, that "fate" was too unpredictable and almost too serious a theme. The Persian words sounded stiff and academic!

But Mira was not willing to sacrifice her first two lines. She kept repeating them. I had a stubborn young poet here.

She started pacing. Every poet's last resort. To pace, throwing out phrases, one after the other. "We stand…," she was saying now. "Stand together… Where, but where?"

"Why not rhyme it?" I urged. I was about to start pacing myself! "Fate. Gate. Anything that goes together!"

Suddenly her eyes widened. She plopped back beside me. "I have it!" she exclaimed. "The future! The future's shining gate!" She leaped to her feet again, her face radiant.

"We cannot see into the future," she explained, "but we twine around each other's fate. You see, Aziz? We stand here, wait here—full of joy!"

And now I saw that my wife had become a poet. A lovely poet, confident of herself again. And she completed her poet's moment, intoning the four lines that were giving her such pleasure.

"We cannot see into the future,
Though we twine around each other's fate.."
But wait here, lovers full of joy,
Beside the future's shining gate."

Without thinking I responded happily—a traditional Arabic phrase that capped her lines. "Allahu-akbar! God is Great!"

It was instinctive. And quickly I added a wish for God's favor on my marriage to this woman who had brought such love to me, and whose child and mine would soon bring more light to our lives. "Lovers full of joy," I murmured.

Mira stood happily gazing at me. "The four lines," she begged. "Could we recite them together?"

"Of course!" I told her. "The words are wonderful—like the poet who created them." And face to face, holding each other's hands, we stood declaring our love beside the shining gate of the future.

I found myself thinking that our two great religions could learn much from this love that bonded us. The intensity of feeling but also the forbearance. The caring and forgiveness. The willingness to share rather than impose ideals or customs. The intellectual communion instead of dogma. The devotion to peace instead of war.

It had become a prayer.

"In the Name of Allah,
The Compassionate, The Merciful"

End

THE PERSIAN JESUIT

A ROMANCE OF INDIA IN THE AGE OF AKBAR

Ray Thomas Smith

San Diego, California

2009

www.ingramcontent.com/pod-product-compliance
Lightning Source LLC
Chambersburg PA
CBHW020612310726
48979CB00008B/1449/J

* 9 7 8 1 4 2 6 9 2 3 6 8 5 *